For Grae,
Jack Fernandez
14 Oct 09

Conquistador

A novel

By

Jack Eugene Fernandez

Bloomington, IN   Milton Keynes, UK
authorHOUSE®

AuthorHouse™
1663 Liberty Drive, Suite 200
Bloomington, IN 47403
www.authorhouse.com
Phone: 1-800-839-8640

AuthorHouse™ UK Ltd.
500 Avebury Boulevard
Central Milton Keynes, MK9 2BE
www.authorhouse.co.uk
Phone: 08001974150

First published by AuthorHouse 8/31/2006

ISBN: 1-4259-5338-7 (sc)

Library of Congress Control Number: 2006906773

Printed in the United States of America
Bloomington, Indiana

This book is printed on acid-free paper.

The characters and situations in this story are purely fictional and have sprung entirely from my imagination. Any similarity to actual persons, living or dead, is coincidental and unintended.

J.E.F.

ACKNOWLEDGEMENTS

I am grateful to the many people who read drafts of the manuscript. Many offered useful suggestions and comments that helped me prepare the final manuscript for publication. I thank especially the following persons: Dr. Lázaro Hernandez, who offered background on Cuba, USF Professors Clinton Dawes, Marvin Alvarez, Willy Reader (deceased), Dennis Killinger, Bruce Bursack, Jim Vastine, Dale Johnson, and many of the members of the USF Women's Club, who, through several book clubs, discussed the book with me. Among these were Sue Vastine, Quinn Bursack, Rose Killinger, Molly and Clark Naylor, Shirley Brown, Lynn Federspiel, Madelynne Johnson. Other friends and acquaintances who read the manuscript were Ángel Rañón, Hammond Powers, Robert Harmon, and my sons Albert, Rudy, and Jack Fernandez. I also thank Ruben Alfaras, a native of Matanzas, Cuba, who offered details of that city and its environs.

Above all I thank Sylvia, my wife of fifty-five years, who suffered through countless drafts, editing and offering encouragement and moral support at every phase of its composition. Without her this project would never have ended.

Finally, I offer my sincere appreciation to the Tampa-Hillsborough County Public Library System for allowing me to reproduce the photograph, *Man standing in Sugar Cane Field, Wachula, Florida 1915*, on the front cover. The back cover photo was taken by the author.

J.E.F.

CHAPTER 1 - ASTURIAS, SPAIN, 1867

*

Havana Sugar firm at 4¼ Cents per Pound

*

Havana Cholera Epidemic Diminishing

*

Pontifical Troops Open Fire on Garibaldians

*

Garibaldi Claims Rights of American Citizen

*

Hurricane Wreaks Destruction on Porto Rico

*

Havana Shipping News:
Arrived, Steamer Raleigh, From New York
Arrived at Cárdenas, Barks Cochran
From Bangor, and Holbrook, From New York
Steamer Naviera to Leave Gigón for
Havana on November 30th

*

As pink bled into the eastern sky Paco watched thick clouds march across the green valley of Peñamellera on that early November morning. Like time itself, those clouds rolled in with the silent roar of a determined army. Paco tried vainly to imagine a warm summer day.

On All Souls Day the previous week he and his parents and every other inhabitant of Colosía attended the ceremonial mass for the dead. Paco sat with Marta and her parents in the pew behind Paco's parents. Slightly taller than Paco, Marta made no attempt to appear smaller. She sat tall, her hand in his, hazel eyes sparkling. The way she tied back her chestnut hair with a black ribbon and a white kerchief over the top exposed the sharp, angular features of her Visigothic ancestors: pointed chin, high cheekbones, thin lips. Her lean, full-breasted figure attracted every young man in the village, but she held Paco's hand as if there were no other. From his calloused hand flowed gentleness and tranquility. Paco combed his long, light brown hair straight back. When he smiled his ruddy cheeks swallowed his blue eyes, and his broad mouth exposed perfectly aligned teeth. His square chin, short thick neck, and solid body carried authority as he stretched back and neck to his full five feet four inches. Spying each other's eyes, each squeezed the other's hand and smiled; their parents pretended not to notice. During Padre Benito's Castilian-accented Latin droning, parishioners fingered rosary beads and sent a vapor of silent prayers heavenward. Through it all Paco and Marta remained in constant physical communion with each other. Called to stand, they rose as one, hand in hand, he stretching to stand tall.

At Padre Benito's final benediction the congregation moved as one, not as they did most Sundays, talking and trading gossip, but with somber resolve.

Like many Spanish villages, Colosía, a jumble of stone houses built against one another, resembled blocks hurled against the mountain. As far as the villagers knew those houses had stood since biblical days. Hard clay streets, if we may call them streets, were merely the leftover spaces around clumps of houses. Because towns grew at will like living organisms, thoroughfares might be narrow enough for a man to touch the walls on opposite sides or broad enough for a plaza. Sprawling across the mountainside, Colosía had few flat spaces. The largest one, near the geographic center of the village, formed a plaza of no discernible geometry. In its center stood a simple stone fountain with a pig of carved stone spouting water from its mouth. A spring under the pig supplied the village, and may have attracted the first settlers to that craggy mountain in Asturias. On one side of the pig's plaza stood two taverns, a harness shop and a blacksmith. Opposite them rose the church whose bell tower could be seen across the entire valley of Peñamellera. On Tuesdays, market day, farmers filled the square with their produce.

But that November morning, all souls day, people flowed out of church like a trickle from the ancient spring. They meandered along separate routes through the village finally coalescing into the road to Panes, where the human river stretched half a kilometer to the small stone-fenced cemetery, finally to pour itself out in gentle eddies around the gravestones.

As they entered, Paco and Marta parted to accompany their parents to the graves of departed relatives. During the hour or so of tears and praying, families weeded graves and trimmed flowers, then prayed some more. Finally the women began to wander back to their homes to prepare lunch, the men to one of the taverns to give life to the ancient proverb, *El muerto al hoyo, el vivo al pollo,* which loosely translated means, "To the grave with the dead; the living to their bread." Paco had gone with the men.

Now, days later in his bedroom, watching the sky strain to lighten, Paco stretched and touched the opposite walls of his bedroom. He pressed his flat palms on the walls and wondered if he could, like Samson, push them down. Sitting on the edge of the bed he put on clothes he had left draped over the chair. Beneath the clothes lay a Bible and a history of the Napoleonic Wars, which Padre Benito had lent him. The small room made it easy to dress in the dark; he could reach all four walls without leaving his bed.

Dodging the tall narrow cabinet next to the door, he walked down the dark cave-like hall to the large kitchen where his mother stood bent over, stuffing pieces of wood into the stove. He knew that no matter how early he rose or how hard he labored she would be there before him and would remain after he had finished his day's work. In the flickering light of an oil lamp beside the stove she did not look well. And no wonder, he thought, this kitchen is even colder than my bedroom.

"Buenos días, Mamá."

She nodded but did not look up, and Paco walked out the front door. The pink glow had not yet stretched into the western sky. He wondered if he had slept. Built on a steep hillside at the lower edge of the village, the house's back door next to Paco's bedroom opened at ground level to the rising earth. The kitchen at the front opened to a small landing that led down a flight of stairs to the road to Panes. During the day the beautiful view from that landing always stopped him, but this opaque morning he shivered down the stairs. At the bottom step he found his wooden shoes and put them on. Another hour would pass before the sun completed its entry.

He pushed open the stable door, and the warm and comforting aroma of manure invited him in. Built to accommodate five animals, the stable now housed only a cow and a mule, though Paco's father promised to buy more cows when Jorge Antonio returned. Paco lit the oil lamp on the wall, and the burning oil added its friendly scent to the stable. Pasiega turned to look. Her blonde hair looked so much like his that he imagined they were related. She turned to him and he stared into her kind, watery brown eyes that pleaded for relief. *"Un momento,"* he said, standing over her and passing his rough palm over her back. The stocky eighteen-year-old wore a heavy shirt and corduroy pants with his broad leather belt pulled tight. His wooden shoes clopped on the stone floor as he moved. Even heavy clothes and wooden shoes could not keep out the damp cold. Straightening his back he passed a finger over his upper lip to feel his new moustache. Let them laugh, he thought. I don't care. Soon I will have great handlebars. He slapped Pasiega's rump. *"Vaca, que ódio te tengo."* It was not the cow he hated, but the ritual. Picking up a broad hoe he pushed the two animals' overnight droppings to the end of the stable near the small window and then shoveled it out the window onto the pile outside. "Each day the same shit," he said aloud. He grabbed a bundle of the previous day's grass from a box near the wall, laid it in the manger before Pasiega, dragged a stool to her side, and sat down. With a handful of grass he wiped off her udder to loosen any dirt or manure she may have lain in and began milking. As always, Pasiega munched passively as he milked, occasionally turning her head in gratitude. "Sure this feels good to you, but not to my hands, and these jets hit the bucket like military drums. You grate my nerves, Pasiega." He liked the steamy-sweet smell of the milk.

"Feels like I have worked through the night," he said aloud, "so dark outside. How many times will I milk you and your descendants before I crack and bend like Papá? The old man is rough and demands much, but he trained me to be a good farmer. If only we could talk of other things occasionally, but he is master and I his apprentice. Ah, but Marta, my beauty. You know, Pasiega, we were only seven years old when I proposed to her. In Señorita Medina's school. She made trouble for me when I pulled her hair … No marriage, though, until I can support her … but I want her now, Pasiega. You know how it is. So beautiful, and her warm hugs drive me crazy. I lost myself that day on the mountain … Was it a dream? No matter. She will have to wait until I earn the right to be called a man. Of course there is the small detail of military service. Inevitable. It will come one day like a shout over the mountain. Almost I hope for it. Oh, God! Anything to get me out of this dark cave of a life … anywhere, to a distant colony; Cuba perhaps or Africa, anywhere away from this stinking village; someplace where I can carve my name into the tree of life … in a bright uniform, riding a horse along a sunny tropical path, Marta behind me, arms tight around my chest, on our right, green Caribbean waters flashing through the fronds of a palm forest; on the left my own mountain green with tobacco. Damn you, Pasiega! Hold your tail. The flies will not kill you."

Throughout the milking he conjured scenes of Cuba, the Canary Islands, and Morocco that he had seen in a magazine at the village barber's: a deserted beach with Marta; then, suddenly, it is not Marta, but an exotic young, dark-skinned native woman clinging to him, kissing him without shame.

He walked up the stairs with the bucket of milk dangling from his hand and left it on the kitchen table. By this time a fire raged in the stove. His father and he liked warm, sweetened milk with their breakfast bread and jam.

"Wash your hands," his mother said.

He looked down, saw how dirty they were, and hid them behind him. Paco believed his mother smiled so rarely because she worked too hard. She worked as if to settle an ancient debt. Taller than Paco, her back bent perpetually, she looked gaunt and pale. Paco could never be sure of the color of her eyes. Light brown, possibly greenish, he thought, but he rarely saw them through the permanent squint that had etched grooves into her chalky flesh. Gray had won its campaign to turn her brown hair the sickly yellow of age. With hands as strong and large and bony as a man's she poured milk from the bucket into a pot, set it on the stove, and laid the bucket on the floor.

Paco walked back down the stairs and out to the small spring by the road to wash. On the way he stopped to look back at his village and said aloud, "*Ay, Colosía*, I don't want to see you even on canvas." Morning was creeping in like the ghost of a dead king returning from his final battle.

A few rays cut through leaden clouds to sink luminous columns into the hill. Drowsy plumes of smoke rising from house chimneys announced that life would continue for yet another day. Paco saw his future in those clouds: whiffs of days joined then split into loose puffs of time carrying him from task to task, hour to hour, day to day, year to year, toward the final vaporization.

After breakfast Paco sat inside the open stable door to sharpen his scythe. A veil of light rain obscured the Panes road and the valley beyond. The road, a pair of reddish-black muddy ruts carved into the green slope, led down the slope to Panes, a crossroads village one kilometer to the northeast. Beyond, the broad slope, punctuated with red-gray boulders of all sizes, tumbled down to the rich valley of Peñamellera, a perfectly flat green expanse nearly twenty kilometers east to west. Across the valley to the north, the majestic sierra rose to protect the rich valley from the clawing Cantabric Sea fifteen kilometers away. Over thirty villages gripped their claws into the sierra and harmonized into the slopes that surrounded the valley. How tough we Asturians are, he thought, to thrive in this harsh land. God must have had men in mind when He made Asturias.

Holding the scythe handle between his knees with the blade facing up, he lifted the stone out of his belt and began to move it in graceful, rhythmic passes across alternating sides of the blade. Oblivious to the roses his mother had planted along the front of the house, he passed the stone across the blade as his mind again disengaged from cold reality to wander over the warm lands of gracefully curving coconut palms he had seen in books. Flinging the scythe and a rake over one shoulder, he laid a rolled-up canvas sheet over his other shoulder and trudged through puddles and wet grass down the hill to the large meadow draped down to the valley floor. He looked out over the field, mentally mapping out the rectangle of rich, dark grass he would carve out during the next half-hour. As the drizzle diminished he began long, smooth motions of his scythe across the ground. He worked with the accuracy of a barber and the rhythm of the steeple clock, always keeping the blade low enough to get the most grass, high enough to leave healthy roots for the next cutting. Finally he unrolled the canvas and raked the grass onto it until he had all he could carry. Then he lifted the corners of the canvas, raised the bundle over his shoulder, and walked back to the stable with the scythe and rake in his other hand. After he had poured some of the green hay into the feeding trough, he patted Pasiega and walked upstairs for another dipper of milk.

"You have much work before you eat, Paco."

He lowered the dipper into the bucket. "Just a little more, Mamá."

"Your poor father works himself to death for you. Go!" She opened the fire door, shattered a piece of firewood against a corner of the iron stove, and threw it into the fire. "To live you must work."

"*Si, Mamá*. Already I go." He downed the milk and walked out the back door and up the hill and saw the sun's spectacular appearance. Like a seductive woman, he thought, promising much, showing little. In leaps he climbed up the hillside to where his father was plowing. He slipped and sank into soggy earth with every step, as if she were sucking him into her bosom. The odor of ripe apples and pears hung on the air. Catching sight of him, his father stopped the mule and waited behind the plow.

"Give me the reins, Papá."

"First we talk." The old man's threadbare *boina* fit his head like a scull cap. His wife had trimmed his gray-white hair so that it hung limply over his ears. He stood bent forward like a rusty hinge and wiped his face with his handkerchief, laid the plow down, still holding the reins, and tried to straighten his back to reach Paco's height. "Jorge Antonio comes home next month."

"Yes, Papá, I am anxious to see him."

"I am getting old, Paco. Soon I will have to turn the farm over to him. He is my eldest now. He and Sara plan to marry soon. You must make plans."

"I will work for him until the army calls."

"You know he became my heir when Samuel died."

"Yes Papá, primogeniture. I have thought much about that. I have decided on a military career."

"A foot soldier? That is stupid!" He threw down the mule's reins. "The army gave Samuel African tuberculosis, and only the grace of God has saved Jorge Antonio in that godforsaken wasteland. I will not give another son to the queen." For a few moments he looked down at the rich, black earth. "My stupid father died on the outskirts of Madrid defending our king against stupid Frenchmen who followed Napoleon. They were all stupid. The crown deprived me of a father and a son. That is enough. I fight only for my own. Let the queen fight her own battles."

"It is a soldier's life to fight, Papá."

"No!"

"It is wrong to avoid military service. I must; the law says..."

"I don't give a damn what the law says. Army—no!"

The anger in his father's voice told Paco the discussion had ended. "How, Papá?"

7

"Eugenio has been in Havana six years. He writes that Cuba overflows with opportunities. You will work for him until you find a good opportunity"

"Why did he write? We have not heard from him in years."

"*Coño!* Because I wrote to him. He is my brother and I asked him to help you."

"But Papá ..."

"It is not only the army, Paco. They may not call you if they fill their quota. Then you will end up in some big ugly city working for pennies, or in a coal mine, or if you are lucky, as a priest fattening yourself on poor people's pennies. Cuba is rich. Eugenio says you can build a fortune there if you fight for it and work hard. That you cannot do here. Padre Benito is making the arrangements."

"But the fare."

"Do not occupy yourself with that, Paco. Now take this mule. We must finish plowing."

Paco picked up the plow and slapped the mule with the reins. He is right. What if the army does not want me? *Coño!* Cuba, the New World! He slapped the mule again to pick up the pace.

In late afternoon Paco led the mule back to the stable under the house, removed the harness and laid out some grass for him. Then he walked up to the kitchen. His mother was not there, so he walked through to the back door. Just outside the house her rose hedge still held a few determined petals. Beyond that lay a half-acre his father had terraced and cleaned for the family garden. All around the garden stood fruit trees—pear, apple, plum, cherry, peach, fig, apricot. Paco found his mother bent over, digging turnips in the garden and asked if she needed help.

She pointed to the nearly full wheelbarrow. "Take these to the shed."

At the west end of the garden stood a chicken coop with eleven hens, and beyond that, a tethered lamb his mother was raising for meat. Around the house, down toward the road, stood the small shed where they stored vegetables, salted hams, sausages, and tools for making and repairing scythe handles, rakes, plows, and harnesses. Paco unloaded the turnips into a box on the floor, stood the wheelbarrow against the wall, and returned to the house to clean up before going to meet Marta in the village square.

*

"I have no choice, Marta. If not Cuba I move to Oviedo or Madrid and starve. The farm goes to Jorge Antonio."

The sun had set and the rain had stopped. Dim torches flickered over the tiny plaza where people milled around awaiting suppertime. Marta and Paco sat by the pig fountain. Seeing her hazel eyes radiating fire, Paco looked down and ran his fingers through the water.

As she spoke, her full breasts heaved. This strong girl was used to getting her way. In the frilly white blouse and wide, black and white skirt typical in Asturian villages, her red cheeks blazed and her lips pursed as she spat out words: "You are just backing out of your promise."

Looking around to see if anyone was listening, he tried to calm her. "I have given you my word! I will send for you as soon as I get established."

"Established? Bah!" She stood and crossed her arms over her chest.

He stood and drew her close. "In Cuba land is abundant, almost free for the taking. I will work hard and make my fortune; then we will live like lords."

Her face turned from anger to sadness. "Please, Paco, stay. You can do the same here."

"I'll send for you in a year; two at the most."

She turned and walked away, her hair bouncing with her firm, determined stride. After a few steps, she turned. "I free you from your promise."

"How can I convince you?"

"There is only one way."

"I am a man, Marta. I will make my own decisions. You must learn to trust me." She turned again and walked toward her house and disappeared from sight into one of the narrow streets. He walked to the nearest tavern.

*

Two weeks later, during supper, Paco's father announced that it was time to leave. Paco's mother stood over the stove turning the chorizo sausages that would follow the beans she had just served them. The smell of frying chorizo drew Paco's attention. Three kerosene lamps pushed against the darkness to reveal rows of potted geraniums on two windowsills. A full moon brought into relief sharp rocks that jutted out of the hillside. At the far wall, flanked by candles, stood a statuette of the Virgin of Covadonga.

"Padre Benito brought a letter today from the army. You have thirty days to report to army headquarters in Oviedo." He waited for the news to sink in. "The arrangements have been made. Your uncle Facundo will drive you to Gijón, where you will board the Naviera, to Havana. Gijón is a hundred and fifty kilometers from here. It will take two weeks. Padre Benito says the Naviera departs on December 7th, three weeks from today. The next ship sails in March. That will be too late."

"But my orders."

"Once you are out of Spain, they cannot touch you. Take the letter. If the authorities stop you, show it. Tell them you are helping your uncle and will report to Oviedo on your way back from Gijón."

"You are asking me to shirk my duty, Papá. A man must do his duty to God and country."

"*Silencio*! Your grandfather and brothers have done enough duty for all of us. I asked Padre Benito months ago to apply for your passport. He brought it today. Here." He handed Paco an envelope. "Money for the passage and one hundred pesetas. It is all I have."

Paco opened the envelope. "I do not need so much, Papá."

"You do nothing but argue. Take it. Tomorrow you will thank me. By the way, Padre Benito said you could keep the books he lent you ... to read on the voyage."

Paco looked at his mother, who had remained silent through the exchange. She scooped up the sausages and placed them on plates with ladlefuls of hot oil as tears rolled down her cheeks.

"At what hour will Facundo be here, Papá?"

"One hour before sunrise. He has a load of apples to sell on the way. You will continue with him to Gijón and help him load the wagon with supplies. Then you board your ship, and he returns with the supplies."

Exhilarated, but still wrestling with conflicting feelings of duty and survival and the inevitable poverty of a younger son, Paco finished his meal silently.

"Do not tell anyone, Paco"

"Why not?"

"Because every other young man in the village will want to go with you. The civil guard is not stupid, so pay attention."

Paco walked to his mother and took her arm. "I will miss you, Mamá."

"Naturally! Who will cook for you and wash your clothes?" Then she embraced him. "Be careful, Paco. The world is full of bad people; trust no one." Then, unclasping the chain with the gold medal that hung around her neck, she snapped it around his. "*La Virgen de Covadonga*. It was of my mother. She will keep you safe."

Paco embraced her and kissed her on both cheeks.

Her eyes overflowed. "May God bless you, Paco."

*

Marta was pacing around the fountain of the pig, every few seconds looking down the hill where Paco would emerge. Seeing him smiling and walking briskly, she frowned and said, "I have news, Paco."

"I, too."

"I tell you mine first. Remember our picnic in the mountains?"

"You must forgive me for that, Marta."

"There is nothing to forgive, Paco. I hesitated to tell you, but …"

"Oh, no!"

"It will not show for a while, but I am, you know … like that."

The possibility had not occurred to him. He did not know what to think, but in an instant he turned. "Then I stay. I will not leave you to face the world alone with a baby."

She took his hand and led him around the plaza. Looking back occasionally at the pig spewing water and avoiding inquiring eyes, neither spoke as they slowly strolled, both their skulls reverberating with unspoken words.

"The army has ordered me to report next month. For one year. We will marry before I leave. When I return, I will work with my brother. You will see; all will be well."

After a few minutes, she began to sob.

"*Que pasa?* Do not worry. I will come back."

"I cannot do it, Paco."

"Do what?"

"I am not … you know. It was Mamá's idea … That is how she tricked Papá. I am not pregnant. Oh, Paco, you do love me. Do not abandon your dream."

He hugged her and when she pushed him away, he said, "I must confess I'm a little disappointed."

She smiled.

"I leave tomorrow. You must not tell anyone for at least a month, not even your parents. I will send for you. Promise me you'll wait."

"I promise. Yes, yes, I promise. I will come tomorrow morning to say goodbye."

"No, we say goodbye tonight."

11

His father stuck his oil lamp into Paco's tiny bedroom the next morning and saw his son in his pressed wool pants and white shirt. Paco turned and smiled as he tied his cravat.

"Have you lost your mind?"

"*Que pasa, Papá?*"

"You might as well announce your escape in the plaza. Put on work clothes."

"Oh … of course."

Shaking his head, Pablo left his son and walked down the hall to the kitchen, where he found his wife bent over lighting the stove. It was as cold as their bedroom. He said nothing and walked out the front door to look for a sign of Facundo. Back in the house he rubbed his hands and told his wife what Paco was wearing. By this time the pungent smell of burning wood had filled the kitchen.

She smiled. "I pressed them last night, but I meant for him to pack them. What a child! He will need God's help in the cutthroat world he's entering."

"Do not occupy yourself, María. God protects innocents."

Paco appeared at that moment in his work clothes. "You were right, Papá. Now I am ready." He even had his rubber boots on and his heavy wool great coat over his arm.

His mother cracked three eggs into the pan of olive oil. "Eat something first."

Paco was too nervous to eat and went to the window to watch for his uncle.

"He is late," his father said and sat at the table staring at his watch. "What passes with him?"

"*Ay, Pablo!* You know my brother has never in his life been on time for anything. He will probably be late to his funeral."

"But soon the sun will rise."

"Here he comes," Paco said, "and with a full wagon."

"Apples, Paco. Let us go down. Hide your bag in the apples."

"First you eat," his mother said, pulling her son back in.

As the mule stopped in front of the house, Pablo said in a loud whisper, "What kept you?"

"Too many apples and only one wife to help. But now I am here."

"Would you like some eggs and coffee?"

"No. Already I have eaten. Better to get past Panes while it is still dark." The tall, thin man's *boina* hung down in front over his thick gray hair. He wore rubber boots over his shoes and a heavy canvas coat over his wool shirt and pants. His bright brown eyes belied his fragile frame of fifty-six years and sparkled with the mischief of an old man who had not forgotten how to relish a good joke.

Running down the stairs, Paco pulled back the canvas cover from the wagon and shoved his bag between some boxes.

Facundo stopped him. "No, put it in this half-full box and lay apples over it so it looks like the others. As Paco followed his uncle's order, Pablo came to him and handed him his gold watch and chain. "Take this. It was my father's. He took it off a French soldier he had killed. The following week my father died of a bullet wound, and a comrade brought it to my mother."

"But Papá, it has much value."

"It helped me dream of the father I never knew. Perhaps it will help you remember me." He did not hide his tears as he hugged his son and kissed him.

Paco slipped the watch into his shirt pocket and fastened the end of the chain to a buttonhole. "I wish I could say goodbye to Jorge Antonio."

"He will understand."

Before Paco could climb to the seat beside his uncle, his mother came downstairs with a package wrapped in cloth. "Some chorizo sausages and cheese," she said, and kissed him. "God be with you, my son."

"Thank you Mamá. I will write and tell you everything."

"*Vamos*," Facundo said, slapping the reins on the gray mule's rump, and the wagon creaked forward with the speed of encroaching old age.

The rocky road to Panes sloped downhill. As they entered Panes they turned west. Facundo smiled, "That was one kilometer. One hundred and forty-nine to go."

At the outskirts of Panes, they saw two civil guards by the road. Their black, three-cornered hats and long capes sent a shudder through Paco.

"What do we do?"

"Calm yourself, Paco." Facundo kept the same slow pace, saluted and said, "*Buenos Días, caballeros.*"

The two men stopped talking to look them over. One was rubbing his hands under his cloak. The other raised his hand for them to stop. "Where do you go?"

Facundo pulled the wagon to a stop. "To sell these apples." He motioned with his hand at the load. "And the sooner the better, or they will kill my mule."

Looking at the animal's drooping head, they laughed. The one in charge motioned them on and turned to his companion and resumed their discussion.

"*Coño*, that was close," Paco said. "I was shaking."

13

"Nerves can make you cautious, but too much caution is also dangerous. You must remain calm and always comport yourself as one who is in the right."

The road west to Cangas de Onís was smoother than the path from Colosía to Panes, but the mountains soon had the mule gasping. They stopped to let her rest and drink water every hour or so or when they passed one of the villages along the way.

By early afternoon the sun had winked through the clouds once or twice through intermittent drizzle. The road joined a small river, and Facundo knew they were approaching Arenas. Taking a sharp curve around a huge outcrop, the large town appeared, and Facundo said, "We'll eat and try to unload these apples. If we cannot, we move on to Cangas de Onís."

"Do not forget, *Tío*, my ship leaves in three weeks."

"Do not occupy yourself, nephew. We will run over with time."

Facundo drove the mule to a livery stable at the town's entrance and asked the attendant where he might find the cider factory. "Past the edge of town, a kilometer on the right. But it will do you no good. Manolo takes his siesta at this hour and does not return until almost sundown," the man said.

"I want to sell my load and move on."

"Manolo does not interrupt his siesta for nothing now that he has a wife. You know how it is." The man burst into a raucous laugh as he walked back into the stable and sat down at his stool by the door.

Facundo understood the factory owner's situation, but he did not want to waste an afternoon with no assurance of a sale. "What do you think, Paco? It may be a waste of time, but if we go on, we will not reach Cangas de Onís today. Let us run the chance. Arenas is just a big village, but let us see what it offers. It is time for lunch anyway."

"We could eat while we drive."

"You worry too much, Paco. Besides, the mule will be grateful to dispose of this load."

"Leave my bag in the wagon?"

"This is an honest man. Your bag is in this box," he said, patting the apples behind him. Then turning to the stable tender, he said, "Permit me to leave my wagon and mule for a couple of hours?"

"Of course. She looks hungry. I feed her?"

"Yes, thank you." Facundo drove the wagon into the stable, and he and Paco stepped down and walked toward the center of town.

Even in the cold November afternoon the streets flowed with people and wagons and burros. Odors of cut grass and fresh manure filled the air. Clouds threatened to disgorge again, but, for the moment, the rain had ceased, though puddles filled depressions in the cobblestone streets. In each of the town's taverns people huddled individually and in small groups around their cider talking about animals, crops or the latest clerical outrage. Facundo pulled Paco into the first tavern. With only a few oil lamps to light the long, narrow room, it resembled a cave with stone walls and floor. At the bar Facundo asked for two glasses of cider. The floor around the bar had pools of spilled cider. Its rich, slightly putrid, fruity aroma hung in the air. The only edibles at the bar were a plate of hardboiled eggs and one of sardines drowned in olive oil. "A ration of each," he told the bartender.

Holding two large glasses by their bottoms with one hand, the middle-aged bartender held them as low as he could reach and, with the other hand, raised the bottle high over his head and poured. Having performed this aeration ritual for many years, he hit the glasses without spilling a drop. The neatly dressed bartender wore a white shirt and black pants and his shiny black hair parted neatly down the middle. He set the two glasses on the counter before the travelers and picked up two small plates on which he painstakingly arranged the rations of fish and eggs. After Facundo had separated each plate into equal halves with his spoon, he and his nephew proceeded to eat their portions from the same plates washing them down with draughts of the murky, weakly alcoholic cider as they speculated on the price apples might fetch.

"What do you expect, *Tio*?"

"Forty-eight boxes, twenty-four reales if we are lucky."

"Half a real each?" Paco said, as his eyes focused on the strapping, young girl with long, light brown hair tied back in a bun. She was serving the tables near the rear of the tavern. He stood over his stool to get a better view. Each time she bent forward to lay down glasses of cider, her loose blouse opened, giving her customers an excellent view of her ample charms. "We stay the night, Uncle?"

His eyes sparkling, Facundo said, "If we stop for every good pair of tits, we will be two months on the road."

Paco sat back and blushed.

After lunch the pair walked around the small plaza, stopping to look into every shop and tavern. Paco seemed to enjoy the adventure. "You will do well in Cuba, Paco," Facundo said. "You may ask how I know. Well, I have observed you since you were born. You are still young, but you are intelligent and curious. You do not know much, but you learn fast. Most importantly, you have *cojones*, like your father. Whatever you intend, you do. I have seen the way you handle animals and your work. I also know Marta tried to trick you into staying. You comported yourself with honor.

15

She admitted her little lie, and you stuck to your plan. It is not easy for a young man your age to push away such a pretty girl."

"How do you know this?"

"My wife and Marta's mother are first cousins. They discuss everything. Colosía is a village, Paco, and villages, like sieves, hold back very little."

"I will send for her, Uncle."

"I know."

After strolling in silence a few moments, Paco said, "So people know?"

"No one has spoken it, but I think so. Remember, very few have not lost a son or brother serving Her Majesty," he said, lifting his cap in mockery. "No one will criticize you. Leaving the country to avoid serving the monarch is one of the oldest and most cherished of Spanish traditions. What good does the army do anyway? In Africa and the Philippines they kill innocent savages who do not harm us. In Cuba, they fight the sons of Spaniards who want to shake loose their oppressive Queen. Yes, my boy, our army exists principally to keep our people under her thumb."

"What worries me, Facundo, is that in Cuba I will still be subject to Spanish law."

"That New World wilderness will swallow you like a grain of wheat. You will find land to farm merely by claiming it. You will be a modern *conquistador*, claiming your territory, not for queen and church, but for yourself. And if Cuba does not suit you, you can find your way to another country, perhaps even North America. Many Asturians have become United States citizens. America has the one commodity all men seek—freedom. Your only concern must be to know what you want because you will without doubt find it."

"You make it sound good, Uncle."

"I speak with authority because I have no first hand experience. I rely on the word of others. Many of the friends of my youth have gone to America, and some have returned, bought homes on large pieces of good Asturian land, and retired like lords. Others have assimilated into the New World as if they were hatched there. Some send for a wife; others marry local women and raise families of Cubans or Mexicans or Argentines."

"How are the local women?"

"Some Spaniards, but also Africans and indigenous Indians. In the colonies people mix easily, and the females, I am told, come out a beautiful *café con leche* color with hot temperaments, eyes that slant and bodies that melt men."

Paco was staring out over the mountains and breathing deeply. "I, too, have heard stories," he said. "Are they true?"

"About the women?"

"That mulatto women are so beautiful."

"I am certain there is much exaggeration, Paco, so do not get too excited. You might injure yourself."

Paco turned his gaze on his uncle's sly grin. Facundo slapped him on the back and laughed.

Two hours had passed before they returned to the livery stable. The attendant had brushed the mule and parked the wagon in a corner. "Now you might find the cider factory owner."

"Good. How much for the service?"

"Ten *centimos* for feed and labor."

"That is not cheap."

"Nor exorbitant," the man said.

Facundo paid him as Paco walked to the mule, led her to the wagon, and hitched her. As he did so, Facundo said to the man, "It is almost dark. Could my nephew and I spend the night here if we do not find a room?"

"If you can stand the animals," the man said. "I do not think they will mind."

Facundo and Paco climbed into the wagon and rode off toward the cider factory. The drizzle resumed half an hour later as they stopped in front of the large, tall stone building with a large rose vine inching across its front wall and a water wheel in back over the river. Manolo, the owner, a large man in his early thirties with droopy moustaches and a menacing gaze, sat in a chair inside the front door with a cigar clenched in his teeth. On the far wall of the large room stood several rows of large wooden barrels and in the middle a huge press with several wooden barrels stacked beside it. Two small, dirty windows filtered scant light into the room. The water wheel turned the press through a geared shaft that protruded through the wall. Above the press hung a pulley with which the man lifted the apples to the mouth of the press.

"I have some apples," Facundo said.

"What kind?" Manolo asked through his cigar.

"The best cider apples you will find in all of Asturias."

"I will judge that," Manolo said, rising. He walked to the wagon and lifted the canvas cover, counted the boxes, opened one, grabbed an apple and bit it. He chewed it and swallowed some and spat out the rest. "Thirty-two reales," he said, and returned to his chair, brushing his hands on his pants.

"I had not planned to give them away," Facundo said.

"They are mediocre at best."

Facundo got back into the wagon, as Paco hesitated, expecting his uncle to jump at the offer. "Let's go, Paco."

As Facundo slapped the mule with the reins, Manolo raised his head and took the cigar out of his mouth. "All right, thirty-five. I have little work. It will warm me during this miserable drizzle."

Facundo stopped the mule and turned to Paco. "What do you think, Paco? We could make better time without them."

"That's up to you, uncle. I have no hurry."

"Forty," Facundo said, "and that is a gift."

"Thirty-seven," Manolo said, holding out his hand for the handshake that would seal the deal, "and not one *real* more."

Getting down from the wagon, Facundo said, "You are a hard man, Señor."

Remembering his box, Paco called his uncle aside. "My bundle, *Tio*."

Facundo turned to Manolo, reached out to shake the miller's hand, and said, "This box I take to my mother."

"Then there are only forty-seven boxes," Manolo said, withdrawing his hand abruptly. "That drops the price to thirty-six and a half reales."

"You are a hard man, *Señor*, but ... *bueno*."

Manolo shook Facundo's hand energetically and said, "Let us unload them."

Facundo backed the wagon to the door and Paco jumped out. "Stay where you are, Uncle. He and I will do it." Paco set to lifting the boxes and handing them down to Manolo, who placed them in a stack near the press. As the last box was stacked, Manolo walked to the back wall, lifted a small iron box from a table, opened it, and counted the silver coins into Facundo's hand. Facundo dropped them into his purse and shook Manolo's hand again. Manolo immediately went to work. Paco and Facundo climbed into the wagon and headed back to the livery stable.

"Manolo is no mathematician, Uncle."

"Not a bad day's work, eh, Paco? We splurge at our next stop."

*

The next morning the owner opened the large livery stable doors with a loud creak and a burst of light. Paco jumped as the animals moved and stomped in their stalls.

He shook his uncle. "Wake up. The man is here."

"The police?"

"No, the owner. It is light. Time to go."

Paco picked up his clothes bag he had used as a pillow, put the books back in and hid it in the box of apples behind the wagon seat. Then he hitched up the gray mule while Facundo talked to the owner:

"How much for the accommodations?"

"How much hay did you eat?" the man asked.

"Very little," Facundo said, smiling.

"No charge then. Much thanks for guarding my property."

Facundo shook the man's hand and asked where they could get breakfast.

"The tavern across the street will serve you coffee if you ask nicely."

"Leave the wagon, Paco. First we eat."

After finishing their bread and coffee they returned to the stable, climbed into the wagon and headed west. The bright, clear blue sky gave Paco the feeling that a miracle was at hand. From where the town ended abruptly, the highway suddenly resembled a loose ribbon dropped across the rocky landscape. The gently curving road opened a vista of their route. To their right the earth gave way to another valley, smaller than Peñamellera, but otherwise similar, dotted with villages and rocks down to its flat bottom. Along with the sun had come a cool breeze. As they bounced and rolled with the sun on their backs Paco buttoned his coat and shoved his hands in its pockets. One valley followed another like a string of emeralds. Occasionally a flock of sheep adorned the pastoral landscape. A few hours later they passed a village to a spot that overlooked still another valley.

"How about some cheese and sausage? Facundo said, parking near an orchard.

"I'd like an apple," Paco said, helping himself to a tree beside the road. "For dessert."

In the evening they stopped at a tavern in a larger but nondescript town and dined on tuna, cherries and cider, where the bartender told them of a livestock fair to be held the next day.

"We must stay for that," Facundo said. Then, seeing Paco's face, he added, "But we have a schedule to keep."

"Too bad," the bartender said. "There is always small game."

"What do you say, Paco? It might be worth a few hours if we could buy some good provisions. Aren't you tired of sausage and cheese?"

"How far have we come?" Paco asked.

"Let me see, about twenty kilometers, I think."

"From where?" the bartender asked.

"Panes," Paco said.

"Twenty-five kilometers."

"That settles it," Facundo said.

Paco was not happy at Facundo's decision, but did not argue. That evening they strolled through the town and ended up at the same tavern drinking cider and talking.

"Don't occupy yourself, Paco. We make good time. At twenty-five kilometers in two days, we will get there in two weeks easily."

"Twelve days, *Tío*, if we keep up the pace."

Facundo looked at his nephew quizzically. "Twelve?"

"Yes. Twenty-five kilometers in two days; six twenty-fives are one-fifty."

"Very good, Paco. Where did you learn that?"

"Don't know. Is it not clear?"

"How did you figure the apples yesterday?"

"You expected twenty-four reales for forty-eight boxes, half a real per box. That is what he deducted for one box. But at thirty-seven reales for the load he should have deducted three-fourths of a real per box, 0.77 real to be exact."

"Amazing, Paco; how did you figure that?"

"Simple, Tío. You divide the price by the number of boxes."

"Divide?"

"Look: thirty-six *reales* is three-fourths of forty-eight. That means he paid you a little more than three-fourths of a real per box because he got only forty-seven."

"I have no idea what that means, Paco, but you must be right, because I got more than I hoped. Such virtuosity will serve you well however you learned it."

The following day, after strolling through the livestock fair for an hour and, deciding not to buy any game, for cooking would waste more time, they bought half a leg of cured ham and departed. Paco sweated great drops of worry watching his uncle stroll so happily in and out of the aisles of goods spread over the town plaza, apparently content to spend the day looking and chatting with no idea how nervous was his nephew.

In Carreña de Cabrales, they bought a small round of the famous, local, very ripe Cabrales cheese and moved on. Paco could not wait to taste it, for he had not had any since he was a small boy. He recalled it pungent, but creamy, rich, and delicious.

The next two days dragged as they traversed the twenty-eight kilometers to Cangas de Onís. The beautiful Romanesque bridge across the meandering river so thrilled Paco that he happily agreed to spend a second night there. Facundo persuaded the proprietor of the livery stable to house them along with their wagon and mule.

They spent their first morning around the ancient bridge, which, from a distance, seemed small until Paco walked to the highest point of its arch. Looking down he could see trout struggling against the current. Walking down the other side of the bridge he examined the ancient stone blocks that had stood through centuries of wear and weather.

Tired of watching Paco walk around the bridge to view it from every angle, Facundo finally managed to drag him away to see the rest of the town. In the afternoon they walked from one tavern to the next on the long thoroughfare along the river, stopping at each for a glass of cider. In the fourth tavern, nearing five o'clock and after a dozen or more glasses of cider, Facundo spotted a familiar face. Moving to him at the bar, he said, "Domingo Hernández?"

"I am the one," the man said, squinting into Facundo's face. "Do I know you?"

"You should. We were boys together in Colosía."

"*Coño!*" the man said. "Facundo! I left Colosía twenty-five years ago."

"Twenty-eight," Facundo said. "We were both twenty-eight at the time. How are you?"

"I came to find work. Now I have a farm, a wife and three daughters."

"That is good. Let me present my nephew, Francisco Iglesias. In Colosía we call him Paco."

They shook hands and Domingo asked the bartender to pour three more glasses of cider. Then, over the next half-hour, Facundo brought him up to date on the people of Colosía. After several more glasses, Domingo invited them to his home for supper. "Conchita will be happy to meet you both."

"Do I know her?" Facundo asked.

"She is from here, but you will like her and my girls."

At ten o'clock that evening they arrived at Domingo's house and found that the wife was not as happy to see them as Domingo had said. "If he had told me sooner I could have prepared something better."

"Anything you prepare will be better than what we have been eating the past four days," Facundo said.

With curled lip the wife returned to the stove to finish the meal. Domingo came in, shook their hands, introduced his wife, Conchita, and sat with them at the kitchen table and passed around a bottle of cider. By the time they had consumed two glasses each, Domingo's daughters appeared and began to set the table. The eldest, María, was about Paco's age and unabashedly smiled at him and started telling him about herself and how many boyfriends she had. She sat so close to him that he did not know how to react. Though flattered, he wanted to be friendly without appearing forward. Raven-black, very straight hair draped around the girl's round face, wide smile, and high, blushing cheeks. What she lacked in beauty she made up in energy. The two younger girls watched their sister and giggled as if they knew what no one else could guess.

Conchita presented tomatoes, fried eggs, potatoes, turnip greens, and finally rice pudding for dessert. Paco showed his appreciation by devouring five eggs.

Two hours later, as Conchita and the girls washed the dishes, Domingo invited them to spend the night. Seeing Conchita's frown, Facundo said they already had accommodations and thanked them for the offer and for the fine repast. They left a little past midnight and wandered around town for a while before they found the livery stable.

Settling into a comfortable spot on the hay in one of the empty stalls Paco said, "*Simpática,* wasn't she."

"Conchita?" his uncle asked with a smile.

"María."

"A man should not play the game with the daughter of a friend, especially one who has offered his home."

"I only meant that she was friendly."

The next morning Facundo said he was glad they would stay another day. "I want to see some farms," he said.

They walked to one on the edge of town and Facundo struck up a conversation with the farmer about his crops and livestock and compared their records of bushels of produce per acre. Less interested, Paco wandered around hoping vainly to find someone his age.

They visited two other farms and ended the afternoon at the tavern on the main road. After three hours and half a dozen glasses of cider each, Facundo said, "I think Conchita has decided that Domingo does not want a drink this day. What about it, Paco? Shall we drop in on them? I think María liked you."

"She talks too much. Besides we need to get an early start tomorrow."

*

On their sixth day out, they left Cangas de Onís and headed north toward Colunga, on the coast. The livery stable owner told them the road wound uphill half the way and then downhill the rest of the way. It turned out to be almost insurmountable for the poor mule, who had to rest even more often than on previous days. As the mule snorted and sweated along a sheer rock wall to their right, Paco saw down the gentle slope to his left a flock of sheep grazing. Near the sheep, under an enormous chestnut tree, sat the shepherd playing what sounded like a flute. "I'm getting hungry," Paco said. "How about stopping? Shepherds are lonely people and usually like company. Let's cheer him up."

Facundo smiled and, leading the mule off the road toward the tree, said, "You are becoming a seasoned traveler." The shepherd saw them and kept playing.

"*Hola, amigo,*" Facundo said. "May we share our lunch with you?"

"With pleasure," the shepherd said, still sitting, watching the wagon lumber to a halt in the shade.

"This looked like a hospitable place to enjoy eating," Facundo said. "May I offer you some of our sausage and cheese?"

"Thank you." The shepherd passed his wine skin to Paco as he sat down.

The travelers opened their food package and spread it before them. As they ate, the shepherd, who looked about Paco's age, asked where they were going.

"Gijón," Paco said.

"That is far," he said. "Over fifty kilometers. I have never seen Gijón."

"Nor have I," Paco said. "It will be my first sight of the ocean."

"I will never see it," the shepherd said. "To follow my sheep is my life. Where they go, I go. They are my children. Sometimes they seem to appreciate me; other times they treat me as a stranger."

"They are only sheep," Facundo said.

"Perhaps I think about them that way because I see so few fellow humans. Mine is a lonely life, but I have plenty of fresh air to breathe and the sun to warm me."

"And your flute," Facundo said. "Did you make it?"

"*Sí, Señor.*"

"Would you play something for us?"

"With much pleasure." The shepherd picked up his flute and began to play an Asturian song about a homesick immigrant in America. As he played, both Facundo and Paco leaned against the tree to listen. In the bright sunlight, the beautiful airy tones wafted over them. Sitting in the still air and strong sun, the musical phrases seemed to rise from the earth. As he played, the shepherd's eyes watered. Finishing the song, he laid the flute down again and picked up the wine skin for a long draft.

"Beautiful," Paco said. "The sadness poured out like honey."

"Thank you. It makes company for me and soothes my children."

"What age do you have?" Paco asked.

"Twenty-one next March."

"Have you done military service?"

At that the shepherd's face stiffened. "Why do you ask?"

"I've been called, and I thought you could tell me about your experiences."

Facundo looked at Paco surprised that he was excited about serving. "Yes," Facundo said, "I advised him to leave the country, but he would not hear of it." Paco stifled a smile.

"I was not called," the shepherd said. "I received my notice two years ago, but they had met their quota and did not want me."

"How lucky!" Facundo said.

"On the contrary. I would have gladly abandoned this grassy prison to see the world. Now never."

"Me too," Paco said. "I hope they send me to Cuba or the Canary Islands. I have a great desire for the tropics."

As they spoke the shepherd watched his flock drift down the slope. Finally he stood. "I must move along. My children have found tastier grass. Have a good trip, and good fortune in the army." He shook their hands and walked down the slope after his sheep.

With some effort, Facundo lifted himself as Paco wrapped the sausage and cheese, and they walked back to the wagon where the mule was grazing in the sun.

By mid-afternoon they decided not to push the mule any further, for she moved, head down, as if each leg weighed a ton. Seeing a village a kilometer or so ahead, Facundo said they would stop there. As the red sun rested a moment on the horizon, a cold breeze began to sweep across the mountain pass. They drove into town and stopped in front of a tavern to ask some men where they could find a livery stable.

"On the far edge of town," said one, "straight ahead."

"*Gracias*," Facundo said, slapping the mule. She looked back as if to be sure, and reluctantly inched forward. At the stable, they almost ran into the proprietor who was brushing a horse near the door.

"*Coño*," the proprietor said. "Be careful."

"Pardon me. I did not see you in the dark."

"Well, what do you want?"

"To board my mule for the night, and if you have room, to let my nephew and me spend the night in one of your stalls."

"The mule yes, but I have no room for people."

"We have stayed in other stables. We do not have enough money to pay for an inn even if we could find one."

"I can put you up in my house, but it will cost you one real for the bed and supper and breakfast tomorrow morning."

"That is a lot of money for one night," Facundo said.

"It is my price."

"Seeing my mule so tired, we have no choice, *Señor.*"

"I will take care of the mule," the man said.

"Where may we wash?" Facundo asked.

"Out back at the pump. My wife will bring soap and towels."

After the man unhitched the mule, Facundo and Paco went inside, where the woman had prepared a bed for them in a small room with a window facing east. "Good," Facundo said. "The sun will wake us early."

"If not, I will," the woman said. "I serve breakfast at seven o'clock."

"Good," Facundo said. "And supper?"

"Ten."

They washed at the pump behind the house and went for a walk. It was another undistinguished Asturian town that offered little more than a tavern or two and a small plaza with a statue of a local man who had returned wealthy from America. Paco walked around the statue and read the inscription at its base fantasizing about the statue they would raise to him one day in Colosía.

On their return they found supper laid out on the crude table. The wife served a salad of lettuce and onions with olive oil and vinegar, then chorizo sausages with potatoes and eggs, and finally apple slices for dessert. Along with the meal she served the cloudiest cider either had ever seen. There was little conversation until Facundo said he had heard that Queen Isabel had recently visited the Pope in Rome. It was an attempt to make polite conversation, for he cared little about the queen or her travels.

The host erupted: "What do I care what that spoiled brat does or where she goes? We work to fill our bellies while she travels and spends money she has not earned."

"True," Facundo said, surprised at the man's outburst.

"The only people who eat like royalty are the priests, the second rank of our country's parasites. We would be far better off without these stinking sons of whores telling us how to conduct our lives. They live on hollow words, while I earn my bread in the sweat of my brow as God dictated."

"And they enslave our colonial natives," Paco said.

"Of course," the man said. "How else could they live so well? And what do they do for us? Nothing! We should govern ourselves like our ancestors did."

"With no government?" Facundo asked.

"No government would be far better than the best government man has ever concocted."

"Perhaps, but life would be hard knowing the villagers down the road could invade you any time they thought it profitable," Facundo said.

"Let them try. We would tear them out of Asturias by their *cojones*," the man said, banging his fist on the table. "They are nothing but cowards and *maricones*."

"I was speaking in general, not about the actual neighboring town."

"Well I speak in specifics. That shitty village has taken our best land. We are left only rocks and heights to till."

"Why don't you move down?" Paco asked.

"I would not live among the stinking bastards."

"Hearing your words, I'm glad we did not to stop there," Facundo said.

"You were wise, friend. It is a terrible place where the priest rules."

"How is that?" Paco asked, intrigued by the man's fury.

"The governor of Asturias in Oviedo chooses the mayor of every town in the region. How do you suppose he makes his selections?"

Paco shrugged.

"The local priests tell him. And you know whom the priest chooses? Whoever will help him control the people."

"That is common, my friend," Facundo said. "I am certain it happens that way in our town."

"Where is that?" the wife asked, hoping to deflect the topic to a calmer one.

"Colosía, near Panes," Paco said.

"Aha!" the man said, slapping his hand on the table. "Padre Benito."

"You know him?" Paco asked.

"No, but as mayor here I learned much about many of our villages. He is like this with the governor in Oviedo," he said, holding his fingers together.

"He has helped me," Paco said.

"Yes, and now you owe him."

"Did the priest select you for mayor?" Paco asked.

"*No, señor!* The governor had to choose me in spite of the priest because the people raised such a stink. They sent a delegation to Oviedo to meet with the governor because the priest's choice was a thief and a *cabrón.* Of course our fine priest won eventually, for I lasted only two years. I promise you one day he and all his brothers will pay."

Facundo had tired of the loud talk and said, "We must get an early start in the morning. Ready for bed, Paco?"

"Would you like some coffee?" the wife asked.

"Always time for coffee," Facundo said

By that time the host, still riled, stood. "I go to the stable," he said.

"May I go with you? I would like some air."

"If you wish. I only go to give the animals a final look."

Out in the darkness the man said, "One day such talk will cost me, but I cannot help it. It is too much, what they do."

"I agree, and I do not think you should worry about trouble. We should all be prepared to act when the time comes. Talk means nothing without action."

"I have acted," the man said, apparently annoyed by Paco's insinuation.

"I can see that, *señor.* You are not the first Asturian I have heard say such things. One day will come an uprising. God willing I will be part of it."

"You are very young," the man said, "but sometimes only the young are willing to take daring action. Take care. Spain depends on you."

*

The next morning the mule seemed content with the gentle, winding, downhill road to Colunga, and she moved at a good pace. It was their seventh day and Paco was anxious to see the ocean. "That man was angry last night."

"He is not alone, Paco."

"Yes, and the colonies are rebelling. Have you heard of any trouble in Cuba?"

"No, but I do not hear much. You will soon know."

The town appeared around a bend in the road at mid-afternoon. Half an hour later they entered Colunga, and Facundo said, "I once had a girlfriend from here; what a beauty! Her parents had come to Colosía to visit their parents. We were both seventeen as I remember."

"I never heard about her," Paco said.

"I learned early not to brag about my conquests. Those who do not believe you will call you liar; those who do will go after her."

"Did that happen to you, Uncle?"

"No, but it happened to a good friend. One morning he took his girlfriend to the mountains to look for snails. When he got her far enough up the mountain, he pulled her into one of the crevices in the rock and kissed her. To his surprise she returned the favor, and things went on from there. They had been going together for nearly a year. Well, with so little resistance, he was soon deep into what he had only dreamed of. It was his first time, and he returned home nervous but ecstatic, floating on a cloud, as he said later. That evening he came to the tavern and bought cider for everyone. Before he realized it he had dropped a hint of his tryst in the mountains. Encouraged by several more glasses of cider, he revealed the whole episode, embellished, of course. Soon his friends were laughing and making up stories of their own. One of the boys said finally, 'You will not mind if I take her out.' That made my friend angry. The rest looked at him surprised. 'Certainly you do not plan to marry her now,' one said. 'If she puts out to you, she will do it with others.' That was certainly not true. The girl loved my friend very much, but hearing that comment, my friend became morose. The thought had not occurred to him. He left the tavern and walked home believing his friends and thinking she should have made him wait until they were married, and she must be a whore, and who knows how many others have had her? Such thoughts plagued the poor boy until he could stand it no longer. He thought of confronting her, but he did not have the courage. Instead he avoided her for several days. She came to his house. His mother, who knew all about it, told her that her son was no longer interested in her. 'You are too free with your most precious possession' she said. 'You have shown what little value you place on it.' The girl ran out of the house crying. Of course my friend learned what his mother had told his girlfriend, and he became furious. But his mother, a very devoted and long suffering woman, calmly said, 'You are angry now, my son, but one day you will thank me. In betraying your love she has saved you from a life of shame.' My friend loved the poor girl with all his heart and was heartbroken. But marrying her now was impossible, for the entire village considered her a whore.

"He was wrong, of course. She loved him so much she was afraid to lose him. They were both immature and acted foolishly, but if you knew how many of our best citizens were born 'prematurely'—those whose parents ate before the table was set—you would be shocked."

"What happened to the girl?"

"Moved to Oviedo. I don't know what became of her."

Paco did not say a word. They rolled and bumped and approached the far edge of Colunga before either of them spoke. Finally, Facundo said, "Don't worry, Paco. Only my wife and I know about Marta. Her mother

28

knows, but she will not say anything. I know you have not told your friends, or I would have heard. Nothing travels like such news. I tell you this because Marta is a good girl and will make you a good wife."

His uncle's thoughts had not occurred to Paco, but he now had to consider them. After another long pause, he said, "Thank you, *Tío*. I will not betray her."

"Betrayal has many faces, Paco."

Paco looked puzzled.

"A woman has to be careful with betrayal because if she betrays her man, he is right to abandon her. It is a law as rigid as nature herself, one of the Commandments. But it is different with a man."

"How?"

"Marta is a normal woman; she cannot expect you to remain chaste during this long separation."

"I have heard that said, but it seems unfair."

"A commendable but ill-advised sense of fairness makes you think that. The problem is simple: no man wants to raise another man's child."

"But what if a man betrays his wife and the other woman bears a child?"

"If the child is indeed his flesh, then, in my opinion, he has responsibility, although some say no. They would say the woman took the risk, and she has to bear the consequences. That, to me, is not manly, though such men usually consider themselves *conquistadores*."

His uncle's words cut Paco with the sharp point of perfect logic. He had never before considered his uncle wise. Witty, sharp, entertaining, yes, but never wise until that moment.

By this time they had passed through the rather dull, ordinary town and were about to exit it.

"We are not stopping in Colunga, *Tío*?"

"Yes, but first I want you to see something."

On the outskirts of town, Facundo turned into a smaller road that ran directly north up a gentle hill. The wagon creaked and tossed as the mule strained up the rise. At the top, they stopped. Before them spread the Atlantic Ocean, called *El Mar Cantábrico,* north of Spain. The sight stunned Paco. He had seen lakes and rivers, but never such a powerful body of water; no, it was surely more than water. That endless, overwhelming ocean would soon become his adversary. The narrow beach before them opened out to immensity itself. Crashing waves capable of grinding boulders into sand were raising a furious mist that resembled a dark apparition hanging over the raging water. Paco imagined his ship tossing like a cork in a roiling sea that could easily swallow him. Stories of entire boatloads of sailors perishing in that raging ocean had stirred him as long as he could remember. All Spaniards had heard such stories. They were part of Conquistador legends. As second thoughts began to smudge Paco's adventurous fantasies, he reminded himself of the courageous men who braved that same ocean with no knowledge of what, if any, land they would find on the other side. Why had they risked their lives? Though he knew well the prescribed answer, for he had heard it countless times in school, around the village square and across the supper table, he could not imagine losing his life. Without life, nothing, he thought. But that conquistador trinity of glory, fame and fortune had permeated every village of the Iberian Peninsula. Now he would seek that trinity wrapped in the fine, New World silk that Spain had uncovered for the Old World four centuries ago.

They drove the wagon down the hill to watch a group of fishermen work on their nets. "It is a big ocean, Paco."

"Is it always this rough, *Tio*?"

"Every time I have seen it, it has looked like this, a furious woman who lures you only to rip you apart as you enter her."

Paco did not like his uncle's jibes. "Other men have crossed it," Paco said, teeth clenched.

"And many have failed." Then Facundo put his hand on Paco's shoulder. "But you will not fail because you have *cojones*."

Facundo decided to splurge by spending that night in an inn. After leaving the mule and wagon in the livery stable, they walked a few doors away to the Pensión España. The stone building looked as if it had once been a private home with a recent two-story addition on one side. The front door opened directly into a small vestibule with a counter, behind which sat the proprietor smoking a cigar, the guest ledger open before him. Through a glass door, Paco saw the dining room. Facundo asked for a room for two. The proprietor ran his fingers down the ledger page, then drew a key from under the counter, looked up, and said, "One real in advance,"

Facundo took the coin out of his wallet and handed it to the man. Without smiling or speaking, the man led them to a room down the hall, a tiny cube with no window and a small bed.

"Where can we wash?" Facundo asked.

"That pan and pitcher on the table. The outhouse is down the hall and out the back door."

Facundo turned to Paco, "We might have been better off at the stable." Paco sat on the bed and bounced a few times to test the mattress. Seeing his nephew smiling, apparently enjoying the accommodations, Facundo said, "You have never stayed in an inn?"

Paco shook his head.

"That explains your enthusiasm."

"We explore the town before it gets dark?"

Paco led his uncle out the door onto the busy street. Colunga had nothing out of the ordinary to commend it except the ocean, and that was what Paco wanted to see. It took them half an hour to reach the long docks in the enclosed bay, where the sun was dipping into the western promontory. As the sky darkened, the haze over the water blurred the horizon. Soon, the red halo above the hidden sun began to bleed across the sky. Although Paco did not see the water come up to kiss the sun and suck it into her depths, he was no less thrilled than if he had seen the sunset in all its glory.

"Perhaps at sea I will see a real sunset," he said.

"They say tropical sunsets are beautiful. Probably the warm air clears the sky. You will find many differences in the tropics."

"*Tio*, I am so excited I cannot wait. What a glorious adventure!"

His uncle smiled, "Come, we will see some of the town."

"In a while, *Tio*." Paco did not move, so his uncle sat on a nearby mooring and watched the sky turn red and then imperceptibly yield to deep blue. Ready to go, Facundo got up as if to walk away, but Paco remained fixed to the spot, dazzled by the transformation.

After a long while, oblivious to his uncle's attempts to leave, he broke the silence. "Look, Uncle, in the east. The sky brightens."

Facundo again sat down. Within minutes, the rosy full moon appeared in the east to cast its crystalline reflection over the water. As they began their stroll back to town the moon had donned her regal halo, and the wet, slate cobblestone street glistened like thousands of tiny moons.

Drizzle had quenched the moonlight as they reached the bustling center. Following the music they reached a tavern where a young man was playing a Spanish bagpipe at a long table lined with other youths. The song ended and, without pausing, the young man launched into a brisk march as the rest listened and tapped their feet. Paco could imagine soldiers marching into battle under the gold and red flag of Spain. The music so thrilled them that the bartender stopped his aerial pouring to listen. All eyes focused on the young man who sat erect and still, pouring out music. At the end of the piece the bartender brought him another glass of cider and patted his shoulder. "You drink free as long as you can play that bagpipe." The crowd cheered.

Paco and Facundo worked their way to the bar and ordered two glasses of cider. The next piece was a jota, during which the men broke into a chorus of rhythmic hand clapping. At the last chord the crowd again applauded and cheered. The music and applause attracted more patrons and soon men had jammed into the tavern to drink and join the singing.

Next morning, their eighth since leaving Colosía, Paco and Facundo sat in the pensión dining room to a breakfast of apples, bread, jam and coffee, after which they walked to the livery stable, paid their bill, and headed west toward Villaviciosa eighteen kilometers away. At first they could see and hear the ocean to their right beneath the cliff, but soon the road turned south into rocky country. As the mule clopped on with her head down, she looked back occasionally as if to show her exhaustion. Facundo indulged her by stopping frequently to rest and drink water, as the day passed with much conversation between the boy and his uncle.

*

With delays in Villaviciosa and in Arroes, both to repair a ruptured wagon wheel, they arrived finally at Gijón at noon of their twelfth day. It rained much those last days, and they were tired, but Paco could not wait to see the port. Gijón, the first real city of their journey, was second in size only to Oviedo, the capital, and had many inns, taverns and restaurants.

"Well," Facundo said, "We made it with nine days to spare."

"Let us go to the port."

"First: business. We must take care of the wagon and mule and find an inn. If that turns out to be as expensive as Colunga, we'll sleep in the stable."

They found a livery stable near the outskirts of the city and left the mule and wagon in the care of an old man who promised to care for both. Then they walked to the center of the city to find an inn. After stopping for cider at two taverns, Facundo saw a pensión that looked modest and comfortable. The Pensión Amistad was away from the center, but busy enough to be interesting and not far from the port. The entrance to the red brick, two-story building was a simple door with the upper half of glass. The sitting room drew them in, where two large windows faced the street so patrons could relax and view the passing parade in warm comfort. The blazing fireplace lent the room a warm glow. Opposite the fireplace stood the concierge's counter. As in Colunga, the concierge demanded the rent of three *reales* in advance.

"But we plan to stay a week at least," Facundo said.

"We require two days deposit and payment by the day as long as you stay," the concierge said. Though polite, he left no doubt about the terms, so Facundo accepted.

Equipped with the customary pan and pitcher, the room was more spacious and comfortable than their earlier one. An indoor privy attached to the building at the end of a narrow hallway was a definite convenience.

Facundo must have known he would not be able to talk Paco into strolling through the city until he had seen the port, so they headed there. After a twenty-minute walk Paco's nerve almost abandoned him at his first glimpse of the raging, giant ocean from the top of the hill. They stood there a moment to take it in and then walked down the hill past several stores and shops to the waterfront, where a large four-master was docked. Paco walked around to the front to see its name then ran back to his uncle, "Uncle, look. La Naviera!"

"Must be in for repairs."

"It is beautiful, Tío; so big. Where do I buy the ticket?"

"We will ask."

A young boy of about twelve dressed in a blue workman' uniform was walking toward them carrying a roll of heavy rope over his shoulder.

"Do you work on this ship?" Paco asked.

Glad for a chance to rest, the boy put down the rope. "La Naviera? No, I wish! I just work the dock."

"Where do I buy a ticket?"

"At the office up that street," he said, pointing up the hill. "She sails day after tomorrow."

"The boy must be wrong," Facundo said. "But if not, it is good we arrived early. Why don't I buy the ticket in my name, to avoid drawing suspicion to you?"

"With no passport, *Tío*?"

"What do you suggest?"

"I don't know, but if that fellow is right, we will have to do it soon."

"Ask for the departure date."

By this time they had reached the office. "Pardon me, sir," Facundo said. "Could you give us information about La Naviera?"

"She sails with the tide the morning after tomorrow."

"We were told December seventh," Paco said.

Offended at having his word questioned, the man said, "It has been changed. She leaves on the thirtieth."

"But why?"

"We found our crew; we leave early. Besides, we are stopping in Tenerife to pick up passengers."

"How much for passage?" Facundo asked.

"What class?"

"The lowest."

"Fifty pesos."

"Thank you," Facundo said, and turned and left.

"Twice as much as Padre Benito said, *Tio.*"

"You have no choice. Let us find a place to think over a glass of cider, to help us decide what to do."

As they walked Paco talked nervously, "Tenerife, Tío! The Canary Islands! *Que bueno!* But the price."

As they turned a corner, Facundo, always on the lookout for a tavern, spotted one that looked hospitable and turned in, ordered two glasses of cider at the bar, and took them to a table and sat down. "Do not worry about the price, Paco."

"I have enough, *Tio.* I will not need any when I meet Eugenio."

"I said not to worry. Now, what about buying the ticket in my name?"

"No. I am the one with the passport; I must do it. If you buy it, they will become suspicious."

"You are right, Paco. We will take care of it tomorrow. We will not think about all that might go wrong. Let us enjoy our evening."

"Please, let us buy the ticket now, Uncle. I want to feel it in my hand."

"Of course, Paco." Facundo swallowed the last of his cider and stood.

Approaching the ticket office they found a civil guard officer standing outside the door. He was wrapped in his cape with his sword scabbard protruding out the back; his three-cornered hat was pulled down over his brow.

Saluting, Facundo smiled, "Good afternoon, officer."

"Good afternoon." The guard touched his hat.

Paco said nothing, smiled politely, and walked into the wooden shack and asked the attendant for a ticket to Havana."

"*Pasaporte, por favor.*"

Paco laid his passport on the counter and glanced at his uncle. The ticket seller leafed through the passport, mumbled Paco's description, as he looked him over, and handed it back. "Fifty *pesos.*"

Paco counted out the coins from his money sack and waited. The man recounted it and put it in a box under the counter and then opened a large book and wrote down Paco's name and description from the passport and then took out a preprinted ticket, filled in the necessary data, placed it in an envelope, and handed it to Paco. "She leaves with the tide, day after tomorrow, the thirtieth. Be on board by six o'clock."

"Yes, Sir."

Stuffing the ticket into his coat pocket, Paco turned and walked out with Facundo. Again they nodded at the civil guard and walked toward the city center. After they had walked two blocks Paco said, "Do not look back, *Tío*, but the guard is following us."

"Probably going home."

"I hope so."

To test the theory, they turned down a side street lined on both sides with large warehouses. Paco carefully looked back after a block; the policeman was still behind them. Facundo again turned toward the original direction and headed for the tavern. Each time they turned, the policeman followed. At the tavern they sat at the same table they had used before and waited for the bartender. Soon the civil guard passed in front of the tavern and stopped, saw them, walked to their table, sat down, and took off his hat without speaking.

"How may we help you, *Señor Guardia*?" Facundo asked, trying to appear nonchalant.

In a quiet voice and looking directly at Paco, the officer said, "You have just bought a ticket on La Naviera."

"That is correct," Facundo said.

"Where are you going?" the officer asked calmly with his fingers interlocked on the table.

"Havana," Paco said in a strong voice, remembering his uncle's advice to act as if he were in the right.

"And your military service?"

Paco felt trapped with no way out. His first thought was that he had planned to join anyway. But suddenly he realized how much he had looked forward to freedom in a new land with fresh opportunities. Serving in the army now under strict regulations in God-knows-where had lost its appeal.

"Have you been excused from service?"

Having remained silent, Facundo now saw a solution: "Officer, the ticket is for me. I did not want anyone to know I was leaving because my wife has relatives in Gijón, and they would stop me."

"Why did this young man show his passport then?"

"Because I do not have one. I must make my way to Cuba to escape that nagging woman. I will be glad to run my risks with the law there."

"Good story and plausible, but a lie. This young man is attempting to evade military service. It is my duty to denounce him to army headquarters. Come with me."

"Please, officer, let us talk," Facundo said, speaking in low tones. "If you will allow him to report on his own, his attempt to leave will not be held against him. He was only following his parents' wishes. You see, they have already lost one son in Morocco and have a second there now. They are sick with worry that they might lose this one." Paco nodded dumbly as Facundo laid out his surprising plan.

"Irrelevant," the officer said. "I, too, and my brothers have served. Every man must answer his summons. It is the law."

Three men sitting at the next table had stopped talking and were listening to their muted conversation. When the officer noticed their silence, he stood and said, "*Vamos.*"

Paco and Facundo followed him out of the tavern and down the street. When they reached a small park the officer stopped. "I have been thinking about this boy's brothers," he said. "I wish I could do something, but my duty is clear."

"There are ways," Facundo said.

"Ways?" The officer looked around to be sure no one was listening.

"As I said, let him report alone."

"Why should I shirk my duty and run the risk of injuring my reputation and position?"

Paco stood back listening, wondering how it would end. If *Tío* convinces the officer, he thought, I will still have to enter the army.

"Officer, I completely agree with you," Facundo said. "It would be foolish to endanger your position for nothing. What would it be worth to take a small chance like this for a good cause?"

The officer stroked his chin as if thinking it over.

"But not merely to let him join the army," Facundo said. "That would be little help, since he will go in anyway if you arrest him. After all, he has not broken the law yet; he still has almost two weeks before he has to report."

The officer looked around again. "For fifty *pesos* I will not stop the boy from leaving."

"That is much money. I do not know if we have it between us." He looked at Paco imploring him with his eyes not to argue.

"Will you throw away this boy's future for a few pesos?" the officer said, shaking his head.

"Will you escort him to the ship? To show your support, so to speak, as if he were a relative, so that no one will suspect him?"

The officer thought for several seconds and said, "Yes, I will do that."

"Then I will give you twenty-five pesos now and the rest when he crosses the gangplank."

"How do I know I will get the rest?"

"You can arrest me and call the police to stop the ship. Once on board, he will clearly be escaping and would go to prison."

"*Bueno.*"

Facundo took out his wallet, but the officer stopped him. "Not here."

"We are staying at the Pensión Amistad. Meet us there in half an hour,"

Turning to walk off, the officer said, "If you are not there I will find you." Paco and Facundo returned to the pensión to wait. In thirty minutes the officer walked into the sitting room and saw them sitting by a window. Without acknowledging him, Facundo stood and walked down the hall to his room. The officer looked to see which door Facundo entered and, in a few moments, followed him, opened the door and entered.

"You will meet us at the dock at 6:00?" Facundo said, handing the policeman the money.

"I will be there. You will have the rest."

The next day passed without incident. Now on their guard, they did not venture far from the pensión and the nearby tavern. In contrast to the rest of their journey, neither Paco nor Facundo felt any desire for conversation. Paco offered to replace the fifty pesos with the remainder of his father's money, but his uncle adamantly refused. "I can think of no better farewell gift."

"But you may lose it and I may still remain. This man may be even more crooked than he acts."

"We must have faith in the greed of our adversaries, Paco." Facundo kept repeating that everything would work out, but Paco felt otherwise, so his uncle finally gave up trying to calm him. Instead he talked about the beautiful city and the ocean, which only made Paco feel worse knowing the life he would miss in prison or the army. A feeling of defeat and resignation had enveloped him as he recalled the words of the man on the mountain pass, "They always win." The civil guard might be playing with us, planning to turn us both in and keep the money. His thoughts drifted to Marta much of the day and how he could explain landing in prison. Feeling he no longer had a future he thought it might have been better to obey the army's order. By sunset, he had sat in the nearby tavern most of the day and had consumed so much cider he could barely stand. After sunset Facundo had to help him to the pensión. Knowing Paco never drank much, his uncle had made no effort to dissuade him, judging it best to let the boy sink into alcoholic oblivion.

Facundo managed to drag Paco to the port at 6:15 the next morning after splashing water on his face and forcing three cups of black coffee down his throat. At the dock they searched for the civil guard. Even with the growing crowd moving about, saying goodbye, and preparing to board or to see someone off, the man should not be difficult to find in his striking uniform. Being taller than average, Facundo could see over most people's heads, but he saw no one in uniform. As they roamed around the boarding area, Paco's anxiety grew, wondering if he would show up at the last minute with a platoon to take him away. Suddenly, Facundo felt a hand on his shoulder. The man stood smiling in full uniform and cape. "I am here to wish our young friend a good trip," he said in a strong voice.

Still suspicious, Facundo looked around for other civil guard officers, but saw none. "Thank you for coming," he said, and shook his hand. Paco also shook the officer's hand and smiled as if they were old friends. Still nervous, Paco said, "Well, it's time."

They shook hands again and Facundo embraced Paco. "I hope we will see each other again, Paco."

"And I also, *Tío*. And thank you for everything. You have taught me much. I wish you could come with me."

"My life is here, Paco. You can thank me and your parents by becoming a credit to them and to Spain in the New World."

Paco crossed the gangplank and looked down from the railing; the officer waved and smiled. Paco saw him turn to Facundo and whisper something, then Facundo holding his hand up and pointing to the gangplank, motioning that it would soon rise.

"But the remainder is due now."

"As soon as they lift the gangplank."

"If you try anything you will land in jail, I promise."

"Just protecting my nephew, officer." Patting his inside breast pocket, he said, "The money is right here and so am I."

They stood waving and trying to talk to Paco across the shouting and waving until a stevedore removed the huge lines from their moorings. The First Mate ordered the sails unfurled, and sailors scrambled over the ship's rigging. Under the eye of the civil guard Facundo stood in thrall at the emotional moment of the great activity urging the massive ship's slow movement. Within minutes the vessel had begun to slide away from the dock and into the bay. The civil guard turned to Facundo, who reached into his coat pocket and withdrew a sack of coins. "Please count them."

The officer pushed his hand back and said, "At your pensión. If it is not correct or if you are not there ..."

"I know: you will find me." Facundo laughed then continued, "*Muchisimas gracias, Señor Guardia.* You have done a good deed. This is the best money I have ever spent." He again shook the officer's hand

and waved again at Paco, who was disappearing into a haze along with La Naviera.

As the faces on deck became indistinguishable, Facundo put his arm around the officer's shoulder. "You are a good man, officer. His parents and I will always remember you. Come, I buy you a glass of cognac."

The officer smiled as they walked away. At the edge of the dock Facundo stopped to look back at the ship. "One moment, please." It had become a blur sinking into the haze, a haloed ghost of a ship. Facundo stood waving for a long time.

"*Vamos*; he cannot see you."

"I know, but final goodbyes take time."

CHAPTER 2 - MATANZAS, CUBA

*

France and Spain Negotiate Alliance

*

Spain to Garrison Rome in the Event of a European War

*

Queen Victoria Arrives Home To Buckingham Palace

*

Queen Isabel of Spain Announces Her
Abdication in Favor of Prince

*

It was still dark when Paco left his clammy steerage compartment to walk out to the deck's port side. After three weeks of fitful sleep and dizziness, he stood at the railing straining bleary eyes against the horizon. The luminous spot he had been watching was yawning into a city that rose as if from primal darkness to cry out its first sign of life in flickering lights and sounds.

An hour later the Naviera slid slowly into the long narrow channel as the blazing solar torch burst behind the great stone fortress's lighthouse. On the opposite side of the channel stood another fort. Paco had read that these two sentries guarded Havana Harbor, the seat of Spanish power in America, for centuries. And during recent years the military gauntlet of Spanish occupation had hardened. As her colonies, one by one, ripped themselves loose from Spain, Queen Isabel II grasped her remaining few closer to her bosom, and, with ever-tighter grip, struggled to keep alive her glorious ancestors' vision of empire.

In the golden-rosy morning, the New World's promise spread across the sky as if for Paco alone. Sleeplessness and seasickness could not dampen his excitement. As the long, narrow channel opened into the immense, sprawling port, Paco gaped at the sight of the great city that lined the broad harbor. But what struck him most were the pink clouds and the golden glow that filled all space, and the soft, green hills in the distance adorned with sultry palms curving with abandon. Cuba looked nothing like his cold, muscular homeland; this warm land felt sensuous, feminine.

It took nearly an hour for stevedores to tie La Naviera to the dock and for passengers to drift out on deck to wait for the gangplank to drop.

Only in the past week had the rough Atlantic lifted its misty veil to reveal the sun in its scorching brilliance. And in that week Paco's face and hands had nearly blistered after so many hours on deck. His chalky, pink-cheeked face now glowed bright red with a new feeling of discomfort. A broad-brimmed hat would be his first purchase.

Some of the buildings looked like those in Asturias—stone with red tile roofs, the cathedral with its bell tower—but most houses were painted in pastels and had larger windows. The new world felt so different that Paco thought it could be a different planet, one closer to the sun. The green Caribbean water felt like a caress after weeks on the mighty Atlantic.

Long before La Naviera docked, most passengers had gathered on deck ready to disembark. Paco stood with them, shifting his bag from one hand to the other near where the gangplank would fall. But as soon as the gangplank dropped and before anyone could exit, a platoon of soldiers in blazing red and gold uniforms marched aboard and set up a long table across the exit. With stern faces, military ceremony and pomp, the soldiers lined up behind the table, where three officers examined disembarking passengers' passports. Paco held his out. The lieutenant flipped through the pages, read carefully the description, and then looked up. "Your military discharge papers?"

"I have not served."

"Your notification of ineligibility then?"

"I have none." Anticipating this possibility, he had decided to claim ignorance, hoping the worst they could do was induct him on the spot, in which case he would already be in paradise. He smiled, tried to appear innocent and managed pretty well to control his emotions as Facundo had taught him.

"Are you sure?" The sergeant squinted suspiciously.

"No, sir. I mean, yes, Sir. I am sure."

"Do you read?"

"Yes, sir."

The sergeant handed him a form. "Complete this."

Paco moved to a spot near the railing and sat with his bag in his lap and filled out the form. It asked for home address, personal data, where he would be staying and for how long. Paco answered everything, including his Uncle Eugenio's address in Matanzas and his parents' address in Colosía and his plan to remain permanently in Cuba. To the question dealing with military service he answered that he had not been called. He finished and returned to the lieutenant who was checking another passenger's passport. The lieutenant looked up, took Paco's form, looked it over, frowned and said, "You will hear from us."

Deflated by the not-so-subtle threat, he recovered his excitement by the time he reached the bottom of the gangplank, where he stopped to take the final step, a step befitting the moment, a ceremonial step upon the new world. Finally standing on land for the first time in six weeks, he felt a great desire to fall down and kiss the ground, but he knew people would think him crazy. There would be time later.

Even before his interrogation, Paco had searched the crowd for his Uncle Eugenio. Standing on the dock, still searching, he felt the ground move beneath him, as if he were still at sea. One of the crew had warned him of that feeling, and he had not believed him.

A small brown dog of nondescript lineage came at him barking and showing his teeth in brief surges of fury. Paco had to smile at the tiny dog's bluster. As he reached down the dog retreated, still barking. Paco extended his hand, and the dog stopped barking and looked at him. Paco snapped his fingers and left his hand out. Cautiously the dog approached and smelled his hand. Paco reached over him to pet him and the dog again retreated. Paco spoke softly until the mutt came to him again and licked his fingers. Paco stroked his head and told him in his gentle voice that he would give him something to eat if he had any. Finally, he stood and continued to look for his uncle.

Strange looking people moved around him, Africans, Chinese, Indians: a human whirlpool. He had heard of the Negroes and, as he had heard, some were as black as coal. But he did not expect them to have such different features. He had imagined they would look like white people, but with black skin. The large lips and broad noses and the tight, curly hair drew his eyes, until he realized one woman had noticed his staring. She appeared to have the mixed color and features of a racial hybrid.

A very thin, very black man approached selling fritters. Paco did not understand him. *"Habla español?"*

The man smiled, *"Claro."*

He was the first Cuban Paco had heard speak. As soon as he realized it was his accent and not a different language, he began to understand. Even though he did not want food, he delighted in the man's speech and wanted to continue the conversation.

"How much?"

"Un centavo," the man said, smiling. "You are a *Gallego*?"

"Asturiano," Paco said.

"Many of you Gallegos in Cuba these days. You like our little country?"

"I said I am Asturian."

"Same thing," the man said, handing Paco the fritter and smiling.

Paco decided not to argue and took the fritter, paid him and turned to look for Eugenio. With the dog still following him, Paco reached down and gave the mutt a small piece of his fritter, which the dog ate in one bite.

After a few minutes walking and looking and chewing, he realized he was wet from perspiration under his wool pants and wool jacket, so he took off the jacket, laid it over one arm, and carried his bag with the other. Sweet, ripe fruit odors mingled with the smell of the sea. Along with fried fritters, semi-sweet and pungent, and other items being sold around him, the scents stretched from appetizing to revolting. A tall, slender young woman in a long, white dress and a broad white hat trimmed with a yellow ribbon attracted Paco's attention. He had first seen her standing by the gangplank with a white parasol as he stepped off. She was clearly waiting for someone to disembark. Lightly tanned, blonde and shapely, she could have been Asturian. Eventually a man, also dressed in white, walked down the gangplank to her. They embraced, kissed on the cheek and walked off together. Paco wondered if he was her husband, sweetheart or a friend or brother. Turning to watch her walk away, Paco saw a man who could be his uncle. He was not sure because of the mob around the gangplank. He stood on his toes trying to see over the crowd, but could not. The man would disappear from his line of sight and then reappear briefly and disappear again. Finally Paco reached him. *"Tío Eugenio!"* he yelled and threw his coat onto his other arm and shook his hand.

"Paco! Almost I did not know you. You have become a man."

"I had twelve years when you left Colosía, *Tío*."

"You look good, Paco, strong and handsome. How went the trip?"

"Fine. Well, not so fine. I threw up almost every day. I think I have lost weight. But here I am."

"Magdalena will fatten you." Then looking down he said, "A friend of yours?"

Paco looked down and saw the mutt wagging his tail enthusiastically. "We just met," Paco said. "I gave him something and now he loves me."

"Want to take him with us?" Eugenio asked.

"Oh, no. He is nice, but I have other things to think about."

At forty-five Eugenio stood tall and slender and quite handsome with his light brown handlebar moustaches, bushy sideburns, and brown hair parted in the middle with a slight curl at the ends. Paco remembered him as gangly and awkward, but now he was a gentleman smoking a long cigar and sporting a white linen suit with a black tie and a broad-brimmed Panama hat pushed back on his head. He was very tan now, and his large blue eyes radiated warmth. They talked on their way to the waiting carriage. The Negro driver sat in the saddle waiting for them. They climbed in and Eugenio told the driver to take them to the train station.

"On the ship I heard something about an insurrection."

"Insurrections in Cuba are as common as coconuts, Paco."

*

The driver wore a white, broad-brimmed hat and a short, blue jacket over a white shirt and tan trousers. Paco smiled as he recalled the wagon ride to Gijón, so different from this fancy carriage with padded seats and a canopy. They drove through the shabby neighborhood that surrounded the docks and then into the heart of the city, past some large buildings and shops and outdoor taverns and stores that sold fruits, chickens, meats, seafood and items Paco had never seen. And everywhere people walked and chatted as in Asturias, but in the warm climate, they seemed more relaxed, open, and hospitable.

"Are we going to see Havana, *Tío*?"

"I do not want to miss our train to Matanzas, Paco."

As the horse trotted on, Paco said, "Is it December in Cuba, *Tío*?"

Eugenio smiled. "It is December everywhere."

"But I have heard that when it is winter in Asturias, it is summer in South America."

"Correct, but Cuba is in the Northern Hemisphere, so it is winter here too, although it will not feel like Asturias."

"To tell the truth, *Tío*, this feels like no season I have ever seen."

"It is like this most of the year—a little hotter in summer, but always a breeze."

"What are the great forts at the mouth of the harbor?"

"The one with the lighthouse is the Morro Castle; the one across it is El Castillo de La Punta."

"This city is more big than Gijón, *Tío*. It must be as big as Oviedo."

"And Madrid. Havana is one of the great cities of the Spanish Empire. We will return to see it with calm after you get settled. Havana is a worthy capital."

"And Matanzas? How far it is?"

"About one hundred kilometers. Two hours by train."

"Fifty kilometers per hour," Paco said. "It took us twelve days to travel one hundred fifty kilometers to Gijón. We will travel as far in one hour as we did there in four days."

"That is the difference between a horse and a train, Paco."

"She was a tired old mule."

"We have those too."

Before they boarded the train Eugenio walked Paco to the engine. "It pulls the train by burning wood from the car behind."

"*Coño! Que grande!* I have heard of them in Spain, but this is the first one I have seen."

With great hissing and puffing the train jerked, and Paco grabbed the armrests. In a few minutes the beast was leaving a trail of gray smoke through the countryside as it took Paco faster than he had ever moved. He held onto the chair, looking out the window as the countryside flew past the noisy beast. He imagined he was riding a charging bull. First the city with row after row of buildings and stores that blurred as they passed; then, within half an hour, they raced through fields and farms of rich green. Paco had never felt such force and speed, like being on a bullet, he thought. He could barely focus on the trees and houses and animals, for they were gone before he could recognize them. Eventually, the monotonous clacking of steel wheels on steel tracks mesmerized him, and he fell asleep with his head against the window. An abrupt slowing with hissing and jarring woke him; he smiled at his uncle and resumed looking at the sights along the track.

At the Matanzas train station Eugenio waved at a Negro waiting astride a horse hitched to a carriage. The man drove to them, dismounted, and placed Paco's bag in the back of the carriage. They climbed in and the driver climbed into his saddle and nudged the horse.

The ride to Eugenio's farm took three quarters of an hour through the city and then south through gentle hills. "Here we are," Eugenio said as they passed through a gate onto a red clay road. The approach to the house was lined with rows of stately royal palms, perfectly aligned like soldiers on guard. Palms normally offer scant shade, but these were so profuse and closely spaced that they cast welcome shadows. With the recent rain the palms drooped slightly, but barely noticeably as befitting soldiers who know how to endure hardship without whimpering. Near the front of the house, the path split into a loop in front of the porch. Around the loop grew a hedge of brightly colored leafy plants so tall that one might take them for small arbors.

A great porch stretched across the front and half way back the side of the house with another like it on the second floor. Round, white columns topped with simple scrolls held up the second floor, and another set above them held up the roof over the second floor porch. A white, wrought iron railing stretched between the columns to enclose both porches, and a red tile roof overhung almost a meter. With the window's slatted shutters open, the breeze kept the sheer curtains billowing constantly. All around the house a hedge of the same large-leaf, multicolored plants wreathed the house. "What are those, *Tío?*"

"Crotons. They grow only in warm climates."

It could have been a big house or a small mansion. Paco could not tell. Beyond the porch a giant bougainvillea vine covered the stucco wall on one side with bright red flowers trumpeting loudly. That vine might once have made the house look homey and charming. Now, growing randomly, it burst like a tropical explosion, reaching the second floor eaves and digging its tentacles around the porch railings. With the recent rain the flowers sagged like old hags straining to lift their arms in prayer. Surrounding the house perhaps ten meters distant, a row of fruit trees, mango, avocado, banana, orange, tamarind, and sapodilla had overgrown their neat placement and now sprawled over the lawn, transmuting the refined, cultured garden of its planter's intent into the jungle of its genetic yearning. Succulent fruit dangled unashamed with the audacity of unbridled life in that tropical womb where every plant fought to smother all others. The fruits were mostly new to Paco, but the crotons caught his eye, especially the red and black ones. He had never before seen such leaves.

Behind the house in the distance stood a field of meter-high cane swaying in the breeze with occasional coconut and royal palms, remnants of past years. Beyond them rose smooth, round green hills that reminded

Paco of women's breasts. As the carriage stopped at the porch Eugenio and Paco stepped out and walked up the four-step geranium-lined entrance directly into the house.

Meeting Paco in the living room, a life size portrait of a tall, slender, young woman smiled down on him. She wore a long white dress with the hem rumpled around her feet. The regal, young woman seemed to be pausing on her journey out of the murky past. With a black lace mantilla over her head and shoulders, she held to her bosom a bouquet of red roses. Her face, milky-white with rosy cheeks, radiated contentment and perception, as her smile betrayed unbearable sadness. Paco thought she was the most beautiful woman in the world and stared for several moments as Eugenio watched with amusement.

Through the arch that led to the dining room, the incarnate Magdalena appeared and took Paco's hands. "Welcome!" she said, with a warm embrace. "How anxious I have been to meet you!" Her exuberant smile caressed Paco, as he looked over her shoulder imagining that she had stepped out of the portrait. Magdalena stood tall, slender, erect, with shiny black hair in a large bun at the back of her head, large brown eyes, and a small, flattering mole on her left cheek. Her white dress swept the floor as she moved. At thirty she was still youthful. Paco had heard that Eugenio, nearly forty when he left Asturias, had married a younger woman, but he did not expect such loveliness.

Lacing her arm in Paco's she said, "Come, dear nephew, lunch awaits us," and led him into the dining room. Then she disappeared into the kitchen and, in a few minutes, emerged followed by a Negro maid carrying a platter of dishes.

As the maid laid out the salad dishes, Paco could not stop admiring her smooth, dark beauty. She was roughly his age with dark skin, but not as dark as the Negroes he had seen at the port, and her hair was not as curly or black, but brown, wavy, and thick. She wore an apron over her long gray dress and a bandana over her hair. She set his plate before him, and he noticed the palms of her hands were as light as his. He looked down at his palms to see their color. In all her movements around the table she never looked at him directly.

Magdalena sat beside Paco at the large table and chatted softly, as the maid served lunch. In Magdalena Paco imagined his Marta, who would one day assume similar duties in his home. His fantasies ran wild over his new tropical paradise.

Sensing Paco's attraction to his wife, Eugenio seemed serious at first, but finally laughed. "I think you will like our climate better than your cold Asturian drizzle," he said. "After lunch we will see the farm."

47

Paco nodded as he chewed and found most of the food the maid put before him quite strange: black beans, rice, fried plantains, and a meat Magdalena called *tasajo*, which she later said was dried horse meat. Paco had not eaten with such enthusiasm since boarding the ship weeks before. He devoured it all.

"The maid is African?" he asked, after she had left the room.

"Lydia? Yes, her mother was."

"And her father?"

"He was white. We know nothing about him." Magdalena looked at her husband sadly. "Anyway, she is ours."

Paco tried to hide his horror at the thought. He surmised the carriage driver was a slave also.

"You talk different," he said. "Were you born here?"

"Yes. My grandparents were Canary Islanders. It is a long story."

"Please tell me."

Sitting back, Magdalena sipped her coffee. "Grandfather arrived in 1779, almost ninety years ago, with the Spanish army. The crown had sent many Canary Islanders to Louisiana to colonize her new possession and establish a sugarcane industry. It was Canary Island's most important crop, and they knew how to grow it. When the British marched into Louisiana the Spanish king ordered troops there to push back the intruders. The Spanish ship stopped in Havana, where the local commander decided they could not beat the enormous British force that had amassed in New Orleans, so they remained in Havana. Later that year my grandfather sailed to the Canary Islands, married my grandmother, and brought her here. The troops never got to Louisiana, and eventually my grandfather was discharged, acquired a piece of this land and made his living growing sugarcane right here in Matanzas. My grandmother bore him fourteen children, of which my father was the fourteenth. Only four reached maturity, however. My father was born in this house in the first year of the new century. My mother emigrated from the Canary Islands as a child. They were married in 1837 and I was born that year. My father was thirty-six; my mother sixteen."

"I had hoped to go to the Canaries with the army, but at least I got to see it. It looks like Cuba."

"Spaniards settled those islands centuries ago for what reason I do not know," she said. "I have not been there, but I'm told it is very beautiful. And you, Paco? How do you like your new country?"

"Very much. Nothing like the cold I am used to."

"Here I have been telling you about ancient history, and we have not asked about your trip. How did it go, Paco?"

"I was seasick much of the first week, but I finally got over it. There is nothing to tell, really ... Oh, yes, a man fell overboard."

"Terrible!" Magdalena said.

"It was during our third week, I believe. I was on the gunwale at the port side talking with the First Mate when the alarm sounded. It was just past sunset. We both ran to the stern as a sailor threw a life preserver out behind the ship. We could not see anyone in the water because it was nearly dark. The First Mate dropped a small boat into the water with two men. Hearing who had fallen in, I asked to go with them. It was a young boy from Gijón; we had become friends. We rowed all around looking, trying not to lose sight of the ship, but nothing. The waves were very high. The First Mate led the search; the other man and I rowed, but nothing. We were so anxious to find the boy that we rowed too far and lost sight of the ship. I must admit, I was scared. But the First Mate was a very good sailor. He remained calm and ordered us to stop rowing and listen, that the ship would sound the alarm if they lost our position. He was right, for we soon heard the horn. We rowed toward the sound and finally spotted her. We had been gone almost an hour."

"You were very brave to volunteer like that," Magdalena said.

"The poor boy had been scared out of his wits the whole trip. He wouldn't venture out near the side of the ship for fear of falling over. I cannot imagine how he managed to fall in. I felt a little bad because ..."

"What?" Magdalena said.

After hesitating Paco continued, "I told him he would get over his fear if he forced himself to stand at the gunwale and look down at the water. He must have been doing that and fell."

"You gave him good advice, Paco," Eugenio said. "Many people have such fears. They must overcome them. The ship must have rocked and caused him to fall."

"You must not hold yourself responsible, Paco," Magdalena said. "I feel for his poor mother."

"So do I, and for him too."

"Well, you must forget all that," she said. "You are with your family. What are your plans in Cuba?"

"Eventually to acquire a farm, but first, I suppose, the army."

"Have you been called?"

"Actually yes, before I left. That is why I came now, to try to escape them. But before I got off the ship in Havana, the soldiers made me register."

"That does not mean they will call you," Eugenio said. "Only if they do not fill their quota. In the meantime, you will work with me and learn about sugarcane. If they call you, you will go; if not, and if you work hard, you may eventually get that farm."

"You think so, really?"

"Certainly. Magdalena's father had no sons, so he left me his land and I have quadrupled it. I will help you when you are ready."

"Thank you, *Tío*."

After lunch they went to the stable and saddled two horses. Within minutes they were trotting along the edge of a cane field that seemed to run for a kilometer along a narrow creek with hills in the distance. They stopped where a dozen very thin black men were cutting cane with machetes. In two smooth motions, they would whack a stalk down near the ground, lop off the top leaves and throw the cane stalks behind them leaving a trail of cane.

"Who is the man with the whip?"

"Manuel, my overseer."

"And the whip?"

"Slaves sometimes need encouragement, Paco."

"I have never seen a man whipped."

"Better not to think of them as men, Paco."

They rode in a direction perpendicular to the farmhouse road and stopped at a hut with several machines and some metal vats. "We have two slaves who stuff the cane between the rollers in one of these presses. The ox hitched to that pole turns the rollers like a crank. The ox pulls the pole in a circle, which turns the cylinders of the press and squeezes out the juice into these containers. We empty the full containers into those large vats over a fire to evaporate the water from the juice. When the syrup is the right thickness we pour it into these cone-shaped pots with a hole in the small end that we plug with a piece of wood. As the pots cool, the molasses sinks to the bottom and we remove it through that hole in the point of the cone. The remaining sugar comes out in lumps that I sell to the agent who, in turn, sells it to wholesalers all over the world."

"Seems simple," Paco said.

"Yes, but it takes much labor."

"Is that the main cost?"

"Without slaves I could not compete."

"It is not right to own a person, *Tío*." Paco stood erect, shoulders back, as if daring his uncle to argue. "They are men and no less human than we."

"I feed and house them. They want for nothing."

"Except freedom."

"Who has freedom? Are you not escaping from the army?"

"This is different, Uncle. They cannot escape."

"Neither can you. I know how you feel, but what remedy remains for us?"

"To farm your own land as we do in Spain."

"Then I would have to live the way I lived there, barely earning my living. I left Asturias with nothing because your father, the eldest brother, was the heir. The rest of us had to fend for ourselves as you are doing. And the heir is the real slave. He must work all his life to stay alive and then leave what little he has to his eldest. Call that freedom?"

"But no one owns him," Paco said.

"The land and the system own him, and if the king calls he must, like a slave, obediently send his sons. In this system the Negroes are not much worse off. Each man must look after himself and his own, Paco. By enslaving a few Africans, I can live well and leave something to each of my children so they can live well. You see things simply, Paco, because life at your age is simple. In a few more years you will see things as they are. Life makes pragmatists of us in the end."

Paco felt he could never become that pragmatic, but he did not want to argue with his host and benefactor. Then he wondered if not arguing was also hypocritical, for was not his reticence a small step toward pragmatism? No, I know what is right and what is wrong, he thought. That will not change.

That evening Magdalena broached the question that had burned her for weeks. They had finished supper and Lydia had cleared the table. Eugenio had lit his cigar, and Lydia had brought out coffee. Having never smoked a cigar, Paco was about to ask Eugenio for one.

"You have a girl in Asturias, I hear," Magdalena said.

"Marta. We will marry as soon as I have money to send for her."

"Is she pretty?"

"Prettiest girl in the valley. Brown hair, hazel eyes and, you know … we have the same age."

"You are young for marriage, Paco," Eugenio said. "Cuba overflows with beautiful girls."

"Others have said the same, but we are for each other," he said. "She waits for me."

"And the army?"

"She will wait."

"Sounds like much waiting," Eugenio said, taking a long draw of his cigar. "You must experience life even as you wait, Paco. Life is short."

Magdalena's sad smile almost brought tears to Paco's eyes as he wondered about the source of her sadness.

Lydia came in to take away the remaining dishes. Paco's eyes followed her movements around the table. As the kitchen door closed behind Lydia, Magdalena said, "Lydia also is pretty."

Eugenio smiled and looked at Paco. He suspected Paco's self-discipline would torment him, but he had said enough. It was up to Paco to follow his plan or to explore the terrain of his adopted land.

"May I try a cigar, *Tío?*"

"Certainly, Paco." Eugenio handed him one from his humidor. "Have you smoked before?"

"No, but it looks good." Taking the cigar, he bit the end off as his uncle had done and stretched to reach one of the candles on the table. He took several puffs and sat again holding the cigar between two fingers.

"You must inhale with caution, Paco. It could choke you or make you sick if you take too much at first."

"I am fine, *Tío,*" Paco said. He took a deep puff into his lungs and immediately began to cough."

"Not like that," Eugenio said. "Like this," He took a mouthful of smoke and then removed the cigar from his mouth and sucked the smoke into his lungs.

"Perhaps later," Paco said.

Magdalena stood to go into the kitchen. "Men!" she muttered as she walked out.

Magdalena had given Paco the corner room at the head of the stairs on the north side, across and down the hall from Eugenio's and Magdalena's bedroom. With windows on two sides and a door to the second floor porch, it was a choice location with a view of the royal palm drive and, in the distance, the road to Matanzas. Magdalena had furnished it simply with a large bed, a chest of drawers, a small desk and chair and an armoire. That evening Paco spent an hour on the porch absorbing the glow of sunset over the city of Matanzas and fantasizing over his new home.

*

The next morning Eugenio woke Paco at sunup. "Your vacation is over, Paco. The hour for work."

Rubbing his eyes he jumped out of bed and went to the window to make sure he had not dreamed his trip. Seeing the sun peering over the horizon, he stood to watch it and thought of Marta. That same sun is nearly overhead where she is now, he thought. How strange, the way it floats over the world like a god. He imagined her smiling and flirting with him, tossing her hair and her skirt. How long, he wondered, before he could hold her again and kiss her?

An obnoxious gust of wind blew into his window, and he tried to identify the odor. Burnt leaves, perhaps, he thought. Behind the burnt odor hung a sour-sweet, fermented fruit odor. At first he thought it had come from the kitchen, but then saw smoke in the distance near a metal-roofed shack.

Hearing footsteps down the stairs, Paco took his father's old watch off the night table, wound it, and laid it down again. Then he jumped into his clothes. In minutes he was standing in the kitchen watching Magdalena supervise Lydia. Eugenio came in through the back door and said, "Today I teach you to cut cane. But first, breakfast."

They sat in the dining room and Lydia brought out the coffee and milk pots, a tray of fresh slices of mango, mamey and papaya, a tray of freshly baked bread, butter, preserved fruit, and orange juice. As she held the bread tray for Paco, she smiled. He nodded and took two buns.

"What are these fruit, Lydia?"

"Mamey and mango, Señor," she said as she laid a slice of each on his plate.

"Thank you," he said, and tasted each of them. "Strong, aren't they?"

"Very rich and nourishing," she said, smiling. "You will soon develop the taste, and you will want nothing else."

Paco found the fruit much sweeter than any he had ever tasted. "I like them, Lydia," he said. Then he turned to Eugenio. "We cut where the men were yesterday?"

"No, a fresh field. I can teach you better if we are alone."

"It does not look complicated, Uncle. I am very good with the scythe"

"A machete is not a scythe, but we shall see. Now eat. The sun gets hot early."

Within minutes they were saddling two horses in the barn behind the house. Paco felt at home in the barn with its familiar smells and tools and animals. They rode out to a cane field beyond the one Paco had seen the day before. In the strong breeze the tall, green cane swayed like waves in mid-ocean. Dismounting and taking out his machete Eugenio said, "It is very sharp, so be careful. Now watch." He grabbed a cane stalk near the middle and severed it near the bottom with a clean stroke. Then, without losing the momentum of the swing, he lifted the machete across the lower leaves and whisked them away with another clean stroke and with a third he topped the cane stalk, threw it behind him, and grabbed another and repeated the movements four times. "Now you," he said.

Paco stepped to the edge of the field, looked at his uncle and bent down and brought the machete down so hard he severed five cane stalks and watched them topple around him before he could raise the machete to cut off the leaves. He turned to Eugenio. "Too hard?"

"Again."

Within five or six strokes he had picked up the rhythm and was cutting the cane as Eugenio had done. Looking up he said, "Like swinging a scythe."

"Actually, Paco, a scythe is more difficult to swing than a machete. Now let us cut for a while and see how we do."

Paco smiled at him knowing he had the advantage of youth.

"You cut here; I'll go across the path," Eugenio said.

With that, Paco started to swing furiously as Eugenio walked across the path and began. Barely aware of the heat and the sun beating on him, Paco left a trail of canes in his wake. He did not look to see how his uncle was faring or how far he had gone into the field. He simply cut with a constant, rapid rhythm, feeling good to be doing man's work after so many weeks, thinking of nothing but the cane, for there was no energy for thinking or musing, only for cutting and the blade in his hand that flew down and across and up like a clock in perfect time.

Paco heard his name and turned to see Eugenio behind him. "How goes it?" Eugenio asked.

"Fine. How much did you cut?"

"Over there."

Paco looked back at his large pile to impress his uncle, but across the path his uncle's pile was nearly twice as big. "*Coño!*" he said.

"It is all in the wrist, Paco. You will catch on." He put his arm around his nephew's dripping shoulder and said, "You have done very well for your first attempt. Not many of my workers do as well even after many years."

"Why should they?" Paco asked. "They have nothing to gain."

"Oh, yes. Hard as this is, I have worse jobs."

Catching a glimpse of a small figure walking toward them, Paco strained to see. "It's Lydia," he said.

"Bringing water, I suppose."

"Good. I'm dry."

The small figure grew as she walked with a clay water jug on her head, holding it steady with one hand. The load smoothed her stride with only a slight swaying at the hips. Paco could not stop staring at the graceful girl glide like a dancer down the dirt path. With her wild mass of hair tied back with twine and a white kerchief over it, her brown face looked long and angular with full lips stretched into a bright smile. She lifted the jug off her head and handed it to Eugenio. He took a long draft and handed it to Paco, who was still staring at her. She had first reminded him of a feral cat, but now, standing in the sun, her brown skin glistened magically: a pale chocolate doll with white teeth and large, green eyes, strangely, exotically beautiful. The way her pink palms contrasted with her dark skin still fascinated Paco, who wondered if she had the same female features as white girls. Of course, she must, he thought. She is a woman like any other, and not so different at that. He handed her the jug and turned to Eugenio. "Shall we continue?"

"My overseer will bring slaves to work this field soon. I just wanted you to know what it takes."

"May I cut some more?"

"Pa' que?"

"I like it."

Eugenio smiled. "If you wish, but I have other work for you."

"Just a while, Uncle," Paco said, as he lifted his machete.

Leading his horse into the barn, Paco was dripping wet. He unsaddled her, put the machete away, and walked to the pump shed. He took off his shirt and splashed his face, chest and arms with water. Magdalena saw him through the window and came out with a towel. "How did it go?" she asked, holding it out.

"Very well. Uncle Eugenio is amazing."

"I sent Lydia out with water. I knew you would be thirsty."

"Yes, much thanks. How many years has she?"

"Twenty-one. I remember the day she was born. She has been mine since she had six years. She is like family."

"Not like property, livestock?"

"Please do not judge us, Paco. Of course she is not livestock. I love her as a sister, but we all must work. She is human and feels pain as we do." Magdalena's face had turned sad.

Paco shook his head in disbelief.

"What is the matter?"

"Horrible," he said, looking out past the barn to the fields. "You love her as a sister, yet you keep her as a slave."

Magdalena began to cry, and Paco said, "I'm sorry, Magdalena. I have no right."

After several minutes she stopped. "No, Paco. I should explain. You see she is my father's daughter. My mother never knew it. Before Lydia's mother died she told Lydia and Lydia told me. I was fifteen. I asked Papá if it was true. He became angry and cursed Lydia's mother for telling her. Later, he admitted it and said he wanted Lydia to be mine because I had a kind heart and would not abuse her. And he told me not to tell Mamá because it would hurt her feelings."

"How did he treat Lydia?"

"Always with respect and kindness, but never friendly or warm. He felt it would be wrong to treat her as a daughter."

"Does Eugenio know?"

"Of course."

Paco handed back the towel.

"Slavery is our national shame, Paco. We all detest it, but without it we could not survive. Also the government will not let us abolish it, for it is the source of our nation's wealth."

"The queen cannot tell you what to do with your personal property."

"Liberating Lydia would ruin her life, Paco. She would have to go to the city and live as best she could, probably as a prostitute."

"She could not live here as your sister?"

"People would not accept her."

"But they must know," he said.

"Perhaps, but we must keep up appearances."

"This is supposed to be a civilized country."

"Simple pragmatism, Paco."

"I have heard that word twice in two days."

"It is not a bad word. Do me a favor, please. Do not reject her."

"What? I have not ..."

"She thinks you do not like her."

"I do not know how to treat a slave."

"She is no less a person than you."

Paco, of course, had found Lydia interesting, and he wanted to talk with her. He wondered if he had indeed been cold to her. "I did not mean to offend."

"I know, Paco. She is ours, but you are ours too. In a different way, of course, but we all belong to each other."

Paco again turned his gaze to the fields. The heat of the sun on the pump shed's metal roof radiated down on them.

"By the way, Paco, Eugenio is waiting for you at the processing plant."

Paco put his shirt on as he ran to the barn and again saddled the mare and rode toward the processing plant, his mind wrestling with Magdalena's revelation. Pushing her away was the last thing he had wanted, but perhaps he had.

As he approached the plant, Paco recognized that morning's odors: burning spent cane stalks under kettles of cane juice. The odor of fermentation must have come from spilled cane juice in puddles and unwashed vats. He dismounted where Eugenio was talking with his overseer. Each had dangling from his belt a whip with a short, wooden handle and several leather strands. Eugenio turned to Paco and introduced Manuel, who shook his hand. Manuel was a head taller than Paco and large and muscular with a thick brown beard and long black hair hanging over his ears. A man in his forties, he stood akimbo with a cigar in his teeth and talked rapidly with a deep, raspy voice. Paco saw clearly why Eugenio had hired him: no worn-out slave would dare challenge this boulder of a man.

Eugenio showed Paco the cane pressing machine, explaining every detail.

"The smell is awful," Paco said.

"You will get used to it, Paco. I barely notice it anymore."

The slaves eyed him suspiciously, thinking he was their new boss. He smiled at one who caught his eye, and the man turned away. Another showed the same reaction. Paco watched two slaves stuff canes into the press as the ox pulled the crank in a circle around them. Soon juice poured out of the spout.

"May I do some?" Paco asked.

Eugenio nodded and Paco walked up to the mouth of the press and grabbed a few stalks of cane and did as the slaves had done. He had to push hard to engage the cane, but once engaged the press drew it in. Eugenio then told Paco to follow him to the evaporators.

With the fires under the roof and the sun overhead, the corrugated metal roof seemed to exhale flames. Paco felt he had descended into infernal damnation. Two slaves kept the fire roaring under the evaporators and stirred the pot to prevent crystallization at the edges. Seeing one of them back away from the pot a moment to wipe his head, Manuel took a step in his direction with his whip in hand. The slave immediately returned to his pot.

Eugenio left Paco with Manuel with instructions to watch the men and keep them working. Then he rode off toward the field where other slaves were cutting.

After four hours in the scorching heat Paco rode home dizzy, his vision yellowed with weakness. He dropped off his horse with buckling knees and held himself up by the saddle as he stood in the barn a few moments. Fumbling with the cinch, he finally got the saddle off the horse and walked to the pump shed, where he hung over the spout, pumped and drank as much water as he could hold. He stood to catch his breath a few seconds then washed and went to his room to change for supper. By the time he reached the top of the stairs he felt better, and his vision had returned to normal. Opening the door to his room he found two pairs of white linen trousers, four shirts, underwear, and some light work clothes neatly laid out on the bed.

Magdalena and Lydia were chatting when he walked into the kitchen a few minutes later.

"Good fit," Magdalena said. "Turn around." He did and she smiled. "I found a man about your size at the store this afternoon. He was my model."

"They feel cool, Magdalena. I threw away my wool clothes. That is, all except my *boina*. It was a gift from Marta."

"You will have little use for it here," Magdalena said. "Why don't you sit on the porch and enjoy the cool evening. Eugenio will join you soon."

Paco walked out to the wide front porch and looked down the rows of royal palms, straight and vertical, like sentinels, and wondered for the thousandth time why he did not grow tall like those palms instead of short like a stump. But that was God's will, not his parents' or his. He could be proud of his strength; solid as an oak, he liked to think.

The sun had gone to its rest and the sky was dissolving into blackness. Paco sat in one of the rocking chairs and watched the last rays die, as the color drained out of the potted flowers near his feet. Even the tall crotons that blocked his view of the path had faded to a nondescript gray. He heard the door open and turned expecting Eugenio, but saw Lydia carrying a tray. "*La Señora* Magdalena said you might like a glass of rum."

"Thank you, Lydia."

Before he could reach for the bottle she picked it up and poured some into a glass of crushed ice with sugar sprinkled over it and placed a lemon slice on top.

"I have never tasted rum, Lydia."

"*El Señor* likes it this way," she said, handing him the glass.

Paco took a sip and said, "Fine, Lydia. Thank you."

"My pleasure is to serve you, Señor Paco."

"I am not used to such formality. Please call me Paco."

"I cannot, Señor."

"Why not?"

"It is not permitted to address *los señores* like that," she said, looking down.

"Even if I ask you to?"

"No, Señor."

"Will you sit with me a while?"

"That also is not permitted. May I bring you anything else?"

"Not now."

Paco rocked in his chair and sipped his rum and watched Lydia open the door and walk in. What a strange country, he thought, but in this setting it is not easy to be angry or to find fault. He lifted one of Eugenio's cigars out of his pocket, bit off the tip and lit it. Sitting alone in his new white linen outfit with a cool drink and a cigar, Paco felt like a gentleman for the first time in his life. Then he thought: Magdalena's sister is not allowed to sit and talk. How strange.

Eugenio stepped out, and Paco stood, as if he had been trespassing. "Please, Paco," he said, sitting with his drink and his cigar. Supper will not be ready for another hour. Well, how do you like our place?"

"It is only one day, but I love it. You are a good teacher, *Tio*."

"And you are a good pupil. The cane smells are not always this strong, but we are pressing."

"It is not that bad. I'll get used to it."

Have you tasted rum before, Paco?"

"No, but I like it."

"Our national drink, distilled fermented cane juice. Not as good as Spanish brandy, but it is ours."

"I like it and everything else I've seen. Such a beautiful country, soft and mild, much easier to live in than Asturias, although I got a little dizzy this afternoon."

"Drink more water. It is essential, Paco."

"I'm fine. Yes, I love Cuba."

"I still miss home," Eugenio said. "I would give anything to see Asturias again."

"Why don't you?"

"Magdalena."

"She would love it."

"That is not the problem. She has always wanted a baby, but ..." he shrugged.

"Maybe you would have better luck there," Paco said smiling.

"She fears my family's scorn."

"They would understand."

Paco and Eugenio chatted for the rest of the hour about Asturias and then about cane and sugar and Cuban politics. Lydia reemerged to ask if they wanted another drink. Eugenio said yes and looked at Paco, who nodded.

After she had poured the drinks and withdrawn, Eugenio said, "Paco, I could use a second overseer. Care to give it a try?"

"I do not know enough."

"You are a fast learner. Before long you will understand the whole operation. Take your time. Follow Manuel a while. When you are ready, I will give you one of the operations. That will relieve him. Your main job will be to keep the slaves working."

"That is what bothers me."

"Why?"

"I will not whip a man, slave or free."

"We rarely use the whip. It is mostly to frighten them."

Pondering the idea Paco realized the whip would be no threat unless he was prepared to use it.

"Think about it, Paco. If you cannot you will never have your own farm. Forget about Asturias."

"I have to think, *Tio.* It is a generous offer, and I appreciate it."

"Take your time. Now let us talk no more of it tonight." He took another sip of his drink and said, "I have no heirs, Paco, at least not yet."

Paco did not know how to respond. He had learned to expect surprises in this strange land. Was his uncle hinting that he might be Eugenio's heir? The possibility filled his brain with fantasies.

"I have seen you work, Paco; your father was right, and you have brains. We shall see. You still have much to learn. We will soon begin replanting, and you will have much work. I knew nothing when I came here, but it is not difficult. In a few months you will know as much as I."

"*Señores*, dinner is served," Lydia said through the open door.

"Come, we talk no more of this tonight."

*

By the end of the following week Paco had begun his plan of shaming the slaves with his endurance and drive. He planned to inspire them by example, hoping they would want to show they were his equal. They watched him cut like a machine, without rest or pause. He spent the following week observing in the processing plant. One day Manuel left him alone. One of the slaves moved to the building and leaned against the wall to talk with another slave. Without his prodding, the ox stopped walking the pole around the press. The slave assigned to feed cane to the press could not work because the press had stopped, so he took advantage of the rest. Paco ran to the ox and slapped him on the rump. The animal jerked his head up, looked back and started to walk. As soon as the press began to turn, the feeder stuffed as much cane as he could into it, and the man standing by the wall ran to the ox and followed it with a stick in his hand. Paco said nothing, but stared at him with the most menacing look he could conjure. He did not remove the whip from his belt, but his message was clear, or so he hoped.

Soon Paco was supervising the press and the evaporators. He showed his results to his uncle that evening. "You have improved output nearly ten percent. What are you doing, Paco?"

"Simple, Uncle. I work harder than they. It shames them to slack off. They are men too; they do not want to look like weaklings."

"Be careful they do not take advantage," Eugenio said.

Paco smiled. "They are working, Uncle."

The day finally came to transport their sugar to the agent. Paco accompanied Eugenio with a caravan of loaded wagons to Matanzas and marveled at the contrast to his trip to Gigón with his uncle Facundo: Now I ride in a slave-driven, covered coach. How things change!

Entering the agent's office Eugenio introduced Paco. Señor Ayala looked Paco over as if he were a slave for sale, evaluating his build, his short stature and his bearing. Wearing a tan linen suit, the short, rotund, middle-aged man was nearly bald, with only a narrow wreath of curly, black hair around his ears, and wore a thick, black moustache and goatee. With his jacket open and his hands in his pockets, his belly hung over his twisted belt as he stood over his desk. The window behind him made it difficult for Paco to make out his facial expression. "Why have you come to Cuba?" he asked, in a thick Spanish accent, looking into Paco's eyes.

"To make my fortune."

"Hah! That is what everybody wants. What makes you think you can handle a fortune?"

"Give me one and I will show you."

"Are you mocking me?"

"Not at all, Señor. Your question has no other answer."

Señor Ayala squinted at him as if ready to chastise him and asked how many acres of cane yielded this load. Paco answered without hesitating.

"How many slaves do you have?" Señor Ayala asked.

"I have no slaves, Señor, but I supervise twelve."

"You do not approve of slavery?"

"No, Señor, but I can work in the system."

After a few seconds staring at Paco, Señor Ayala broke out smiling. Still looking at Paco he said, "This boy will do well, Iglesias."

"I am convinced of it."

They talked a while, mostly Señor Ayala and Eugenio haggling about the price. They finally agreed and shook hands, and Eugenio and Paco went outside and supervised the slaves as they unloaded the sugar.

Back home, Eugenio took Paco to his office next to his bedroom and opened the ledger to enter the day's sale and explain how he kept the books. As he recorded his entry, Paco stood behind him reading the figures over his shoulder. They included the number of acres cut, liters of juice pressed and kilograms of sugar produced. Standing there Paco calculated in his head how much Eugenio had earned per acre. Before Eugenio had finished the calculations Paco said, "That is forty-five and a half pesos per acre, Uncle."

"Wait, I am not finished."

Paco said nothing as Eugenio continued for several more minutes. He then turned and looked at Paco. "Close. Forty-seven and a half per acre."

"You have made an error, Uncle."

"What?" To demonstrate how to do the calculation, Eugenio ran through the column of figures aloud. He caught his error and turned to Paco. "How did you know?"

"I add the figures in my head. It is not difficult."

"Ah-hah. Well, if you can do that, I guess you can understand the books."

Paco smiled with satisfaction and sat by his uncle.

Eugenio drove off the next morning and told Paco and Manuel to tend to the workers. "I will return soon. Have them clean up the plant while I am gone."

After breakfast Paco walked to the back porch saying he was going to the plant.

Magdalena said, "I will send Lydia with water."

"Thank you." A few minutes later she watched him lead the men toward the boiling shed.

Less than an hour later Lydia appeared outside the fenced-off part of the outdoor boiling area. Paco walked to her as she lifted the water jug off her head and handed it to him. Wearing a long gingham dress, white kerchief over her tied-back hair, she looked tired and hot.

"Please sit down a minute, Lydia." Taking the jug he handed it to one of the workers and told him to pass it around. While the workers drank, Paco asked Lydia if she was well."

"*Sí, Señor.* A little warm, nothing more."

"It is a long walk from the house."

"I am used to it."

"You are very good to me, Lydia. I appreciate it."

"It is easy to be good to you, Señor." She looked down as she spoke.

"Can we talk sometime?"

"Of course, Señor. Whenever you wish. About what?"

"I want you to tell me about Cuba."

She smiled. "I would like that."

"We would have to sit down together, Lydia."

She looked puzzled. "We can talk while I work, Señor."

"Can't we chat alone?"

"Better while I work, Señor."

By that time one of the slaves returned the water pot to Lydia and she stood.

"After supper?" Paco asked.

She nodded and walked back to the house.

Eugenio returned late that afternoon and asked for Paco. "He is still with the workers," Magdalena said. As he mounted his horse, she said, "Tell him it is almost time for supper."

Paco was saddling his horse as Eugenio rode up. "*Hola, Tío.* I was just leaving."

"The place looks good. Come, we ride back together."

Eugenio could barely contain himself as they walked their horses behind the slaves. "I have bought the land I have been haggling over for almost a year," he said. "We'll plant it as soon as we finish replanting the rest. In the meantime, I want you to take two men and get started. But not until I seal the deal … in the next day or two."

"We will need more men."

"I will buy two more slaves."

At supper Paco watched Lydia's every move in the dining room, waiting for her to finish her duties. When the kitchen work was almost complete Magdalena retired to the living room, where Eugenio and Paco had lit cigars. Eugenio opened his newspaper, Magdalena sat down to read, and Paco stood and walked into the kitchen. Magdalena smiled as he passed. Lydia remained silent while he stood near the table with his back to the swinging door that led to the dining room. He did not see Magdalena standing at the swinging door holding it slightly open to look in. "Would you help me with something outside?" Paco asked.

Looking past Paco for Magdalena's nod, Lydia said, "Of course, Señor."

She turned and hung a shiny brass pot next to several others on the wall by the stove, so each pot hung in its ordered place, large to small, as one might expect in an army kitchen. "This is the neatest room in the house."

"I work hard to make it so; though some people come in and leave a mess, and I have to tidy up after them."

Knowing she was talking about Magdalena, Paco smiled. Hanging pots of flowers flanked each window, and trays of flowers lined the windowsills. With large windows the room stayed cool even when the stove was hot. The neatness fascinated Paco: sparkling tile floor, clean with not a speck or crumb to spoil the pattern, varnished table in the center covered with a white tablecloth. Lydia used that table to roll out pastry and bread dough; it, too, was immaculate. As Paco waited for Lydia to finish putting away the last of the silver, he watched her hands. Slowly, carefully, as if she were handling delicate surgical instruments, she wiped each piece and placed it in its slot in the silverware case. She finished and turned to him, smiled, and led him to the back porch and down the steps.

"I came from a small village in Asturias," Paco said. "Know where that is?"

"I have heard of it."

"Near the north coast of Spain. Very cold, not like here."

"I have never seen another country, but I think Cuba is beautiful," she said.

Paco led her toward the barn. "Let us stroll and talk. All right?"

"*Sí, Señor.*"

As they wandered toward the cane field he blurted out, "In Spain we have no slaves. This is all new and shocking to me." He immediately felt he had overstepped.

She looked at him with pity. "No need to apologize, Señor. It is not your fault."

Her directness so startled Paco that he hesitated. Finally he said, "Thank you, Lydia."

After a long pause, she said, "La Señora told you I am her sister. She loves me and I her. I am proudest of her, perhaps, because she does good even if it defies custom."

Paco nodded.

"You want to know about slaves? Would you like to see their quarters?"

"If it is permitted."

A light breeze ushered in the cool, clear evening as the slave quarters came into view around the barn. Paco felt good talking, finally, with this fascinating girl. In only a few months he had learned about sugarcane processing and was even imagining his own farm. It seemed impossible.

Only yesterday, so to speak, he had milked cows and cut grass on the cold slopes of his rocky homeland. Even with the evil blemish of slavery, Cuba was every bit the tropical paradise he had envisioned, and here he was finally walking and talking with the exotic girl of his cold, dark morning fantasies. Then the thought of being an overseer tightened his throat.

An elderly slave woman sitting on a straight-back chair outside her palm frond-thatched hut stood up as they approached. It was third in a tight row of seven huts aligned behind the barn and out of sight of the house. Of course, Paco thought, they would not want to sit on their back porch with their cigars and rum and watch their slaves wallow in poverty.

"Good evening," Paco said.

The thin, bent woman stood and nodded with a stern jerk of her head and walked inside drawing aside the cords that protected the entrance against insects.

"Please tell her to stay."

"She is my mother's sister. Please sit down."

Paco sat and looked down the path in front of the huts while Lydia brought out another chair for herself. Inside, a hammock swayed gently over the bare earth floor. Even in the semidarkness the old woman's profile stood clear against the sky through the back window. She was sitting before a small table that held a statue of the Virgin, two candles, and several small pieces Paco could not discern. The flickering candlelight danced an arabesque across her face. Beneath Paco's feet, constant use had worn the grass down to hard packed dirt. With the sliver of crescent moon that hung above them, he could slice through the darkness that hung over the field. In the barn to his right, silhouetted farm animals moved gently, while to his left, along the row of huts, three slaves sat silent. He imagined they were straining to hear their conversation.

"I see only one hammock. Where do you sleep?"

"This is my aunt's hut. I sleep in the main house in a room across the hall from Señora Magdalena's room. My mother and my aunt used to live here. They cooked for *los señores*. Now my aunt cleans the house and washes clothes."

"And your mother?"

"She developed a cough that got worse and worse. Finally she began to cough up blood. I was only five and remember little of her. She was brought here from Africa as a young woman."

"Did she talk about that?"

"Very little. She talked mostly about the African religion."

"It must have been hard, losing your mother so young."

"Her brother died young too, before I was born, of back-breaking work and beatings." Her sweet voice now unsheathed a bitterness that Paco had not heard before. "Forgive me," she said, looking down.

"Have you ever been beaten?"

"No, Señor." She smiled. "I am Señora Magdalena's sister."

"Do you address her that way when you are alone?"

"Yes, Señor."

"Seems strange for sisters."

"If I pretend to be her equal, soon I will begin to believe it, Señor."

Paco wanted to argue, but could not formulate a logical response.

"I avoid unhappiness because it hurts me here," she said, putting her hand on her breast."

"I do not understand all this," he said.

"I live well; I have a good room and eat the same food as you. The señores provide for us, but I am special."

"And your future?"

"Future?" She thought a long while.

"Don't you want a family and a home?"

Tears came to her eyes, and she put her hand on her breast and turned away. "Whatever God wills," she said.

"Please do not think I ..."

"You want to know about slave families?"

"Yes."

"A priest marries us, but with so few women, marriage is rare. The greatest difference is that our babies belong to the *hacendado*."

The thought revolted Paco. "How can a woman accept that?" he said.

"That is how it is."

Her emotionless tone sent a chill through Paco. "That is wrong," he said.

"Talk of right and wrong does not change what is."

"Many countries are fighting slavery. The United States just ended a long civil war over it."

"Men fight; men die. That is what is. Here they fight against Spain. Where is Spain exactly?"

"A long way across the ocean." He pointed northeast.

"Is it pretty?"

"Yes, but where I lived, very cold and hard."

"Is that why you left?"

"No, for opportunity. Cuba is better."

She smiled. "For you, yes."

Looking into her green eyes, Paco realized opportunity meant more slaves. "Yes, Lydia, and your people should share it."

"I do not like to think about that, Señor."

"You should."

She remained silent.

"Does my uncle beat his slaves?"

"Rarely."

"Lydia, you are intelligent and beautiful. You should aspire to more."

"What is aspire?"

"To want a better life."

"I want only to serve Señora and Señor Eugenio and you, Señor."

"That is not enough. What about you?"

"That is all I want."

"Are you married?"

"No."

"Do you have a sweetheart?"

"Never."

"Why not?"

"Perhaps it has to do with aspire, Señor."

Seeing her aunt standing at the entrance to the hut, Lydia said, "I have to go now. Pardon me?"

"Of course, Lydia."

*

The next afternoon, Eugenio and Paco came home for lunch to find Magdalena waiting for them at the back porch. "You have two letters, Paco."

Paco took them in his hands and smiled at Marta's name on the first envelope. Flipping to the second with stubby fingers, the official army letterhead stunned him. "At last, my sentence," he said, laying it aside and opening Marta's. As he read, Magdalena and Eugenio feigned nonchalance, but they did not leave, and Paco knew they were anxious to hear his news. "Jorge Antonio is back from the army, and he is healthy, thank God. Everyone is also fine."

"That is all?" Magdalena asked.

"She wants to come to Cuba so we can get married." He had expected her to remind him of his promise, but not this soon. Saying no more, he stuffed Marta's letter into his shirt pocket and opened the second letter. "The army wants me too, no doubt," he said. But as he read, his heart began to race. "Their quota … is filled. They don't need me." He threw the letter into the air and jumped up.

"Wonderful," Magdalena said. "We celebrate tonight with a good supper and a bottle of Rioja wine."

With the excitement, Paco only picked at his lunch as he rattled off his litany: how he had planned to volunteer in the army and changed his mind and how Facundo drove him to Gijón and the ocean voyage and landing and confronting the soldiers and finding this tropical paradise. "And the sword hangs over me no longer. Now I can really get down to work."

"Work no, Paco. We go to Matanzas this very afternoon. We take the day off to celebrate, see the town and enjoy loafing so you can absorb the good news."

"Good idea, Uncle."

"Just be sure to find your way back," Magdalena said.

Matanzas was much smaller than Havana, but it had a cathedral, a castle and the taverns, shops, and stores one would find in any Spanish city. The houses looked Spanish, except for ubiquitous front porches for socializing and the large windows to let in light and air. Relaxed and smiling in the carriage, Paco took in the sights hungrily remembering the tensions of that earlier wagon ride from Colosía to Gijón. Eugenio asked the driver to stop at his favorite sidewalk café across the square from the cathedral. "Wait here," he told the driver. Finding a table in the shade of a large sapodilla tree, Eugenio said, "What will you have, Paco?"

"I have not tasted cider since I left Asturias."

"And you probably won't taste it here. This is sugarcane country; that means rum."

"*Hola, Señor Eugenio*," the waiter said. "It makes much time that we do not see you in Matanzas."

"Much work, José, but today we celebrate with cider. Do you have any?"

"*Si, Señor. Sidra Asturiana.*"

"Good. A bottle, please."

The waiter quickly returned with a chilled bottle of cider clearer than Paco had ever seen. He removed the cork with a pop and poured until the glasses overflowed with bubbles.

"This is not cider."

"The best," Eugenio said. "*Sidra champanada.* Taste it."

With his first sip Paco made a face. Then he took another. "Not bad, Tío. Tastes like cider, but with bubbles, and look how clear." He bent over to read the label. "Villaviciosa," he said. "We passed through there on our way to Gijón." Wearing the white linen outfit Magdalena had bought him, he felt handsome. His moustache had filled out, blonde and sparse but clearly visible now.

For over an hour they sat in the shade drinking cider and talking about Asturias. Paco did not miss home as much as Eugenio did. Though the New World had fulfilled its promise, Eugenio kept repeating, "One day ... One day, perhaps. And you, Paco, do you not miss your parents?"

"Of course, but I have no desire to return to clawing the earth for my existence. I am glad to be here."

The sadness in Eugenio's face clashed with the bright sunny day. Try as he might, Paco could not sympathize. "I cannot believe it. The weight has been lifted. The army does not want me. I must do something ... something to celebrate my future."

Eugenio tilted back his hat, and his face again beamed. "Do not neglect your present, Paco. Your future does not yet exist, and it will slip away as you stumble into it. You live here and now, in the present. The present is all there is. *Hay que disfrutar!*"

"De-fruit, what a strange word, Uncle."

"Not strange at all, Paco. It means to enjoy the fruits of life, of which Cuba has many, including a temperate climate and lively and uninhibited people. Cubans are not cold, hard and tight like us *Asturianos.* They are warm and loose, and the women are delicious. Have you not noticed how they move, like soft, gentle fruit swaying in the breeze, begging to be plucked and devoured?"

"I guess so."

"To live here without enjoying all the tropics offers is the greatest error. Look at that lovely mulatta, Paco. Skin reddish-bronze like a ripe mango."

"She is a Negro, Uncle."

"Some say you have not lived until you have had one."

"Have you?"

"I work hard; I enjoy everything."

"What are they like?"

"Warm, meaty, delicious."

Paco sat silent, digesting his uncle's words. "What about Magdalena?"

"She knows I love her. I am as devoted as any husband. Look, my boy, you can enjoy the fruits of the island without buying an orchard."

"I do not think I could go with another woman knowing Marta waits for me."

"She cannot mind what she does not know."

"That is what Facundo said."

"Marriage is a lifetime contract, Paco, but it does not mean that you must turn away from God's delights. Take Lydia. She is pretty and quite willing."

"How do you know?"

"Her eyes, Paco. They shine for you. Haven't you noticed? She knows her role."

"But she is Magdalena's sister

"Ah, so you know."

"She is family."

"Yes. Would you shy away if she were a white family member?"

"That would be different, Uncle."

"Oh?" he smiled. "But do not worry. You are betrothed and you will marry Marta. In the meantime, *disfrutar*." He slapped Paco's back.

Paco could ignore the obvious no longer. "It is wrong to enslave human beings, Uncle. But I suppose once you accept slavery, then what you say makes sense."

"I did not create slavery, and I did not bring those poor wretches here. I feel the same as you, Paco. I do not like it, but without them I would still be chopping the rocky hills of Asturias for my daily bread."

"Pragmatism?" Paco said with cynicism.

"Exactly. Idealism makes you feel proud and successful as you watch your family starve. I know many such idealistic paupers with principle. But let us not argue. You will not understand right and wrong or even your own beliefs until you have faced reality and necessity."

As they finished their second bottle of cider Paco said he would like to see the town. They stood, Eugenio paid the bill with a good tip, and they walked out of the shady café and into the bright, mid-afternoon sun. "I know a place full of beautiful girls. All shades, whatever you like. What do you say?"

Not wanting to seem unappreciative or prudish, Paco nodded.

The two-story house was a good stroll away in a prosperous neighborhood, flanked on one side by a bank and on the other by a barbershop. A tall, handsome, middle-aged woman opened the door. "Welcome, *Señores*. What is your pleasure?"

"A drink and a place to chat a while," Eugenio said.

"One of the girls will tend to you."

They sat on a sofa at one end of the large living room, which had a piano along the long wall and several plush chairs and three other sofas and several small tables scattered about. Two other men were sitting with two girls having a drink and smoking.

"What now?" Paco asked.

"*Disfrutar.*"

As the time passed and they finished their second rum, a pretty young girl, no more than sixteen, bronze colored with barely noticeable African features, approached them. "*La Señora* said you wanted to see me."

Paco looked puzzled, so Eugenio said, "Yes, my dear. Sit down here by my nephew." Then Eugenio stood and went to a sofa at the other end of the long parlor, where several girls were talking. The girl put her hand on Paco's knee. "I'm called Gloria."

"I am Paco."

"This is my first week."

"I have never been to a place like this."

"Like to go to my room and talk a while first?"

They stood and she led him up the stairs. He did not really want to go with her, but curiosity and excitement had him by the throat, and his heart beat furiously as he ascended the stairs behind the well-endowed young girl. Her loose fitting dress hung slightly below the knees and afforded glimpses of parts of the female body Paco had only imagined. She held a door open and he walked into a simple room with a bed, a nightstand table, a vanity with a large mirror, and a pan and water pitcher on a small dresser. A window overlooked the small back yard, a large privy, and a house beyond. Paco stood by the door waiting for the girl to do something. She sat on the edge of the bed and patted the spot beside her, trying her best to act sophisticated, though obviously awkward and nervous.

"If you do not mind," Paco said, "We talk a while?"

She nodded and smiled.

Paco sat on a small bench by the vanity and interlocked his fingers around his knees. Two thoughts twisted around each other in his mind: if I do not want to do this, why am I so excited? And why this feeling of violation? She is attractive and willing. How many times have I dreamed of being in a room with a beautiful, willing woman? But my honor, my integrity? As he looked at her, he wondered why she would choose to do this and guessed she might also have misgivings. They did not speak, but sat looking at each other, then not looking at each other. He felt as uncomfortable and out of place as he ever had. Finally he stood. "Thank you for inviting me, but better I go."

"Am I not pretty?"

"Very pretty, but I am betrothed to a girl from my village in Asturias. It is not right."

She smiled. "My father was from Galícia. I never met him, but my mother told me he went back to Spain after the army released him."

"Did your mother work in a place like this?"

She looked down. "Yes, but she became pregnant with me and left. My father visited her several times. He left Cuba before I was born."

Paco sat beside her and put his arm around her shoulder. "Thank you for telling me." He took out the amount Eugenio said they charged, and laid it on the bed. "I go now. You are a good girl."

"But I have not earned this, Señor."

"You have, and much thanks." With that, he stood and returned downstairs.

"You work fast," Eugenio said.

"It does not take long if you know what you're doing." Then he asked one of the girls for another glass of rum.

Having lost count of the glasses of rum he drank during the afternoon, Paco found himself relaxed and enjoyed teaching the girls some dances of his village. Gloria joined them and Paco sat with her, but he could not think of anything to say. Eventually she asked him about Asturias, and he began telling her about Colosía and life on his father's farm. He toyed with the thought of inviting her upstairs again, and for the next hour the thought never left him. Even as he talked about his village, his brain was weighing the prospects: She is pretty and sexy, and I want to, but I must not. She's so young, so innocent. True, she is a prostitute, but she is too young to know what she is doing. She will end badly, but I cannot help her. But I must not fool myself. As much as I hate to admit it, I am afraid, but of what I cannot say.

As the conversation turned to his boat trip and how sick he had gotten, he watched her—parted lips, smiling adoringly. Then he knew why he could not go upstairs with her. She was relieved; he had helped the poor girl.

Watching the scene from the next sofa, Eugenio stood, walked to him, bent down, and whispered, "Don't forget where you are and what she is."

"What?"

"You're here to *disfrutar*, not fall in love."

Paco frowned and said nothing, and Eugenio returned to his conversation.

In late afternoon Eugenio walked upstairs with his favorite girl. Paco remained with Gloria. After a long while Eugenio returned neatly dressed, and had another glass of rum. He downed it and asked Paco if he was ready.

"If you are, Uncle."

The carriage and driver were waiting. Eugenio got in and said, "Home, but do not rush. As they rode down the cobbled streets, Eugenio and Paco laughed at everything, especially the girls so willing, so accommodating.

"Why did you say I shouldn't fall in love, Uncle?"

"You looked more like a lover than a patron."

"She is nice. I don't think she has ever done it."

"You mean, before you?"

"Please don't laugh, but ... we only talked."

Eugenio laughed aloud and threw his head back.

"It is not funny, Uncle."

"She is the innocent type. Some men like them sweet and innocent. Like having a virgin. Others like the raunchy ones, tough and talking dirty."

"Have you seen her before?"

"Of course. She' nice, all right."

"Have you done it with her?"

"No, but a friend of mine has many times."

For a while Paco was silent, but soon, at his uncle's taunts, he began to laugh with him.

They stepped down from the carriage, both wobbling, and walked in, each with his arm over the other's shoulder.

"Aha!" Magdalena said, rising from her chair in the living room. "I see you had a good time."

"The best," Eugenio said. "We saw all of Matanzas and baptized every café."

"Hungry?"

They sat at the table and waited with smiles on their faces.

*

Slaves knew their white overseer, Manuel, as *El Oso* because, like a bear, he was hairy, bearded, big-boned, tough, and had large, nicotine-stained, widely separated teeth. Walking, he resembled a round-shouldered, lumbering bear. Manuel had only to look at a slave and the man would bend to the work as hard as he could. Manuel rarely used the whip, but it was always visible and he liked to pat it as he gave orders. He would grasp the handle as he spoke. That little gesture, as much as his appearance, inspired dread. A year had passed since he used it, and two other slaves had to carry the whipped man away, his back sliced open and bleeding. As his fellow workers carried him, Manuel took out a handkerchief and wiped the blood off the whip and hooked it back on his belt. He looked up to see the slaves staring at him. He again touched his whip and they immediately fell to their work. The first day Paco worked with Manuel, he explained how he kept the slaves in line.

Though Paco disliked this treatment of the slaves, he managed to smile. "Does it bother you that they call you *Oso*?"

"They do not call me that to my face," he said, showing his brown teeth through a grin. "They can call me what they want as long as I don't hear."

"Uncle Eugenio wants me to take some of the men to start clearing and replanting."

"You left your whip in the barn," Manuel said.

"I won't need it."

"You cannot tame these animals with kindness, Paco."

Paco ignored him and led the men away.

Clearing took almost a month of backbreaking work from first light until the men could not see what they were doing. On the cleared field they planted pieces of cane saved from the previous harvest, each piece with one node. Paco worked along with the slaves, even though Manuel had advised against it. "It is slave work. You will undermine the process."

"But I want to show them how much one man can do."

"Already they know, and they do not give a damn. Your job is to make them work, not do it yourself."

"Let me try this, Manuel. Just for a while."

Manuel walked off shaking his head. Paco set about to plant with fury. At first the slaves followed his pace, but before long Manuel returned and stopped him.

"Look behind you, Paco."

Turning, Paco saw the nearest slave twenty meters behind. Saying nothing he walked to the slaves. "You have to work faster. It is easier to work faster, and you finish earlier."

One of the slaves, a thin, short man of indeterminate age, muttered under his breath, "We will work until night no matter how fast we plant, Señor."

Hand on his whip, Manuel growled, "No back talk."

"No, Manuel. He was only giving his opinion, but he works well. Watch him."

Again Manuel walked away muttering, but Paco would not be deterred.

As the sun dipped into the horizon, Paco yelled out, "All right. Time to quit."

Manuel came to him. "We have another hour of light."

"They will work better tomorrow if we let them rest."

Manuel shook his head. "I will have to tell Eugenio."

"I accept responsibility."

74

At supper that evening Eugenio wasted no time. "Manuel tells me you dismissed the slaves early."

"They needed rest. They worked well today, Uncle."

"You do not know enough to change the rules."

"You can't work men until they drop, Uncle."

"While they rest they do not work; that means production drops. We can make them work at the same pace whether they rest or not."

"But Uncle, it is inhuman to work them to death. They worked almost eighteen hours today."

"Eighteen is minimal." Laying down his fork and looking directly at Paco, he said, "It is simple: a slave costs 300 to 400 pesos. It costs less to work them hard and replace dead ones than to extend their lives a few years by working them less."

Paco pushed his chair back, ready to get up. "That's horrible!"

Eugenio picked up his fork and looked down at his plate. "Finish your supper, and do not play the fool. Our purpose is to make money, not to pamper slaves."

Magdalena had kept quiet during the discussion, but now stepped in. "You are a kind and gentle young man, Paco. Those are good qualities in a person, but ..."

"What is the value of a fortune bought with such suffering?" Paco said.

"If you do not feel you can handle it, Paco, I can find another overseer."

"No, Eugenio," Magdalena said. "Paco is kind and only wants to do good. Perhaps kindness is better than the whip. Give him a chance."

Eugenio was still frowning, and Paco was looking into his plate.

"Come, boys, Lydia prepared this nice supper," Magdalena said. "Enjoy it and stop arguing."

Eugenio put his hand on Paco's shoulder. "Experience will teach more than words."

Next morning Paco led his crew to the field before the sun had shown itself. The morning glow grew by the minute, and by the time they got to the field day had dawned. Paco told them to get started and paced around to push them whenever they slowed down.

By mid-morning Lydia appeared with a jug of water on her head. Paco took the jug from her and had a long drink, then passed it to the worker nearest him. "I am preparing a nice lunch, Señor."

Paco smiled. "I am hungry already." Her dress was damp in spots from perspiration.

"I liked talking the other night."

"Can we do it again?"

"Of course, Señor." Then she took the jug from the last man who drank from it, said no more, and walked back to the house.

"Can we rest, Señor?" one of the slaves asked.

"A few minutes only. Until I tell you."

The men all dropped where they were standing and lay flat on the earth. By the time Paco called them to get up, several were asleep. "Come on," he yelled, "Up. There is much work to do."

The men slowly rose and got back to the planting, but they did not hit the same pace. They were moving slowly now, stopping to wipe their brows or to rub their backs. Paco felt sorry for them, but he knew he had to push them. "I have given you a rest. Now work."

Two of them frowned at him and did not move. Paco immediately realized the situation could become dangerous. "If this is how you thank me, I know how to make you hurry."

The men seemed surprised, for Paco had no whip, and they suspected he would not use it if he did. He went to the biggest of the slaves, a man who stood a head taller than he and whom the others looked up to. "Pick up the canes and get started."

The man stood motionless looking down on him. Almost without realizing it, Paco sent his fist into the man's stomach. The punch was so hard and fast that the slave doubled over and fell to the ground. "Anyone else?" Paco asked, turning to the rest.

Without looking directly at Paco, they all went to where they had left off. The man on the ground was still struggling to get his breath. Paco reached down to offer a hand, but the man's teeth were clenched. He pushed away Paco's hand and stood without help and went back to work. Paco said no more.

That evening he said nothing about the incident until Eugenio mentioned it. "I hear you had trouble with one of the slaves."

"No trouble."

"What happened?"

"I gave them a few minutes rest and one of them would not return to work until I convinced him."

"We never let them rest, Paco. They come to expect it."

"I saw no harm."

"You must learn: they do not respond to kindness."

"I still think they will."

"You had to beat him."

"You seem to know everything."

"I want you to learn, Paco, but there is a limit to how much I can invest in your education."

"Are my men not producing?"

"So far, but I worry about morale."

"There is no morale, Uncle. I hope to develop some."

"Favors soon become rights."

"Uncle, I want a chance. Can I have it?"

"To a point, Paco, but then …"

"Thank you, Uncle."

Paco thought about that discussion as he lay in bed that night: I did not use the whip, but I beat a man and may have ruined my first opportunity. Perhaps Uncle Eugenio is right, but how can I win their loyalty and dedication through beatings? I'll carry the damn whip and prevent another beating.

The next morning Paco awoke and went to the window as usual to watch the sun. He imagined how it looked in Asturias and what Marta was doing. She is cooking lunch now, he thought, and while I am eating lunch she will be at the plaza waiting for me to appear. He smiled at the thought of her waiting for him because it reminded him that soon she would wait no longer, nor would he. His eyes loosened their grip on the horizon and the grand lifting of the day's curtain. He dressed and went down for breakfast.

He fastened the whip to his belt that morning before he led the slaves to the planting. Without making a show of it or stroking it or handling it, he would merely show he had thought of using it. Why do they not see that I want to treat them well? They heard me argue with Manuel about working them late.

No slave failed to notice his whip, but it seemed to have no effect. One or two even smiled at it. The morning went well. They worked hard and planted nearly half of the field. Lydia came out in mid-morning with a jug of water. Paco was happy to see her, but saw that the slaves also were glad, probably expecting another rest period. He drank, handed the water jug to one of them, chatted with Lydia a few minutes. The slaves took the opportunity to rest a moment. After a few moments he turned and said, "All right, back to work."

One of them, a thin, tall man, said, "I am sick, Señor."

"What is it?"

"My chest hurts."

Paco told him to sit in the shade of a tree not far from where they were planting. "I will check on you in a few minutes."

Another came to him with the same complaint. "How is it that two of you are sick?"

Three others gathered around him complaining of pains. "This will not do. Get back to work, all of you."

"What about the man under the tree?" the second complainer asked.

"That is not your affair. Now go!" At that he put his hand on the whip.

All eyes followed his movements, waiting to see if he would loosen the whip and let it fly. The large man who had challenged him the previous day stood in front of the others. "I have a stomach ache," he said, "from yesterday." The man's voice and demeanor were strong, not that of a man in pain.

"What is your name?"

"My African name is Ali."

"Well, Ali, perhaps you did not learn enough yesterday and need another lesson."

"But I have a pain here," he said, pointing to the pit of his stomach.

The men watched in admiration.

"If only some of you are claiming to be sick, why are the rest of you standing there?"

No one said anything. A few moved toward the planting and several remained to listen.

"I cannot work," Ali said.

"You will work, and now." Paco removed the whip from his belt and held it hanging at his thigh.

"Would you whip a sick man?" Ali asked in a cynical tone.

"I will if you do not move."

"But I am sick." Ali stood in a threatening stance, clearly challenging Paco's authority.

The whip fell to earth as Paco's fist came up under the man's chin so hard Ali staggered back and spit a tooth into his hand. He looked at Paco with fury and strutted toward him with his fists tightly balled. As he came within range Paco again smashed the side of Ali's face as the African grabbed Paco's other wrist, but the blow was so hard that Ali lost his grip. At that point Paco attacked him repeatedly with both fists one after another until Ali could no longer stand and fell to the ground. Pointing to two men, Paco said, "Now he is sick. Pick him up, and take him to his hut. And tell him to be at work after lunch." The other men had already begun to move to their work. Paco looked down and saw his knuckles were bloody. He wiped the blood off and tried not to show he was injured.

78

That evening Paco did not wait for Eugenio to bring up the incident. "Uncle, I beat up the same man again today. I do not think he will cause anymore trouble."

"The difference between today's beating and the whip is that you are hurt too. It is stupid, Paco. You are hurt, and the worker cannot work. But worse, by fighting you have treated him as an equal. Don't you see? You are an overseer, not a coworker. The whip is the only discipline they understand. It is the weapon a master uses with a slave or any other animal. You would not punch a pig or an ox, would you?"

"I don't know, Uncle. This whole business has stirred me up. I will think on it. If I cannot do the work, I will tell you. I will not be a burden."

After supper Eugenio went to Matanzas for the evening, and Paco sat on the porch alone thinking about his choices. Soon Magdalena joined him.

"Kindness often brings suffering, Paco," she said, "but I do admire your charity and respect for human beings."

Without looking at her, Paco said, "Thank you, Magdalena."

"It is not easy to live in our Savior's image, Paco."

"This has nothing to do with religion, Magdalena. I just don't believe one man should own another."

"Neither did Christ, Paco."

"Doesn't it worry you that Eugenio does not follow Christ's teaching, Magdalena? And how does Christ feel about those poor slaves?" Tears were running down her cheeks.

"Those slaves are the same as us in His eyes, Paco, possibly better for their suffering. All of us, no matter how much wealth we accumulate, live immersed in disappointment and frustration."

"Certainly not you, Magdalena."

"Yes, I too. I lack the one thing that would give my life worth; that is my disappointment."

Paco nodded, recalling what Eugenio had told him.

"Our true reward will not come in this world. Those slaves will find their reward as surely as you and I."

After a long silence, Magdalena excused herself and walked inside.

Paco went to his room, washed his face, undressed and blew out the oil lamp on the table by his bed. His second floor room was down the hall and across from Eugenio's and Magdalena's bedroom. Lying in bed under a sheet with the windows open, he thought about the fight and its effects on the men and Eugenio's business and what it meant to Magdalena. Clearly Eugenio's sin worries her, he thought. Such a simple woman! To live by such simple rules; no, living by them is not easy; only reciting them is easy. How can I live by rules that deny me all I want? Magdalena does not live by them either, for she owns her sister. Surely that is worse. No, Magdalena is not free from sin either. But she is kind and loving; I'm glad she doesn't feel I did wrong with Ali. Eugenio is right; I treated Ali as an equal.

*

As thoughts tumbled in his swirling brain, he heard the door open slowly and turned to see the figure of a woman in a nightgown outlined by the open door. She came toward him and stood by the bed.

"Lydia?"

"I heard of your trouble today. I thought you might need me."

"It was nothing."

She sat on the bed. "You did the others a great favor. Ali bullies them."

"Did I do wrong, Lydia?"

"Of course not. Ali treats the others worse than Manuel does, Señor. He must learn his place. But what about you?"

"My hand hurts a little. That's all." He lifted his hand and opened and closed it a few times.

She took it and held it in hers and kissed it and then massaged it gently. "I want to help you," she said.

"This is a strange time for you to come here."

"Do you mind?"

"No."

With one hand she unbuttoned the top of her nightgown and then took his hand and held it to her bare breast. He was surprised but did not pull away and did not move his hand for a long while. Then he started to massage her breasts. She felt warm and moist and breathed deeply, as did he. Soon she took off her gown and lay beside him and rubbed his chest, still holding his hand on her breast. By this time, Paco no longer felt he must control himself. He rolled on her and, with her help, managed to do what he had wanted to do since he first saw her. He was happy and excited in her embrace and held her tight as they moved together. The curtains billowed with the breeze, he moved, she moved, they kissed, he ran his fingers through her thick hair. They moved as if by some heavenly directive that drives the young to thrust out all inhibition and reason and belief, and trust only that deep, inherited intelligence that springs from primitive, inarticulate lineage, and complete that which they will not think about until the damp, spent postlude.

80

After a long while in which he nearly fell asleep, he rolled over and lay next to her. They were no longer heaving. They did not speak.

"Please do not think this places any obligation," she whispered.

"I do not think anything. Lydia, I have wanted to be with you since the first time I saw you."

"Remember we are master and slave, Señor."

"I don't like to think that."

"But do not forget it."

"Why did you come?"

"To comfort you, and because I knew you wanted me." He looked at her strangely, and she added, "And I you."

Her words were so sweet and calm that he kissed her again. "Is that why?"

"Pleasing you is my only wish, *señor.*"

"And Magdalena?"

"She does not mind."

"Does she know?"

"Please, Señor, no questions." Saying that, she rolled onto him and started kissing him. Their moist bodies grew hotter. Before he knew what was happening, they were moving again, entangled in each other's sweaty bodies like snakes. It took longer this time, and it was better.

"Oh, Lydia, I need you."

"Please, do not make trouble for me."

"How?"

"By forgetting the difference between us."

"We could erase it," he said, not knowing exactly what he meant.

She stood and put on her gown. "Impossible, Señor. I must go."

"Please, not yet. I will not ask any more questions."

She sat again on his bed, and he held her hand.

"*Señor*, I really must go."

She left Paco trying to grasp the fullness of what had happened. Not what had happened, for that was clear, but why? Finally, he fell asleep and dreamed of clear green water and swaying palms.

He awoke irritated by the pink glow streaming through the window. Rather than watch the sunrise as he usually did, he closed the drapes and dressed. Fingers of light leaked through the cracks and stabbed his eyes like daggers of treason. The sun was pointing his flaming finger of judgment at Paco. Instead of thinking about treason he wanted to think about the delicious night and Lydia's surprise visit, but the image of Marta would not leave him.

By the time he walked into the dining room, he felt better.

Magdalena smiled. "You look happy. You must be feeling better." Her eyes sparkled.

For a fleeting instant Paco wondered if she knew. He did feel good and did not want to arouse his feelings of guilt. As he exchanged good mornings with his hosts her knowing smile found him. He soon convinced himself he was merely feeling like a guilty child who thinks everyone is looking at him. To distract any suspicions he turned to Eugenio. "I will control the slaves, Eugenio. There will be no problem."

Eugenio smiled. "Good."

Eugenio's assurance did not entirely convince Paco, however.

After breakfast Paco went out back to saddle his horse and, before mounting, took the whip off the wall hook and put it on his belt and rode to join Manuel, who was leading the slaves to the field. *"Buenos días, Manuel,"* he said as he joined him.

Manuel looked at the whip at Paco's side and smiled. "Take this bunch to that field to finish planting," he said, pointing. "I will work the others here."

Determined to keep his leadership position, Ali walked in front of Paco's crew. Paco did not react, but stayed behind them, nudging the stragglers with his horse. The men seemed more tired and slower than usual. Paco dismounted and pointed to the where they would start. Noticing Ali's malicious squint, Paco felt he might face a new challenge, so he braced himself and kept his hand on the whip. Seeing Ali looking at him, he unfastened it and held it at his side for a while, slapping it gently on his thigh. Ali stooped to begin planting, the others followed. Work progressed smoothly after that.

Before long Eugenio rode up. "How goes it?" he asked without getting down.

"Fine."

"The trouble maker?"

Paco pointed to Ali.

"I thought so. He has caused trouble ever since I got him. I'll sell him. The others will work better without him."

"Good idea, but can you?"

"I know a man who buys trouble makers like him. He pays little, but this one is worthless anyway."

"What will they do with him?"

"Clear forests or break rocks in quarries. The slaves know."

"The ultimate punishment?"

"Not quite. He will live. I see your whip. Good."

"You were right, Uncle. They will test me, and I am ready."

Eugenio smiled, put his hand on Paco's shoulder, and galloped off.

That night Lydia again appeared. Saying nothing, she walked in silently, took off her gown and slipped under the covers with Paco. She came every night that week. As the week passed he pined for her more each night, fantasizing throughout the heat of the day about the warm, glorious night to come. He would retire early each evening not caring whether he aroused suspicion. If Magdalena knew anything she revealed nothing. Eugenio seemed to accept his explanation of exhaustion after the hot day.

As Paco waited for her in bed, thoughts raced through his mind of the wonderful girl who seemed to live only for him, and her hot passion that asked only to please with luscious lips and soft belly and thighs that held him in her vise. Never before had he met a girl so anxious to give herself. He stopped mentioning love or marriage because every time he did she would frown and withdraw. Instead, he found it more pleasant to respect her wishes and ask nothing. His only problem was the haunting phantom of Marta's face that appeared every time he closed his eyes: beautiful, blonde, young, eager, dressed in virginal white. And he had betrayed her. But everyone had urged him with the repeated, *"disfrutar,"* even Lydia. How could it be wrong to enjoy something so good? Why not *disfrutar,* as long as he still kept his promise of marriage and family with the woman he had cherished since childhood? Lydia was his love slave, his comfort in this time of sexual famine. But feelings for Lydia had begun to grow. She had come to him as a compliant slave who wished only to serve her master, but he wanted to believe that she had come with love.

*

Marta's next letter arrived the following week. Magdalena met Paco with it as he rode in from the field. As soon as he finished washing at the pump shed she handed hin a towel and then the letter. Throwing the towel over his shoulder he tore part of the letter trying to rip open the envelope. Magdalena stood by smiling as he read.

"Any news?"

"Marta is fine and so are our parents. Jorge Antonio is working hard with Papá and expects to marry soon ... Oh, and she says her mother will not let her come unless she is married."

"Oh."

"I am not ready, Magdalena. I have nothing. Besides, I cannot go home now. The army would surely take me. What passes with that woman? She does not trust me?"

"She is a mother, Paco. Cautious for her daughter."

"Well, they will both wait."

"Marry her by proxy."

"What?"

"I had a friend who wanted to marry her sweetheart, but he lived in Argentina. Her mother would not let her go to him until they were married. He could not afford to travel here and back, so they performed the wedding in Matanzas with a stand-in for the young man and some witnesses—a civil ceremony. Anyway, it was done, and everyone signed the documents, and they sent the papers for the young man to sign. Soon the documents came back and they were legally married. To satisfy the family, they married in church later in Buenos Aires."

"Marta always worried I might not send for her … Perhaps."

"Don't you love her?"

"Of course."

During supper two hours later, Eugenio brought up the subject: "Magdalena says you might marry soon. Don't you know marriage is the severest form of slavery?"

"Don't make fun of me, Uncle."

"Eugenio!" Magdalena said. "Please, Lydia is in the kitchen."

"Marry her, Paco," Eugenio said, laughing. "A good wife is a great asset."

"I will, Uncle, eventually."

During the discussion Lydia served the dessert with no visible reaction. She returned to the kitchen, and Eugenio said, "I did not want to tell you yet, but I have named you heir to part of my farm, Paco. Thirty acres. Not much, but a start."

"That is generous, Uncle, but I do not want to look forward to your …"

"I know, Paco, but you need some security. You can treat the parcel as your own, to plant and harvest. And use my processing plant."

Imagining his own farm with beautiful cane leaning with the breeze lifted Paco's spirits, but there were still too many questions, and they all came down to Marta and Lydia. What if she became with child? How would Marta take it? He had always detested the kind of deception that now smothered him.

"Thank you, Uncle. I will live up to your faith in me."

That evening Lydia came to him as usual, but she did not get into bed. "I am sorry, but it is my time of the month. Forgive me. I just came to tell you."

Relieved, Paco talked about his work and how well it was going. He casually brought up his feelings towards her. She abruptly stood and excused herself. He tried to stop her, but she did not respond and walked out and shut the door behind her.

She did not return to his room the following week. As much as he enjoyed her visits, he did not take her absence as a rebuke. The frolic had gone on long enough, he thought. Better to stop before it goes too far. But she came to him again late one evening and sat in a chair near the bed. He held open the sheet invitingly.

"No more, Señor. You will marry soon, and I want Señora Marta to like me."

"You are right, Lydia, and I appreciate your generosity, but … one last night together?"

"Please, I do not wish to deny you, Señor Paco."

He reached for her hand, brought her close, and kissed her cheek. "You are an angel, Lydia. I will always love you."

She rose and left and came no more.

CHAPTER 3 - BABIES AND REVOLUTION - OCTOBER 1868

*

Louisiana Senate Ousts E.L. Jewell and

Installs A Mulatto Named Pinchback

*

Deposing of Spanish Queen and Her Designated

Heir Causes Uncertainty in Europe

*

By late February the cane in Paco's thirty acres stood knee high. Riding along the parcel filled him with so much joy that he broke into a gallop yelling, "Mine, all mine." His joy felt boundless. How could it have happened in so short a time? Riding across his farm, the farm he had dreamed of? And more land than his father's or that his father could ever dream of owning. He was a modern conquistador, machete in hand, hacking a highway to his New World fortune through a brilliant lush green world.

Then, in mid-gallop, the image of Marta appeared to him, and thoughts of all the work this farm would mean, and the superimposed shadowy image of Lydia appearing nocturnally—a spectre of love and lust. How could he separate the two?

Magdalena was relentless talking about the proxy marriage as if it were all arranged. With her prodding, Paco finally wrote asking Marta to propose it to Padre Benito. Two months later she answered that he was willing, and that her mother did not like the idea, but Padre Benito convinced her. It was not until several letters had sailed across the Atlantic that the wedding took place in the church of Colosía on May 5th with Paco's father as Paco's stand in. A month later the papers arrived in the mail. Paco signed them with Eugenio and Magdalena as witnesses and mailed them back the same day.

In her next letter Marta wrote that she could not leave right away because her mother had come down with smallpox. Paco shuddered recalling the last smallpox epidemic that ravaged the valley, and how wagons would come through the paths picking up bodies and carting them away like stacks of logs. Paco wrote begging her to take care and then waited anxiously. In late June she wrote that she would leave in two weeks. He realized she was on the ocean at that very moment. Suddenly a mixture of fear, happiness and anxiety gripped him, as he wondered how both these women could live in the same house.

That evening at supper he told Eugenio about the letter, but he had already heard. Before Paco could finish, Eugenio raised his wine glass for a toast to their happiness.

Lydia served the meal as usual with no show of emotion. But she wore a different type of dress, a loose, unbecoming one with no waistline. Knowing she could not be hiding a belly, he thought it strange. Magdalena noticed his curiosity and, as soon as Lydia had left the room, she whispered that Lydia was pregnant. Paco's face dropped. She put her hand on his and said, "Lydia is very happy, Paco. Do not spoil it."

He tried to hide his feeling of anger and betrayal, realizing Magdalena must have known all along, and Lydia had lied about her period. He could not comprehend how they could act as though it was none of his business.

"I will not spoil anything, Magdalena."

After supper Paco walked into the kitchen. Two clean pots lay on the stove, so he assumed Lydia had left in a hurry. Not wanting to ask where she had gone, he walked to her aunt's hut and found her sitting outside talking. She stifened and told her aunt to leave.

"Magdalena told me you are in a family way."

"*Sí, Señor.*"

"Is it mine?"

"Please do not ask, Señor."

"Is it?"

"You were within your rights, Señor."

"*Coño!* Answer me!"

"Yes, Señor," she said, her head down.

"Then the child is my responsibility."

"Forgive me, Señor," she said with defiance, "but the responsibility is mine alone."

"You are carrying my child."

She stood and walked into the hut without speaking. Paco also stood wondering if he should follow her in and settle the question, but he was not sure what the question was. What would I do with a baby? What will Marta think, and Eugenio and Magdalena? I must talk with them. He turned and walked back to the house more confused than ever.

Magdalena was reading in the living room; Eugenio had gone to town for the evening. "Magdalena, I have just learned that I am the father."

"I know, Paco."

"She told you?"

Hesitating, she said, "Even if she hadn't, I could see it in your face."

"This is terrible."

"Oh no, Paco. A new life is always wonderful."

"Don't you see, Marta is coming."

"Paco, you must not cloud such happiness."

"I do not feel happy!"

"Lydia carries a new soul within her. Nothing in this world is more joyful. Think of it, Paco, a new human being to bring happiness to you both. If it were mine I would be ecstatic. Oh, Paco, I am ecstatic!" Magdalena had her palm to her breast and her eyes upward, as if in thanksgiving.

Paco looked at her as if she were crazy. "But what will I do with Marta?"

"Nothing, Paco. Lydia is the mother. The baby will be fine."

"No child of mine will be a slave."

"Do not worry about that. You are married now."

"But I am the father."

"Lydia will live with us as always. The child will be part of our family."

"You did not hear. Not a slave!"

"Of course, Paco. The child will be free; he will live as our own."

"What would he be in this house if not a slave?"

"Eugenio and I will adopt him legally."

"Why would you do that?"

Magdalena's calm happiness changed to excitement: "Oh, Paco, it would be wonderful finally to have a child. You will see him every day. Marta does not have to know and neither will the child. Marry Marta and worry no more about this baby. It will have everything. Oh, Paco, I have dreamed of nothing else since Lydia told me. I am so grateful."

"You knew I was the father from the beginning?"

"Forgive me, but it was the only way."

"The only way for what?"

"Like me, she wanted a child, but not with a slave. She wanted a white child, so her baby could have a normal life."

"So she used me. You thought of everything. Is Eugenio's will part of the plan too?"

"Eugenio knew nothing until this evening. He truly thinks of you as a son."

"You have been good to me, Magdalena. I do not want to hurt you, but Lydia has used me and you have helped her. That is hard to bear."

"How has it hurt you, Paco?"

"You and she have saddled me with a responsibility I cannot discharge."

"Would you abandon Marta to marry a mulatta slave?"

"That is cruel, Magdalena."

"The last thing I want, Paco, is to hurt you. You are kind and generous, but you must be pragmatic."

"That odious word again."

"*Ay, Paco.*"

From that day Paco saw Lydia only at mealtime and avoided her at other times. She, in turn, responded with aloof courtesy. Occasionally he would walk in on Magdalena and Lydia in the kitchen, and they would stop talking and turn to their work until he left.

It all makes sense now, he thought. She has what she wants and no longer needs my services. Wanted only to serve and comfort me—lies! And that ugly word. She is the greatest pragmatist of all, a willing slave who manipulates her masters. I have to give her credit; though, she is clever and wily and scheming and ruthless; an opportunist. But I must not alienate her—for my baby, I will not lose my baby. Pragmatism, I am yours! Mamá, you were right: "Trust no one."

*

The night before Marta's arrival, Paco barely slept. Her ship was due to dock at eleven in the morning. She had written to ask, mysteriously and

89

without explanation, that Paco not bring Eugenio and Magdalena to the port, but they would not hear of it.

The beautiful late July morning was refreshingly cool with a light breeze and a clear blue sky. He could not have ordered a more perfect introduction to her new home. Eugenio reserved a honeymoon suite at the Hotel Inglaterra in Havana.

The ship slid into Havana harbor like a swan on a placid pond. Paco could barely talk or stand still. They stood as close to the ship as they could for a glimpse of Marta, as stevedores secured the ship. She was not to be seen. Finally the gangplank dropped into place, and the police marched aboard. Paco searched the passengers' smiling faces, but no Marta. People waved at their friends and families and threw flowers and kisses. Still no Marta.

Nearly half an hour passed before passengers began to move down the gangplank. As the mob laughed and talked and shouted and shuffled down the narrow walkway, Paco saw a young woman enter the gangplank who might have been Marta. He was not sure because she wore a broad black hat and veil. She reached the bottom step before she saw Paco and waved. Seeing her dressed so sedately in mourning, Paco felt a flash of dread, wondering who had died. Ignoring his feelings he rushed to her and embraced her and almost knocked off her hat. She embraced him passionately, crying, nervously holding her hat. He held her out and moved to lift the veil, but she stopped him. "Paco, I told you not to bring them."

"They would not listen. They want to meet you, Marta."

Eugenio took her hands: "*Bienvenido,* Marta. We are happy to have you with us at last. Permit me to present my wife, Magdalena."

Magdalena hugged her and Marta returned the gesture, but somewhat stiffly. "Come, let us get a look at you, my dear," Magdalena said.

"Let us move away from the sun, Paco," Marta said, walking away from the ship.

"*Que pasa?*" he asked, following her.

She pulled him away. "Please, Paco. I do not mean to be rude, but please."

"Of course." He turned and told Eugenio and Magdalena that they needed to talk alone.

"Of course. We will wait at the café near the gate." Turning to Magdalena Eugenio whispered, "She is not dressed as a bride."

"Of course not, Eugenio. Someone has died. Poor girl."

Marta and Paco walked to the building to wait for her luggage at customs. "What is it, for God's sake?"

Pushing him into a corner of the large room, she lifted her veil. Paco's jaw went slack. She was almost unrecognizable with pockmarks and stretched skin around her mouth and chin. Paco could not speak. Expecting his reaction she spoke softly through tears, "I could not write it in a letter. I came down with the smallpox shortly after Mamá did. She died after a week. My father almost died with worry about me. It was terrible for everybody. Dozens died in Peñamellera. You remember the last outbreak? Well this one was worse. Everyone thought I would die, but eventually I improved and, after weeks of suffering with horrible sores, I began to feel better and finally recovered, but it left me ..."

"I'm sorry about your mother. I did not know."

"Please let me finish." She wiped her eyes. "I will never look like the Marta you knew. I release you from our marriage, and I will not be angry if you send me back. In fact, I will be relieved because if I stay I will always believe you kept me out of a sense of obligation."

As Paco listened he tried to recall her clear pink skin and radiant eyes. They were now mountains of hideous red scars. She had lost weight and resembled skin stretched over bones. Paco felt so sorry for her and wanted to hug her, but he could not. He stood looking at her knowing, in spite of how he felt, that he must be a man and not a spoiled child with a broken toy. She looked so sad that he grabbed her and hugged her as tight as he could. She began to sob as she stood in his arms, her arms hanging down her sides. "I love you, Marta and I want you to be my wife. I do not care that your face has changed. You have much more than a pretty face. We will fatten you up and soon you will be your old self."

She sobbed, "You must be sure."

"Of course. Eugenio has reserved us a honeymoon suite in Havana's best hotel. But first you must meet them. They are good people. Do not worry. Come."

"But I am so ashamed."

"Of what? Are you not my girl from Colosía?"

"No, Paco. I am someone else. I see it every day in the mirror."

"Enough!" He took her hand and led her out of the building and to the café where Eugenio and Magdalena waited. Eugenio was drinking beer and Magdalena a fruit punch. Marta had pulled the veil down over her face.

Rising, Eugenio said, "Please have something to drink."

Knowing there was no use in delaying the inevitable and adding to Marta's anxiety, Paco said, "Marta is recovering from smallpox."

She looked down.

"Her disfigurement embarrasses her. I told her it makes no difference to me, and it will make no difference to you." He turned to Marta. "Please, Marta, meet your new aunt and uncle."

Marta's tears had drenched her veil. Slowly, tentatively she lifted the veil and pulled it back over her hat. Neither Eugenio nor Magdalena showed the least sign of revulsion. Paco felt proud of Marta's courage knowing that raising that veil was perhaps the most difficult thing she had ever done.

"My uncle died of smallpox in Colosía," Eugenio said, "but thank God some cousins survived, and soon no one noticed the scars."

Magdalena could not hold back her tears. She moved her chair next to Marta's and put her arms around her. "Paco is right, Marta. It makes no difference. My tears are only for your suffering."

"You are very kind, but people will see me as a freak."

"Only the blind will see that, Marta," Magdalena said. "Those who have sight will see a very beautiful girl."

Marta smiled weakly and looked at Eugenio. Before she could speak he said, "I remember you. You were Paco's girlfriend even before I left Colosía. I know your parents well. How are they?"

"And I remember you, Eugenio. Mamá died a few weeks ago. Papá has not gotten over it. The loss of my mother has left him an old man. It was difficult to leave him."

"Perhaps he can come for a visit or perhaps to stay," Eugenio said.

"He will never leave Peñamellera, Eugenio."

"I often think of going back. Perhaps one day," Eugenio said.

Magdalena put her hand on his and said, "One day, Eugenio."

"Uncle, I think Marta might like a Daiquirí. I know I would."

During the next hour in the café Eugenio talked about Cuba and the sugarcane business, and Magdalena described life on the farm. By that time Marta was smiling. Eugenio and Magdalena drove them to the Hotel Inglaterra on the Paséo del Prado and registered them in the honeymoon suite. He kept Marta's large suitcase containing her belongings, and Marta kept a small bag, which she gave to the bellboy. Eugenio said, "Honeymoons are for couples, not crowds. We go now." They all said goodbye and Eugenio and Magdalena drove away waving back at the young couple.

"Shall we see our room?" Paco asked.

"May we leave the bags and go for a walk. It is a beautiful day, and I would like to see some of the city."

"Only if you leave the veil."

She nodded.

"Good. I have not seen Havana either. We will see it together."

Feeling Marta at his side the next morning, he asked if she had been awake long.

"A while," she said, turning to face him.

He wanted to look at her, but hesitated and hated himself for that. On those mornings in the Hotel Inglaterra, he had forced himself to smile and to laugh though he did not want to. Back home, he thought, life will resume, and I will love her as always. Only her surface has changed, not her inner self, but that rough surface tightenes my stomach every time my eyes fall on her.

Now, back home, he awoke, threw back the covers, stood and took her hands. She smiled as he led her to the window to look out on the plantation. "This is what I have done every morning since I got here." The red sun was still enmeshed in the palm trees at the edge of the plantation. "I would look at the same sun that was shining on you in Asturias at that very moment, but it was midday there. I tried to imagine us thousands of miles apart and warmed by the same sun."

Their silhouette against the open window resembled two children, she thin with long flowing hair, he thick and muscular, stretching to her height. She put her arm around his shoulder as she looked out the window and tried to imagine herself in Asturias at midday as Paco watched the sun climb over the Cuban horizon. "From now on, Paco, it will rise and set on us together."

Paco kissed her and they stood a few minutes longer contemplating the immense drama unfolding before them. While the sun cleared the trees Paco dressed, and Marta sat on the bed and talked of home and how glad she was finally to be with him. "But Paco, I am an outsider ..."

"You are family, Marta."

"... in the house of another woman."

"Give Magdalena a chance."

"I will, Paco. I love you and I will do everything to make them love me."

"They do already. Now I must get to work. See you downstairs."

Marta remained at the dining room table feeling uncomfortably out of place. Paco had explained that Lydia was Magdalena's slave sister. Though the enigma of a woman whose sister was her slave intrigued her, Marta accepted their relationship. Lydia especially fascinated her, the way she moved and served them, treating everyone with formal respect wrapped in what Marta perceived as chilly superiority. In Lydia's quiet, detached demeanor Marta saw a clever, determined woman who understood her world completely, perhaps better than her half sister understood hers. Lydia expressed no noticeable reaction or curiosity to Marta's pock marks.

Magdalena walked through the swinging door and Marta followed her to find the kitchen as immaculately clean and neat as Paco had said. Lydia was still washing and drying the last of the kettles and putting each in its proper place. Magdalena gingerly, using two fingers, picked up a pot from the table and took it to the tub where Lydia was washing. Lydia looked up and Marta reflexively raised her hand to her face and, as quickly, brought it down. Magdalena noticed but said nothing. Studying Lydia's belly, Marta's eyes went to Magdalena with a quizzical look. Magdalena shook her head and gestured out the door.

Marta picked up two pots from the stove to take to Lydia, but Magdalena stopped her. "You are not here to work, my dear. You must devote yourself to enjoying Paco and life in your new home."

"I cannot stand by and watch others work."

"Nonsense," Magdalena said. "We have lots of help."

"Sometimes more than we need," Lydia said.

"Come now, Lydia. I would love to help you."

"Perhaps *Señora* Marta would like to see the rest of the house and the gardens."

Turning to Marta, Magdalena said, "She does not like me interfering in her kitchen. What can I do? Come, we must not upset her."

On their way to the porch Marta stopped at the door to admire the large portrait. She had already seen it, but, bombarded with welcoming gestures and speeches, she had not had a chance to look at it carefully. The eyes were magnetic. The image was of a lady of breeding, nobility perhaps, with seriousness emanating from her beautiful visage. And the mantilla added old world, mystical charm.

"Eugenio commissioned an artist in Havana to paint it. Do you like it?"

"Oh, yes. It is beautiful, a perfect reproduction, Magdalena."

"Thank you. Perhaps Paco can have yours made."

Marta lifted her hand to her face and turned away.

"Forgive me, Marta. I did not mean to hurt you." The tears that filled her eyes could not wash away what she immediately realized were unkind words, and she put her arms around Marta. "I only meant that you are beautiful enough for a portrait. Try to forget what cannot be changed. Anyone can see your true beauty."

"Do not occupy yourself, Magdalena. It is just that ..."

"I know. Beauty is a woman's most important asset. We feel defenseless if it is threatened."

"I am not defenseless, Magdalena," Marta said, eyes flashing. "I have much more to offer than clear skin. I am not a bumpkin whose only goal in life is to catch a man."

"Of course not, my dear. I only meant ..."

"Please, Magdalena ..."

"Paco no longer notices it."

"I wish," Marta said, and walked out to the edge of the porch and looked down the path.

"Let us sit and I will tell you about the farm."

"I want to be of use, Magdalena."

"You must learn to live as a lady."

"I cannot be what I am not."

"You are a lady. You will soon settle in and find much to interest you."

"First I must make Paco glad that I came."

"He is a new man already."

"Tell me about Lydia. Is her husband a slave?" Marta asked.

"She is not married. The father was a Spaniard."

"Was?"

"He returned to Spain."

"And left her to have the baby? What a brute!"

"Not really." Seeing Marta's puzzled face, Magdalena continued, "Every woman wants a baby, but the babies of slave women are slaves also. But with a white father, well, you know the saying: '*La raza avanza.*'"

"*No comprendo.*"

"Lydia is half white; the baby will be three-quarters white. It will pass for white"

"How mathematical."

"We shall see, Marta. We can only hope. I plan to rear her baby as my own. Lydia will care for it, of course."

"You are very generous, Magdalena."

"Lydia is ..." Magdalena hesitated, but knew she would have to tell her. "... my half sister. My father ... well, you know. So the baby is my blood also."

"Paco told me."

"I am glad."

"And she never identified the father?"

"Only that she was glad he left."

"*Por diós?* Why?"

"Lydia is very pretty; white men often keep mulatta mistresses."

"And she did not want to stay with him?"

"Her life is with us. She planned it all." Magdalena came close and whispered behind her hand: "Her African aunt consulted her mystical shells to learn when her fertile time would be." Seeing Marta's puzzled look, she continued, "Santería, the African religion. I do not believe in it, of course, but it worked."

"I have much to learn about Cuba."

"Cuba is not so strange. People are the same everywhere. Only their customs differ."

"Paco feels quite good here with you and Eugenio."

"I have not been able to have a baby, Marta. That is my great shame and disappointment. But we welcome you and Paco as family, just as we welcome Lydia and her baby. I pray you will always live with us, but if someday you want your own home, well then ..." She put her crocheting away. "Tell me, what do you like to do?"

"In Asturias I cooked and washed clothes and milked the cows and tended the garden. I will help with anything."

"That is slave work. For the moment enjoy your new home."

"Did her pregnancy make you angry?"

"Heavens no. It will be the baby I never had. Besides, it is quite common with those people, I'm afraid."

"Those people? But she is your sister."

"And I love her very much, Marta. We each have our station in life. Lydia is happy with hers."

"She seems very competent," Marta said. "A very good cook."

"Yes, but sometimes her competence gets tiresome. I wish she could take things easier. But she is a fine person and will be a good mother."

"How does she feel about the baby's father?"

"Never mentions him."

"Was she in love with him?"

"Oh, no."

"I see."

"This is a different culture, Marta. Try not to pass judgment, my dear. It will only worry you and make you unhappy."

As she looked at Magdalena, Marta's thoughts hovered around the grand portrait in the living room. The artist failed to capture Magdalena's flitting like a butterfly between reason and fantasy. Nor had the artist caught her deep-rooted superiority neatly wrapped in tissues of humility and kindness. How could a woman refer to her sister like that?

"Marta, as much as I try, I have been horrible today. First I hurt your feelings. Then, a moment ago, I referred to Lydia as one of 'those people.' I beg God's forgiveness and yours for that. It shows that I see myself as better than her, but she is the far better person, for she has given much more in her life than I. And now she will bring to light a new life, the one thing I cannot do. I do not want to envy her, Marta. Oh, how I hate myself at times like these."

No words passed between them for a long while. Then, with tears running down her cheeks, Magdalena returned to her crocheting.

"I never learned to crochet," Marta said. "May I see your work?"

Looking at Marta with eyes that melted the younger woman, Magdalena said, "Of course, dear. Come."

Magdalena's room at the southeast corner of the second floor had a large bed by the door and two large windows on each outside wall. On her side of the bed stood a small table completely covered with pills, powders, ointments, salves, a half-liter bottle of rubbing alcohol, and two small, unlabeled boxes. Beyond that stood a dresser with a pan and pitcher, soap dish, shampoo, skin lotion, hair oil, two brushes, combs of various sizes, a bowl of dusting powder and a wadded towel. The items covered the dresser top much like those on the small table, unordered, as if dropped there. Marta expected something to fall to the floor as they talked. Against the east wall, between two large windows stood an armoire. One of the doors apparently could not close because of the bulky dresses crammed inside. Under the south window along the floor stood a row of shoes of various colors. In the middle of the inside wall, a door led to Eugenio's office.

"Eugenio keeps his clothes in his office, through that door. I'm afraid I have monopolized the entire bedroom." Then she opened a dresser drawer and lifted out a stack of crocheted items and spread them over the bed: doilies, a bedspread, two dresses, and a pair of unfinished booties. "For Lydia's baby," she said, holding up the booties.

"These are beautiful, Magdalena. Would you teach me?"

"With much delight, my dear. We start tomorrow morning after breakfast."

Paco came home late that afternoon and found Marta in their bedroom. "You look sad. Are you all right?"

Her face brightened. "I am now that you are here."

The sight of her deformity shocked Paco, and a feeling of pity crept along his skin. "Sorry I could not come to lunch," he said, embracing her.

"I missed you. They will not let me help with the housework. Lydia does not want anyone in the kitchen, not even Magdalena. Anyway, we sat on the porch and talked. Poor Magdalena, such a kind and gentle soul; how lonely her life seems. I think Lydia's baby will lighten her life.

Anyway, she took me to her room to see her crocheting. Tomorrow she will teach me."

"Life is different here, Marta. Slaves do everything."

"Magdalena would need a crew of slaves to clean her room. You should have seen the mess."

"I've caught glimpses of it from Eugenio's office."

The idea of slavery did not bother Marta as it did Paco. He started to tell her how he felt, but didn't, not wanting to add to the discomfort of her new surroundings. Instead, he took her downstairs to the porch, where they sat and chatted until Lydia brought him a rum drink. "May I fix you one, *Señora* Marta?"

"No, thank you, Lydia."

At supper Magdalena and Eugenio peppered her with questions about Asturias. Marta recounted their wedding, "such as it was," as she put it, and how the poor priest appeared so nervous conducting a wedding with the bridegroom missing, and how Paco's mother, poor thing, frowned throughout, apparently anticipating what her friends and family would think of the bizarre ceremony.

"In Asturias I liked the livestock fairs best," Eugenio said. "People from all over Peñamellera would bring their animals to sell—cows, horses, mules, everything."

"Oh, yes, Eugenio," Marta said. "I used to tend the field of beets and corn we planted to feed the animals."

"You actually planted crops for the animals?" Magdalena asked.

Eugenio jumped in: "*Absolutamente!* They ate as well as we did; sometimes better. In Asturias animals are more productive than people."

They all laughed as Marta and Paco nodded agreement. Just then Marta's face clouded over. She was no longer nodding and smiling, but became sad and quiet. Before long she was sobbing. Magdalena stood over her and stroked her hair. Marta wiped her eyes and calmed down. In a whisper she said, "I am sorry, but it was one week after the wedding that the smallpox hit our valley. Mamá was one of the first ones to come down. No one else in my house got it until, a week later, I came down." Paco took her hand and smiled sadly. Marta straightened her shoulders and lifted her head and continued, "I was remembering Padre Benito's homily the Sunday before I left. He read out the names of those who had died in Colosía. He said nearly half the inhabitants of the valley of Peñamellera had perished."

They were all silent when Lydia walked in with a tray of Spanish candies. "Some *turrones* to celebrate Señora Marta's arrival."

Marta smiled, "I don't remember the last time I tasted *turrones*. Thank you, Lydia. And when is the baby due?"

"About a month, *Señora*."

"The booties are almost finished," Magdalena said, holding one up.

Lydia smiled politely and said, "Very pretty," and walked back through the swinging door.

Paco knew Magdalena would not say anything to implicate him, but the thought of confessing to Marta sent a shudder through him. He asked Eugenio, "How long before we start cutting cane?

"Two weeks; perhaps sooner."

"How much do you think it will bring?"

Eugenio smiled, "You will be well pleased, nephew."

After supper Eugenio and Paco took their glasses of cognac and cigars to the front porch. A minute later Marta and Magdalena joined them. Marta did not sit, saying she was going to her room. "Not yet," Magdalena said. "I want to show you something I started today." She pulled out of her knitting box the beginning of a black mantilla. "For you," she said.

"How beautiful, Magdalena. Like the one in your portrait."

"I saw you admiring it," Magdalena said. "You will look beautiful in it."

"Perhaps soon I will learn to make something."

"In no time, my dear."

*

That night Paco slipped into bed and kissed her with feelings of fear and trepidation. He loved her, but the scars coverd her entire body. Everywhere he touched she felt like a reptile. But he would not let her notice his revulsion; she was self-conscious enough. Love will overcome this feeling, he thought. She is, after all, the woman I have always wanted.

But during those times in their bedroom locked in each other's arms, Lydia would force herself into his brain, and he could not keep her out. She would rise like a flame behind his eyelids to ignite a satanic inferno. In those moments he told himself how much he loved Marta and tried to remember how she looked in her Asturian dress and blouse, so beautiful and voluptuous, so alive and ready, not the thin, frail, withdrawn creature that lay in his arms. Then Lydia would appear like a hissing feral cat of the night, arousing him in excitingly revolting ways with her hands, her lips, her legs, her black soul sucking out his very life, and he would sink into Marta with force and anger and hate and ecstasy and love and feelings of calamity.

By her second week in Matanzas, Marta's frustration at doing nothing had reached a crisis. She had tried to help in the kitchen and with the rest of the house, but Magdalena insisted on transforming her into a lady of leisure. Marta stood at the porch railing one morning and fingered one of the leaves on a plant that had overgrown the railing. The strong thick leaf looked as if it had been dyed red and black. She went down the front steps to the plant and found weeds covering the ground. Inspired, she went to the kitchen and asked Lydia where they kept the gardening tools.

"In the barn, *Señora*. Why?"

"I want to do something with the crotons out front."

"*Señora* Magdalena will have someone take care of it."

Marta smiled and walked out the back door to the barn and found a hoe, a wooden rake much like the ones she used in Asturias, a pair of clippers, and a small hand shovel. By the time she had walked around the house to the front porch Magdalena was sitting on one of the rockers.

"What are you doing, Marta?"

"These plants need help."

"One of the field hands does that."

"Not well enough, it seems."

"But, Marta ..."

"I love gardening, Magdalena . Surely you cannot deprive me of this little pleasure."

"If you put it that way, I suppose not, but at least let me bring you a hat. This sun will make you black."

Magdalena returned to find Marta had pulled out several clumps of weeds around one of the hedge plants and had moved to the next. Magdalena handed her a broad-brimmed straw hat and a pair of garden gloves. "Thank you, Magdalena." She put on the hat and fastened the string under her chin, and then she slipped on the gloves.

Three hours later Marta dragged a large bag full of weeds and branches to a pile near the barn and returned to admire her work. The spindly crotons were now neatly trimmed and the reddish-black earth around them contrasted beautifully with the bright hedge. There was still the rest of the front of the house to do, but that would wait until tomorrow. After returning the tools to the barn she went to the pump shed pleasantly tired, removed the gloves and hat, and washed for supper.

By the end of the week, she had cleaned and trimmed the rest of the hedge to a height that opened the view of the road to anyone sitting on the rockers. She also planted a row of border flowers to separate the crotons from the lawn.

"This porch has not looked this good in years, Marta," Magdalena said that evening. "We have not seen the path from here in a long time. I congratulate you."

"Yes, Marta; you have carved out a little piece of Asturias right here in Matanzas," Paco said.

She smiled. "Next the bougainvillea. It grows too wild."

Three weeks later the cane swayed like giants in the wind, and Paco could hardly wait to begin the harvest. He was sure he would clear more money from those thirty acres than Eugenio would from any comparable parcel. His slaves were far from happy, though. He had worked himself and them harder and more steadily than they ever had. But for them the result, far from gratifying, was merely more work with the presses.

Pressing went well, especially without Ali. His departure caused a strange reaction among the slaves. Paco's announcement that Eugenio had sold Ali evoked muttering with a mixture of elation and horror. They were glad to be rid of him, but knew where he had gone. Paco felt sorry for them, but he did not let up. His future rested on their backs.

After harvesting the crop and processing it down to sugar, Paco, with Eugenio, led the wagons to Matanzas for the sale. *Señor* Ayala was as jovial as before and happy to see them. He offered them rum as they chatted, but Paco refused, not wanting to impair his judgment during his first important transaction. Ayala understood and continued the banter.

An hour later, Paco and Eugenio walked out of his office with the most money Paco had ever held in his hands. He laughed with glee and handed it to Eugenio.

"It is yours, Paco."

"Are you sure, Uncle?"

He slapped Paco's back and pushed him toward the wagons and watched, hands in his pockets, hat tipped back, a smile on his face, as Paco supervised the unloading. Paco admired his uncle in his neat white linen suit and shiny patent leather white shoes.

With the money stuffed into his pocket Paco climbed into the carriage, and Eugenio's driver drove them back to the farm. The slaves followed in the empty sugar wagons.

"How does Marta like Cuba?"

"I'm worried; she seems withdrawn. She always talked much and had strong opinions. I hope she finds her old self soon."

"Magdalena is good at bringing out the best in people."

*

A week later Paco came down to breakfast and didn't find his uncle. "And Eugenio?"

"He had a bad night," Magdalena said.

"Nothing serious, I hope."

"I think not. Chills, a slight fever, and a headache."

"Anything I can do?"

"No. I left him sleeping. Probably something he ate."

"In that case I will start clearing my acreage for the next planting."

That evening at supper, Eugenio still had not come down. "He is no better?" Paco said.

"No. His head and stomach ache. If he is not better tomorrow I will call Doctor Fuentes."

"Why don't you call him now?"

"He said not to. You know Eugenio. Says being sick is for sissies."

"Any idea what it might be?"

"My first thought was smallpox," Marta said, "but this is different."

Paco went to Eugenio's room, knocked gently, and heard, "Come in." "How are you feeling?"

"Fine. Just a headache and an upset stomach."

"I'll call the doctor."

"No, no. I'll be fine by morning."

Eugenio did not smile and his voice was weak. Paco did not want to go against him, but felt he must.

After a few minutes, Paco realized Eugenio was in no mood for talking, so he left.

The following morning Marta and Paco came down to breakfast and found Magdalena waiting for them at the foot of the stairs. "Please, Paco. I think we should call the doctor."

"What happened?" Marta asked.

"His temperature is up and he has developed red spots all over."

"What do you think it is?" Paco said.

"Lydia says typhoid fever."

Paco went out the back door and called the driver, who came running. "Go to Matanzas and fetch Doctor Fuentes immediately. Tell him *Señor* Eugenio needs him. And hurry."

Meanwhile, Marta had led Magdalena into the dining room. "We must eat something, Magdalena."

"I cannot."

"Nonsense. Lydia, bring her something, please."

Lydia frowned at being ordered by this newcomer, but she pushed through the swinging door and soon returned with coffee and some bread and pastries. With Marta's urging, Magdalena sipped some coffee and picked at one of the pastries. Paco returned and said he would stay until Doctor Fuentes came.

"No, go to your duties. I will send for you if I need you."

"I wait; then I go."

Paco wondered about visiting Eugenio's room, knowing how contagious the disease was. He took Marta's hand as they waited at the dining room table. Magdalena went into the kitchen to talk with Lydia. Paco told Marta to stay away from Eugenio's room.

"If they need me I will go and do whatever they ask."

Paco kissed her and smiled. In less than an hour the doctor was there. Paco led him to Eugenio's room.

"Where is Magdalena?"

"I will send her up." Paco walked in the kitchen and told Magdalena, she ran up the stairs.

"Marta, I go to work now. Send someone right away if I'm needed."

Magdalena cried through lunch. Between sobs she reported the doctor's opinion that it was a severe case of typhoid fever. "He wants to watch him closely ... says he will probably worsen ... before he improves. What will I do, Paco?"

"He is strong, Magdalena. Don't worry."

Eugenio got progressively worse, as the doctor had predicted. Paco went in to talk with him each day, but Eugenio was so weak he could barely respond. By the end of the third week, he had lost weight and his breathing was labored. One afternoon Magdalena ran down the stairs saying he had passed blood, but his fever was down. In the morning the fever had climbed again and he was bleeding.

Doctor Fuentes came every day, but one morning, after examining him, he walked downstairs and said Eugenio's condition was grave. "I was afraid this would happen."

"What?" Paco asked.

"Pneumonia. He has little chance now." He shook his head. "I will stay as long as I can, but ..."

Magdalena suddenly broke into hysterical sobbing and fell into the sofa. Marta on one side and Lydia on the other tried to comfort her. Paco found himself unable to focus clearly with tears welling in his eyes. A moment later Lydia's aunt, who was cleaning Eugenio's room, rushed down the stairs and, through heavy breaths, said: "*Señora* Magdalena, *Señor* Eugenio calls you."

From the top of the stairs Magdalena shouted for Paco to fetch Eugenio's attorney, *Señor* López. "And tell him to hurry, Paco, please."

Paco ran out the back door and yelled for the driver. "Go to Matanzas as fast as you can and bring *Señor* López. Tell him *Señor* Eugenio must talk with him right away."

"Why the attorney?" Paco asked, returning to the living room.

"He did not say," Magdalena said. "Come, he wants to see us both."

Eugenio looked like a rosy cadaver, splotched, very thin and breathing with great difficulty. "How do you feel, Uncle?"

"I … revise my will … leave all my holdings … to you and Magdalena … jointly … not half to each, … but joint owners. Paco I want your word … you will … keep Magdalena for … as long as … she lives."

"No, Eugenio. This land is Magdalena's. It was her father's. I have no right."

"I have … reasons, Paco. With you as … part owner you will … run it well … and with her as part … owner, you will … treat her well."

"I will do that anyway, Uncle."

"I know, but … this arrangement … make her … less dependent … more secure … and you more … willing to work hard. Well, Magdalena?"

"My father worked hard for this land, Eugenio. I love Paco as a son, but …"

"You have my word that I will work the land and keep Magdalena as my mother. She is the rightful owner."

"*Coño!* … no … argument." Eugenio was barely audible. "I have … thought much. It is … my right, and best … for her. She is my … main concern. I want the farm … to flourish. She cannot … but … you can, Paco. You have … talent and … ambition."

Paco tried again to object, but Magdalena interrupted, "He is right, Paco. I consent gladly."

Señor López arrived in half an hour, and Magdalena escorted him to Eugenio's room. Eugenio asked her and Paco to stay as he explained what he wanted. López wrote down what Eugenio said and agreed to draw up the will.

"Do it here … now?" Eugenio said.

"Of course."

"Come with me, *Señor*," Magdalena said, leading him through the door to Eugenio's desk."

López finished and reread the document, then took it back into Eugenio's room for his signature.

Eugenio signed and whispered, "Magdalena and … Paco … sign also … and López … as witnesses."

They all signed, and Eugenio closed his eyes and fell asleep.

It was a long week with Doctor Fuentes coming each morning mostly to comfort the family. Four days later, before breakfast, Magdalena came down excitedly saying that Eugenio's fever had dropped: "He is improving."

Within a few minutes Doctor Fuentes came down the stairs. "He is gone. Stopped breathing the moment you left."

Magdalena ran upstairs into the room, bent over and shook him hard, yelling for him to wake up. Doctor Fuentes ran in and stopped her. "He is gone, Magdalena. It is over. Come, we go downstairs. I will send someone to take care of him."

She came down the stairs crying, waving her arms in anguish. At the bottom step she plopped down with her head in her hands. "What will I do? I cannot live without him."

"You feel that way now," Doctor Fuentes said, "but you will live as we all must until comes your time, as it comes for each of us."

"Oh, doctor, how can you say that?"

"For him and for your family."

She stopped crying and sat looking out the window.

That was July 3, 1869.

*

By the last week of August Lydia's pregnancy was dragging her down, though she tried not to show it. With her pregnancy had come an enormous weight gain; She looked swollen, rotund, and lumpy. The sprightly young girl of a few months ago now strained to haul her belly and newly corpulent body from task to task. Her legs felt weaker. Standing over the sink had become an ordeal, in which she alternated between standing sideways and stretching out her arms. No one dared complain when meals dragged out over hours. They knew her too well to comment until one day before supper. Magdalena walked into the kitchen and found Lydia sitting at the table with her head in her hands and a sink full of kettles. Magdalena gingerly said, "Lydia, dear, let auntie help a little."

"I do my work, you do yours if you have any," Lydia said, standing and walking to the sink.

"But you are tired."

"This is my kitchen. Go somewhere else to entertain yourself."

"I only want to help, dear."

With her hand pressed against her back, Lydia turned and disappeared into the dining room leaving the door swinging like a fan.

At supper Magdalena whispered to the others, "Even at such a delicate time she will not ease up."

"Is she afraid to lose her position?" Marta asked.

"She knows better than that."

"Perhaps she feels the baby will be a burden on you," Paco said.

"But I look forward to the baby."

"Do you think she worries she will have to share her baby?" Marta said.

"How could she possibly?" Magdalena said. With her voice cracking she said, "Haven't I suffered enough?"

"I meant no disrespect, Magdalena."

Recovering her composure Magdalena said, "I know, my dear. You are only trying to comfort me."

Later, in their bedroom, Paco returned to the subject. "I think you were right about Lydia."

"She does not trust anyone," Marta said.

"I think you are right. Magdalena wants to play mother while Lydia washes the diapers."

"In all fairness, Paco, after Eugenio's death, this baby is a godsend. Lydia knows reality, though. She erupted the other day because Magdalena said the baby would be an Iglesias, reared with privileges. Lydia knows an aristocrat could never have a slave for a mother. I think Lydia will hold her ground and to hell with Magdalena and her loneliness."

Paco had little sympathy for Lydia, but he said no more for fear of arousing suspicion. He smiled knowing Lydia would also have reason to worry about him. As far as he was concerned Lydia could play the slave as long as his baby was free and well cared for.

As her days drew close Lydia ground herself down with self-torture over every possibility her frantic mind could imagine. Though not proud of enjoying such simple justice, Paco smiled recalling how she planned her pregnancy with the cunning of a lion. And now she would have to guard the carcass alone against the world.

The hour struck with loud scrambling in the kitchen as Paco descended the stairs to breakfast. Through the kitchen door he heard Magdalena say, "I will call the doctor. Try to keep her calm!" She ran into the living room, stopped, and returned to the kitchen and out the back door to find the carriage driver. "Hurry, fetch Doctor Fuentes ... and please tell him to hurry."

"What will I tell him?"

"That we need him right away. It is urgent."

In the kitchen Paco found Lydia seated at the table moaning with her head in one hand and the other holding her belly. Marta sat beside her with her arm around her shoulder. "Is she all right?" Paco asked.

"The pains started two hours ago," Marta said. "It could be any time."

Lydia let out another moan and stiffened. As the pain eased Marta helped her up and walked her to the living room and sat her on the sofa. "Would you rather go to your room?"

Lydia nodded and Marta and Paco helped her up the stairs. Lydia looked at Paco as they laid her in bed. "Thank you, *Señor* Paco. And you too, *señora* Marta."

Marta placed a pillow beneath Lydia's head and said Doctor Fuentes would soon be there.

"Will you call my aunt, please?"

Paco ran down the stairs and out to the slaves' huts and found the old woman. "Lydia is in labor. You understand my wife knows nothing about the father, and she must not find out."

Nodding nervously, the old woman rushed into the hut, picked up a small bundle and emerged a moment later hobbling as fast as her bowed legs could take her toward the house.

"Lydia is in her room," Paco said. "I'll wait for the doctor here."

Paco met Doctor Fuentes at the door and sent him upstairs. Before going back into the fields he stopped in the kitchen, poured a cup of café con leche, and sat down to drink it. Minutes later he was in the barn, saddling his horse.

Four hours later, Paco returned for lunch and found the doctor sitting with Magdalena in the kitchen drinking a cup of black coffee. Clearly angry he told Magdalena, "You should not have called me. Don't you realize what you've done?"

"Lydia is family, doctor. I could not let her have her baby in a hut with no doctor or hygiene."

"It is just not proper. If not for Eugenio's recent passing I would have left. Slaves have their own doctors."

"Doctor, I want to bring her up as mine. Can I adopt her legally?"

"What about the mother?"

"She agrees. She wants the best for the baby."

"I could talk with López the attorney. He can arrange it if the mother agrees ... But she is a slave, Magdalena."

"Does that matter?"

"I don't know," Doctor Fuentes said. "You are very generous to do this."

"I will never have one of my own. This baby is the answer to my prayers."

"The father was white, no?"

"Yes, but we do not know who he was." Seeing Paco standing at the door, she smiled, "Come, Paco. Lunch is ready."

"And Marta?"

"With Lydia. She was a great help, Paco. She is quite a girl. You are lucky."

"I know. I'll wash and be right back."

"Want to see Lydia's baby?" Marta asked, as he reached the back door.

"Not now. They are well, no?"

"Fine. Doctor Fuentes said she had a smooth delivery. I was surprised at how fast she came."

"Good. I will take my food with me. The men are ready to start replanting."

Doctor Fuentes smiled as Paco went out the door. "Typical. Men find little interest in other people's babies."

"He has much on his mind these days, especially since Eugenio died," Magdalena said.

Paco wanted very much to see the baby, but he did not want to see Lydia. He hated the fact that this baby would forever bind them together. Most of all he feared Marta would find out and leave him, and he would end up with that predator.

"I have to be going, Magdalena," Doctor Fuentes said. "Call if you need me, but remember what I told you."

"Thank you for coming, Doctor. We are all grateful."

"You must see the baby," Marta said, coming out to the porch.

Hesitant but curious, Paco followed her into the house and upstairs. Lydia's room was sparse, but neat and well arranged with lace curtains and wicker furniture, certainly not a typical slave's room. Lying in bed, propped up by three pillows and with the baby in her arms, Lydia smiled and looked down at the baby as if to show her off.

"How do you feel, Lydia?"

"Very good, *Señor* Paco. The doctor said I had an easy birth."

"She is very pretty, Lydia. What will you call her?"

"Isabel, *Señor.*"

"After the queen," Marta said. "How lovely."

"I have much work," Paco said. "Congratulations, Lydia."

"Thank you, *Señor.*"

Marta walked down with Paco and out to the back porch. "She is very happy, Paco, and very lucky to have such a beautiful baby."

"We will have a beautiful baby one day, Marta."

She kissed and embraced him and held on to him for a long time. Finally, he said, "I really must go."

"I wait for you with much desire, Paco." They kissed again and he went to the barn to saddle his horse.

That evening Marta kept looking out the kitchen window for him and brought a towel to the water pump shed as he rode up. He unsaddled the horse and walked to the shed. He kissed her and she recounted her day: "The gardening will have to wait. I spent most of the day with Lydia and the baby. How strange, Paco; she will not say one word about the father. All she said was that he returned to Spain."

"She's probably embarrassed," he said. "Or fears he will take the baby."

"But she won't give a straight answer. Always deflects my questions and changes the subject."

"That's Lydia."

"I asked what he looked like. She said only that he was tall and very handsome and then turned away saying she was tired and sleepy."

"Uh-huh."

"Half an hour later she was sitting up by the baby bed stroking and singing softly to her."

"Never having had a baby, I cannot judge her behavior," Paco said. "But I do love you. Let's discuss that."

"Good."

*

By March, it was clear Paco would need another overseer and asked Manuel if he knew of anyone who could handle the job. Manuel said his cousin who worked for another cane grower was not happy there.

"I would not want to raid a neighbor."

"He does not get along with his boss," Manuel said. "Neither of them would be sorry if he left."

"Perhaps I should talk to his employer."

"I could do that for you."

"Who is he?"

"Don Miguel Alonso."

"He owns the next farm to the south. I will ride over now." Manuel obviously wanted to negotiate, but Paco wanted to know why they did not get along.

Within a quarter of an hour he trotted into Miguel Alonso's farm and asked at the main house to see him. The servant who answered the door said he was due for lunch soon and asked him to wait, but Paco said he would wander around the hacienda and have a look around.

Behind the house stood a large barn occupied by several horses and cows. The tall cane plants beyond the barn stretched into the distance. Paco walked into the barn and found a Negro brushing a beautiful bay mare. "I am looking for don Miguel. Can you tell me where he is?"

The man looked at him quizzically and continued brushing. Finally he replied, "Don Miguel is in the field, *Señor*. His overseer is behind the barn. Maybe he can help you."

Paco found the tall slender man looking at the cane field, pacing, apparently waiting for someone or something. The man had broad shoulders and a wide straw hat that covered his mane of light brown hair. His moustache stuck out from his face like needles. The man's stare made Paco feel threatened.

"What?" he said, in a gruff, high-pitched voice.

"I am waiting for don Miguel. The servant in the house said he would return soon, so I was just looking around at his magnificent hacienda."

"Magnificent, yes, but not for long."

"Who are you?"

"Enrique Peluso, don Miguel's overseer, at least for the moment."

"I do not understand."

"I am not afraid to talk, *Señor*, but whom do I address?"

"Paco Iglesias from the next hacienda."

"Ah, yes. My cousin Manuel has told me about you."

Paco had suspected he was Manuel's cousin from his bad humor. "He says you want to move."

"And the sooner the better."

"I need a second overseer. I came to talk with your boss about you."

"From what I have heard from my cousin, I am not too sure I am interested."

"And why not?"

"Don Miguel is a pansy. He does not like to work the slaves the way we must. He keeps me from doing what he pays me to do, and I don't like it."

"And Manuel has told you I am the same?"

"Frankly, yes, although he has said lately that you are learning."

"I must say you are frank, Peluso. I like that."

"Flattery is not what I want, *Señor* Iglesias. The only reason I would consider it is that you pay Manuel more than I get here."

"Your pay would be the same as his."

"Will I be allowed to work the slaves properly?"

"Only if you do it to my advantage. I will not have a sadist working for me, and since you are frank, I will be too. You sound like a man who enjoys laying on a good beating."

"No, *Señor*. I do not like it, but I will not let them mock or defy me. All the talk of rebellion against Spain these days seems to have filled them with desire to challenge authority. But no, I do not enjoying beating them."

"If you understand that I want maximum productivity with minimum property damage, you have the job."

"I will have to think on it. Perhaps you should talk with don Miguel first. Then you will be more sure."

"Good idea."

"*Bueno.* He comes now." Enrique pointed to the cane field where a horseman was trotting toward the barn.

With dark hair and eyes, the handsome young man smiled broadly. "Hello. You are Paco Iglesias from the hacienda north of here. How can I be of service?"

"Have we met?"

"Yes, once with Eugenio."

"I am in need of a second overseer. My overseer has a cousin who works for you. I just met him. Manuel told me you were not happy with him."

"He does his job, but I don't like the way he whips the slaves, and he doesn't like me. Also he's rude and talks down to me. I was on the verge of firing him this morning, but decided to think it over. That's why he is loafing behind the barn."

"I would not hire him without your consent, don Miguel. Good neighbor relations are far more important."

"I like him very much, Paco. I'd hate to lose such a man. I already lost one, and good workers are not plentiful, but this one I cannot manage. Take him with my blessing."

Paco got the impression from the man's demeanor and the sadness in his voice that he had more than a boss's interest in his overseer. Don Miguel was a handsome man of average height, shiny black hair and smooth skin, slightly feminine in the way he talked and moved. Paco remembered one or two such men in Asturias, and he smiled.

"If you are sure, I will talk with him again," Paco said.

"Please help yourself, Paco. I am happy to meet you after all this time."

"Perhaps you and your wife will have supper with us soon."

"I am not married, Paco. I live here with my mother, but I look forward to becoming friends."

They shook hands and Paco walked back around the barn to talk with Enrique Peluso, who was sitting against the barn smoking a cigar. "Well?"

"Do you want the job on my terms?"

"Maximum productivity, minimum property damage? Fine."

"Can you start tomorrow, eight o'clock?"

"Yes. I will see Manuel this evening." He stood and shook Paco's hand.

On his return Paco found Manuel working the men in the field. "I hired your cousin."

"You will be glad. Enrique is a good man."

"His trouble with his boss bothers me," Paco said. "Don Miguel clearly did not want to lose him, but he cannot manage him. Gave me his blessing. Is there more?"

"I do not like to gossip, *Señor* Paco, but don Miguel was very friendly with one of the slaves, if you know what I mean, very friendly. Well, the slave talked back one day, and Enrique gave him a whipping. Of course, he did no serious damage. The man could walk afterwards. Enrique figured the slave felt invincible because he was the owner's lover. Don Miguel was furious. Called Enrique a sadist and an evil monster. Then, crying, he ran off. That knocked Enrique off the burro, as they say."

"I figured something like that."

"That is not all. After that don Miguel became very solicitous of Enrique. Bought him things, you know, shirts and a beautiful belt with a silver buckle. Enrique told him to keep them and called him a fairy to his face. My cousin is very outspoken, as you may have seen."

Paco could barely keep from laughing. "It all makes sense now. Thank you, Manuel. I will tell no one."

*

After supper, Paco wanted to show Marta the cane field, but she wanted to see the garden out front first. "Look, already the weeds are back," she said, bending down to pull out a clump.

He took her arm, smiled and told her the weeds could wait. He led her around the house and toward the cane field. The sun hung over the tallest canes; the temperature had dropped slightly.

Marta fanned herself with her hand and said, "I'm still not used to this Cuban heat."

"Your Asturian blood will soon thin.

"You know, Paco, I am not one to complain, but … well, I try to help with the baby, but it is impossible. Lydia is so jealous she won't let Magdalena near Isabel. She barks at Magdalena without mercy. I feel like an intruder."

Paco chuckled.

"It is not funny, Paco. Poor Magdalena loves that baby so much it makes me want to cry."

"I'm laughing at Lydia, not Magdalena."

"This afternoon, while Lydia was in the kitchen, Magdalena went to see the baby. I saw her from the hall and went in to have a look. She picked Isabel up and cradled her and started to sing the most beautiful song I have ever heard. A Cuban lullaby I think. She just stood rocking and singing gently. It was beautiful; I was mesmerized. Magdalena saw me and continued singing and turned Isabel to me so I could see her. She was so proud. Then she walked to the window and held her up. I think she wanted the baby to see the royal palms and green hills. Magdalena stood there smiling, as happy as I have ever seen her. Lydia stormed in with her arms out saying she would take her. Poor Magdalena actually looked guilty. To ease the tension I said, 'She is beautiful, Lydia.' Lydia turned to me and said, 'It is her bedtime. Why do you keep her awake?' Magdalena handed Lydia the baby as if it were an offering to an angry god. I felt terrible for her and said, 'She was quite awake when we came in, Lydia.' Again she turned to me with fury. 'Don't you have anything better to do, *Señora* Marta, than play with my baby?' Then Magdalena said, 'We love your baby and want to enjoy her. Of course, you are her mother. There is no reason for jealousy.' At that Lydia blew up. 'If I am jealous,' she said, 'it is because you, *Señora* Magdalena, are a thief, trying to steal my child by pretending to be her mother. And what is this woman doing here? Can't she have her own, or is she as dry as you?'"

"*Coño!*" Paco said. Knowing Marta's temper and intolerance for stupidity. "What did you do?"

"I controlled myself, Paco. The fight was between sisters. I just happened to be in the way. I only spoke because I felt sorry for poor Magdalena."

"You said nothing?"

"I told her I had tried to help her, but I would not intrude again."

"Then what?"

"By that time the baby was screaming, probably frightened at all the yelling and tugging, *pobrecita*. Magdalena led me out, and you would not believe what she said. 'Be patient with her, Marta. She is a good person who has suffered much in her life. She loves Isabel very much and only wants the best for her.'"

Soon Marta smiled and snuggled up to him with her arm wrapped around his and said, "Maybe Magdalena is right, Paco, but I wonder. About an hour later Lydia came to my room and apologized. I could tell she was still angry, but she said, 'I am sorry, *Señora* Marta. I said bad things that I regret. Please forgive me.' I wish she would not treat me so formally. Anyway, I knew it was Magdalena she was really mad at."

"Reminds me of the story in Don Quixote," he said, "Sancho Panza becomes governor and they bring two women to him with a baby, both claiming to be the mother. Do you remember?"

"I never read it."

"Well, after they presented their cases Sancho said, 'Cut the baby in half and give half to each mother.' One of the women said, 'Good. That is fair.' The other cried and said, 'No, don't hurt him. Let her have him.' To which Sancho said, 'Here is the mother, the one who would rather give him up than hurt him. Give the baby to her.'"

Marta was smiling now. "I guess responsibility can make a sage even of Sancho Panza. Are you saying Magdalena was the sage this afternoon?"

"No, I was thinking of her as the real mother," Paco said. "She is the only person I know who seems to take the teachings of Christ seriously."

"In spite of her position and breeding she sometimes seems sad, as if she carried the sins of the world on her shoulders. You are right, Paco. She is saintly."

"Or a simpleton. Sometimes the difference is hard to see."

"Do not say that, Paco. Her heart is pure and without malice, truly Christ-like."

"One small miracle would convince me." Then he said, "Remember our walks in the hills around Colosía? It could be drizzling or sunny. We didn't care."

She held his arm tighter. "I remember, but I am glad to be here with you. Wherever you are is where I want to be."

In her eyes Paco saw her old beauty. Her pock marks had strangely vanished in the waning light. Having regained her weight and energy she looked lovely.

"Remember the day we made love in the mountains?"

"How could I forget, Paco?"

He stopped. "Do you realize we have never made love in the cane?

Holding his hand she pulled him into the field and knelt down on the thatch among the tall canes and pulled him down to her. Before he could speak they were wrapped in each other, kissing and touching, and the breeze blew over them, and the canes whispered, and the sky blushed.

Afterwards, lying together gazing into the red sky, Marta said, "I have news for you, Paco. We are going to have a baby. I wanted to be sure before I told you."

"My God! We shouldn't have ..."

"It was good, Paco, better than good."

He kissed her again, thinking that this was truly a land of surprises.

CHAPTER 4 – REBELLION, 1868

*

October 10: Carlos Manuel de Céspedes
Calls for Cuban Revolution

*

October 11: Rebels Take Yara. Revolution Spreads

*

October 19: Céspedes Takes City of Bayamó

*

Paco opened the newspaper that October morning seven months later to read the blaring headline: "Céspedes Calls for Revolt Against Spain." The story told of a lawyer named Carlos Manuel de Céspedes who had raised his voice for revolution and had been seconded by a group of patriots meeting in a plantation in eastern Cuba. Within one week, the rebels had taken a town named Yara, leading people to call the rebellion "*El Grito de Yara,*" the Cry from Yara. So far, the only skirmishes had occurred in Oriente, the eastern province, whose thick, dense mountains favored guerrilla fighting. The landowners there seemed more dedicated to winning independence from Spain than those in the richer, western provinces.

This news excited Paco. The landowners' call for freedom, with which he sympathized, had combined with a call from poor whites and blacks to abolish slavery. Of course the call for abolition did not sit well with the landowners. As much as he hated slavery, Paco could not convince himself that his hacienda and his way of life could survive abolition. Abolition would force growers to hire salaried men. Housing and boarding slaves cost almost nothing compared with the wages free laborers would demand. Ideals teetered on the sharp fulcrum of pragmatism. At breakfast he asked Magdalena if she had heard about the revolt.

"Yes. It is all you hear in Matanzas."

"And abolition?"

"It will ruin us."

"Slavery is horrible," Marta said with defiance, waiting for rebuttal. With her huge belly she now sat sideways at the table and she did not exhibit her usual good humor.

Only one year earlier Paco would have agreed with her, but his opinion had softened now that he was responsible for a large plantation and a family of six. Many times he had recalled with bitterness Eugenio's opinion that it is easy to have strong ideals when you have nothing to lose.

No one responded to Marta's challenge, but the conversation continued to needle in and out of the rebellion, how long it would last, and whether it would reach Matanzas. As they ate and talked don Miguel Alonso appeared at the front door. Lydia's aunt opened for him. He asked to see Paco.

Paco heard don Miguel's voice and walked out to welcome him.

"Paco, have you heard?"

"The rebellion? We were just talking about it. Won't you join us for coffee?"

Paco introduced him to Marta and Magdalena and then stepped to the kitchen door and told Lydia they had a guest.

"I heard something last evening," don Miguel said, staring at Marta's belly, "and this morning's newspaper had little else. Hope it doesn't spread here. My slaves are restless. My overseer says it's the rebellion."

"We will have to guard them even more now," Paco said.

"I don't believe in war," don Miguel said.

"I am a Spaniard, as is my wife, but Spain has brought it on herself. The rebels have a right to revolt."

"It's true that Spain's taxes hurt us, but losing our slaves would be worse," don Miguel said.

"Then you are in favor of freedom from Spain?" Paco said.

117

"Of course, but not at any cost. People should not die for economics."

"Oppression makes men brave," Paco said.

"Exaggerations!" don Miguel said. "Do you feel oppressed? I certainly don't."

"No, but hunger is the vilest form of oppression. And what of the poor slaves?"

"My only problem with slaves is they don't want to work."

Marta could control herself no longer: "Would you if you had been torn from your family and brought here to live like an animal and work eighteen to twenty hours each day?"

Don Miguel's jaw fell with the shock of a woman entering a men's discussion. Magdalena tried to hide her discomfort by laying her hand on Marta's, but Marta drew away.

"The African serves no other purpose, *Señora* Iglesias. It's clear that God put them here to serve the white man."

"And why did God put the white man here, don Miguel?"

Don Miguel stammered. Finally, after a few seconds, he said, "To improve the world for humanity."

Without hesitation Marta said, "You mean white humanity."

Paco smiled at his wife's attack and sat back to enjoy it.

"I do not mean to sound hard or unfeeling, *Señora*. I am known as kind and just. I care deeply for my slaves. But we Cubans of means have created prosperity in our Cuba; we provide wealth and employment to many. What if we abolished slavery and Cuba could no longer compete in the world sugar market? What would happen to us, poor and rich?"

"We would have to dirty our hands," she said. "That would be no great tragedy."

Don Miguel turned to Paco for help, but found only a smile. Finally he stood. "I really must go. Thank you for the coffee and the pleasant conversation. *Señora* Iglesias, you have some interesting ideas. You must meet my mother. She would like you."

"I would love to."

"We heard you were expecting. When is the blessed day?"

"Two more months," she said. "But it feels like two years."

He smiled, said goodbye, and left.

Magdalena, who had said nothing throughout the discussion, said, "You are outspoken, Marta."

"I could not take such shit!"

"We women must maintain decorum, for our self-respect."

"By swallowing stupidity? You can keep that kind of self-respect."

118

"Oh, dear," Magdalena said. "I'd better go help Lydia."

Paco's and Marta's smiles split into laughter.

Within two weeks talk of rebellion had swamped the island like a tidal wave. People seemed willing to fight, especially slaves who would gladly risk their lives for freedom. Worried that his slaves might get caught up, Paco called them together and told them that, come what may, they would soon gain their freedom, but it would have to come gradually.

As best anyone could gather from the pamphlets and the Matanzas newspaper, most intellectual leaders of the rebellion came from Oriente Province. These farm and factory entrepreneurs had bristled for years under heavy Spanish taxes on their products. Spain, they said, kept colonial entrepreneurs on a short leash. "We are her slaves," one said. These upper class men knew they would have to proceed with care, for supporting the rebellion could prove dangerous. They all knew the Captain General in Havana, the governor of the colony, could and would use Spanish soldiers to enforce Spain's laws.

Paco tried to remain neutral and continued to run the hacienda as usual. The new overseer, Enrique, was working well. He was not excessively cruel, and between him and Manuel they controlled the slaves with very few whippings. By December Marta had begun to comprehend that abolition of slavery would indeed ruin them. She still did not like to see men and women mistreated, but had begun to understand the price of compassion.

Paco and Marta spent many hours talking about slavery and rebellion, usually alone, where they could express themselves without riling Magdalena or Lydia. Lydia, for her part, said nothing about the rebellion. No one could imagine that she approved of slavery, but she kept her feelings to herself. During discussions of slaves and slavery she remained aloof, but listened attentively.

It was a rainy evening, and Marta and Paco were sitting in the front porch watching the light rain that fell like a blessing on the green land.

"This afternoon Lydia nearly pushed Magdalena down to get at the baby."

Paco puffed his cigar and rocked.

"After lunch, Magdalena went to her room to crochet, and I went to see the baby. Lydia was nursing her when I came in. I asked if I could hold her when she was through. She said she would sleep after nursing, but that I could later. After she finished and put Isabel to bed, I asked if we could sit a while and talk. Know what she said?"

"She refused."

"How did you know?"

"She did the same to me. She plays the slave who knows her place, but she has arranged her place exactly as she likes it."

"I know. And she bosses Magdalena, as if she were the slave."

"Magdalena told me how she connived to become pregnant. It had to be a light-skinned Spaniard."

"Well, you can't blame her for not wanting her child to become a slave."

"She got her wish, Paco. Beautiful and no one would take her for an African; light skin and hair and greenish eyes. Truly amazing."

Paco said nothing.

"Another thing," she said. "Lydia resents Magdalena for more than the baby."

"They are sisters, remember," Paco said. "Sisters always fight."

"Magdalena should threaten to sell her. Wouldn't that shake Lydia?"

"*Coño!* Magdalena is not capable."

"I know."

*

Next morning, as Paco walked toward the barn, Manuel ran to him. "*Señor* Paco, three slaves have escaped."

Paco stopped, to make sure he had heard right.

"I woke them this morning and found three missing. The others all claim they know nothing. Maybe I can whip them into telling. What do you want to do?"

"Go find them."

"Good. I leave right away."

"No, Manuel. You and Enrique stay and keep a tight guard. Others will follow if those three get away."

Paco returned to the house and found Lydia in the kitchen. He told her what he had just heard and asked if she knew anything.

"No, *Señor.*" She did not look up and continued to scrub a large pot.

"Look, Lydia. I know you don't want to hurt your friends, but if you know something, tell me. If I don't bring them back, they will surely end up worse than here. Also, the rest will do the same, and we will be ruined. Magdalena and you, too."

She continued to scrub for a moment longer, apparently thinking it over. Finally she passed her hand over her brow and said: "They went to join the rebels, *Señor.*"

"Where?"

"Oriente. They followed the river out of Matanzas." Then, with a frightened expression, "Please do not say I told, *Señor.* They will hate me."

"I won't, Lydia. And thanks."

Paco ran up to his room where Marta was fixing the bed. "Three slaves escaped. I must go."

She put her arms around his neck. "Can't you send one of the overseers?"

"It is my responsibility. Imagine what will happen if I do not bring them back."

"Be careful, Paco." Then she hugged him tightly.

He ran downstairs looking for Magdalena and found her sitting on the front porch sewing. Sitting beside her he told her what happened omitting what Lydia had said. "You must take over until I get back."

"Oh, Paco. I cannot order men."

"You do not have to do any work. Manuel and Enrique will handle the men. Just be present and let them know you are in charge. I will not be long."

She looked so frightened and worried that Paco said, "Just check on the overseers once in a while, Magdalena. They know what to do."

"I will try, Paco, but …"

"I remember Uncle Eugenio had a pistol."

"I will get it." He followed her up the stairs into Eugenio's office, which Paco now used. She opened a box in one of the cabinets behind his desk and took out the revolver. Never having noticed the box, Paco was surprised. "Here, Paco, and a box of bullets."

"Thank you, Magdalena. I hope I do not have to use it, but I may not be able to coax them back without it."

Returning to his bedroom he found Marta preparing a change of clothes. He took them, kissed her and said goodbye. She smiled her slightly bent smile and he left. Downstairs he found Lydia, who was waiting with a package of food.

"Thank you, Lydia. I have not told Marta or Magdalena what you said."

"Thank you, *Señor.* Be careful."

As soon as Paco had left, Magdalena came to Marta's room and sat down. Marta looked surprised because Magdalena had never come in like that.

"What is the matter, Magdalena?"

"I cannot do it, Marta."

"Do what?"

"Paco asked me to run the hacienda while he is gone, but I cannot."

"Why not? You are strong and capable."

"No, no. I always depended on Eugenio and Lydia, and now Paco. I am afraid."

"Nonsense. Come downstairs. We will talk with Manuel."

"Now?"

"Right now."

"But what will I say?"

"Tell him to call you if there is trouble. Let him know you are in charge."

Marta took her by the hand and led her down the stairs to the living room. Seeing how she hesitated, Marta let go her hand and continued into the kitchen and out the back porch not even looking to see if Magdalena was following. She was. Enrique was mounting his horse to lead a crew of slaves out. "Go on, call him," Marta said.

"I cannot." She put her hands to her face.

"Enrique!" Marta yelled. "*Un momento, por favor.*"

He told the men to wait and trotted back to where the women were standing. "Yes, *Señora?*"

Seeing that Magdalena was not going to speak, Marta said, "Enrique, Paco said you and Manuel will control the men."

"Absolutely, *Señora.*"

"It is a difficult time. Others may try to escape. I will hold you and Manuel responsible."

He glared at her, rolling the cigar from side to side in his mouth, as if he were forming the words to curse her. She glared back with her jaw set tight, and he turned his horse and rode back to the men and continued his trek to the field.

"That was wonderful, Marta. You are so brave. You do it. Please."

"You are the owner," Marta said.

"And as owner I appoint you to do whatever you must."

Seeing her on the verge of tears, Marta realized it was probably better not to force her. "Of course, Magdalena," and she embraced the trembling woman.

"I am lucky to have you, Marta. I need your courage and your strength."

It felt good to be trusted, but Marta's confidence was mostly pretense. Still, she knew Paco would expect her to try.

During the workers' lunch period Marta walked out to the field to see how the day was going. The men were sitting down under the boiling shed and Enrique was sitting alone under a tree eating his lunch. He stood as Marta approached.

"Please sit down and finish your lunch," she said. "I only wanted to see if there were any problems."

"Not yet, *Señora*."

"Good, and Manuel?"

"I saw him a while ago. Everything is fine."

"How will you make sure they do not leave during the night?"

"Manuel and I plan to take shifts standing guard. We discussed it with *Señor* Paco before he left."

"Please call me if there is anything."

"Yes, *Señora*."

Marta returned to the kitchen and sat sideways at the table to accommodate her huge belly

"Lunch will be ready in a few minutes, *Señora*."

"This load is getting heavier by the day."

"The burden of motherhood."

"Do you think any of the others will try to escape?"

"I do not know, *Señora*. I have little to do with them."

"We may be at war soon," Marta said, trying to make conversation.

"I know nothing of war and fighting, *Señora*."

"The people have good reason to rebel."

"I know only the kitchen and tending my baby."

"Perhaps you should interest yourself more, Lydia. This is your country too."

"I have no control over such things, *Señora*."

"There he goes again, kicking me."

"You are lucky to feel that kick. Poor Magdalena will never feel it."

"She is a good woman."

"She worries too much. Not that I am complaining, *Señora*."

"Did she want a baby very much?"

"Oh yes, *Señora*. She would have done anything for a belly like yours."

"Poor thing. That is why she takes such interest in Isabel?"

"Sometimes she … "

"What?"

"Nothing, *Señora*, just the way she looks at your belly."

"What do you mean?"

"I think she envies us."

Marta suddenly wondered why she was telling her this. Perhaps Magdalena had said something, but she had never even dropped a hint.

Throughout the conversation Lydia did not look at her, but continued cooking and preparing the plates and spoke in a matter of fact tone. Marta felt Lydia was trying to tell her something. "What should I do?" Marta asked.

"Nothing, *Señora*. It is not your problem."

Marta got up and went to her room to freshen up, but she could not shake the thought that Magdalena envied her. She had not shown it, so Marta could not ask her about it. Finally she tried to put it out of her mind, since there was nothing she could do.

A week passed with no word from Paco and no trouble from the slaves. Manuel and Enrique managed them well, standing nightly guard in shifts and reporting to Marta every morning, noon, and evening.

Marta sensed nothing strange in Magdalena, but wondered, and the suspicion changed her feelings. I am only human, after all, she thought. Envy generates odium, and no one likes to be despised, especially for having a baby. If she felt that way then she is not the person I thought she was. Marta began to feel uncomfortable around Magdalena and avoided intimate conversations. One morning a few days later, after they had eaten and Marta had finished fixing her room, she walked down to the dining room looking for Lydia and overheard her talking with Magdalena in the kitchen. Thinking it would be nice to join them Marta approached the closed door, but before she opened it she heard her name and stopped to listen.

"How could she think I resent her baby?"

"I could be wrong, *Señora*. It is only an opinion."

"Has she said anything?"

"No, but haven't you noticed how she avoids you? What else could it be?"

At that moment Marta understood everything. Without listening any further she pushed open the door and walked in, and the conversation stopped dead. Marta looked at Lydia and said, "You should be ashamed. You told me Magdalena resented my belly, and it has worried me for days. Now you tell another lie. If you had not planted the idea it would never have occurred to me." She turned to Magdalena. "Magdalena, you have been good to me, and I know Lydia is your sister and you love her, but she is a liar. I do not know why she does this, except out of envy. You can decide what to believe, but I will not put up with deception."

"Why would I do such a thing, *Señora* Marta?" Lydia said, almost crying.

"I do not know what is in your heart, but what you told Magdalena just now is a lie."

"Stop, please!" Magdalena said in tears. "We will forget it and be friends. No harm has been done."

But Marta was not ready to forget. "I was beginning to feel you did not like me before I heard her lying through the door, Magdalena. It is difficult enough to be here alone, a foreigner with my husband gone. I will not live with such meanness. You better talk to your sister, Magdalena."

"I will, I will. Please calm down, Marta. Everything will be fine."

"I have to see to the men," Marta said and walked out the back door. Soon she was perspiring and breathing heavily. She found Manuel standing near the men cutting cane. "Good morning, *Señora.*"

"Manuel, I ..." she could not finish. The sudden pain in her belly felt as if it would knock her down. She bent over and he caught her. "What is it, *Señora*?"

She looked down to see water dripping down her legs. "Oh, God! Please Manuel ... help me."

Marta's vision blurred. Manuel picked her up and carried her all the way to the house, her head flopping up and down as he ran, sweating and puffing. Magdalena was standing on the back porch watching. Still holding Marta, Manuel told her what had happened. "Where shall I put her?"

"In the living room, Manuel. Come."

As they entered the house Marta's eyes could not focus; she saw light moving across the ceiling and heard Lydia telling the carriage driver to hurry. Marta's clothes were wet with the water and sweat. Then she passed out.

The next thing she remembered was lying in her bed with her knees up and Doctor Fuentes bending over her and Lydia and Magdalena moving around the room like kites in the air and the doctor shouting, "More water, and more towels ... *Pronto, pronto!*" It seemed like hours with the pains coming more and more rapidly, one upon the other, and Doctor Fuentes saying, "Don't push ... No ... Wait ... Hold it," and, frightened and trying to understand what was happening, Marta tried to hold the baby back, and she was yelling, "When, Doctor? Please! The pain! Oh, Paco, where are you? Paco! Paco!" Then later, the doctor saying, "Now ... Push ... Push ... Yes, that's it ... Push ... Fine ... Yes ... Fine ... That's it."

Then the pain stopped and ... relief ... and then the most beautiful sound she had ever heard. She was still puffing. Lydia and Magdalena were standing at the foot of the bed, smiling, arms around each other's waist. "A boy," Magdalena said. "A beautiful boy."

"You can sit down now, *Señora* Magdalena," Lydia said. "I will take over."

Then the doctor laid the baby in Marta's arms. "It is a boy?"
He opened the little blanket. "Yes, see?"

*

Neither Lydia nor Magdalena could do enough for Marta the following
two weeks. They spent hours with her each day, bringing her soup and
milk, always milk, and sitting to talk and looking at the baby and holding
him and rocking him. Lydia, especially, worked tirelessly to make Marta's
recovery as easy as possible and soon convinced Marta she was truly sorry
for the lies she had told. Marta slept much and nursed the baby and felt
wonderful. Every day Lydia brought Isabel into Marta's room to nurse her
while Marta did the same, and they talked. It was the first time Marta had
felt comfortable with her.

"What will you call him?" Lydia asked one afternoon.

"I like Pablo, after Paco's father, but I will wait until he returns. We
talked a few times about names, and I had the feeling he did not like Pablo,
but I will try anyway. He never told me what name he liked."

About two weeks after the baby was born, the doctor said Marta
could get up, and she walked downstairs. It was time for breakfast, and
she wanted to eat with Magdalena in the dining room. Lydia held a chair
for her.

"The baby is asleep and I have freedom, at least for a while."

"Is he all right alone?" Magdalena asked. "Perhaps I should go to
him."

"Oh, no. He knows how to let me know when he wants something."

Marta stood and said, "How would you like me to make *fabada
asturiana*, the way my mother taught me?"

"Are you strong enough?" Magdalena said.

"Absolutely. I refuse to become an invalid."

"Well, if you like," she said, looking quizzically at Lydia.

"I will make it, *Señora*. I have made it often."

"Only an Asturian can make it correctly. For lunch tomorrow? The
beans have to soak."

Lydia said no more.

"I will see what we need," Marta said. "If we need something I will
go to Matanzas."

"We have everything, *Señora*: white beans, onion, potatoes, ham,
chorizo, morcilla, and olive oil. Marta told her morcilla was not authentic
Asturian. Lydia made a face that showed a mixture of surprise and offense
and walked into the kitchen. After breakfast Marta washed the beans to

remove any pebbles and put them under water for the next morning. Then she went to Lydia and embraced her. "Thank you for everything, Lydia."

She smiled and kissed Marta's cheek.

"I would like to sit on the porch," Marta said.

Magdalena followed her out to the rockers. "It is nice of you to help," she said.

"After all you have done for me? Besides, I love the kitchen. I did all the cooking for my family."

"It is a beautiful morning," Magdalena said.

"Yes, a fine time to thank you again for making me feel at home. It is not easy moving to a new country with new people, but you have made it easy."

"Have you decided on a name?"

"I wait for Paco."

"Pablo is a good name."

"I only wish he were here."

"I am sure he is all right."

"I wanted the baby to wait for him, but you and Lydia were wonderful."

"Marta, I am glad you said what you did to Lydia that day. It has helped her."

"Perhaps I was brutal, but I have never been able to keep silent in the face of wrong."

"I wish I could do that, but I worry too much about others' feelings."

"Asturias is a rough country. You have to be tough to survive."

"You and Lydia are strong," Magdalena said. "I admire you both, and Paco, too. The way he has taken charge of the hacienda as if he had been born to it. And now, you." She turned and kissed Marta. "I am very happy to have another sister, Marta."

The following day, Manuel came to Marta during breakfast, saying the slaves were restless and difficult to control. "They have slowed down and do as little as they can. I have used the whip, but I cannot whip them all."

Marta got up and led him out of the house to where he had left the slaves standing near the barn. Every one seemed drenched in gloom and bitterness.

"I am here to tell you that my husband has promised me that you will all be freed in a short time, rebellion or no. He has many details to work out yet, but soon he will fulfill his promise. As I understand his plan, you will be able to stay and work for pay or leave as free men to work or join

127

the rebels. I ask one thing: wait. If we lose this crop, my husband will not be able to offer anything. Stay and be patient. He will return soon."

Seeing them nodding and looking at her with anticipation, she said to Manuel: "Go now. They understand. And treat them well." Then she walked back to the house calmly and with as much dignity as she could muster. In the kitchen she stopped and looked out the window. Manuel, on horseback, was following the slaves to work.

*

Paco followed the Canimar River southeast out of Matanzas through lush, green country, stopping in every village to question anyone he could stop. Occasionally someone who had seen the slaves would point the way. On the way, the reported sightings became more and more recent, which meant the slaves had slowed their pace. Paco carried the pistol at his side, mostly to show he was serious. He had never shot a man and hoped he never would, but he would leave nothing to chance. The threesome's trail took him east, and he cursed them throughout the length of Matanzas Province. It would be a long way to Oriente, but he felt certain he would catch them before they reached their destination.

Near the end of the second week Paco reached Colón, where he spent the night inquiring about the men, resting and looking around. The next day, heading for Arabos, he stopped in a small village, got off his horse and asked his usual questions, knowing that if he did not catch them soon it was because he had passed them. He dismounted at a covered fruit stand on the plaza, where two men sat in the shade of the store's overhanging metal roof playing chess. Paco described the three men. The older of the two said, "I saw three Negroes this very morning. They asked for the road to Oriente, so I pointed the way. I told them to follow the railroad tracks. They looked pretty nervous and their clothes were tattered, so I figured they were runaway slaves going to join the rebels." The old man spoke with enthusiasm and great animation, waving his arms and pointing vigorously, apparently glad to have someone new to talk with. His friend, the fruit stand owner, without looking up from the chessboard finally made his move and took a sip of his *café con leche* and looked at Paco.

"You are right," Paco said. "They belong to me."

"I knew it," the old man said, slamming the table and rattling the chessboard.

"*Coño!*" the owner said. "Every time you are about to lose you try to knock them over. Play fair if you want me to play with you!"

"By the way," the old man said, ignoring his friend, "one of the men was coughing, almost choking, and very thin. He looked pretty bad."

"That's one of them. How long ago?"

"Not even an hour," he said, shrugging and raising his arms. "We had just sat down to play. Right, Luis?"

The owner nodded, still studying the board.

"Thank you." Paco remounted and headed in the direction the old man said.

Knowing a sick comrade would hinder their escape Paco slowed his pace to avoid announcing his presence by galloping. After letting the horse walk for less than half an hour he spotted them on a hill silhouetted against the sunlit sky trudging the lonely road with cane fields on either side. The two on the outside held up the middle one. They heard Paco's horse and looked back. One of the men pushed the other two into the cane field, but it was too thick to move through. Paco rode up with his pistol drawn and said, "Stop or I kill you." Armando, the sick one, fell to a sitting position with his arms and legs interlaced through the cane stalks. Only the cane kept him up. He looked so forlorn and thin that Paco felt pity for him and dismounted.

"Help him up," Paco said. "We go back now. But first, we stop at the village to eat."

Seeing Armando's weak condition Paco helped him onto his horse behind the saddle. Armando was obviously grateful and thanked Paco profusely. The others were not as glad to see him, but hunger and the pistol offered overwhelming encouragement. Back at the village they found the same two men still sitting at the fruit stand staring at the chessboard. They had moved the table to follow the shade.

"Aha! You caught 'em," the old man said. "Going to use the whip?"

His malicious smile annoyed Paco. "We need something to eat," he said, picking out some mangoes, bananas, and oranges. He paid the owner and asked where they could find some meat.

"Across the plaza, over there," the owner said. "They have ham, sausage, cheese, bread; everything."

Paco bought the fruit, crossed the plaza with the three, bought some chorizo sausage, milk and bread, and rode out until they found a shade tree just past the edge of the village. He spread the food under the tree, and they all ate their fill with little conversation. Armando found it difficult to eat with his coughing. It must have been days since their last meal, judging by the way the others devoured their food almost whole. They finished and resumed their journey. The two slaves walked ahead of Paco, who, with Armando, rode the horse.

Later that afternoon, passing through another village, they encountered a platoon of soldiers guarding the main exit of the village.

"Halt!" the sergeant said, holding up one hand. "Identify yourselves."

"I am Paco Iglesias. I am returning with my escaped slaves."

"You are a Spaniard."

"Yes, *Asturiano*. I own a sugar plantation near Matanzas. That is where I go."

"How do I know you are not joining the rebels?"

"Sergeant, these men had intended to do that, but I caught them. They belong to me."

"There are many people joining them these days, even Spaniards. They are traitors and will be treated as such," the sergeant said, looking them over. "If you are lying, it will go badly for you."

"Damn it, Sergeant. I own a plantation. Why would I join the rebels who are trying to ruin my business?"

"*Bueno, bueno!*" With his hand he signaled for them to pass.

As they rode off, Paco thought, Such arrogance to talk to me like that, a fellow Spaniard. No wonder people are rebelling.

Armando grabbed Paco's shoulders and started to cough. Soon he was coughing violently until he bent over to the side and threw up a large amount of blood. Paco immediately dismounted and helped him to the ground. They were near a farmhouse, so he helped Armando to the house to rest a while. By the time the four of them arrived Armando had calmed down, but the ordeal had weakened him even more. A thin, old woman with thick gray hair in a bun came out to see what they wanted. Paco explained why they had stopped. Without a moment's hesitation she wiped her hands on her apron and invited them in. The old woman brought Armando some *tilo*, a slightly narcotic plant infusion. As he drank she called Paco aside and said, "This man has tuberculosis. I am sure of it. My husband died of it last year."

Paco already suspected it and thanked her for her generosity. She then made coffee with milk for the rest of them and asked them to sit and drink. The two others were glad to have coffee after so long.

"I would offer more, but I have no more. The soldiers have taken everything."

"I am sorry, Señora. I did not know they were raiding small farms."

"They take everything they can get, the cutthroat bullies."

After they finished the coffee, Paco helped Armando back up on the horse and they continued. By now it was quite hot and Armando was leaning more and more on Paco. In late afternoon Paco decided to stop in the next town that had a jail where he could lock up the men for the night and sleep peacefully.

They passed two villages before they found one with a jail. A man in the plaza led them to it. Paco knocked on the door and a short, thin man of about fifty, wearing a broad straw hat, came out smiling. "*Si, Señor?*"

"I am looking for a jail."

"This is the only jail within a radius of twenty kilometers. This must be the one you seek."

"And who are you, Señor?"

"I am in charge. We do not get many customers," he smiled, "for which I thank God."

"Can you put up three slaves overnight for me?"

"Have they broken the law, *Señor?*"

"They tried to escape from my hacienda. I will pay."

"Well, in that case, I think I can accommodate them," the jailer said, inviting Paco in. He reached into the drawer of the little table where he was sitting and took out a key. Paco stood looking around at the tiny stone building. The small office had one window and opened to a cell through a barred door. The cell had no windows. A print of Queen Isabel II hung on the wall over the small table. Someone had painted a moustache, which had been crudely wiped off. The jailer led the three men into the cell, locked the door, and put the key back in the drawer, assuring Paco that they would be safe until he came for them in the morning.

"Will you feed them?"

"*Si, Señor.* My wife will bring them something."

"Thank you. Pay you tomorrow?"

"Of course, *Señor.*"

"Where can I spend the night?"

"We have no hotel, *Señor*, but you can stay in my son's house. He has an extra room he sometimes rents."

"You are very kind."

The next morning Paco found the jailer excited. "He is dead, *Señor*, the skinny one. Died during the night."

One of the slaves explained, "He coughed much during the night. After a while he quieted down and I thought I would finally be able to sleep. But when I awoke this morning he was not breathing." The man was almost in tears. "He has been sick with the cough for a long time, *Señor* Paco. Nobody said anything because they were afraid you would sell him like Ali."

Suddenly feeling sick, Paco turned and walked out. He could not face them, wishing they had told him before. Oh, God! What a miserable despot I've become. He walked down the road for a while and then stopped at a bar and ordered a glass of rum. Standing at the bar he drank it down in one gulp and returned to the jail to retrieve his property. He thought: my property!

That afternoon they encountered a group of men, black and white, going east, singing and laughing. They stopped to talk.

The first words their leader said was, "We are going to Oriente to join the fight against the whore-son Spaniards."

Paco smiled, "We are headed to Matanzas."

Hearing Paco's accent the man said, "You are a Spaniard."

"Yes, but I live in Matanzas."

"Do you know what you are doing to our people?"

"I hear stories," Paco said, "but I am not one of them."

"They are not satisfied to kill men; they kill women and children as well, sometimes people who are minding their own business. They are sadistic bastards."

"Most war stories are exaggerated," Paco said, "but they always carry some truth."

"Exaggerated, hell! I have seen it."

"You have fought them?"

"Not yet, but we will soon. Say, you won't denounce us, will you?"

"Have no fear."

"We fear nothing!" the man said. "We are prepared to die for freedom."

"I will not denounce you, and I wish you well."

They continued on their way, mumbling among themselves. Paco did not want to linger, thinking his slaves might take it into their heads to join them. He could see their eyes brighten as they listened to the leader's flamboyant speech.

"*Vamos!*" Paco said, and started the horse walking again behind the two slaves.

For two days they walked, each night stopping where Paco could lock up his slaves. Armando's death had dampened the others' enthusiasm for rebellion. They walked as if into oblivion, with no destination, no end, except the end of life. A few times Paco got off the horse and walked with them, to talk, to exchange ideas, but they did not want to talk. It was as though they did not want to think or imagine or dream, but only to walk into nothingness, as if they would gladly meet death at the end of the road.

Early the next morning they found a village that had been burned, every house destroyed, some still smoldering. Only the shell of the stone church remained with its roof no more than charred sticks. Looking around for anyone still alive who could tell him what had happened, Paco found an old man lying against the church wall. He had been hurt, but not as badly as he thought.

"*Que Pasó?*" Paco asked the old man.

"The bastards came and killed everyone and burned everything!" His voice cracked.

"Why?" Paco could not imagine soldiers killing a whole village.

"They said we helped the rebels who came through last month."

"Did you?"

"A few did. Most had nothing to do with it."

"And the bodies?"

"Behind the church, executed. A few tried to get away, but the soldiers shot them on the spot. I'm the only one left. I played dead and fooled them. You will find the others behind the church."

Carlos, Ricardo, and Paco walked around the church and found twenty-nine bodies, men women and children. There were even two babies lying distorted and unrecognizably mangled, as if they had been smashed against the church wall. "Come," Paco said. "We bury them."

Carlos bent over and vomited. He had little to lose, but heaved for several minutes before he could stand. Ricardo helped him. They stood to find Paco digging with an iron cross he found in the church. "Here," he said. "We dig a trench and bury them together."

Carlos went from house to house looking for shovels. In a few minutes he returned with three, and they all dug. Soon the old man came around the church to see what they were doing. He left and returned with another shovel and joined the work.

On their way out of the village three hours later, Carlos walked by Paco's horse as if he wanted to say something. After about a kilometer he said, "*Señor*, you do not have to worry about finding a jail for us. I think we go with you gladly."

"Good, Carlos. That was pretty bad back there, no?"

"Bad enough to keep me away from the Spanish soldiers, *Señor*."

"Well, Carlos, things may soon get better, I hope, for everybody."

By mid-afternoon a village appeared over a slight rise in the road. Paco stepped up his pace, anxious to rest a while. The road went down a slight slope that hid the village until they reached the top of the next rise. From the hill top Paco saw a crowd of people moving about. "Soldiers!" Carlos said.

Suddenly the movements slowed and became more ceremonial. Four soldiers stood at attention with burning torches. The rest of the platoon stood four men against the church wall. The man in charge ordered five soldiers to form opposite the prisoners, no more than four meters away. The man in charge raised his sword and the soldiers raised their rifles. The leader stood by them with his sword raised to give the order to shoot. Without thinking, Paco fired his pistol three times in the air as he spurred his horse to move in random directions. He yelled as loud as he could, "Get them! Get the sons of whores!" As he ran the horse in circles he called to Carlos and Ricardo to spread out and yell all the obscenities they could think of. "Yell! Move around and try to sound like a platoon of rebels. But keep moving." He fired three more shots and reloaded.

The soldiers abandoned the execution and ran up the hill toward them. "Follow me into the woods," Paco said to Carlos and Ricardo, as quietly as you can. "We do not want them to hear us."

By the time the soldiers reached the top of the hill, Paco and the two slaves had moved deep into the thick woods and were circling back to the village. Paco's only plan was to get there before the soldiers could return, hoping he could mobilize the villagers to fight. Later he would have a difficult time trying to recall exactly what he thought. Everything happened fast, as if a different person had jumped into his body. They moved as quickly as they could, pushing aside tree branches and bushes. With all the obstructions Paco's horse could not move as fast as the men, but they managed to stay together. They could hear the soldiers breaking branches and yelling to each other where they had been a few minutes before. As the voices became fainter Paco knew they had taken a wrong turn. He and the two slaves ran, ducking and weaving around trees. Paco rode as fast as he dared, and the slaves stayed with him. He no longer worried that they might desert, for they knew the soldiers would kill them if they caught them.

Paco and the two slaves made it into the village from the side almost opposite where the soldiers had run out, but found no one. Paco ran into several of the houses saying in a low voice, "We want to help. Come out. Quick!"

Soon a few emerged with machetes, and one of them said, "Where are the rest?"

"We are only three," Paco said.

"My God! We are lost!"

"Not necessarily," Paco said. "Do what I say and we may have a chance. Quickly, get all the weapons you can find, spread out and hide in the houses. They will return to the plaza, and we will have them surrounded. Then we will give them the big surprise. Now run; tell the others."

"They were about to shoot us," another man said.

"Two or three of you: let them find you. They will try to resume the executions. While they busy themselves with lining you up, the rest of us, on my command, will run out yelling. We will kill as many as we can. Do you have machetes for us?"

Someone produced three machetes. Paco reloaded his pistol and poured a handful of bullets from the box into his pocket. He grabbed a machete in his right hand and the gun in his left.

Before long they heard the soldiers marching back. Paco saw out the window of his hut that they were spiritless and drenched in perspiration. Standing in the middle of the plaza the sergeant began to yell, "Come out, immediately, or we will burn down the whole damned village."

One at a time, as instructed, four men emerged, the same four who had been awaiting execution. Paco immediately recognized one of them, the large Negro, Ali. Grabbing them the soldiers led them to the same church wall and lined them up as before. "Where are the others?" the sergeant yelled.

"They left. We did not want to leave our farms," one of the villagers said.

"Good. We will finish what we started and then find them." He ordered five soldiers to line up as executioners. Before he could raise his sword to give the order to fire, Paco began yelling and the townspeople poured out of their huts like wild savages swinging their machetes. A few had only ax handles and some gave extra machetes to the condemned men. The villagers outnumbered the soldiers ten to one, and swinging wildly, those cane cutters severed a dozen arms, legs and even two heads in the scramble before the soldiers could fire the first shot. One managed to fire his rifle as another hit him. The bullet hit Ali in the foot. An instant later Paco fired his pistol and dropped the soldier. Although he could barely stand, Ali continued to swing his machete. Paco moved in his direction swinging his machete at anyone who came near while holding his pistol ready. It felt as if that they fought for an hour, for time seemed to slow down. Actually in less than a minute all the soldiers lay dead or mortally wounded.

In the shattering silence after the yelling and swinging were over, Paco stood looking around, his heart pounding, feeling an animalistic elation. He counted twelve soldiers on the ground, two still writhing, including the sergeant, most of them with great gashes on their bodies or missing limbs. He looked down and saw he was standing in a pool of blood and his clothes were drenched in blood and sweat. Except Ali, none of the villagers seemed to be hurt seriously, only scratches and bruises.

Paco called the villagers together. "More soldiers will certainly come. They will find their compatriots missing, and then they will kill everybody they can find and burn everything."

"What will you do?" one man asked.

"We are returning to Matanzas," Paco said. "You must all leave this place immediately. Get away. Go to another village or to Matanzas or Havana, where there is no fighting. Anywhere, but get away from here."

The villagers nodded and began to move away from the devastation. "Perhaps we should burn our houses."

Paco nodded gravely. "Good idea. You will not be able to return anyway."

With their help, the villagers gathered what they could take with them and then lit fires in all the huts. Everyone stood at the edge of the village looking at the blazes for a few minutes. The wind shifted and smoke almost overpowered them. Several of the women and a few men cried as they watched their homes enveloped in flames. Finally they began to wander off in various directions.

Paco looked at Ali, who was sitting against a tree. "Can you walk?"

"I do not think so, *Señor* Paco."

His foot was bleeding. Paco squatted and bound the wound tightly with his handkerchief and said, "Come with us."

He said nothing, but stood as best he could and nodded. "I will try, *Señor.*"

Paco walked his horse to him and helped him up. Ali looked at Paco strangely, curiously, but said nothing and climbed up behind the saddle.

As they were about to leave, four of the white men of the village and a Negro returned from the path they had taken. "May we join you, *Señor?*" the Negro asked.

"I am not a rebel," Paco said. "I am going back to Matanzas to work my farm."

"We do not want to fight, *Señor*, but we would rather be with you than in a strange village where we know no one."

"Are you a slave?" Paco asked the Black man.

"No, *Señor.* I have papers."

"Come then."

They stopped the first time they found a river in which to bathe and wash their clothes. Until then they stayed off the roads knowing their bloody clothes would alert everyone of their encounter.

Ali looked weak and his foot was horribly swollen. Paco bathed Ali's foot in the river, washed his handkerchief and wrapped his foot with a dry cloth from his saddlebag. He would get him to a doctor back in Matanzas.

Ali spoke little during the trip, but in camp that night, after Paco had bound his foot, he said, "*Señor*, you have been very good to me. I will be forever in your debt."

"You are free, Ali. Eugenio sold you. As soon as you are well you may go wherever you wish."

"Thank you, *Señor*, but I will stay and serve you."

"We will see. Now go to sleep."

*

They reached the hacienda at noon the next day. Paco had been gone twenty-six days. Lydia heard his horse and the men talking and came out and started jumping. "Oh, *Señor*, you are back! *Que bueno!*"

Paco helped Ali into the back porch and sat him down and turned to Lydia. "It is good to be back, Lydia."

"It is very good to see you, *Señor*. I fix something special to eat."

"Thank you, Lydia, but first send the driver for Doctor Fuentes. This man is wounded and needs help. Tell him to hurry."

"*Señora* Magdalena took the carriage to Matanzas."

Paco ran out to the field and found Manuel. "Send one of the slaves to fetch Doctor Fuentes. I have a wounded man here."

"Who?"

"Ali. We had trouble with some soldiers."

"The others cannot stand him, *Señor*."

"Do not tell them who it is. Now hurry."

Returning to the house Paco asked Lydia where Marta was.

"Upstairs with the baby,"

Thinking she meant Isabel, Paco ran upstairs to his bedroom and found Marta nursing their baby. She motioned for him to come. "I just knew it was you, Paco. Look at our son. He has only a few days." The baby jerked with her movements.

"My God! He came early."

"I wanted him to wait, but he said no."

Paco kissed her and looked into eyes moist with happiness. She lifted the baby to him. As he took him in his arms the baby began to cry. "Do not cry. I am your *Papá*." After a few seconds he handed him back. "He is beautiful, Marta, but I think he is still hungry. How do you feel?"

"Wonderful. He is beautiful. Just like you, Paco."

"He is beautiful like his *Mamita*. You look better than before, Marta."

"This baby would make anyone feel good. He is perfect. Sleeps and eats well and has good lungs."

"I heard them. I will spend the rest of the day with you, but I have a wounded man downstairs. Doctor Fuentes is on his way. I must go down to meet him."

"What happened?"

"Shot in the foot. I have much to tell."

"I too."

Paco and Marta talked about the baby, neither wanting to begin their story knowing they would have to stop for the doctor. Finally, after a long while, they heard a carriage approach, and Paco excused himself.

"Where is the patient?" Doctor Fuentes asked. He had let himself in and was standing in the living room. Paco led him to the porch without explaining. Catching sight of Ali, Doctor Fuentes pulled Paco back in. "No slaves. Your cook was special, but this: no!" He started toward the front door.

"One moment, Doctor. This man was shot defending the people of a village from soldiers who were about to execute them and burn their village."

Doctor Fuentes stopped, but did not turn. "Where?"

"A nondescript village two days east. I don't know the name, but it does not matter. It has burned to the ground. I have passed nearly a month looking for runaway slaves. This man is not one of them. He is a free man."

"He was fighting the Spaniards?"

"Yes, and bravely. They had him before a firing squad when I happened along."

"*Bueno.*"

Having heard their conversation from the porch, Ali said, "Doctor, in no time *Señor* Paco organized the entire village, and we overpowered a platoon of armed soldiers, and with no more than machetes and sticks. I have never seen such bravery, Doctor."

Doctor Fuentes smiled. "Well, well. So Paco is a hero."

"I could not stand by and let them kill women and children."

By this time Doctor Fuentes had unwrapped Ali's foot. He examined the toe and pressed his finger into the flesh. It left an indentation, as if the flesh were dead. "My God! Gangrene. I will have to amputate right away or he will lose the foot, possibly the leg."

"Then hurry, Doctor," Paco said.

"I'll know better at the hospital."

"Can't you do it here?"

"Not if you want him to survive."

"Will he cause a problem?"

"I will arrange it. Get someone to help my driver lift him into my carriage."

In a few minutes the doctor's driver was galloping toward town. Paco walked up to the front porch and found Marta waiting at the door. They sat in the rockers, and she placed the baby in his arms. As she talked, Paco looked at the baby, "My boy. I can hardly believe it. He is beautiful; look, blue eyes. And look at his head, covered with fuzz."

He heard little of what Marta said until she began to talk about the slave slowdown and how she resolved it.

"Where was Magdalena?"

"She could not do it and asked me. Did I do right?"

"Perfectly. I should have known. You are a good commander."

She smiled. "I will try not to command you more than absolutely necessary."

That afternoon Paco drove to the hospital and found Doctor Fuentes. "I had to amputate his big toe. God willing, I will not have to cut more. It looks good, but we will not know for a few days."

"How does he feel?"

"Since he came out of the anesthesia all he could talk about was you and your heroism. He wants to work for you and prays you will let him."

"Eugenio had to sell him because he caused problems."

"I only report what he said."

"We shall see."

"Be careful, Paco. If the army finds out what you did, they will come after you."

"They know where to find me, Doctor. Thanks for helping Ali. He is a good man after all."

That evening Paco walked downstairs to find Magdalena and Marta waiting for him in the dining room. Before him was a green salad, a large platter of rice, and one of black beans. In a few minutes Lydia brought in a sumptuous platter of roast pig surrounded by fried plantains. Paco's mind flashed to the pig fountain in the plaza of Colosía. He sat in awe of the overwhelming meal. He had not enjoyed a decent meal in weeks. "A work of art, Lydia. Fit for royalty."

"The pig was *Señora* Magdalena's idea, *Señor* Paco. She wanted to welcome you with something special."

"Well you certainly have." Turning to Magdalena, "We have decided to name our baby Eugenio."

Magdalena stood, walked to Paco and kissed him and then Marta. Her eyes were tearing. "You make me very happy. Your uncle would be delighted." Returning to her chair she asked Lydia to bring out the bottle of Asturian cider. "I bought it this morning in Matanzas for your homecoming, Paco."

Lydia returned with the chilled bottle of cider, trying to open it. "Here, let me," Paco said. Ceremoniously, he popped the cork and then stood and filled each glass with the bubbly liquid. "In Asturias they pour the still cider over the shoulder to aerate it. I never tasted the sparkling cider till I came to Cuba. I don't think it needs aeration, so I will pour it like champagne. Bring a glass for yourself, Lydia," he said.

"No, thank you, *Señor*."

"A glass, I said." She went into the kitchen and returned with another glass. He filled her glass and Magdalena raised hers and toasted, "To our babies, Isabel and Eugenio, and to our returning hero."

Paco's eyes went to Lydia as she drank with the rest. She did not smile like the others, but drank silently, emptied her glass, and returned to the kitchen.

"Tell Magdalena about your travels, Paco."

He recounted the journey and how he followed the slaves' trail. As he spoke he saw a shadow under the door to the kitchen and realized Lydia was listening. "Lydia!"

She stuck her head through the door, and Paco told her to come in and sit down where she could listen comfortably.

"Oh, no, Señor. I have work to do."

"Sit down and listen."

His tone could not be denied. She sat at a chair by the wall.

He told of wandering through town after town hearing of the slaves' passing and then pursuing their trail, and of finding rebels on their way to fight, and of villages that had been destroyed, and of burying the bodies, and finally the skirmish with soldiers.

"Señor Paco, the slaves say you are a hero."

"Who said that?"

"Everybody, Señor. Probably the men you brought."

"I am so proud of you, Paco," Magdalena said. "Eugenio would have wanted to join the rebels."

"But, Paco," Marta said. "If this gets around, the army may take you for a rebel leader."

"I am neither a rebel nor a leader, but I could not let them commit such atrocities."

"I hope they understand."

"They will."

Magdalena's smile and pride clouded over. "Do you think they will come?"

"Probably, but do not occupy yourself; I will explain. Now let us finish this grand meal."

Lydia returned to the kitchen.

*

The army did not wait long. Shortly after dawn a knock at the front door brought Marta down the stairs. Magdelena and Lydia were talking in the kitchen and did not hear. Marta opened the door to four soldiers with stone faces. The captain saluted her and said, "*El Señor Iglesias, por favor.*"

"He is out back, Captain. Please come in and sit down. I will call him."

Standing at the barn door talking with Manuel, Paco heard Marta call him from the back porch. Her voice carried such urgency that he stopped his conversation and came running. "Soldiers, Paco. Be careful."

Walking through the house to the living room he extended his hand to the captain. "Good morning. How may I be of service?"

The four soldiers were still standing. The captain was looking at the painting of Magdalena with a pleasant smile on his face, but as he turned to Paco his smile curled into a scowl. "Señor Iglesias, we have learned that you led an attack on a platoon of Spanish soldiers last week in a village east of here."

"You have heard correctly, Captain."

The captain was surprised at his admission, and it took him several seconds to form the next question. "Then you are with the rebels?"

"No, Captain. I care nothing for their cause. I am a farmer and businessman. I care only for my family and my business."

"Why then?"

"I was coming to that, Captain." Taking two cigars out of the humidor, Paco handed him one and bit the tip off the other. He lit both recalling Facundo's admonition to act as if you are in the right and never appear defensive.

"Captain, I left my farm four weeks ago to pursue three slaves who had escaped to join the rebels. It took me two weeks to find them, and then

141

another week and a half to bring them home at gunpoint. On our return we came through a village that had been burned and all but one of the villagers killed and left to rot on the ground; women and children too. The survivor told me Spanish soldiers did it. I had heard of such things, but, as a Spaniard, I did not believe them. We buried the bodies and continued on our way home. A day or two later we came to a village where Spanish soldiers were about to execute four villagers. Two others held flaming torches ready to burn the village. Seeing them line the villagers against the church wall and the sergeant prepared to execute them, I fired my pistol several times and created as much disturbance and noise as I could. They came after us. We circled through the woods and reached the village ahead of them, where I told the villagers to hide. In a few minutes the soldiers returned and found the four villagers. They lined them up again to proceed with the execution. At that moment, on my orders, the entire village erupted from all directions with machetes and sticks."

"Then you did participate in the attack on the soldiers?"

"Of course. They were going to kill innocent people, babies like mine. Captain, if you and your soldiers came here threatening to kill my family, I hope someone would come in and stop you, and I think you would feel the same."

"Those innocent people aided a band of rebels the previous week."

"Does that justify soldiers of the Royal Spanish Army to kill children and women? If so, then I am ashamed to be a Spaniard. What rule of war allows such atrocities?"

"The rebels also commit atrocities, Señor Iglesias.

"But they are rabble, Captain, not disciplined soldiers led by educated, courageous officers like you."

After thinking a moment, the captain said, "I also have heard of atrocities. I do not approve, Señor, but I cannot question my superiors."

"I can."

"I ask you again: are you with the rebels, Señor Iglesias?"

"No, and I do not intend to join them or allow any of my slaves to do so. I leave the killing to you, Captain."

"Do I have your word on that, Señor Iglesias?"

"Yes."

The captain looked at him for a long moment and said, "I will report what you have told me. Your reputation as a respected citizen of Matanzas confirms what you say, so do not worry. My men and I will be on our way now."

They shook hands, and the soldiers left.

Marta had watched the exchange with clenched jaws, saying nothing. As the sound of their horses' hooves died away, Paco went to the kitchen, took a bottle of brandy from the pantry, poured himself a glass, took a long drink, and sat down. Marta sat with him and held his cold hands. Lydia continued her duties as if nothing had happened.

"Will he come back?" Marta asked.

"I think not."

"But you admitted everything."

"What can he do? Kill me? Lock me up? Where would it stop? The army has nothing to gain. He knows where I am."

"But others might want to fight seeing you were not punished."

"The army may go after them. I have no interest in the rebellion, Marta. The captain is not stupid; he saw that. As I said, he knows where I am and can watch me all he wants."

His absence had taken its toll on Paco. Now home finally, fatigue overcame him, and he slept two hours that morning. On awaking he went to the front porch to survey his estate and digest all that had happened during the past two years. It felt like a dream from which he would awake in Asturias in a drizzle. Manuel came to talk with him that morning, but Paco asked him to carry on as before, and they would talk later. He could not bring himself to enter into a serious discussion. He wanted only to think and not think, to dream and to keep from dreaming. Paco had never felt as detached from the present as he did those two days after his return, but as morning dissolved into afternoon and afternoon into evening and evening darkened his vision, he began to talk of the farm and to ask what had happened during his absence.

He spent much of those two days on the front porch thinking quietly. Marta sat with him much of the time, but also left him alone because she could see that he needed solitude. With the porch as his sanatorium and the gorgeous royal palms as his therapists, exhaustion and jangled nerves soon relaxed.

The next afternoon he received a message from Doctor Fuentes that Ali was well enough to return home. His carriage driver drove Paco to the hospital where he found Ali smiling in his room. With his foot still bandaged he limped, but seemed strong and energetic. After thanking Doctor Fuentes and paying the bill, Paco brought the carriage to the entrance, and they headed for the farm. On the way, Ali said little except to repeat how grateful he was to Paco and the doctor.

"They treated me well. They expect me to recover completely. I may have a limp, but I do not mind. Better to limp than to rot in the earth."

"You can stay as long as you like, Ali, but when you are well you must leave and make a life for yourself."

"I would like to work for you, Señor Paco. I will do whatever you say; you do not have to pay me. If you could let me use a small plot of land to grow vegetables, I will grow enough to feed myself and your family."

"Do you know how to grow things?"

"Oh yes, Señor. I was a farmer in Africa. I can grow anything."

"I can arrange that, Ali, and for the others too."

"The slaves?"

"Why not? It would help all of us."

Ali said nothing more about it.

Paco left Ali off at the barn where Lydia had prepared him a pallet as Paco had asked.

Upstairs, Paco found Marta nursing Genio and recounted Ali's plan to grow vegetables.

"Is that a good idea?"

"I have promised the slaves I would free them. With so much talk of rebellion and fighting, they need distraction. If they leave I will have to hire free men to replace them. If I free them and hire them even at low pay, how will they live? But if I continue to provide a place to live and let them grow their own food, the cost will be nearly nothing. They would be happier and healthier, and also might find it advantageous to stay. I would get cheap labor for the cost of letting them use some of the land, of which we have plenty."

"Perhaps, Paco."

"Let us see what Ali does and how the others react. Now, I think I have rested enough. It is time to see to my farm." He kissed her and Genio and walked out and shut the door. As he started down the stairs he heard Lydia's voice coming from her room.

"I am Mamá, not you. And Isabel is not your slave. You will not take her."

Paco could not hear the response.

"I do not care how much you love her. She is mine and mine alone. I bore her with great pain. What did you do? She may call you Tía if you like, but not Mamá."

Silence.

"It was not just baby talk. You have always wanted Isabel for yourself."

Silence.

144

"Well remember, Señora Magdalena, you do not own her. That was the agreement … I will not be quiet. I speak the truth, and I do not care who hears it."

Paco stood a moment longer waiting for another outburst, and as he started down the stairs, she began again. "Only his son he sees. For him this one does not exist, but she is as much his as the boy."

Paco burst into her room without knocking. They both stopped, mouths agape. Magdalena was pale and Lydia was perspiring and her breast heaving. Paco shut the door behind him and spoke in a soft voice: "I have heard all you said, Lydia. If Marta has heard, you will be out of this house, baby or no baby. Do you understand?"

"Please, Paco. She meant nothing," Magdalena said.

"I think she meant for Marta to hear. I repeat, Lydia. If she hears or if she has already heard, I will put you out."

Lydia picked up Isabel and walked out the door. Magdalena was crying so hard that Paco stayed a few moments longer. "I do not know what Lydia wants, Magdalena, but she has much malice. I have seen it and so has Marta. I will not tolerate it."

"Being a slave makes her defensive, Paco. Do not be hard on her. She means no harm."

"I think she does, Magdalena. I will do nothing against her, but if Marta learns what she must not learn, I promise I will throw Lydia out of this house."

"She is only a poor slave."

"She is not poor and is obviously not a slave, Magdalena. She controls more in this house than either you or Marta. I warn you, Magdalena, if you cannot rein her in, I will." Then he walked out and down the stairs and out back to the barn to find his overseers.

On returning that evening, Lydia had supper waiting. As he walked through the kitchen she greeted him warmly as if no words had been spoken.

Paco said, "*Buenas tardes*," and went through and up the stairs. Marta was nursing Genio. "Marta! You were nursing him when I left. Have you been feeding him all day?"

Her laugh startled the baby. "He is as hungry for me as you are. How would you like it if Lydia had no supper ready?"

"I would not care as long as I had you."

She reached for his hand and kissed it. "I am very lucky."

"No more than I."

They sat together and talked softly until she finished. By that time Genio was sound asleep in her arms. She put him in his bed and they walked down to supper.

As Lydia came in to pick up the first course dishes Paco said, "Where is Isabel? I rarely see her."

"In her room, Señor Paco."

"Why don't you bring her down? She is old enough to take her place at our table."

"That is right, Lydia," Magdalena said. "What is supper without children?"

Marta smiled and nodded.

Without another word, Lydia went upstairs and, a moment later, came down with Isabel in her arms.

"Bring her here, Lydia," Paco said. Lydia held her for Paco to see. He reached over and passed his hand over Isabel's head. She smiled. Her light brown hair was no longer fuzz, but real hair, soft, wavy and chestnut color, and her greenish eyes sparkled. She let out a gurgling sound and burped and then smiled. "She is beautiful, Lydia."

"Gracias, Señor."

Paco looked at Marta; her eyes smiled warmly.

Magdalena said, "I will take her, Lydia."

Lydia handed Isabel to Magdalena and went back into the kitchen to bring out the second course.

CHAPTER 5 – CHILDREN, 1879

*

*April 12, 1869: Carlos Manuel de Céspedes
Elected President of Rebel Cuban Republic*

*

*November 27, 1871: Spanish Soldiers Execute
Eight Medical Students in Havana*

*

*February 27, 1874: Spanish Troops Kill
Céspedes in His Hideout in Sierra Maestra
Mountains. Cubans Call It Assassination*

*

*Spain's King Alfonso to Wed Archduchess
Marie Christine of Austria*

*

February 10, 1878: Ten Years War
Ends with Pact of Zanjón.
Cubans Win Amnesty, Political Reforms,
and Parliamentary Representation.
200,000 Lives Lost

*

"What are we making today, Lydia?"

"Yemas de coco for dessert, Genio."

"Oh, goodie! Egg yolks with coconut."

"Bring some eggs. Then you will separate the yolks and beat them."

The chubby ten-year-old ran out the back door and out to the chicken coop behind the barn. Loose, dark hair bouncing as he ran, he slung open the chicken coop gate and then carefully closed it, remembering that last week he had left it open and then spent half an hour chasing chickens around the yard. He walked as fast as he could, carefully holding the egg basket, to the kitchen, where Lydia was grating the coconut. Genio sat at the table, cracked an egg, let the white spill over the shells into a bowl as he poured the yolk back and forth from one half shell to the other, and then dropped the clean yolk into a second bowl. He repeated the process eleven times and then beat the egg yolks with a whisk until they were smooth. Finally he added the sugar and put the mixture into a pot on the stove and stood by it, stirring it with a wooden spoon.

"Careful it doesn't burn, Genio."

The gentle odor of coconut wafted through the house. Genio looked at Lydia occasionally, and she would shake her head and say, "Not yet," or correct him, or nod approval. When the mixture was thick enough she handed him the grated coconut and some powdered sugar, which he added, stirred the mixture, and poured the mass on the marble countertop to wait for it to cool enough to handle. He touched it several times to check the temperature, and finally began to form it into little balls in the palms of his hands until he had twenty-eight spherical candies.

As Paco approached the pump shed to wash before lunch, the aromatic coconut odor drew his head to the kitchen window. He washed, dried, and went into the kitchen to see what delicacy Lydia had prepared. The sight of his son wearing a flower-decorated apron covered with powdered sugar was more than he could stand. He grabbed the boy by the hand and walked him to the pump shed, stuck his head under the spout, and pumped the handle. Genio was crying, but Paco pumped with one hand and held him under the gushing water with the other until all the sugar had dissolved away. Then he told him to march into the house and get ready for lunch. Crying, Genio left a trail of water as he stomped through the living room and up the stairs.

Paco returned to the kitchen and said, "Lydia, I've told you not to encourage him."

"Genio loves to cook. What is wrong with letting him help?"

"I will not have my son grow into a kettle-loving ninny doing woman's work." Then he walked to the front porch to wait for lunch. Soon after he had lit a cigar, Marta came out and sat with him. "I heard Genio crying," she said.

"And he will cry until he learns he is a man and not a woman."

"He's just a little boy, Paco."

"You are too easy on him. That's why he is such a baby."

"He is still a little boy."

"And his little brother?"

"Ignacio is playing with Isabel."

"There you have it. Genio has no playmates. A ten-year-old boy should have boys his age to play with."

At that moment they heard a loud cry. Taking the cigar out of his mouth he said, "Not Genio again!"

"No, it's Isabel." She opened the front door and found Isabel sitting on the living room floor sobbing, "He hit me." Ignacio was standing over her laughing.

"She was pulling me, trying to take me to her room. Then she hit me, so I hit her back."

Lydia ran in, stood over Ignacio, and raised her hand to slap him, but Marta moved between them, took Ignacio's hand, and walked him upstairs. Paco followed Marta and Ignacio to their room.

Before Marta could say another word Paco grabbed Ignacio by the shoulders and said, "It is unmanly and cowardly to hit a girl."

"She is almost twice his age, Paco. A girl's slap can hurt as much as a boy's."

"I will not allow it." Paco yanked Ignacio by the arm, laid him over his lap, and spanked him. Soon Paco's face had broken out in perspiration; his chest heaved.

"We have to live together, Paco. We must try to get along." Then she took Ignacio's hand and led him to the door. "Go play, and stay out of trouble." After he had left she said, "You saw how furious Lydia was."

"To hell with Lydia. And she better not touch my son." At that, he went down to the dining room. Lydia was laying out the lunch and Paco sat down to eat. "I have too much work to wait for everyone to finish crying."

"*Si, Señor Paco.*"

That evening Paco looked across the table at his daughter. She was beautiful; her green eyes sparkled with mischief. Longing to pick her up and kiss her, his guilt multiplied, not only for failing his daughter, but also for deceiving his loving wife. At times like these, all the children together, the weight of his guilt pushed him deep into his chair, and he would stare into his plate as the others chatted. He stuffed himself to dull his guilt and detested himself for denying his daughter to save himself, knowing he should have thought first of her. That feeling pressed him ever deeper until he felt trapped in a cage separated from his daughter by iron bars of regret.

Next to Paco sat Genio, eating voraciously, and beyond, seven-year-old Ignacio, who preferred to play with his food than eat it. Across from Genio sat the pale, noble Magdalena, delicate and beautiful as ever, and next to her, Isabel, frowning. Magdalena held a forkful of rice before the little girl's mouth, looking at her imploringly as if she could imagine no greater happiness than to see Isabel eat another mouthful.

"Please, Isabel. To grow strong and intelligent."

Genio, barely aware of the conversation, continued to stuff himself. "This is good, Tía Magdalena. More rice and beans, and some plantains?"

"Of course. See, Isabel, how well Genio eats. He will grow big and strong."

"He's fat and weak, Tía. Want me to show you?"

"Please, Isabel. Eat your supper. You can play later."

"Genio!" Marta said, "Remember dessert is coming."

"I always have room for dessert, Mamá."

"You will get fat."

"Growing children must eat, Marta," Magdalena said. "He will lose the baby fat when he begins to stretch out."

"Genio has baby fat; Genio has baby fat," Isabel chanted.

Through the conversation Paco kept his eyes on his plate, waiting for the bickering to end. "Enough!" he said finally. "Isabel, eat what you want." Then turning to the rest, "Supper should be a time for pleasant conversation."

"But, Paco," Magdalena said.

"No child has ever starved in the presence of food. For heaven sake, let us have peace."

"Of course, Paco," Magdalena said.

By this time Lydia had heard the talk and came in. "Isabel, finish your plate or else."

"But Mamá, I'm not hungry."

"Do not come to me later begging for a snack." Lydia's eyes flashed the determination that Isabel had come to respect.

"All right, Mamá." She picked up her fork and picked out several beans and put them in her mouth.

Finally everyone finished dessert. Lydia picked up Isabel's dish. "Go do your school work. You do not belong in the kitchen."

"I want to talk with you, Mamá."

"Later."

"But Mamá."

Lydia said no more and backed into the swinging door holding a stack of dishes. Isabel followed her in. "Why can't I help?"

"You are not a servant."

"Why don't you sit on the porch with the others?"

"We are different, Isabel. You are a member of the family, not a servant."

"So are you, Mamá."

"They won't make a slave of you."

"Am I a slave just for helping you?"

"You are as good as any of them, Isabel. I was born into slavery, but not you. You are white. You are as good as anybody. Never forget that."

"Tía Marta works in the garden, and she's not a slave."

"That is different. She is the wife of the owner."

"But she likes to work. What's the difference?"

"Go. I am busy."

The talk of being a slave puzzled Isabel. Of course I'm not a slave, she thought. And why does she always say I am as good as they?

She walked out to the porch where the rest of the family sat.

"Want to play, Genio?

"All right."

She led him to the driveway. "Hide and seek?"

"Sure."

"Genio, do you think you are better than me?"

"No. Why?"

"I just wondered. "Do they tell you that you are as good as other people?"

"No. Why?"

"Well, I'm better than you."

"No you're not."   He crossed his arms across his chest.

"Sure I am; I'm not a big sissy like you."

Genio turned to leave, and she slapped his behind and yelled, "You're it!" and ran off, weaving around the royal palms. Genio closed his eyes and started to count.

Paco stood and took Marta's hand. "A little walk?" She nodded and followed as Magdalena gathered up her crocheting and walked into the kitchen, where she found Lydia straightening the pots on the wall.

"Why did you send her out?"

"I will not have her cleaning other peoples' garbage."

"Don't be so sensitive, Lydia. I thought she would enjoy working with you. She likes being with you."

"No matter how much you try, she will not go down this road."

"Try? I was thinking only of her, Lydia. You spend so little time with her."

Lydia stopped and turned to her sister. "Mind your own business. She is my daughter, not yours."

"Why do you treat me like this? I only want to help you both. She has no father to guide her."

"And she never will. Remember that, Magdalena: never! I wait for the day he decides to act like the father he never was. That is the day I fix him."

"Paco would give anything to be her father openly. He loves her very much."

"Bah!"

"I see his face when you yell at her. It pains him, Lydia."

"Just like my father. Had his fun and left me to my real mother to do the dirty work. I certainly cannot count on you."

"That's not fair. I would have done anything for you and you know it."

"You asked Papá to make me your slave. Is that the way you help a sister?"

Teary-eyed, Magdalena said, "What could I do? You have no idea what I went through."

"I know you are the heir and I am the slave who is not worth a shit!"

"*Ay*, Lydia, I cannot bear such anger."

Lydia walked out the back door and left her sister crying at the kitchen table.

*

Soon after Paco and Marta returned from their stroll, don Miguel dropped in. His weekly visits had become an enjoyable routine for both Paco and him. They would play dominoes for an hour or two and chat over coffee. This evening don Miguel seemed withdrawn. Paco led him to the living room, where Paco had a small table ready with a box of dominoes, some paper, a pencil and cigars. He handed don Miguel a cigar and sat at the table, but Miguel remained standing.

"*Que pasa, Miguel?* Do you not want to play tonight?"

"Yes, of course." Don Miguel sat down and they shuffled the dominoes over the table. Each took ten and stood them up. Paco lit don Miguel's cigar and his.

"What a disaster this war has been," don Miguel said.

"Why? The fighting never reached us; we are still in business. We have had good fortune."

"But we're still under Spain's thumb, and the rebels are still rumbling. Nothing has changed."

"As long as they leave me alone, I care nothing about who runs the country."

"But they won't leave you alone, don't you see? The war failed because the Creole landowners never came to terms with the common people."

"Right! We would be hypocrits to rebel at Spanish oppression while we continue to oppress slaves. Now play."

"I'm sorry, Paco, I can't concentrate on dominoes; so much hangs over us."

"But the war is over."

"Macéo is organizing an offensive in Oriente."

"Let him. Look, Miguel, I do not like Spain's taxes any more than you, but I will not risk what I have for a vague ideal. To me it makes no difference who wins. Both Spaniards and Cubans know how to use power to enrich themselves. And to do so they will have to keep us in business. That is reality."

"And abolition?"

"It is coming. The United States abolished slavery almost fifteen years ago. Our only hope is to mechanize. Machines can do nearly everything slaves do. We must be pragmatic. Slavery will die; we must not die with it."

"But why should Spaniards rule us from thousands of miles away? They don't understand or care about us."

"We are all Spaniards, Miguel. Even you Creoles, children of Spaniards, were born under the flag of Spain."

"You are a *Peninsular*, Paco. You will never see things from the Creole point of view."

"What are you talking about? My children are Creoles." Paco took a long draw on his cigar. "I see things as they are, Miguel. I simply do not have your faith in local rule. Will a Cuban government give us lower taxes? Do you really think they will be able to maintain order and peace by catering to the poor? So they abolish slavery, what then?"

Don Miguel shrugged.

"And what about life in a half-black, half-white nation? Can you imagine our culture crushed under the heel of the African savage?"

"You've changed, Paco."

"And that revolt in your slave camp, Miguel? Whose side did you take?"

"We stopped it."

"Bah! The Spanish Army stopped it. Look, nobody has tried more than I. I let them use my land; they worked it a while and gave up. They knew I would feed them, so why should they work extra to feed themselves? They smell weakness in generosity."

"That plan was destined to fail, Paco. They have never been taught to do for themselves. They need guidance."

"Like Ali who swore eternal love and gratitude? In less than a month the ungrateful bastard disappeared without even waving goodbye. Two weeks later rebels took him prisoner for stealing a rifle and left a note on a tree in my cane field warning me to control my slaves. They are worse than your awful Spanish tyrants. Who knows where Ali is? Rebels, bah! Rabble is a better word! I planned to make him an overseer. How stupid I was! But no more!" He was shouting as he stopped and banged his fist on the table, knocking dominoes onto the floor. He forced himself to calm down by taking a long draw from his cigar. "I came here thinking Negroes were like us, but with dark skin. Another stupidity! They are not like us. They would not be slaves if they were good for anything else. Can you really imagine them governing?"

Don Miguel's face showed disbelief. "I know Negro landowners."

"All Mulattos. Do you know any pure African landowners?"

Don Miguel shrugged and said, "I remember a conversation with Marta years ago. She wondered how we could expect Africans to work after being torn away from their homes and forced to live under unimaginably horrible conditions. Would you work diligently? These men remember their former lives as free men, Paco. Strange; I disagreed with Marta then, but she was right, as was my mother."

"I agreed with her too, Miguel, but these ten years have taught me more than any university could. The world is not clean and good as I once thought. It is dirty and mean and vile. We try to stay clean in this dirty world, but it is impossible."

"Ay, Paco. Such disillusionment is depressing."

"Keep your illusions then." Paco knew he could not explain his disillusionment. It had shattered under the crushing blow of a daughter he could not acknowledge and a lie that stabbed him every time he looked into Marta's trusting eyes. Until that moment he had not understood the depth of his anger. In a mild voice he said, "I have tried, Miguel, but ..."

Isabel emerged from the kitchen and walked through the living room behind don Miguel and up the stairs, her eyes locked on the floor. Paco felt a cold shudder trying to recall exactly what he had said that she might have heard.

"How are Marta and the children?" don Miguel asked.

"Fine, *gracias a Diós*. Marta got over her two miscarriages. She had me worried, but I should have known better. She is a tough *Asturiana*. Never gave up until we got Ignacio. Can you believe he started school already? Tough, all boy." Paco smiled as he spoke of his younger son. He wanted to tell him about Isabel, but couldn't. He wondered how long he would have to live his deception. "And your mother?"

"Not at all well, *pobrecita*. She can barely walk. I have taken her to the best doctors in Havana, but she does not respond."

"She is quite old."

"She'll be ninety next month. But she has always been an ox, an *Asturiana* like Marta. I always admired her drive and energy; now she is a pitiful sight." Don Miguel's eyes filled. "She was the one who finally made me see how cruelly we treat slaves and how wrong it is. It was our only disagreement, but now ..."

"You are lucky to have her, Miguel. I have not seen my parents in years. One day, perhaps."

*

After lunch the next day Paco took Ignacio to the field to watch the men cut cane. Sitting on the saddle in front of his father, Ignacio watched the men cut for a while. Paco could see he was enthralled. The boy turned to Paco. "May I, Papá?"

"You are too little, Ignacio. When you get a little older."

"I am seven, Papá," he said, lifting one leg and sliding off the horse and staring at his father.

Paco dismounted, "All right, I will show you."

"I know how. Give me your machete."

Seeing the little boy with his fists on his sides like a little man, Paco handed him the machete with a big smile. "Be careful, it is very sharp," he said, thinking the boy could barely hold it up. But he had already grabbed it with both hands and swung it as hard as he could. It bounced off the cane, but the blade made a slash on one of the stalks. He stooped down to look at it and said, "I cut it, Papá," jumping up and down. He lifted the machete again to cut some more, but Paco took the blade out of his hands, picked him up, and explained that he was too young for such a dangerous blade. As he spoke Ignacio punched his nose as hard as he could. Even though it hurt, Paco burst out laughing. Seeing his father laughing, Ignacio laughed too and punched him again. Paco stopped laughing, put him back in the saddle and rode back to the house smiling, thinking, What a boy!

Genio was a different matter, a disappointment, a sack of fat with no backbone, unfit for man's work. Genio never wanted to go to the field with his father. The last time Paco took him, he cried until Paco brought him back. Paco became so angry he walked away and left him crying by the pump shed. All Genio seemed to enjoy was playing with Isabel and cooking. And Isabel led him by the nose all day long. Every time Paco saw him playing with Isabel he wanted to whip him. He never did, of course, though he imagined a good whipping might teach him to be a man and not a whimpering lackey to a girl.

Genio and Isabel attended school together. That Autumn Marta enrolled Ignacio. The school was small, with only two classrooms—one for children ages six to eight, the other for those nine to twelve. The teacher assigned Genio and Isabel to the same desk hoping that studious, quiet Genio would calm Isabel. She was always talking and getting into trouble, usually with the boys. One morning, finding Isabel and a boy behind the school kissing, the teacher summoned Magdalena for a conference. Señorita Ayala, tall and thin as a cane stalk, was waiting for her with her face squeezed into a prune frown. "Señora Iglesias, Isabel must straighten up, or I will have to expel her."

"Por Diós! Que pasó?"

As the teacher related what she had seen, Magdalena put her hand to her mouth in shock. "I cannot believe it."

"She is disrespectful and does not mind. I have reached the end of my patience."

"Please do not expel her, Señorita Ayala. If you give her another chance I will see that she changes."

"I will not have her undermining my work and leading other children down the wrong path. I sat her with Genio thinking he would keep her quiet. He is such a good and polite boy, but it has not helped. I will not have her contaminate the others."

"Isabel is a good girl, Señorita, but I understand your position. Let me try."

"One more chance, Señora Iglesias, but only one more."

"Thank you."

"Is she your daughter? I ask because I told her I would call you, and she said you were her aunt."

"I adopted her as a baby."

"What is her background?"

"Is that important?"

"If I am to help her and teach her."

"She is the daughter of one of my slaves."

"And her father was white?"

"Yes."

"That explains much."

"What do you mean?"

"What can you expect from the daughter of a slave woman and no father present?"

"You should not pass judgment, Señorita Ayala."

"What you call judgment, I call fact."

"You must not hold her parentage against her."

"I am a teacher, Señora Iglesias, not a judge. Thank you for confiding."

That afternoon Magdalena found Lydia in the kitchen. As she related what the teacher had said, Lydia grew livid. "Remember, Lydia, she is a child, and we must help her."

"What do you mean by that?" Lydia's teeth were clenched tight.

"Do not hit her, Lydia. She is a baby."

"We have been through this many times. You are the cause. You never want to punish her when she needs it."

Magdalena began to cry. "Please, Lydia ..."

"You may be the legal mother, but I bore her, and I will discipline her. You will not shield her from me anymore. Understand? The only reason I agreed to the adoption was so my daughter could get the inheritance I was denied."

Magdalena left the kitchen crying and went to her room.

A few minutes later Magdalena heard screaming and crying from Lydia's room and put her hands over her ears. If only she would spank her with her hand, she said to herself, instead of that leather belt. Magdalena could not stand the thought of Isabel being whipped with a leather strap like a slave. "How could she?" she said aloud through her sobs. "Lydia, of all people, whipping her own baby like an overseer." She ran to Lydia's room and threw open the door. "Stop! Please stop!"

Tears streamed down Lydia's cheeks as she looked up. "I told you to stay out. To your room!"

"Whip me, Lydia; I am to blame, not her, please."

"To your room, I said!"

Magdalena ran out the door like a little girl running from her own whipping. In a moment the crying started again, and Magdalena ran downstairs and out the back porch to escape the screams.

At mid-afternoon Isabel found a deck of cards in her mother's room and called Ignacio to play with her.

"Let's call Genio," Ignacio said.

"Forget that sissy! He's in the kitchen with my mother pretending he's a girl."

They sat at a small table in Isabel's room and Isabel started to deal. "What will we play?"

"Casino's the only game you know, little dummy."

"Don't call me dummy."

She had dealt the cards and Ignacio picked up two jacks with the one from his hand and Isabel said, "You cheated!"

"No I didn't. Look, a jack like the others."

"I don't care," she said, throwing down her cards.

"I don't let slaves talk to me like that."

"I am not a slave."

He nodded. "Just like your mother."

Isabel reached over and slapped him across the face. He stood, took two steps back and ran at her and butted his head into her stomach. She fell holding her stomach trying to catch her breath.

Having heard the yelling from her room and the word, slave, Lydia stormed in and grabbed Ignacio by the ear. He swung at her and missed.

"Slaves can't hit free children."

"I'll kill you, you miserable brat."

"Please don't, Mamá, don't kill him."

Lydia pushed her away. "Mind your own business." Turning to Ignacio she said, "You may think you're better than Isabel, brat, but you are just shit."

"I'll tell Mamá," he said, still swinging.

"Good, and tell her what you just said."

He took another swipe at her and missing. "Mean old nigger."

Lydia gave him a slap that left his cheek bright red. "To your mother, brat." She grabbed him by the ear and took him downstairs to the porch, where Marta was sewing. Bursting out the front door, Lydia said, "There she is. Now tell her what you said."

"Lydia hit me," Ignacio said, crying.

"Tell her why, or I hit you again."

Marta dropped her sewing and stood. "No more hitting."

"Tell her." Lydia was screaming.

"I just said she was mean."

"The rest!" Lydia said.

"I hate you, you mean old nigger."

Marta grabbed Ignacio and pulled him to her. "You will never talk to Lydia or anybody else like that." Then turning to Lydia, "I apologize, Lydia. I will take care of him. But if you ever hit him again I personally will knock your teeth out."

"It started because he knocked Isabel down, knocked the breath out of her."

"What did your father say about hitting Isabel, Ignacio?" Marta said, still holding him by the arm.

"Well, are you going to punish him or not?" Lydia was raging.

"I'll do that without your help."

"You need something."

"I said I would handle him, now leave us and remember what I said."

Lydia stared at Marta and down at Ignacio and back again and turned and walked back to the door. She opened it she ran into Isabel and pushed her out of the way as she marched into the kitchen and pushed the swinging door so hard it slammed against the wall.

Marta said, "You know I have to punish you."

"I don't care. Isabel can't call me a cheater."

"Her words will not hurt you, Ignacio, but hitting her in the stomach can, and badly. You must never do that again."

"Well, go ahead, punish me."

"What you said to Lydia is very serious. Your father will have to deal with you."

Ignacio began to cry. "You're mean, Mamá."

"Go to your room and stay there until he comes home."

"There's nothing to do in my room."

"Good, you will have time to think over what you have done."

About an hour later Paco returned from the field and found Marta on the porch. "Why the long face," he said, as he kissed her.

Marta told him the story. Paco stood and walked to the edge of the porch to look down the palm-lined path. "I cannot allow her to hit our son, Marta, but his behavior was intolerable. I will not allow him to talk that way to anybody, adult or child. What did you do to him?"

"He is waiting in his room for you to punish him."

He walked to the door.

"What are you going to do?"

"My belt."

"Please, Paco. He is still a baby."

"Today he becomes a man."

Paco found Ignacio sitting at the window seat looking out the window. "Your mother told me."

"Lydia hit me first and ..."

"I know all I need to know. You cannot talk to anybody that way. You will respect her and everybody."

"What are you going to do?"

Paco took off his belt. "Come here."

Ignacio looked at the belt that dangled from his father's hand for a moment and then walked to him and lay over his lap.

Marveling at Ignacio's courage, Paco no longer wanted to do what he could not avoid. Ignacio said nothing throughout the whipping and did not cry. Paco said no more and walked down toward the porch to talk with Marta. As he passed Isabel sitting on the living room floor she said, "*Hola, Tío Paco.*"

"How are you, Isabelita?"

"Ignacio hit me today." She was looking up at him imploringly.

"I know, and I have punished him."

"Play casino with me, Tío Paco?"

"Not now, Isabel."

"You never play with me like you do with Ignacio and Genio."

"Later." Stopping, he looked back at her knowing she was right. He told himself he loved her, but how could he say it? His feelings swirled in a broth of love and suspicion and trust and lies and anger at lying. Unable to coagulate his feelings into solid action he knew he should stop and play with her. But he went to his wife wondering how long he could walk this fine line between deception and truth, between father and disinterested uncle. But uncles play with their nieces too.

"And Ignacio?" Marta said, as he opened the front door.

"I told him to play outside and to stay away from Isabel for a while."

"Did he cry?"

"Not a whimper. What a boy!"

Marta had tears in her eyes, knowing that crying was not the only way a boy can express anger. During the silent minutes that followed, Paco recalled a mild winter day a year before Ignacio was born, the day he took Isabel and Genio on a carriage ride through the plantation, hoping to interest the boy in the farm. Instead Genio sulked the whole way, saying he was helping Lydia in the kitchen and wanted to go back. "She's making a cake," he said over and over. Isabel ignored him and enjoyed the ride. Paco enjoyed her interest and her questions, but also noticed her eyes fill with admiration during a drive past a group of men cutting cane. She lit up at the sight of sweaty black workers wielding their machetes against the great sea of cane, as if she wanted to be with them. Her interest seemed to lie with them and not the cane or the farm. But he hacked away such thoughts, wishing that circumstances could have been different for them.

The following afternoon after school, Isabel went looking for Ignacio.

"Where are you going?" Genio asked, as he gathered up the game he wanted to play with her.

"To find Ignacio. He's more fun than you, little sissy."

Genio threw the game on the floor and started to cry. He cried so hard that he finally fell on the floor, kicking and pounding his fists against the floor as if he had been robbed of his most precious possession. Ignacio heard the yelling and found Isabel standing over Genio laughing. Ignacio joined the laughter, which made Genio angrier. Hearing the ruckus, Marta came down and broke up the scene. She took Genio upstairs and Isabel and Ignacio began the game Genio had wanted to play.

As Marta walked Genio up the stairs, Lydia pushed the kitchen door open to watch the little fat boy crying and dragging himself up the stairs with his shirttail hanging out and his pants drooping. She stood at the door chuckling, with one hand holding the swinging door open, the other fisted on her waist. She looked at Magdalena, who had come in from the porch, and smiled. Marta took Genio to his room and then returned to the porch wondering how anyone could enjoy seeing a poor boy cry. She thinks she helps her daughter, but she is only teaching her to be mean, Marta thought.

Next morning before breakfast Paco and Ignacio were sitting in the living room enjoying the smell of brewing coffee, and Magdalena came in. "Your laces are loose, Ignacio," she said and stooped down to tie them. As she did, she said, "I wish you could have known your great-uncle Eugenio. He was quite a man."

"What is great-uncle, Tía?"

"Your father's uncle. He came from Asturias like your father and your mother. Your father's father and he were brothers. He brought your father here."

"Was he brave, Tía?"

"Oh, yes, and very intelligent." She finished tying the laces and bent over and kissed Ignacio on the cheek. Walking in with the breakfast Lydia stopped to stare with murderous eyes at Magdalena. She set down the tray, spun around and returned to the kitchen slamming the door against the wall. Magdalena followed her in and began speaking in soft tones that Paco and Ignacio could not hear. Paco did not have to. He knew she was begging forgiveness.

CHAPTER 6 -
ADOLESCENCE - 1889

*

Spanish Cortes Installs Its First Cuban Representative

*

1886: Spain Abolishes Slavery in Cuba

*

To Paco the years had flipped past like book pages in a breeze. The Ten Years War had ended, and slavery was a mad memory. Spain still guarded her Caribbean Jewel as a jealous lover his virgin bride, and the bride's anger simmered.

Paco discouraged talk of rebellion and refused to accept the disaster most landowners expected. He bought machinery that did the job faster and with fewer workers, and his business prospered. With slavery no longer an emotionally explosive reality, his heart again beat in rhythm with the rebels, even as his brain resisted. But more importantly, he felt good about doing business without exploiting other human beings.

As he gradually freed his slaves, Paco hired Cubans and immigrant Spaniards to operate his new machinery. He preferred Spaniards because they knew hunger and did not shy away from work. The Cubans of both races worked well, but they would occasionally disappear for days at a time to be with their families.

Paco's sons tugged at politics in opposite ways. An ardent rebel sympathizer, Genio published letters regularly in Havana and Matanzas newspapers in spite of Paco's continual warnings that they would hurt business. At times Paco felt Genio was more interested in hurting him than in freedom. Genio had never shown the slightest interest in sugar cane. He loved the arts and writing and spent countless hours talking with likeminded friends. Paco could not comprehend how his son had become so oblivious to the business that most affected his family.

Even at seventeen Ignacio was already a man in his father's eyes. Lately he had started parting his blonde hair down the middle like his father's and was nurturing sideburns and a moustache. Looking at him directly, Paco felt he was seeing his mirror image as a youngster, except that Ignacio was a head taller. Ignacio could cut cane as well as any man and liked to tinker with the machines and talk with the overseers. Obviously preparing to run the business, Ignacio rose like a star in his father's firmament. Paco loved to watch him work, either swinging his machete, driving the workers, or adjusting a steam press. Sometimes Ignacio's ambition teetered on the edge of excess, especially in his tendency to rile workers unnecessarily.

Manuel's first complaint had been calculated and mild. "Señor Paco, Ignacio demands much of the workers. These men are not slaves. If we're not careful we will lose them."

"He expects them to work as he works."

"I know, Señor, but …"

"We pay them to work." And with such simplicity Paco dismissed his son's excesses.

It was Isabel who concerned Paco most. At twenty, she was a beauty with green eyes and long, thick, chestnut colored hair that flowed in loose waves over her shoulders. But it was her voluptuous figure that turned men's heads on every street. When she knew someone was watching she would sway and strut even more. She liked to hear their comments as she walked past them. She would usually flip back her hair in a gesture that said, "Don't you wish." She favored large brimmed hats and tight-fitting clothes that flattered her figure.

Isabel had struggled for years to break free from what she saw as unbearable tyranny. Seeing herself a free spirit born to roam and to experience life to the fullest, she identified with the rebels. Her two mothers had laced her world with the barbed wire of a military prison. And her jailers, Magdalena and Lydia, thought her rebellious, unladylike behavior would lead her to damnation. It was only in the past year that they had allowed her to go to Matanzas without them, and that was only for an hour and with the carriage driver as guard. That small morsel of freedom had followed a violent argument, at the end of which, Magdalena finally convinced Lydia to let her go to avoid complete alienation.

The following day Lydia tried to appease her daughter by taking her into the kitchen. "Come, we talk while I cook." Sun was streaming in the wide window over the worktable, and the sweet smell of gardenias filled the kitchen.

"How many times do I have to tell you I'm not interested in cooking?" Isabel said, in her rapid, machine-gun accent. She was standing by the table as her mother took a jar of grain out of the pantry.

"One day you will be glad you learned. Now watch."

"I can't wait for that day."

"You talk of nothing but men. Aren't you ashamed to be so brazen?"

"What else is there?"

"I will make fritters. You like fritters, don't you?" Lydia kneaded furiously.

"Yes, and always someone cooks them for me."

"Spoiled brat! You and your fast talk. Sometimes I can barely understand your silly jabbering. When are you going to learn that you must earn your bread?"

"Why should I? You and Tía Magdalena do that for me."

"Well, from now on you will learn to work."

"What kind of work?" Isabel asked, hoping she meant a job in town.

"Fix your own bed, comb your own hair, and bathe yourself."

"And what will the servants do?"

Lydia kept kneading the mass of dough without looking up.

"If that's all for today's lesson, I have better things to do than listen to another sermon."

Lydia walked around the worktable and slapped Isabel with a powdery hand, leaving a handprint of white dust on her cheek. "So I have nothing to teach you?"

Isabel wiped her face with one hand and smiled. "Thank you, Mamá. You are an excellent teacher."

Hearing the commotion in the kitchen, Magdalena came in with a frantic expression in her eyes. "What is the matter?"

"None of your business," Lydia said.

"How is it not my business, Lydia? I am her legal mother."

"Like hell you are. Did you bear her? Did you feel the pains you pathetic simpleton?"

Magdalena started to cry. Standing with her hands over her face she could not respond.

"That is right," Isabel said. "You are not my mother." Then, seeing Lydia nodding approval, she continued, "And neither are you. No mother hits her child like you do. Marta never hits Genio."

"His father does," Lydia said. "I have seen him."

"Well I don't have a father. Are you supposed to be my father and my mother?"

"I do what I must. You don't need a father. And as for that Paco Pipsqueek ..."

"*Ay*, don't talk like that, Lydia," Magdalena said. "He is the *Hacendado*. We must respect him."

"You respect him enough for all of us."

"I've had enough of you both. I have two mothers too many." She pushed the swinging door crashing into the wall and went to her room and spent the rest of the day stirring a boiling mixture of listlessness and anger into a bitter brew.

The following day she rose early. Saying nothing she found the driver and ordered him to take her to Matanzas. The driver returned to the barn an hour later. Magdalena called him to the back porch and asked where he had taken Isabel.

"Matanzas, Señora. I let her off near the new hotel on the plaza, and she sent me home."

"Did she tell you what time to pick her up?"

"No, Señora. I asked, but she said nothing and walked away."

"How will she get home?"

The driver shrugged.

"Stupid questions," Lydia said as she passed Magdalena on her way to the pump shed to fetch water.

That evening Isabel did not appear for supper and Magdalena panicked. Storming into the kitchen she said, "Where could she be?"

"How do I know? Let me worry about her."

"But I can't stand it. Something may have happened."

"How many times do I have to tell you that I do not know. It is your nagging that has made her so rebellious."

"I love her, Lydia. How can you say such a thing?"

"You will never understand your place."

"I love her as much as any mother. Don't be jealous; I know you do not like me to say it, but ..."

"Get out of here and leave me alone. I'm tired of your whining."

Magdalena ran out of the kitchen crying and went to her room.

The next morning Magdalena opened Isabel's door and found her bed had not been slept in. She ran downstairs and out the back door and found the carriage driver. "Go look for Isabel. Go down every street and alley until you find her. And do not come back without her."

"But, Señora, she may not be in the street. If she is indoors I will not see her."

"Please, do not argue. Go!"

It was almost sundown when the driver returned. The horse dragged the carriage behind her as if it weighed a ton. The driver sat slumped in his seat with the reins hanging loose, as the horse led herself into the barn.

No longer as disinterested, Lydia was waiting with Magdalena, and both ran out to the barn as they heard the carriage and horse lumber in.

"Did you see her?" Magdalena asked.

"No, Señora. I drove along every street more than once. I did not stop. I did not even eat. I never saw her."

"Go back and look again," Lydia said.

The man looked at Lydia as if she had spoken a foreign tongue.

"But Lydia ..." he said.

"You can return tomorrow," Magdalena said. "Go get something to eat."

"I told him to go."

"Please, Lydia, do you not see both man and horse are tired?"

"Get another horse then."

"Come, Lydia." She took Lydia's arm and led her inside. "Tomorrow."

*

Four days later Isabel appeared. Marta and Magdalena were sewing on the porch and looked up to see a well-dressed young man stop his carriage in front of the house. Wearing a new hat and dress covered with lace and frills, Isabel stepped down. Both the ladies dumbly watched the young man, who did not move from his seat. She turned to face him. He smiled at her and flipped the reins and continued on his way.

Magdalena turned to Marta and whispered, "Did you see that? He did not help her out or escort her to the door. He did not even greet us."

"Where have you been, my dear?" Magdalena said.

"Matanzas."

"With whom?"

"Friends."

"Who was that young man?"

"A friend."

"We were worried sick. What were you doing?"

"Getting away from your nagging."

"I do not deserve that, Isabel. I was terribly worried."

"Don't you see I'm fine?"

"Where did you get that dress?"

"Bought it. What do you think?" She twirled around to show it off.

"Well, dear, it looks … it is not your style," Magdalena said.

Isabel turned to make it balloon out and said, "I love it."

"Go see your mother. She has been worried sick."

"After I wash up."

Isabel walked into the living room and stopped under the portrait of Magdalena when her mother opened the kitchen door. Without speaking, Lydia walked to her and slapped her so hard on the face she nearly knocked her down. "Never leave again without telling me where you are going. And take that dress off. You look like a whore."

Isabel regained her balance and raised her arm as if to slap her back, but stopped, turned, and walked upstairs to her room. By this time both Magdalena and Marta had come in. Standing with her fists jammed into her sides, Lydia's solid form expanded and contracted like a bellows, as tears of rage filled her eyes. Magdalena approached her and put her arm around her shoulder. Lydia pushed her away and disappeared into the kitchen. Magdalena followed her. Marta returned to the porch.

That afternoon Marta met Paco in the living room, took his arm, and led him upstairs.

"What is it?"

She raised her hand as if to say, "Wait." In their bedroom she recounted Isabel's arrival. He tried to appear detached, but the story tore into the pit of his stomach. As she spoke he rose and went to the window and looked out so she would not see his face. His fists were so tight he thought they would explode. As much as he wanted to do something, no action made sense. To approach Isabel and chastise her seemed useless at this point, and she would certainly rebuke him as she had Magdalena and Lydia.

Marta finished and he said, "I am going to wash and dress for supper. See you downstairs." He went down to the pump shed to wash and then walked behind the barn and stood thinking about his daughter and his horrible secret, the worst pact he had ever made.

Supper passed with few words. Even Genio and Ignacio kept silent, their eyes shifting back and forth from Lydia to Isabel to Magdalena. Serving the meal in complete silence and with a face sterner than usual, Lydia drew a shroud of silent fury over the supper. She served each person without acknowledgment. Isabel's nonchalance was too strained and obvious to convince anyone. "What are you sewing, Tía? It's lovely."

"A navy blue mantilla for you, dear. Like it?"

"Yes. Thank you, Tía."

"Why don't you make Genio and me something?" Ignacio asked with a smirk.

"It is not easy to sew for boys. Perhaps a shirt one day."

Ignacio winked at Isabel as Magdalena spoke. After supper Paco went to the living room to read. Isabel came through and stopped to look at Magdalena's portrait. She stood there a long time, tilting her head this way and that, imagining herself with a mantilla like the one in the portrait. Then she tilted her head back in a haughty gesture as Paco watched over his book. She passed her hand over her arm and looked at it and then raised her eyes to the portrait again. Then she turned abruptly and walked to the porch. As soon as Paco had resumed his reading Ignacio walked past him and opened the front door and sat with Isabel. "Pretty good, Isabel. You go off on a binge and she makes you a mantilla. You should go for a month next time."

"Oh, shut up."

At first their conversation irritated Paco, but soon the dialogue took a strange turn.

"You're disgusting. Keep your nose out of my business."

"Is that where I had it?" Ignacio was rocking hard, making strong, exaggerated rocking motions. "Have a good time?"

"Leave me alone."

"Come on. You can tell your little cousin."

"Evelio's worthless. All he wanted to do was drink brandy."

"Didn't want anything else?"

"How would you like to spend hours watching a fool sleep off his binge?"

"You could have left."

"I almost did, but he woke up and told me of a stupid dream he had, and we started to laugh, and everything was good again."

"Did you play hide the chorizo?"

Paco put down his book and walked outside. "Nice evening."

"Yes, Tío Paco."

"Ignacio, go to my room and fetch me a cigar." Paco knew Ignacio did not like the role of errand boy. Ignacio stalked out and Paco said, "Tell me with whom you travel, and I'll tell you who you are, Isabel."

"Ah, how I love proverbs. So full of wisdom."

"People look down on girls who spend so much time with a man. Don't you ever expect to marry?"

"No!"

"Why not?"

"You're not my father. I have enough with two mothers. So stuff your questions." She stood, went inside and disappeared upstairs.

He had watched Magdalena and Lydia fight over her and knew in his soul that they had made a wild animal of his daughter. Yes, she needs a father, he thought. He went inside and heard Magdalena and Marta upstairs talking. Probably about their embroidery, he thought. In the kitchen he found Lydia scrubbing a pot. The room smelled of garlic and gardenia.

"Are you very angry with Isabel?"

"What do you think?"

"It is time she knew ..."

Lydia dropped the pot and turned to him. Her eyes overflowed with hatred. "If you tell her you will never see either of us again. Understand?"

Seeing her assume her bulldog stance, he wondered what he had found attractive in her. "But why, Lydia? She has you and Magdalena, but no father. She needs a father, especially now."

"She has me and needs nothing more, least of all a father."

"That is unfair, Lydia. Who knows what she will do next. Neither you nor Magdalena has been able to rein her in. She needs me now more than ever."

"You will never see us again."

"But why?"

"Because someone has been trying to take her from me since she was born. First Magdalena with her sweet, cuddling, childish shit, and now you. You have stayed in the background, but I always knew you wanted her too. Well, you won't have her!"

She picked up the pot and resumed scrubbing. He knew from her tone that it was no use. "What if I tell Marta? Perhaps she could better understand my feelings."

"Tell anyone and you will never see us again." Her words struck the pot like metal on metal.

"All right, but think it over. I have no desire to take her from you, only to help her."

Saying nothing she scrubbed so hard that soon she was puffing and perspiring visibly.

Paco returned to the front porch. Marta and Magdalena were still upstairs, but soon Magdalena came down to the kitchen. A minute later Marta opened the porch door looking for Paco.

"Quiet supper," she said.

"Yes."

"Poor Magdalena is very upset. Doesn't know what to do."

"What can she do? Lydia does not tolerate meddling."

"Have you talked with Genio today?" Marta asked.

"No. Why?"

"He wants to enroll in the University."

"I know." In a singsong tone he said, "To study literature and philosophy."

"Talk with him, Paco."

"He knows what I think."

"Let him go, Paco. He's twenty."

"I will not pay for him to dabble in philosophy and spend his days talking nonsense with other lazy intellectuals. If he wants to become a lawyer or a doctor or an engineer, fine."

"He's not interested in those things."

"Then he will work like a man."

"You are just angry because he doesn't want to farm."

"I wish he did, but I would never force him."

"You leave him little choice, Paco."

"More than I had. Must I remind you?"

"Your uncle helped you."

"I want Genio to do something worthwhile, not spend four or five years in Havana living like a rich brat. If he wants to study philosophy, let him pay for it."

"You know he can't."

"Why not?"

"Why so hard? You can afford it."

"We cannot solve his problem."

"Don't be angry, Paco."

"I'm not."

She got up and reached for his hand and said, "How about a walk?"

Without enthusiasm he rose and they walked down the path between the royal palms toward the main road. With the moon full they could see every frond and even their colors. Marta walked close grasping his arm. Paco remembered a day twenty-odd years ago walking along an Asturian mountain road to the cemetery. How life changes. The beautiful path they trod belonged to him now. As they walked between the straight rows of palms, everything in his sight was his. Marta looked lovely in the moonlight, her scars barely noticeable.

"You are part of me, Marta."

"We are part of each other." She held his arm tighter.

"You have become more beautiful."

"Even with the extra weight and the rest …?"

"They are barely noticeable, and your figure is … how do I say it?"

"You don't have to."

"Marta, you are the best thing that ever happened to me."

She said nothing and rested her head on his shoulder.

Throughout his compliments his thoughts had never strayed far from Lydia. As they walked an apparition appeared, the ghost of a girl disguised as one person, but hiding an inscrutable phantom. After twenty years she had remained a stranger whom he would probably never understand. And Magdalena who strove so hard to please and to help everyone. Paco visualized her portrait in the living room and how it had impressed him; such an imposing presence, regal, beautiful, secure, commanding; so different from the all-good, suffering woman who seemed to want only to be kind. She was kind, gentle, generous, warm and still beautiful. It was as if Magdalena in her goodness had held back the evil that makes a person ugly. Perhaps, he thought, Magdalena's beauty added to Lydia's anger. Magdalena had received her inheritance in every form, even physical beauty. She had aged gracefully while Lydia had bloated into a chunky icebox with spindly legs, hard and cold and cracked with anger.

He spotted a spider web stretched between two palms. In the middle of the round, beautifully delicate web sat the spider: black, wrinkled, motionless. Paco could not take his eyes off the fluffy web moving gently in the breeze with the host riding patiently in the center. Suddenly a fly flew into the web, and, before Paco could be sure what he had seen, the spider dashed over it and, with fleeting motions of its appendages like flying fingers of a hand, extruded more of its silky webbing and, in a bare second, wrapped the insect into a white mummy. Having finished its work, the spider crawled back to its center to await another victim. Paco felt sympathy for the poor, trapped insect and imagined himself bound by Lydia's evil web.

Marta squeezed his hand. "You've wandered."

"Just thinking how lucky I am."

"I, too."

A cloud had passed across the moon and moved on, illuminating her face. "You are more beautiful than ever."

"She snuggled close and said, "Why don't we go to bed?"

*

Next morning Paco had almost finished breakfast when Genio came in wearing a white suit. Having stretched the jacket to button it had cut deep creases under the arms. But even in the tight fitting suit he looked neater than usual, especially with his well-oiled, dark wavy hair. His thick, black moustache added breadth to his chubby face.

"Good morning, Papá," he said, as he sat down.

Paco wanted to get to work, but decided to broach the issue. "I hear the rebels are starting up again."

"Yes, Papá. There is much talk in Matanzas. Havana too."

"Think they will get anywhere?"

"Something has to change. The depression is terrible."

"Spain will pull us out eventually, especially if we start acting like a loyal colony and quit this talk of rebellion."

"Why should we depend on Spain to solve our problems?"

"Like it or not, Genio, we are Spaniards."

"We must be free, Papá. What right do they have to punish people for speaking against them? Americans can speak freely and assemble— legally. They have freedom."

"To a point, Genio. Even Americans must work for their living."

With sadness Genio said, "Work is all you think of, Papá. There's more to life."

"Such as?"

"Family, friends, the intellect, the soul."

"Those cannot exist without work. As to the intellect, it is for making your living first and for leisure second."

"Please, Papá, not more stories of Asturias. This is Cuba, a rich land full of starving people."

"There is much wrong with Cuba, Genio, but nothing that hard work cannot solve. Only when Cubans decide to develop the nation's natural riches will they be free."

"I want very much to attend the University in Havana. May I?"

"To study what?"

"Philosophy and letters. I want to write."

"How will you earn your living? Working for a newspaper?"

"If I have to. I want to write novels and books on philosophy."

"From what I know most writers have never attended a university. They write about the life they have lived."

"I know, Papá, but the university can teach me much."

"Why not law or medicine? Earn your living helping others. Lawyers help people solve problems; doctors cure the sick. How better to help humanity?"

"Those things don't interest me. I want to understand the great thinkers and their ideas."

"Understand this, Genio: I do not push you merely for my pleasure or to save money. I want you to move toward a good living so you can support a family. Don't you want that?"

"Of course, but ..."

"Damn it, Genio. It is not only money you will squander studying noble ideas and writing tracts nobody will ever read. To make a mark in this world you must touch people in concrete ways."

"And if I work to pay for my studies?"

Paco thought a moment. "I would not object."

"Then I have your permission?"

"How do you plan to live until you find a job?"

"My friend José has offered to put me up in his home for a while. His parents moved to Havana after the Americans bought their farm."

"Oh, yes, the Álvarez family. Too bad about them."

"Nobody else could afford to buy them out. You see, Papá, Spain's terrible taxes are sinking well-to-do Cubans as well."

"You are a Spaniard, damn it."

"No, Papá. I am a Cuban and proud of it."

"I cannot deny my homeland, Genio. I was born a Spaniard and will die one. I love Cuba too, but to me Cuba is a colony of the Spanish empire."

"We should be free. I hate to go against you, Papá, but I must. I feel about Cuba the way you feel about Asturias."

"You are right about the depression, Genio, but it cannot last. I have managed to stay afloat."

"You're one of the few, Papá, and I'm proud of you for it."

"What are José parents doing?"

"His father works for the American company that bought his farm. As an administrator, I think."

"José is a good boy. I do not want you to become a parasite."

"I promise. Only until I earn some money."

Genio stood and shook his father's hand and then left the dining room and took the stairs two at a time. Paco was surprised to see his son's corpulent mass move so rapidly. Genio had continued to gain weight through his teen years, and now, at twenty, he had become a short, flabby lad, no taller than his father, and kind and thoughtful. Worried that any strong personality could turn him, Paco realized his son had entered manhood and would have to make his own way. Perhaps living alone in a big city would teach him more than a father could with words and advice.

Paco walked to the barn, saddled a horse and rode to the field. As he approached the work crew he saw Manuel and Ignacio talking, arms waving, and the workmen standing around them. Seeing Paco coming Manuel told the men to get back to work. They were planting new cane, and it was hot and steamy, with rain clouds gathering as if to rinse the dusty land clean.

"*Que pasó?*"

"*Nada, Señor Paco,*" Manuel said. "Ignacio and I were having a discussion."

"Discussion, hell," Ignacio said. "He told me to leave, but I won't."

"Go to the house, Ignacio," Paco said. "We will talk there."

"But ..."

"To the house."

After Ignacio had disappeared into a cloud of dust, Paco told the men, who had stopped again, to get back to work.

Manuel took Paco aside and said, "He drives me and the men crazy, Señor Paco."

"At his age he thinks he knows everything, Manuel. Leave him to me. Just get this field planted. It looks like rain."

"*Si, Señor Paco.*"

Paco remounted and rode back to the house and found Ignacio in the kitchen talking with Lydia. Seeing Ignacio so serious and Lydia smiling, Paco knew she was enjoying the boy's troubles.

"Come, Ignacio, to the porch. Lydia, will you please bring us coffee?"

They sat in the porch rockers and Paco took out two cigars, offered Ignacio one, and bit the end off the other. Ignacio smiled broadly. "You have never offered me a cigar before, Papá."

"It's time you learned to enjoy a good smoke."

Ignacio bit off the end as he had seen his father do hundreds of times, and Paco lit both cigars. Ignacio drew three or four puffs and took the cigar in his fingers and rocked back in his chair. They both took several more puffs and rocked gently in the still, humid air. Ignacio continued puffing for a while and then stopped and held the cigar between his fingers. After a while Paco turned to him and said, "Don't you like it?"

"Made me a little dizzy, that's all. I'm fine."

"Don't inhale. Just blow it out. You will learn to inhale in time."

At that admonition, Ignacio took a deep puff and inhaled it as if to show his father. Soon his eyes opened wide and his mouth turned into a frown.

"What's wrong?"

"I don't feel well, Papá. Must be the sun. It's been pretty hot."

"What happened with Manuel?"

"He doesn't want me to work the men hard." Ignacio still looked weak and held the cigar away.

"If you push them too far they will do less. They know what they can do."

"Excuse me, Papá. I'll be right back." He ran into the house and out the back door. Paco stood at the front door until he heard the loud heaving he expected. A few minutes later Ignacio returned without the cigar.

"Are you all right?"

"Yes, Papá. I'm fine now."

"The cigar?"

"Oh no. I just didn't feel well."

"You cannot pick up a cigar and smoke it without learning how, Ignacio. Like most things, just because you can light a cigar and pull a few puffs does not mean you know how to smoke. Men smoke, but smoking does not make you a man. It is like supervising workers. Being in a position to tell men what to do does not make you a supervisor."

"Is that why you gave me the cigar, Papá? To embarrass me?"

"I want you to understand a simple principle, Ignacio: Doing man's work is not the same as being a man. I am very proud of the way you are developing. You have the makings of a good businessman. Genio has no interests in any of that. You will probably run this place better than I one day. But you need to mature; that means working and listening to your elders. In fifty years Manuel could not learn to run this farm. He lacks ability. He is a good man and can teach you much, but he is limited. You are not, Ignacio, except in experience. Do you understand?"

"I understand you're trying to make a fool of me. We both know I can handle any job on this farm. I can do Manuel's job and I want it. Why the excuses?"

"You will run this farm soon enough. No seventeen-year-old should take over such a job, even one as talented as you."

"I will not wait forever, Papá."

"Good."

Before lunch Paco related their conversation to Marta.

"Give him something, Paco, or he will become disheartened."

"Seventeen is too young, for heaven's sake."

"You were a boy when you took over this place. Not much older than he. You do not want him to think you don't trust him, or worse, that you envy him."

"You know better."

"Then show him. Let him do something."

*

After lunch don Miguel appeared at the front door. Magdalena, who knew him well by now, let him in. "How are you, Magdalena?"

"Very well, don Miguel. Nice to see you."

"Is Paco in?"

"Of course. Please sit down; I will call him."

Short and stubby, but muscular and fit, Paco came bouncing down the stairs smiling at his old friend, a cigar clenched in his teeth. His hair had not thinned noticeably and still held its light brown color. Parted in the middle with a slight curl at the ends it adorned the face of a man of substance. "Too early for dominoes, Miguel."

"I came to say goodbye."

"Vacation?"

"No, Paco. I've lost my farm. It'll be sold at auction in a few days."

"Foreclosure? I knew you were having troubles, but …"

"You're one of the few left, Paco. Depression has the island by the throat, and, now that Spain and America have raised tariffs against each other, I lose money with every load I sell."

"But you just bought new equipment."

"That dragged me down even faster. The payments came due just as sales and prices dropped. Horrible!"

"I think I can hold out until the economy stabilizes."

"I don't see that happening, Paco."

"It started when the Americans became our main customer and supplier. Now they control us. Next comes annexation."

"Nothing could be worse than this, Paco."

"Spain cannot give up her most important colony, Miguel."

"To Spain we're only income, nothing else. She paid her war debts out of our ribs. Now, with sugar prices cut to half, we're doomed. Even my bank—one of the biggest in Cuba—closed. How have you managed, Paco?"

"I put half of my money in Madrid and the rest in New York. I knew our banks would never make it through the war."

"Very smart, Paco. The Bank of Santa Catalina paid ten cents on the peso. Almost wiped me out." Don Miguel lowered his head as if in dejection and said, "It doesn't matter anymore, Paco. First Mamá and now the farm; there is nothing left."

Paco could see don Miguel was becoming morose. "Come now, Miguel, you are strong and healthy, and you are not poor."

"What does money matter, Paco, without the people and home that make life ... more than an exercise in bookkeeping?"

"How much will it take to pay off your debt?"

"Let's drop it, Paco. *No importa.*"

"Come on; how much?"

Don Miguel looked at Paco. "About a tenth the value of the property. Why?"

"I will lend it to you."

"That's generous, Paco, but I couldn't pay you back. Not in today's economy."

"Things always pick up."

"Not this time. Besides, I'm through farming. With Mamá gone I'm getting out of Matanzas, moving to Havana. She left me well fixed. Why don't you make a bid? The Atkins Company people have hovered over me like vultures."

"How about selling it to me, and I can pay the debt before it goes to auction. That way I won't have to bid, and you will get something."

"That's very generous, Paco."

"How much?"

"I don't know. What do you think?"

"How about double the amount of the debt?"

"That's too generous."

"Done."

*

Next morning, Paco looked into Genio's room and saw him packing. "Leaving so soon?"

"The school term starts in a few weeks, Papá. I'll have to find something before then."

Paco felt pity for the poor boy, so excited, so nervous and overweight. He knew he would be an easy mark for any big city sharpie. Seeing innocence and weakness beaming from Genio's face, Paco wanted to grab him and make him stay so he could take care of him, even as he realized that would only doom him to perpetual dependence. To become a man he would have to go alone and face his father's fears. Of course, Genio was too young and full of enthusiasm to harbor such fears. He saw only the good in people.

"Good luck, son. If you have trouble finding a job, write. I have friends in Havana who could use a bright young man."

"Thank you, Papá. You are very good to me."

"I'll take you to the train."

"The driver is waiting. You have too much work."

"Nonsense. I have plenty time,"

"I must take charge of my life, Papá."

Encouraged, Paco said no more, shook his son's hand, and embraced him. "Write, Genio."

"Of course, Papá."

Paco went to his office, sat at his desk, and opened his account ledger, not looking for anything in particular. His mind was not on the accounts, but on Genio's future. He had considered telling don Miguel to look after him, but knowing Miguel's attraction to young men, he decided not to tell either that the other had moved to Havana. After a few minutes he heard the horse and carriage and went to the window in Genio's room and saw the driver lifting suitcases in and Marta kissing Genio and handing him a lunch package for the trip. Marta watched him drive off, then walked back to Magdalena with tears running down her cheeks. Magdalena, with her endless supply of tears, was also crying. Paco was surprised to see Marta weeping. My strong, fierce *Asturiana*! He thought.

At breakfast Marta and Magdalena were both quiet. Paco envisioned their thoughts of Genio's trip shuttling back and forth across the table, like threads on a loom, weaving feelings of calamity.

"Where are Ignacio and Isabel?" Paco asked.

"Ignacio ate early and left. Would you like me to call Isabel?" Magdalena pushed her chair back to get up.

"No. Let her sleep."

As she was serving, Lydia stopped momentarily with her tray in her hands and looked around the table. Everyone thought she would ask about her daughter, but instead, she served in silence and returned to the kitchen.

179

Having realized that Marta was right, Paco decided to offer Ignacio a more responsible job. He finished his breakfast rapidly and rode out and found him talking with some of the workers. Manuel was standing off to one side ignoring him.

"*Hola*, Ignacio. I want to talk with you."

He was explaining to two young Spaniards how to run the steam press. "What is it, Papá?"

"Everything all right?"

"Perfect. Why?"

"Can you come to the house with me?"

"In just a moment," Ignacio said, and turned to the two men to make sure they got the machine running.

Ignacio led the way at a gallop, seemingly in a hurry. They stopped at the barn and put away the horses. "Will we be a while, Papá?"

Paco nodded; they unsaddled and walked to the house and up to Paco's office, where he led Ignacio to the south window.

"From here I can see the barn and the fields and, with my spyglass, the whole farm. Feast your eyes, Ignacio. Our world."

"Beautiful!"

"It will be yours one day. I arrived here with nothing but the clothes I was wearing. Now it is all mine."

"And Magdalena's."

"The responsibility is mine for now. I have been thinking: perhaps it is time you assumed some responsibility."

Ignacio smiled cynically, as if to say, about time.

"I want you to oversee the entire manufacturing process—cane pressing to sugar. How about it?"

"Gladly, Papá. May I work with you on the books too?"

"The books are complicated and take time. I tried to get Genio interested, but ... Well, you are the one."

"What about Isabel?" Ignacio said.

"She is not an heir."

"Magdalena might disagree."

"Do not worry about that, Ignacio. Isabel is a woman and will not inherit the farm. She will be well cared for. Now, what is your vision?"

"To make this farm even bigger, enormous, the biggest in the island. I want to make Hacienda Iglesias the greatest in Cuba. To create a shipping line that will take our sugar to all parts of the world." He was swinging his arms dramatically and his eyes were bulging.

"I like your vision, Ignacio. In fact I have just arranged to buy don Miguel's plantation."

"More land's a good start," Ignacio said.

"Don't blur a good plan with unbridled ambition, Ignacio. Calculate your plan in detail, lay it out, and carry it out step by step."

"Nothing important happens gradually; revolution's the only way."

"I'm not talking about war."

"Me neither. The rebels can go to hell for all I care."

"I cannot argue with anything you say, son. I like your vision. Together we can make it reality."

"It is my vision, Papá. I'll bring it about." He turned and looked out the window.

"*Que pasa?*" his father asked. "Don't you want to work together?"

"We will work together until I take the reins, Papá. The day it becomes mine I'll make my revolution."

"Well, you will just have to wait. You have just finished school; not even legal age. You are nothing but a snot-nose boy with grandiose ideas and baby hair for whiskers. Get the hell out of here and go back to work. You are in charge of manufacturing. Let us see if you can revolutionize that by bringing in as much sugar as Manuel and Enrique."

"Papá, I ..."

"Out!"

After he left Marta came in. "What's wrong?"

"Spoiled brat!"

"*Que pasó?*"

"Leave me. I have much work."

Knowing how far to push him, she left without another word.

Looking out the window Paco pondered his future: Can I handle him? He is tougher than anybody I have known. For a while back there I wondered if he was planning a coup. He has a damned good vision ... Calm down and think intelligently. He pushed too hard, but that's his brash youth. But I am older, as bright, as energetic, but not brash. Age will win. Yet ... Napoleon was a general at twenty; Alexander the Great was a teenager. God, what do I face with this blood of mine?

Paco stayed in the house that day working on his books and writing letters. He had not heard from Asturias in months, since his mother died. His father had died five years before, so he wrote to his brother. After lunch he took a carriage to Matanzas to wander the streets and drink a few glasses of beer.

Alone, Marta went to her room to gather her thread and needles to take to the porch. Glancing out the window she saw Ignacio riding toward the house. She yelled out asking him to come up to her. In less than a minute he walked into her room, anger spread across his face.

"*Que Pasa?*" she asked.

"He thinks I'm still a baby. Won't let me do anything."

"But he put you in charge of the operation."

"He wouldn't explain the books. I want more that an overseer's job, Mamá. I need to understand it all."

"One day, Ignacio, and you will do well, but your father still has much to teach you."

"Bah! I can learn the way he did."

"You underestimate your father, Ignacio. He wants very much to see you succeed, but you are still young."

"He was younger."

"He had no choice; no one else could. Listen to him and have patience."

"Why do you always take his side? It would be nice if you had a mind of your own."

"I do, Ignacio. I side with him because he is right. If you were right, I would side with you."

"Hah! You're his lackey."

"I am nobody's lackey. Your father is right. You are demonstrating it by your tone."

Ignacio turned and stalked out of the room and slammed the door behind him.

*

Matanzas had grown since Paco first saw it that December day twenty-three years ago. Its bay still fascinated him. His thoughts wove patterns over the terrain of his mind: Genio in Havana studying philosophy, Ignacio in the fields working like a field hand with his eye on conquest, and rebellious Isabel.

With the immediacy of his sons' demands, Isabel reappeared out of a foggy corner of Paco's consciousness. Ignacio was right: Isabel is as much an heir as he and Genio. Did that annoy him? Was he showing me he understood the situation or was he plotting to eliminate her from the picture?

Paco could not be sure and was afraid to probe, but he would find a way to help her without turning the property over to her or breaking it up. He knew one thing: a person so dedicated to diversion could not be a good manager. But who knows what else she thinks of? Something bothered her enough to drive her away for four days. Paco knew her two mothers, hovering over her every movement, had spoiled her and had probably driven her to rebellion. Who knows what phantoms inhabit the poor girl's mind? Paco could not bear the possibilities that battered his brain. Perhaps she was just finding her own way, like Genio. Perhaps her only recourse was escape. Poor Isabel!

He spent two hours in Uncle Eugenio's favorite little bar. The waiters all knew him, and it was a good place to spend the afternoon. He played dominoes for a while with some acquaintances and recalled the day his uncle took him to the brothel. What a day that was! Uncle never knew I did nothing but talk to that frightened girl. Oh, to be eighteen again and know what I know now, Tío Facundo used to say. It always sounded silly. Of course you cannot relive your youth, and if you could, you could not bring all you had learned with you. You would make the same mistakes all over again.

"Another beer, Señor Paco?"

"No, Jaime. My check please, and include my domino mates."

"Stay as long as you like, Señor Paco. The place is yours."

Paco paid and walked to the waterfront recalling his first glimpse of the ocean, so different from the calm Caribbean. That Atlantic beast threatening to swallow him whole almost changed his future. Ignacio sees things differently. If he had seen the ocean I saw in Gijón that day he would have jumped in and swum to America. What a man!

Paco got home shortly before supper and went to his office. As he sat down Marta burst in. "Isabel has left."

"Not again!"

"To Havana. She left a note for Magdalena telling her not to send anyone after her."

"When?"

"Before sunup. Ignacio helped her. And, by the way, I spoke with him this morning right after you left. You are right, Paco. He is not ready to take charge."

Seeing through Ignacio's scheme Paco growled, "Where is he?"

"In the field, I suppose."

He started toward the door, but she held him. "Wait, there is more: Magdalena told Lydia, and she started the biggest row I have ever seen. Yelled terrible things at Magdalena."

"She blames Magdalena?"

"Because Isabel left the note for Magdalena."

"She'll get over it. I have to see Ignacio."

Paco went downstairs and out to the barn, saddled a horse, and rode off to the processing plant at a gallop. He found Ignacio standing over the young immigrants feeding cane to the press, showing them how to feed more cane in less time. He saw Paco and stopped. "What is it, Papá?"

Paco took him aside trying to control himself. After a few seconds, watching his face for any expression of guilt, Paco said, "I understand you helped Isabel leave."

"That's right."

"Why?"

"She asked me to."

"Did it have anything to do with our conversation this morning?"

"What do you mean?"

"About her being an heir?"

"What?"

Paco looked at him unbelieving, thinking, He's smart, perhaps too smart for his own good. "Was it to get another heir out of the picture?"

"How can you ask that, Papá?"

"Answer me."

"I'd never do that. She's like a sister." He turned and walked away. Then he stopped and turned. "I'm ashamed of you, Papá. You really do hate me."

"I told you she was not a threat."

"And I believed you. I've been thinking about our conversation too. I'll take my vision elsewhere."

He went to his horse, saddled it, and rode off toward the house, leaving Paco wondering about the words that had passed each other missing their mark. Slowly he mounted his horse and returned to the house, where he found Ignacio in his room packing a suitcase.

"What are you doing?"

"Guess."

"If you don't get back to work, I will ..."

"What? Fire me? Hit me? Go ahead, try."

He towered over his father by nearly a foot and faced him toe to toe. "I asked you a simple question, Ignacio. I did not fire you. Why are you making such a drama?"

"You don't trust me, and now it's clear that you hate me. I can't continue to work here."

"You are wrong. I have trusted you with a good part of the family business. As to liking you, you have always been my special favorite. For a smart boy you are exceptionally stupid. Do you not see what I am trying to do?"

"I see only that you want me under your thumb, quiet and docile, like Mamá."

Paco stood before him like an idiot, not knowing what to say. What could he do with this boy-man? Paco sat in a chair near the bed. Seeing his father sitting, Ignacio stared at him, enraged, as he sat on the edge of the bed looking out the window. They remained like that for several minutes. Paco tried to divine what was going through Ignacio's mind and could barely recall what he himself was thinking minutes afterward. Finally he stood and lifted Ignacio by the shoulders. "Ignacio, please listen and try to understand: You are my only heir to this farm. Eugenio and Isabel will inherit some wealth, but not the farm. The farm is yours. You are the only one who can breathe life into my fondest dreams. The last thing I wanted was to have you think I lack trust in you. That impression came from my desire for you to learn all you could before jumping in as *hacendado*. Above all you must believe that. No plantation is worth a son. I have let Genio go because he needs to experience life. I hope he does well in the university. The way I see it, at worst he will waste a few years studying useless things and become a man in the process. You were a man already in the womb. You are the one."

Paco finished his speech and lowered his head wondering if his son would attack again. Instead, Ignacio put his arm over Paco's shoulder. "I did not know you felt that way, Papá. Of course I'll stay. But you must believe I didn't try to get her out of the way."

"I do, Ignacio. I do." They embraced for a long time.

"What are you going to do about her?" Ignacio said.

"She does not want us to interfere. I will respect her wish, but I will ask Genio to stay in contact with her."

Ignacio started out the back door, and Paco asked where he was going.

"I left those men working. If I don't get back they'll be sleeping."

Watching Ignacio ride off at full gallop, Paco went to the pump shed to wash his face and try to cool off. Magdalena came out and offered him a cup of coffee, and he followed her into the kitchen.

"And Lydia?" Paco said.

"Visiting her sick aunt in the slave quarters."

"I hear she's furious."

"Quite." She poured black coffee into a demitasse and handed it to him. "I have been thinking, Paco. Isabel is my legal charge and heir. Perhaps you could find something for her in the farm ..."

"Where is Marta?"

"Upstairs, sewing."

"I have given much thought to Isabel, Magdalena, but a ship can have only one captain. Of the three only Ignacio is qualified. He will be a successful *hacendado* at the proper time. Genio is not interested. He wants a different life. I hope he can achieve something worthwhile and live happily. As for Isabel, she also has shown no interest in the farm. I think she is an unhappy girl who does not know what she wants. We can only give her the freedom she seeks and hope she finds what she is looking for. I promise you she will inherit her rightful portion in cash and possibly some of our Matanzas property, but not the farm."

"Lydia worries she will end up with nothing as she did."

"Did Lydia ask you to talk to me?"

"Well, yes. She is afraid Isabel will end up dependent on us, as she has."

"Lydia lives exactly the life she wants. She could have been part of our family, but she refused."

"She is a complicated woman, Paco. You are right, of course, but she needs me to look after her."

"Don't you realize she controls you?"

"Don't say that, Paco. I think only of her and Isabel."

"I know, but I must be fair to all of us."

"Please remember poor Isabel has no father to lean on."

"That is not my fault, Magdalena."

*

Genio's small apartment reminded Paco of his house in Colosía, though this one was cleaner and tidier. Genio escorted his father into the small sitting room and then to the tiny bedroom, barely large enough for a single bed. A desk and chair dominated the sitting room with a short bookcase about half full of books on each side of the desk. An empty trash basket peered out from under the desk, and a pencil and a clean pad of paper lay neatly on the desktop. Paco passed his hand over the desktop and smiled at Genio, who had recently wiped it clean. The boy's neatness always surprised his father, and he looked around, taking in everything with approval. The best part of the bedroom was the window that overlooked a neighbor's landscaped garden filled with mango, coconut, mamey, and sapodilla trees. The pungent scent of ripe fruit filled his rooms with tropical sweetness laced with a hint of decay. The formal photograph of Paco seated with Marta standing behind him and their two young boys standing by his sides recalled simpler times. Every time Paco saw that photograph he thought of the daughter who should have stood with them. He looked at the photograph trying not to think of Isabel, but of Genio, who, in spite of his apparent lack of direction and ambition, had a kind heart.

"You look thinner. Are you eating well?"

"Yes, Papá."

"Need money?"

"A few hours each evening at Sánchez's Men's shop keeps me eating."

"I have to sign papers for the don Miguel farm tomorrow morning. After that my day is yours. How about showing me Havana?"

"Great, Papá! But this evening we go to *El Gallo de Oro*. I want you to meet my friends."

"The Golden Rooster, eh? Sounds intriguing. How go the studies?"

"Good. I have four very good professors and one who is a little boring, but they all know their subject."

They chatted about trivial things for almost half an hour before Paco asked about Isabel.

"I saw her the other day. She rooms with a girlfriend in a nice area on the edge of El Vedado."

"How is she?"

"All right, I guess. I took her to supper."

"What does she do for money?"

"Still had some you sent her and has some leads on jobs."

"Such as?"

Genio shrugged.

"Are you sure she is all right? You sound unsure."

"Well … she's drinking … I don't like to tell tales, but … well, a lot."

"How do you know?"

"The other night I walked past an expensive restaurant, looked in the window and there she was with a fellow. Both of them looked pretty drunk. People were staring. It's her first taste of freedom, and she hasn't yet figured it out."

"Give me her address. I'll go see her tomorrow."

"I'm glad, Papá."

With that comment Paco saw that Genio was worried.

"I'm hungry. Where is that Golden Rooster?"

They walked down two floors to the street below, where buggies and clopping horses were moving in all directions, as pedestrians were doing their best to dodge them. The deep red, drooping sun filled the crowded streets with a golden radiance.

After three blocks dodging people through a middle class neighborhood they found *El Gallo de Oro*, a crowded hole in the wall that ran deep into the building with two potted palms on either side of the entrance and a bar just inside against one wall. Four small tables filled the narrow space between the café and the street, so people had to spill onto the street to get past. Before venturing in, Genio peered in for a moment.

"There they are. Come."

The three young men were sitting around a table smoking cigars and nursing glasses of beer. "Papá," Genio said, "I present my university friends: Manuel, Horacio, and Hector." Manuel was a small boy, short and thin, who looked no older than fifteen or sixteen. His dark, smooth-skinned face bore a solemnity that had worn away the smile seemingly forever. Horacio, tall, thin and also dark with tight, curly black hair, wore a thin moustache that stretched across his wide face with his smile. Hector was older, perhaps in his mid twenties, and the leader of the group judging by his commanding presence. Blonde with light brown eyes, he stood tall, was solidly built and wore a flat straw hat pushed back on his head.

Paco shook their hands and sat down. "I invite you all to supper."

Hector stood, raised his glass, removed his hat and put it over his heart and said, "On behalf of my friends, Señor Iglesias, I accept the honor of your hospitality with the greatest pleasure."

"Genio, your friends are very formal."

"Give them time."

Paco ordered a beer and one for Genio, and Hector offered them cigars. "I assume we have time for a cigar before supper?"

"Always time for a cigar," Paco said.

The waiter returned with the beer, and they chatted about the university and about Havana. All three were Havana natives and lived with their parents. Paco told them of his flight from Colosía and how Havana had changed since he arrived.

"As a Spaniard, what do you think of Cuban freedom, Señor Iglesias?" Horacio asked. "Genio says he's not sure how you feel."

"That's because I have mixed feelings." Paco had heard of student debates and was eager to test himself against these young intellectuals. "I prefer to remain a Spanish citizen. I might be more enthusiastic about Cuban freedom if not for the problems it would bring."

"Such as?" Horacio said.

"Anarchy, Horacio. We Spaniards, all of us, have an affinity for anarchy."

"We're Cubans, Señor Iglesias," Hector said.

"I meant as a people. Cubans are Spanish by blood, heritage and tradition and carry our Spanish ancestors' traits."

"That's true," Manuel said, "but there is a great difference between Cubans and Spaniards."

"And for good reason," Paco said. "Cubans are born into the hospitable tropics, a warm, gentle environment, and feel more relaxed and secure than those of us who were reared in the bitter extremes of Iberia. But we have the same blood, like the English and the Americans. Their Common Law heritage, more than anything else, keeps them free. We have no such tradition. Each Hispanic person, in his heart, lives by his own laws. We are all anarchists at heart."

"That is true, Sir," Hector said, "but what does that particular truth have to do with our freedom? You say our freedom would be dangerous because of our leanings toward anarchy, but if Spaniards have the same heritage, why are we better off under Spain?"

"Our wine is bitter, but it is our wine?"

Watching Genio smile throughout the discussion, Paco could not tell whether he was anticipating his annihilation or his victory.

"Ah, you have read Martí," Hector said; then turning to Genio, "You have underestimated your father. I am now convinced he is a revolutionary like the rest of us."

"Not quite," Paco said. "To me a revolutionary is one who fights for his beliefs, and I am not ready to fight. Talk is cheap, gentlemen."

Genio slapped Hector's shoulder. "You're dead, Hector."

"Not yet, my friend," he said. Turning to Paco, he pushed his hat back and continued, "Would you call José Martí a revolutionary?"

"Yes."

"He only talks," Hector said.

"Martí talks to the people through his writings. For that they exiled him to Madrid, where he continued writing and talking. The pen is his weapon. If he were to take up arms he and those stupid enough to follow him would be wiped out. He has enough sense first to seek money and support. The pen is his cannon."

"Are you challenging us to do the same?" Manuel asked.

"Not at all. I chose not to join the rebels in the Ten Years War. It was not worth risking everything for a questionable dream, which, if fulfilled, would not help me and mine. I work for my family and for Cuba by continuing to farm. I produce sugar and sell it. That is how I contribute to Cuba's well being."

"Genio says you fought, Señor Iglesias," Manuel said.

"Genio should not tell part of the story without the rest. I did, but not for the rebellion. I fought to keep some villagers from being slaughtered, and I would do it again."

"So there is something worth fighting for?" Hector asked.

"Of course. Tell me, what in Cuban freedom is worth dying for? How does Spain harm us? Whose life is threatened?"

They all looked at Hector.

"Killing is not the only infamy, Señor Iglesias," Hector said. "Unfair and crippling taxation, denial of free speech and assembly, a military government, no jury trials. In other words, they deny us important rights to which we are justly entitled."

"And the right to make money?" Paco asked.

For the first time Hector showed anger. "Are you saying money is our cause?"

"No, Hector. I believe you are idealistic and honorable men who want to improve Cuba. But many rebels die without understanding why. I know I sound cynical, but I have seen men kill for nothing and die for the same nothing. I also see old men sending young men to die."

"I think I understand," Horacio said. He turned to Hector who was still sulking. "You fool, he is just trying to tell you to understand what you risk your life for before you risk it."

"I could not have said it better," Paco said. "Now, is anybody else hungry?"

Paco put his arm around Hector's shoulder and said, "What career are you preparing for?"

"Law."

"What kind of practice do you plan?"

"International law," he said, seriously and with conviction. "I think relations between nations is the most challenging career of all."

"I agree, Hector. Not only the relations between Spain and Cuba, but also between Cuba and the United States. The way we are going, our most important relationship will soon be with the United States."

Hector smiled in agreement.

*

Next day Paco went to Isabel's apartment and knocked on the door. Hearing no answer he knocked again. He put his ear to the door and heard a noise. He knocked again and waited. Isabel opened the door and looked at him as if he were a stranger.

"May I come in?"

"Of course, Tío."

With the curtains drawn on the two large windows of the spacious living room Paco could barely see where he was walking. As he took a few steps he accidentally kicked a bottle that went spinning under the sofa. "Sorry. I did not see it."

"That's all right," she said, taking a kimono off the couch so he could sit. "What brings you here?"

"I had business and wanted to see you and Genio. How are you getting along?"

"Fine. I haven't had a chance to clean up. You caught me by surprise."

Clothes were draped over chairs, a second empty rum bottle stood on the end table next to two ashtrays full of cigar butts. From the way Isabel moved Paco could see she was wearing nothing underneath her silk robe tied around the waist.

"Genio gave me your address."

"He's sweet. Took me to supper one evening to a place called *El Gallo de Oro*. What a dump! If he invites you, don't go."

"Too late. We ate there last night."

"Well, it's the thought that counts, I suppose," she said, reaching for a long, thin cigar and lighting it. "Oh, I'm sorry. Care for one?"

"Sure, thanks."

She lit his cigar and hers and sat down beside him. "You have a nice place here," he said.

"It's really my friend's. I help with the rent until I can find my own apartment."

"Is your money holding out?"

"Oh yes, fine. And thanks for the check. It came in handy." She took a long drag.

"You smoke now, I see."

"I do as I please now," she said smiling.

"What do you want, Isabel?"

"To live my life without nagging."

Paco detected the belligerency behind her words and sensed she was ready for a fight. "It's nice to make your own rules," he said. "But that brings its own problems."

"Please, Tío, don't start."

"I won't. I'm just happy to see you healthy and happy."

"I'm both. How's Mamá? Angry, I'm sure."

"The way you left shocked us all."

"There was no other way. She'd have raised hell."

"Probably."

"And Tía Magdalena? And Marta? Are they well?"

"Yes, yes. They all miss you."

"Listen, Tío, I really don't care how much anybody misses me. I don't live for their comfort, and you can tell them that."

They heard a knock on the door.

"*Un momento, Tío.*"

She opened the door slightly and whispered, "You're early."

"You said two o'clock," the middle-aged man said, looking at his watch, "and it's half past."

"I can't now. Come back in an hour."

"I can't. It's now or nothing."

She walked him out and closed the door behind her. After a few minutes she returned and, before closing the door, said, "Thanks, Carlos. I'll make it up to you."

"Who was that?"

"A friend. We had a date, but I can see him another time."

"I don't want to spoil your plans."

"It's all right, Tío. He'll be back."

"Are you going together?"

"Just a friend."

"Is he from Matanzas?"

"Havana."

"Who is he?"

"Why all the questions? Don't you understand I won't put up with spying?"

"I just like to know who your friends are."

"Drop it!"

"Have you found a job?"

"Not yet, but I'm looking."

"What kind of work do you seek?"

She looked at him as if she would yell at him again, but said, "Anything. I'd prefer an entertainment job, you know, singer or dancer, something like that."

"Sounds like fun. Good luck."

"Look, Tío, I have this appointment, you know. And I have to dress and tidy up. Could we meet again later?"

"Sure, Isabel. I leave tomorrow morning, but I'll return often. Next time."

"Next time, let me know."

"Of course."

As soon as he walked in the door, both Lydia and Magdalena accosted him.

"How is she?" Their voices stumbled into each other's like a poorly rehearsed operatic duet.

"Fine, living with a girl friend. They share the rent in a nice apartment in a good neighborhood."

"Does she look all right? Is she eating well?" Magdalena asked.

"She looks healthy. I did not have time to take her to dinner. Next time."

Lydia asked nothing, which gave Paco the impression she shared his suspicions about Isabel's activities. Paco said nothing about the condition of the apartment or the strange visitor, whom he suspected was both less and more than a friend. He talked with Magdalena for a while, answered most of her questions, and went upstairs to see Marta.

After a hug and kiss, Marta asked how Genio and Isabel were.

"The ladies only asked about Isabel. Genio is fine. I met three of his friends. Nice boys. He is happy and seems to be doing well."

Paco described his apartment and how clean he kept it. Then he told her about Isabel and her angry reaction to his questions. Telling her about the visitor drew a sad frown. "That sounds bad."

"I know. Next month I go back. She will not put me off."

*

As the month passed Paco's worry grew. Neither of Genio's next two letters mentioned Isabel, even though Paco had asked about her. Paco had written to her also, but she never responded.

In Havana he went directly to Genio's apartment. Genio spoke excitedly about his university work and especially about the history professor who spoke so eloquently of patriotism and rebellion. "He says it's just a matter of time before the revolution resumes. He's brilliant, Papá. Knows everything. He was wounded in the Ten Years War in Camagüey. He's fine now, but, well, he's great!"

It was clear Genio had set his sights on the upcoming rebellion. Knowing he could not stop him by demands or advice, Paco turned the conversation to Isabel. "Have you seen her lately?"

"She's disappeared."

"Left Havana?"

"Moved."

"What about her roommate?"

"Doesn't know either."

"Did she say whether she left Havana?"

"I think she's still here."

"Please, tell me what you know."

"Not much. Her roommate said she was still in town, but wouldn't say where."

"Listen, Genio, if you know something, don't keep it from me. I may be the only one who can help her."

"I know, Papá, but ..."

"I leave it to your conscience." Paco lit a cigar. "Have one?"

"Sure, Papá."

Paco handed him one and lit it for him, and they both took several draws without looking at each other. "I guess I won't see her," Paco said. "And I promised I would."

Genio's face had become serious, but he said nothing.

"Where shall we eat tonight? *El Gallo de Oro?*"

"If you like, Papá. Look, I would like to tell you more, but ..."

"I won't press you, Genio, but if you want to help her ..."

"It's you, not her I'm concerned about."

"That bad?"

"She's in a bad house," he said, looking at the floor.

"Give me the address at supper, and I will see her tomorrow."

"Please, Papá. Don't go there."

"I must, Genio."

Animated discussion did not enliven that evening's supper. Both Paco and Genio could think of nothing but Isabel and her bleak future. Paco slept poorly that night. Before waking, he dreamed he had fallen into a dry, brown canyon from which there was no escape. High in one tall tree hung a ripe fruit, luscious and gigantic, but he could not reach it or shake it loose, and he was starving. He jumped out of bed and washed his face, trying to wipe away the thoughts that had trampled his peace. At the department of agriculture that morning he floundered through his business, sleepwalking through negotiations over rights to sell directly to foreign buyers. Afterwards, he stopped for a quick lunch and went in search of Isabel.

By mid-afternoon Paco found the address Genio gave him. The large house on the edge of the prominent Vedado district looked like the home of a prosperous businessman. Two large royal palms stood in the front yard, and the porch reached around the front and sides of the house. The yellow brick, two-story house with white trim blended into the affluent neighborhood. Paco knocked on the door and waited until a pleasant looking, middle-aged woman opened. "Yes, Señor?"

"I am looking for Isabel Iglesias."

"She's occupied right now, but you're welcome to come in and wait. May I offer you a glass of rum?"

"Thank you," he said, and walked in. The place was well decorated, not garish as he had expected, but in good taste with beautiful landscape paintings on the walls and comfortable plush furniture throughout the several waiting rooms. A pretty, young girl brought him a Daiquirí and asked if she could sit with him.

"Thank you, but I am waiting for someone."

About half an hour later Paco saw a middle-aged man walk down the ornate staircase, sliding his hand along the polished mahogany banister as if caressing it. Behind him came Isabel dressed in a short-skirted dress with a plunging neckline. The man reached the bottom of the stairs, turned, and said something to her that made her giggle. Straightening his tie she said goodbye and looked around the room until her eyes fell on Paco. She drew a breath and then a scowl crawled across her face as she walked toward him.

"What the hell are you doing here?"

"I told you I would see you on my next trip to Havana."

"So now you know." She sat down and folded her arms across her chest.

"Yes, and I will not ask what you do here because you detest questions."

"I'll tell you anyway. I earn a good living, I meet nice people, I answer to no one, and I love it."

"Sounds like perfection."

Her reaction showed she did not understand how to take his comment. "For me, yes."

"Well, it is not! I will ask no questions, but I will say this: you are coming home with me."

"Like hell," she said, standing.

Paco stood and said, "Sit down. I have more."

"Suppose I'm not interested?"

"I think you will be."

She sat and looked at him as if daring him to say anything important.

"There is something I should have told you long ago. Everyone concerned, including myself, thought it was better for you not to know. That was a mistake."

Her eyes squinted with curiosity.

"Who is your father?"

"A bastard who abandoned my mother and me before I was born. What else do I need to know?"

"You are almost right, but not completely. Your father never returned to Spain."

"What?"

"He has lived near you since you were born. He saw you the first day you breathed and has watched over you every day of your life. And he has loved you all that time, but he was never able to tell you."

"Why not?"

"Because everyone thought it better for you and for his wife, who does not know."

"So to protect his wife?"

"Partly, but mainly to protect you."

"Bah! Lies. I have no father."

"Damn it, Isabel. It's me!"

She looked at him as if she would laugh. Then she looked down at the floor. Not knowing what to say, he waited. She finally looked up with tears streaming down her cheeks. A dam had burst. She raised her fists and hit him as hard as she could. Barely realizing what she was doing, he grabbed her hands and brought her to him to embrace her. "I do not blame you, Isabel. You are right to hate me. I behaved badly, but I have always loved you. You must believe that. I have always looked on you as my daughter."

She could not stop staring at him. "I suppose you think that makes a difference?"

"Please, Isabel," he said, trying to comfort her.

"Leave me alone. I want you to go." She got up and disappeared into the darkness at the top of the stairs.

The woman who brought Paco in had seen the commotion and came to him. "What is wrong, señor?"

He shook his head. "May I wait here for her?"

"Are you going upstairs to her?"

"I think so, but not right away. I'll have another rum."

"Certainly." She walked upstairs and disappeared.

In a few minutes the same girl brought another daiquiri. Paco lit a cigar and sipped his drink for a long time. Finally the middle-aged woman came down and said, "Please go up. Room six. Isabel waits for you."

He put his drink and cigar down and took the stairs two at a time, glad Isabel wanted to see him. He hoped it meant she had got over her anger and wanted to talk, daughter to father. He found number six and knocked on the door.

"Come in."

He found her sitting on her bed. She had stopped crying and stood as he entered. "Isabel, I …"

Before he could say another word she said, "I don't want to hear anymore. If you are my father, you are an even bigger bastard than I thought. You let me think my father was an irresponsible son of a bitch all these years. You made me an orphan for your own selfish good. Now you want to take over my life. Where were you when I needed a father to protect me from those witches? Where were you when I needed a father to teach me about love? Now you come with your miserable apology. Well it's too late. I no longer need a father, you bastard! You can go to hell!"

"I don't blame you, Isabel, but …"

"Get out!"

Try as he might, tears had blurred his vision. He stood and turned to walk out. At the door he turned again and said, "Please, Isabel. I love you and always will. Don't turn away from me."

"Out!"

Instead of leaving that afternoon Paco decided to see Genio first. The awful secret was out, and there was no holding it any longer. The guilt he felt was unbearable. Isabel was right, he thought. I behaved horribly. I must make amends.

He stood at Genio's door in complete dread before knocking. Genio came out in his robe with his hair uncombed. "*Que pasa?* I thought you were leaving on the afternoon train."

"I had to see you. I just saw Isabel. It was awful; just as you said." He stopped to wipe his brow with a handkerchief.

"Sit down, Papá."

Paco sat on the living room sofa.

"I was about to make some coffee. How about some?"

"No, thanks, Genio. Son, I told Isabel about her father."

Genio looked at him waiting. "Yes?"

"I'm her father." He waited for the news to sink in. "We kept it secret for several reasons that you could probably guess, and I don't want to go into details. She hates me now. Said I made her an orphan. It was horrible."

Genio looked down for a moment and then at his father. "Papá, you did what you thought was right. You've always cared for her. If she doesn't realize that, it's her fault, not yours."

"But she hates me, Genio."

"She will figure it out, Papá. Don't worry. I've never met a more honorable man than you. I am proud to be your son."

Paco stood and embraced him. "Thank you, son."

*

During the train ride back he rehearsed what he would tell Marta. As well as he knew her he could not guess how she would react. Still, he had no choice. It would be his first step toward winning back his daughter.

He reached the house as the sun was setting. Lydia and Magdalena were waiting on the front porch. He told them he had not had time to visit Isabel, but would do so next trip.

"Did Genio say anything about her?" Magdalena asked.

"No, except that he had not seen her in a couple of weeks."

"She must have moved, because one of my letters came back unanswered," Lydia said. "Do you have her new address?"

"No."

He left them on the porch and went directly upstairs. Marta put down the book she was reading and smiled. "How good to have you back! I have missed you terribly. All they talk about is Isabel. How is she?"

"They barraged me before I could sit down. Let's go for a walk, Marta. We have not walked together in a long time."

She stood, took his arm, and walked him downstairs and out the front door. "We will return soon," Paco said.

"How is Genio?" Marta asked.

"He seems to be doing very well. He likes his professors, especially one who talks of revolution. I think he has mesmerized our son."

"Revolutions attract the young."

"I saw Isabel." Paco hesitated, almost changed his mind, but instead said, "She lives in a brothel."

Marta put her hand to her lips and walked in silence for a time. Finally she said, "She just wants to torment them."

"That is not all," he said, not knowing how to continue.

She looked at him strangely, and in her face he saw the trust and love he had come to take for granted. It almost stopped him, but then, "Marta, I told her about her father."

"What about him? Paco, you look so strange."

"Do you love me, Marta?" Without waiting for her answer he said, "I hope you will forgive me. I am her father."

She kept walking. They walked a long way before she spoke. "I often wondered why you showed so little interest in her and yet worried so much about her, and why you always took her side against our boys."

He could not speak.

"Frankly I suspected something, the way you and Lydia barely exchanged a word. Are you seeing each other?"

"Of course not! It was as I told you years ago. She planned it all in detail. She never wanted a man, just a white baby. I finally realized her scheme and felt used, no, furious. I agreed to remain silent only if Magdalena would bring up the baby as a member of the family, and, of course, to protect you. I was afraid you would hate me."

"Protect yourself, you mean."

"They encouraged me and made it so easy. I must have looked like the ideal man for her scheme—white, young and stupid. Lydia was very kind and gentle then, always going out of her way to be sweet, so unlike her usual way. Then, one night, she came to my room unannounced. I was shocked of course, not knowing what she wanted. She was anything but subtle. She returned every night for two weeks, until she knew for certain she was pregnant. Then she stopped, saying it was her time of the month."

"Didn't you realize what she was doing?"

"No. She said she wanted only to serve me, but she used me. I could have killed her I was so angry. She was carrying my baby, and I couldn't even talk about the child. It had nothing to do with you, Marta. She was here ... I was lonely. I missed you so much. I did not mean to hurt you, but I hurt Isabel even more. She hates me and blames me for making her an orphan, and she is right. Now you will blame me for my faithlessness, and you will be right. Lydia and Magdalena convinced me that it would hurt Isabel to know, and if she knew, you would soon find out."

"You should have told me."

"I know that now."

"It hurts to think of you loving another, Paco. You have thrust a knife into my heart."

"I never loved her or anyone but you. It was brute, childish lust, not love."

As he walked he became aware of the processing plant's sickening, sweet odor, and he wanted to run away from its all-pervasive presence, to take a ship somewhere, Asturias, perhaps, anywhere away from this place. With a new beginning he would make it up to Marta, start a new life free of deception. No, he thought, I must do it right here in this pungent alembic where ruthlessness boils us down to human bagasse. In Asturias we struggled to live. What do we struggle for here?

She walked on beside him saying nothing. With the moon directly overhead like a beacon lighting her world for the first time, her head filled with confusion—hating him for the times she had stood by him, feeling betrayed by the terrible secret, wanting children so badly and having two beautiful sons, wanting him so much and fearing she would lose him, and lying about the smallpox, and he accepting her horrible scars that she could not show him at the port, and knowing how she disgusted him, and he accepting her and learning to love her again, and all these years being ardent lovers.

"We are even, Paco. I've always felt guilty for surprising you with my smallpox. I could have told you, but I, too, was afraid. Love needs trust, and neither of us had yet learned to trust. Perhaps we have both learned to trust enough to confess finally."

Paco stopped and embraced her. "You have never looked as beautiful as you do now. I have never wanted any other woman."

"I know, Paco."

That evening they made love. With the windows open and the breeze blowing, the curtains rolled like waves on the ocean. The two days since Paco had left for Havana felt like months. Now, lying in bed, a tropical breeze caressing their warm bodies, they were again lovers, but now free, for both had shed a lingering guilt. For the first time, Lydia did not come between Paco and his wife. He had allowed Lydia's demands to eat away at his judgment, but now that the task of healing had begun he would show Marta that she was his only love, as he would show his daughter that she had a loving father. He could see now the degree to which guilt had come between him and both these women. With his bands loosened he rejoiced.

"I think I should return to Havana. See if she has thought things over."

"Good idea. Are you going to tell the ladies?"

"Not till I see Isabel."

"Good."

The next morning Paco ate breakfast with Ignacio, Magdalena and Marta as always. Afterwards he announced he would return to Havana.

"But you just arrived," Magdalena said.

"I left some unfinished business. I will be back in a day or two."

As the carriage picked him up a half hour later, Marta said, "Maybe I could help. Isabel likes me."

Paco had wanted to invite her, but he feared his recent confession might have turned her against Isabel. "I think you could. How long will it take to get ready?"

"A minute," she said, running up the porch steps, "I don't need much. Be right down. Also I'll ask Lydia to prepare some food for Genio."

Paco sat back in the coach and lit a cigar as she disappeared into the house.

*

They arrived in Havana shortly after noon and checked into the Hotel Inglaterra. Barely aware of distant thunder and black clouds smothering the horizon, they took a carriage to Genio's apartment, where Paco left Marta with her bundle of meat, plantains and black beans. A light drizzle had dampened the traffic, so the ride to Isabel's place took less time than before. On the way he rehearsed what he would say as the horse clopped rhythmically along the street: Don't be aggressive. She'll object and perhaps even be rude and abusive, but don't relent. At the house he told the driver, "I should not be long, but if I am, wait."

The driver looked amazed at this man who had just left his wife and come to a brothel.

Paco walked up to the porch and knocked on the door. The same woman opened it.

"I'm sorry, Señor, but Isabel told me to say she does not want to see you."

"I know, but I want to see her. May I come in?"

"Of course, Señor. Please sit down. I'll call her."

The room was nearly empty with only two girls talking at a sofa across the room. They quickly saw he was not interested in their seductive smiles and resumed their conversation. In a few minutes the woman returned and sat with Paco. "She will not come down, Señor."

Saying nothing Paco stood and ascended the stairs two at a time to room six and knocked.

"Yes?"

"It is Paco."

"Go away. Didn't Evelina tell you?"

"I won't be long."

She came to the door, opened it and walked back in. "What?" she barked.

"I brought Marta. She is with Genio."

"Does she know where I am?"

"Yes."

She turned in anger and shook her fists above her head.

"Do not concern yourself," he said. "I did not tell your mother or Magdalena."

"Why not?"

201

"What would I tell them?"

"That I lived too long in that mausoleum."

"Marta sympathizes with you."

"She's always been kind. More than those meddling witches."

"We all love you; only we show it in different ways."

"Not my mother. She loves only herself."

Paco felt the same way, but said, "That is harsh, Isabel."

"Why don't you just say what you came to say and leave?"

"I came to do, not to say."

She crossed her arms in defiance.

"Think what you are doing, Isabel. Is money so important that you would sell your body to strangers?"

"You think this is for money? Fool!"

"Why, then?"

"Why should men have all the fun? I'll never saddle myself to one bastard for life like the good little ninnies. I have my fun; they can keep the housework and ass-kissing."

"I don't believe that," he said. "Inside you is much that is good and true and loving."

"The only thing inside me right now is an old man's juice, and I can wash that out with vinegar and water. If you'd like a piece, just say the word."

Without realizing what he had done, he watched her careen backward onto her bed. Paco looked down at his stinging hand that had slapped her as if without his permission. Her teeth clenched through a smile of crystalline hatred. With her eyes flooded she stood and walked slowly toward him and slapped his face as hard as she could. Then she did it again and again, and he offered no resistance. Finally she turned and walked to the table by her bed and lifted one of her cigars out of a box and lit it with shaking hands.

"You've done what you came for. Now leave."

"Forgive me, Isabel. I don't know what made me do that."

"I do. You're a man, a bastard, a *cabrón* and a *pendejo*. You are *mierda*, as a man and as a father."

Paco turned and walked into the hall and down the steps and out the front door to the waiting carriage. It had begun to drizzle, so the driver had raised the top. Paco got in, told the driver to take him back to Genio's address, and sat back in the seat and began to sob so hard he thought the driver would turn to look. He did not.

"How could you do such a stupid thing?" Marta said.

"I completely understand, Papá. She's infuriating. Sometimes she makes me so angry I want to do the same."

"Your mother is right, Genio. I am older and should know better, but something blinded me. She said the most horrible things. My vision blurred, and I became a savage."

"Let me go to her," Marta said. "Perhaps I can reach her."

"I doubt it, Marta, but try if you want. You cannot do any worse."

Marta gathered her purse and left, as Genio poured a glass of rum with some ice and lemon and handed it to his father.

"You are very kind, son."

They tried to converse, but they could not cut through the silence between them. Finally Paco said he would lie down a while. Genio said he would go out for a newspaper and disappeared.

Genio was sitting at his desk with the newspaper spread before him when Paco opened his eyes. He got up and stretched as Marta walked in, drenched. By her slow, spent appearance Paco knew she had not succeeded.

"What happened?"

"Nothing. What a horrible place. The woman did not want to let me in. I had to explain I was your wife. She complained that Isabel had spent the whole afternoon in her room. She was mad because Isabel was not bringing in money. Horrible!"

"Did you see her?"

"Yes. She was very sweet, but she will not come home. I never realized how much she hates her mother. And she called Magdalena a 'gutless zero.' She will never come home."

At the phrase, gutless zero, Paco recalled Magdalena's portrait in the living room and how stately and confident and full of wisdom she looked.

"I have never felt so helpless, Marta."

"Me too. We will have to depend on Genio." She reached over and grasped his hand. "See her often, Genio. Let her know we love her."

"I will, Mamá."

*

The train ride back to Matanzas was quiet and uneventful. They spoke little, each trapped in a web of recollections. Every once in a while Marta would take his hand as if to communicate beyond words. Past the window rain fell in a monotonous haze over the land, blackening the air.

"I have learned one thing, Marta. Genio is quite a man. I always felt he was my failure, the son who would not farm or work or do any of the things I liked. But he is profoundly good and decent."

"Why does that surprise you?"

"I don't know. Maybe I had a different idea of what a man should be. He has chosen study as his route to maturity. I ridiculed his free Cuba ideas, but they showed he cares passionately for something outside himself. I guess I'm proud of my chubby, unattractive son."

"I think he's quite attractive."

Driving into the hacienda Paco wondered aloud how he should break the news.

"There is no way to make it painless. Want me to do it?"

"No," he said, lighting a cigar and blowing out a breath of smoke as if it were his last. "I have shirked my duty long enough."

The two women had seen the carriage enter the path and swarmed around them as Paco set down their two small suitcases on the porch.

Magdalena was the first to speak: "Is she eating well?"

"Sit down," he said. Then, in a gentle tone he took a long draw on his cigar. "Isabel has rebelled against all of us. The life she has chosen is exciting to her and horribly repellent to us. Both Marta and I separately tried, but we could not convince her to come home. I think we have no choice but to respect her wish to be left alone. One day, perhaps, she will realize her error."

The two sat rapt. With her jaws tightly clamped and the muscles in her face twitching, Lydia seemed ready to explode. Magdalena sat slumped in her chair in abject sadness, cheeks streaked with tears. Both understood what Paco had avoided saying, and neither would voice the word.

"She seems happy," he said, as an afterthought.

Lydia stood and walked away. "As far as I am concerned, she can stay there. I never want to see her again."

Magdalena broke into violent sobbing, and Marta put her arms around her and rocked her like a baby. Swirling in smoke, Paco's head looked like a mummy's wrapped in fine gauze. He sat still as an exhumed cadaver, holding back tears. Finally he stood and put his hand on Magdalena's shoulder, patted it, and went into the kitchen, where Lydia was cutting onions as if they were human heads. She looked up. "You told her, didn't you?"

"She had a right to know."

Paco had felt Lydia's hatred before and was prepared. She wiped her hand on her apron and passed it over her hair and then continued cutting onions.

"You are my greatest mistake, Paco."

He did not answer and returned to the living room. Marta had taken Magdalena upstairs, so he went out back to find Ignacio. He saddled his horse in the barn and rode out to the steam press shed. Ignacio had been supervising the men who worked the press and walked to his father as he dismounted.

"Did you get don Miguel's hacienda?"

"Yes."

"At your price?"

"I saw Isabel and Genio."

"But what about the land?"

"Isabel works in a brothel."

Ignacio paused a moment. "I'm not surprised. She always liked the wild side of life. Is she well?"

"You don't understand, Ignacio. Women in that profession have short lives."

"She enjoys it. What's so good about living a long and boring life?"

"How can you be so cold?"

"What are you upset about? She's not your daughter."

Paco had often felt like hitting Ignacio, and the urge almost overpowered him. Recalling his recent blow-up with Isabel he controlled himself. "She is my daughter, Ignacio, but even if she were not, I have lived in the same house with her all her life; how could I not care about her."

Ignacio looked at his father dumbfounded. "She's my sister. What do you know!" He put his arm over Paco's shoulder. "I didn't know. I'm sorry, Papá."

"I also saw Genio. He's doing well. Likes studying and has good friends."

"Revolutionaries, I'll bet."

"Why do you say that?"

"Genio always limped on that foot. There's talk of a new rebellion. Think he'll get dragged into it?"

"I hope not."

"It may be the best thing. Might give him a purpose and maybe a little ambition."

"I have to get back. Later you can give me a report on what has happened since I left."

CHAPTER 7 - SIX YEARS LATER, APRIL 1895

*

Spain Cancels U.S. - Cuba Trade Pact and
Increases Taxes and Trade Restrictions

*

José Martí Addresses Cigar Makers in Tampa, Florida.
Raising Money for Cuban Freedom

*

September 1895: Martí Declares
Cuban War of Independence

*

Spain's Reconcentration Program Forces
hundreds of Thousands of Cubans into Cities.
Thousands Die of Starvation and Disease

*

Paco joined Magdalena and Marta at the table and opened his newspaper. The headline in large print read, "Martí Returns." Paco wanted to read the article, but Lydia came in with her tray. He folded the paper, smiled, and said, "Good Morning." The years had not been kind to her. The shapely young woman had grown even more solid and chunky. She reminded Paco of a chest of drawers with spindly legs. Even at forty-nine, wrinkles had squeezed her face into a dried prune with cheekbones pushing against bronze skin. She still wore her thick, brown, gray-streaked, wavy hair tied in a bun that hung on her neck. She did not respond, but served the breakfast and then pushed the swinging door into the kitchen.

"Looks like another beautiful spring day," Paco said.

"I saw some dark clouds on the horizon," Magdalena said.

"We need the rain," he said.

"What do you hear from Genio?" Magdalena said.

"He graduates on the seventh of June," Marta said.

"It is a shame he married so hastily. I wanted to give them a party," Magdalena said. "But we will make it a double celebration—graduation and wedding with lots of people. I love a big party; don't you, Marta?"

Remembering the village fiestas in Colosía years earlier, Marta said, "That would be nice."

"Celia is beautiful and cultured, Marta. Genio chose well."

"If only she were not such a revolutionary," Marta said.

Having finished serving the juice, coffee and rolls, Lydia walked toward the kitchen, but before she opened the swinging door, she said, "All for the boys; nothing for the girl."

"You never even mention her name, Lydia," Paco said, as the swinging door closed behind her.

Magdalena shrugged. "Pay no attention, Paco. She is all bluster, but she thinks of nothing but Isabel."

"One would never know it," Marta said. "How can she cut her off like that?"

Before Magdalena could reply Lydia burst open the kitchen door and stood over the table with her fists jammed into her hips. "How I treat my daughter is my business. Tend to your own; I will tend to mine."

"She belongs to all of us, Lydia," Magdalena said. "We worry about her too."

Glaring at Paco she spit out, "Hypocrites!" Then she turned and disappeared.

Marta and Magdalena both looked at Paco. "She certainly leaves no doubt about whom she blames," he said.

"No one is to blame," Magdalena said. "We all did our best."

"This discussion is growing whiskers," Paco said and got up.

"But you have not eaten," Marta said.

Without answering he continued out the back door to the barn, saddled his horse and rode out. Scenes like that had become common, and they angered Paco more than he would admit.

Seeing Ignacio in the distance he rode toward him thinking, I am the owner, and he treats me as his lackey. Paco considered turning the farm over to him so he could relax, but it had grown to one of the largest plantations in the western part of the island; surely he could not hand his hothead son such responsibility. Ignacio had matured in intelligence, size, and strength, but he had also grown more obstinate. But Paco knew that Ignacio must one day take the reins. His only hope was to retain control until Ignacio mellowed as much as he would.

Ignacio called from the shade of the press building, "*Hola, Papá.*"

"Everything all right?"

"Everything is not my assignment; my operation is going well, as always."

"Good. Did you see the newspaper this morning?"

"Just the headline. So Martí's back. *La gran mierda.*"

"He must be important if the Spaniards hate him so much, Ignacio. Lots of people consider him Cuba's savior."

"A great fool is more like it. Does he really think he can succeed against the odds?"

"You never know. He has raised much money from the exile communities in the States and Latin America."

"But we're the ones who count, sugar producers and tobacco men, and we aren't stupid enough to support him."

"Don't be so sure, Ignacio. Spain no longer stands behind us, except for more taxes."

"I'll stick with the money. Money is power. Martí may get cigar makers' pennies, but Spain has the factory owners' dollars. I'd rather see the United States take us over than the rabble. Americans know how to run a country."

"Funny," Paco said. "Martí said he would prefer Spain to American annexation."

"Not me. Spanish rule or annexation for me."

"Genio thinks Martí is a genius."

"Hah! His dream will burst soon enough. Besides, now that he's married and graduating, he won't have time for such foolishness."

"Have you read his pamphlets? I only hope he does not ruin his chances for a good position."

"He will, like everything else."

"He has done well."

"Wait till the Captain General sees his pamphlets."

"You mean your friend, the Spaniard you want to keep in control?"

"I have no friends, only allies and enemies."

"Those are the words of an old man, Ignacio."

"Not old, Papá, mature."

"Revolution means bloodshed, Ignacio. But Spain has oppressed us for years."

"I don't feel oppressed, Papá; least of all by Spain."

"I have to get back. See you tonight."

That evening Paco retrieved the newspaper and sat down on the front porch to read it. The article recounted that on April 11th, José Martí had landed on a rocky beach called La Playita in the eastern part of the island after braving a raging storm during the night passage from Haiti. Martí, General Máximo Gómez, the leading general of the Ten Years War, and several other leaders had made the trip in a yacht after their call to arms in February. In March, the second most important general, Antonio Macéo, the Black leader who almost single-handedly carried the Ten Years War in the east, returned from forced exile. Now, with Martí home for the first time in fifteen years, hostilities were imminent. The Spanish government was amassing troops all over the island in anticipation.

Paco put the paper down and stood with a sudden urge to see Genio, who was sure to join the rebels, perhaps already had. Paco knew he would not be able to dissuade him, but he might offer help and advice.

That evening Paco told Marta about the impending rebellion, and she agreed that he should go to their son.

"Will you see Isabel too?"

"I'll try."

*

The early train arrived in Havana at ten o'clock. Paco found Celia alone in Genio's apartment.

"*Hola, Señor Iglesias.* How good to see you," she said, leading him into their small living room. "Business in Havana?"

"No, just to see you and Genio."

"Have you heard about Martí?"

"I saw the headlines in Matanzas."

You've come to try to talk Genio out of going."

"Frankly, yes."

"We're working as hard as we can for the revolution."

"I know."

"We live for the revolution, Señor Iglesias. It comes before all else."

She spoke and stood with her arms hanging down like a military leader at attention, snapping orders.

"I know how devoted you both are, but I have lived through civil war. There is nothing worse, Celia. People become animals, worse than animals. Animals do not kill their own."

"No sacrifice is too great. All devoted revolutionaries feel that way. We would willingly die for *Cuba libre*."

"Do you expect Genio soon?"

"Yes. I'm preparing lunch. Please eat with us."

"Thank you, yes."

Genio walked in about an hour later. Paco was in the kitchen with Celia as she cooked, chatting about life on the farm and about Magdalena and Marta and the rest. Seeing his father, Genio's face lit up. "How good to see you, Papá. I did not know you were coming."

"He wants to stop the revolution, Genio," Celia said, smiling.

Paco frowned at her comment, but did not respond. "How go the studies?"

"Very good, Papá. Just a few weeks more."

"Any jobs?"

"A small law firm here in Havana wants me to join them."

"Excellent. How do you like Havana, Celia?"

"I love it. My parents live only an hour away."

"If you have no plans, I'd like to take you to supper."

"That would be very kind of you."

Paco was reluctant to bring up the subject of the revolution, recalling Celia's earlier reaction. Near the end of their meal in the Hotel Inglaterra dining room, he said, "Now that Martí has come home, they expect the revolution to start soon."

"Within days, I hope, Papá. All the major players are present, Macéo, Gómez, and now Martí. It will be glorious."

"How do you feel about American annexation?"

Celia looked as if she would explode. She fidgeted with her hair, moved around in her chair and fumbled with the menu. Genio had asked her to let him carry the argument, but it seemed she would not be able to contain herself.

"That's the only point where Martí and I disagree," Genio said. "America would be better than Spain. But independence is our only real hope. If the U.S. takes us over, we will remain a colony. It's time we became our own masters, made our own laws, and charted our own course. You see that, don't you, Papá?"

"I see you will make a good lawyer, Genio. You argue well. Doesn't he, Celia?"

She smiled for the first time since sitting down. In the crowded dining room the chatter of people distracted them, so they could barely hear each other. It seemed the news had animated everybody. They talked about the revolution for a long time before the food came. It was evident Genio was not going to change course. He and Celia seemed happy with each other and with their work, so Paco made no further attempts to divert him.

After supper, Genio took them to El Gallo de Oro where they found a louder crowd. Manuel, Horacio and Hector were there with a few others debating the coming revolution. Manuel greeted Paco as an old friend. Hector tried to draw him into the debate, but Paco deflected the subject to another, for he was in no mood to hear about the glorious revolution that might cost him his son.

Next morning Paco awoke on the living room sofa. Genio and Celia had insisted he stay with them, even though he had reserved a room at the Hotel Inglaterra. A little stiff after sleeping on the narrow, lumpy sofa, he stretched and smelled coffee. He dressed and went in to find Genio and Celia waiting for him.

Looking at the kitchen clock he said, "You should have called me."

"Not the way you were sleeping," Genio said. "For a while we thought you had died."

"You slept well?" Celia asked.

"Quite well. Never this late."

After a breakfast of fruit, bread and coffee, he gathered his things and left for the train station. Paco's acceptance of Genio's revolutionary zeal had softened Celia.

Paco spent most of the trip back imagining his son cutting his way through eastern mountain brush, out of breath, sweating and panting. Before long, he had worked himself into a frantic state and couldn't sit still. With a mighty effort, he forced himself to think about the farm and Marta. Before long he was wandering through his youthful days in Asturias with his parents, milking the cow on a cold morning, and meeting Marta in the evenings at the village plaza. But no sooner had he calmed down, than he was again with Genio, praying he would not find his way into the fighting and cursing his young friends and General Gómez, and Macéo and Martí, and even Celia.

During the next month letters flew back and forth between Matanzas and Havana. Genio was still publishing articles trying to awaken the people to the cause of revolution. On the twentieth of May a headline blared: "Martí Shot." The brief article read:

> "Martí and General Gómez were in Dos Ríos preparing to begin an offensive when Royal soldiers attacked a nearby camp. Leaving with his troops, General Gómez ordered Martí to remain with the rear-guard, but Martí disobeyed and rode forth to his first military encounter. As he entered a narrow pass, a platoon of soldiers waiting in ambush shot him down. A companion, Angel de la Guardia, made several unsuccessful attempts to rescue him. Later General Gómez attempted to retake Martí's body, but he also failed. According to reports, the Spaniards have taken him to Santiago de Cuba."

Paco returned to his room, asked Marta to pack a small bag, and handed her the article. "I must see Genio right away before he does something impulsive."

Within minutes he was in his carriage headed to the train station. After the three longest hours of his life, stopping interminably at each town, and then finding a carriage to take him to his son, he knocked on Genio's door. Celia opened and embraced him. "I'm so happy to see you, Señor Iglesias," she said, leading him by the hand into the living room. "I'll fix some coffee." Paco was so anxious about Genio that he had forgotten to eat breakfast. At the mention of coffee he followed her and sat at the kitchen table.

"You must have heard about Martí," she said.

"This morning."

"Genio left yesterday."

"Oh no! Where?"

"Santiago de Cuba. With Hector, Horacio and Manuel. They've all joined Macéo's unit."

"My God!" He put his head in his hands. "But his graduation? He could have waited a few days."

"You couldn't have stopped him, Señor Iglesias. I tried."

"Please, no more formalities; call me Paco. You tried to stop him?"

"You know how much I've written and spoken for months, doing everything I could to help the revolution, but the day he told me he had joined and began packing his suitcase, everything changed. I felt helpless, devastated. In my mind I saw him lying dead in some mountain forest, or standing before a firing squad. Please believe me, I tried, I really did."

She began to sob. Paco held her to him, and she cried on his shoulder.

"When a man makes up his mind, there is nothing anyone can do," he said.

"You don't hate me?"

"Of course not."

"What shall I do?" she asked through sobs.

"Go to your parents until he returns."

"And leave it all to him? I couldn't, especially now. The doctor confirmed it a few days ago. I'm with child."

"Why, that's wonderful!"

"I sent you and Marta a letter day before yesterday. We didn't know during your last trip and wanted to be sure before we told you. That same afternoon we got the news about Martí. The next day Genio was gone."

"All the more reason to go home."

"I can't abandon him now; I must carry on."

"What can you do here that you cannot do at home?"

"They don't even want to hear the word, revolution. We argue all the time about it. They want us to remain a colony."

"As you know, I've had mixed feelings, but now that Genio is in it I am for the revolution."

"Then you understand why I can't go home to be pampered while Genio risks his life?"

"You are a woman, Celia."

"This woman can do more than you imagine."

"I know, Celia, it is just that, … Well, now that I am here, how about lunch?"

"Yes, thank you."

*

Before going to the train station, Paco decided to see Isabel again even if only for a moment. He was so filled with Genio and his action that he could barely think about Isabel, but he tried if only to avoid thinking about his son.

Seeing Paco, the woman's face stiffened. *"Buenas tardes, Señor."*

Walking in past her he said, "I must see Isabel."

"She is no longer here, Señor."

"Where, then?"

"She left no forwarding address."

"I am her father, Señora; it is important."

"I know, Señor. Truly I wish I could help you, but I can't. Please excuse me."

Paco stood staring at her for a moment and then thanked her, turned and walked out to the carriage.

At breakfast the next morning Paco reported on his trip to Havana. It had rained most of the night and the sun was just breaking through the viscous air. Though the house had been damp all night, the air, now unusually clear and fresh, blew through like a blessing. Magdalena's interest and excitement over the latest news of the revolution surprised Paco. She had heard of Martí's death and wondered how that would affect the war. When he told her Genio had joined the rebels, her smile unraveled. Thoughts of adventure and idealistic struggle melted into a vision of the young man in the thick of fighting. Until that moment the revolution had been an abstraction, a game to talk about and watch from afar. But now the abstraction had crystallized into brittle reality. Paco related what Celia had said and how her pregnancy had changed her feelings and attitude.

"The fingers of reality have tightened around her neck," Paco said. "Genio's marching off to battle has trampled their beautiful rhetoric into ashes."

Lydia stood listening after serving breakfast. As Paco related that Genio and his friends had joined General Antonio Macéo, a smile crept over Lydia's lips. Seeing him looking, her smile broadened. He knew she was gloating over his troubles, for he was the person she most hated, and she would let him know how she felt. He tried to ignore her and told of trying to talk Celia into going home to her parents and of her refusal.

"She is a strong and determined young woman," Paco said. "But her brave talk of glorious revolution has changed. Describing her horrible vision of Genio lying dead and covered in blood on a lonely battlefield, she cried."

As he related Celia's feelings Magdalena began to sob silently.

"Sorry, Magdalena. I did not mean to stir you."

With Lydia smiling and nodding knowingly at the end of the room with her arms crossed over her chest, Paco could stand it no longer.

"You have heard something funny, Lydia?" he growled through his teeth.

"Not funny, Señor Paco; fascinating. How do you feel knowing your son is walking into this deadly madness?"

"Proud, Lydia."

"I hope he gets his reward," Ignacio said.

"Meaning?" Paco asked.

"Idealists rarely benefit. They reward those who stay home and talk."

"I'm sick of your cynicism, Ignacio. What made you so hard?"

"I'm just pragmatic, Papá. You know I'm against this revolution. They can't win. Spanish soldiers will overwhelm them in days. But that doesn't mean I don't care about my brother."

"He is doing what he believes in, as I assume you are," Paco said.

"No one is criticizing you, Ignacio," his mother said.

"I am!" Paco shouted. "There is too much cynicism and anger and meanness. This room overflows with it, and I am sick of it."

"What are you talking about, Papá? Must I agree with you to be considered a member of the family?"

"Not just you, Ignacio," he said. Then, staring at Lydia, "I tried to see Isabel yesterday before I left."

Lydia's face collapsed into an ugly, twisted frown, and she turned toward the kitchen.

"I was going to wait to tell you in private, Lydia, but you seem to enjoy bad news."

She stopped and stood holding the swinging door ajar.

"I went to her house. The madam told me she left."

She turned at the word, madam. "Where?"

"She doesn't know."

"Is she still in Havana?"

Paco shrugged.

"Why you did not tell me last night?"

"Because until this moment you have not even wanted to hear her name."

"*Sinvergüenza!* How dare you talk to me like that? I am her mother, not an ignorant slave. Tell me!"

He stood, walked to her and led her into the kitchen and out to the back porch expecting her to resist, but she followed meekly. Out of earshot of the rest, he said, "Lydia, the woman said she had left with no forwarding address, but I think she knows more."

"What do you think?"

"I really do not know; perhaps she is sick."

Lydia fell into a rocking chair, put her hands to her face, sobbing hysterically and began to hit herself on the chest and head and to pull her hair.

"Stop it! That won't help," he said, grabbing her hands.

"What know you of help?"

"She is our daughter, Lydia, not yours alone, and I feel bad too. I have visited her on every trip to Havana, anything to keep in touch. I am still trying and will continue no matter what you say or do."

She looked at him and again started to cry violently as he stood watching. Finally she said, "I go crazy. I don't know what to do. I have tried to erase her from my soul, but I cannot. I hate everybody. I want only to die."

He raised and embraced her. She continued to cry in his arms. It was their first physical contact since before Marta came. Finally she backed away. "I must see her."

"I will take you to Havana, and together we will find her."

"Marta too," she said.

"Of course, and Magdalena."

"No, not Magdalena."

"She would be very hurt."

"I don't care. This time she will not come between us."

"Get ready. We leave right away."

Finding Marta and Magdalena on the front porch, Paco asked where Ignacio was."

"He said he had much to do and left," Marta said.

Paco told them Lydia wanted to go to Havana to find Isabel, and he would take her. Magdalena smiled and said, *"Gracias a Diós!* I have worried so much about both of them."

"I too," Paco said. We leave right away."

After thinking a few moments Magdalena said, "Paco, as much as I want to see Isabel, I think it would do them both much good to be alone together; I will stay."

"But you love Isabel too," Marta said.

"Think how Lydia has suffered," Magdalena said. "She needs to be alone with her daughter."

"That is very thoughtful, Magdalena," Paco said, glad he did not have to relate Lydia's sentiment.

"Marta and I will stay and look after Ignacio," Magdalena said. "Do not worry."

"Marta is going with us."

Marta looked at him with surprise.

"Yes, we have business in Havana. Come, Marta. We must get ready."

In their room Paco told Marta that Lydia did not want Magdalena to go. "Magdalena saved me the embarrassment of telling her."

"How different two sisters can be!"

An hour later, as Lydia, Marta and Paco were climbing into the carriage for the ride to the train station, Marta saw Magdalena looking out the living room window and went back in. "Won't you come out to say goodbye?"

"I cannot, Marta," she said, her eyes filling. "Tell Isabel I miss her and explain why I stayed."

"Please, Magdalena, come out and say goodbye."

Magdalena looked at Marta with a sad smile and said, "Of course."

Marta led Magdalena to the carriage. As Marta climbed to her seat, Magdalena reached over and took Lydia's hand. "Goodbye, my sister. Tell Isabel I will come later and that I love her as I do you."

Lydia looked down at her sister and without smiling said, "If we find her I will tell her."

*

Never having seen Havana, Lydia did not like the rush of carriages and horses clopping through the streets and people crowding the sidewalks, talking and shouting to each other. In her simple dress and severe hairdo, she held her bag close to her bosom with both hands and looked around as if afraid she would miss something. She waited outside the train station for Paco to find a carriage.

Lydia had never been inside a hotel and was shocked by the large room she had all to herself adjoining Marta and Paco's room. Both rooms had a balcony overlooking a busy street and a plaza. Marta unpacked and knocked on Lydia's door. After several knocks Lydia came out smiling. "Sorry, Señora Marta, I was on the balcony looking at the city. How beautiful it is from up here!"

"Yes, isn't it? We are ready whenever you are."

"I am ready."

They drove directly to the house on the edge of El Vedado. Paco asked Marta and Lydia to stay in the carriage until he could talk to the madam. His knock on the door brought her out. The middle-aged, brown haired woman saw Paco, and her bright face melted to a frown. She blinked her blue eyes several times and said, "I already told you, *Señor*; I cannot help you."

"*Señora*, Isabel's mother has come from Matanzas. She is in the carriage and is out of her mind with worry," he said, pointing to the street. "Please talk with her."

"I told you I know nothing about Isabel. She left a month ago, and that is all."

"Please wait, I'll get her," Paco said, and walked down the steps to the carriage and brought Lydia onto the porch. The woman stood wide-mouthed as Lydia approached. "I didn't know Isabel as well as I thought," she said, shaking Lydia's hand and staring into her face. "I thought the other woman who came here was her mother."

"That was my wife," Paco said.

With added surprise, the woman smiled and said, "Isabel made me promise."

"Think, Señora," Paco said. "How can you keep such a promise?"

"Come into my office," the woman said, leading them in with her arm around Lydia's shoulder.

"I must see my daughter," Lydia said. "Please tell me where she is."

The woman could not keep from staring at Lydia. Her eyes darted between Lydia and Paco.

"If we are going inside, I will get my wife," he said. He went down again and asked Marta to come in and told the driver to wait. Once inside the woman's office they all sat down.

"I remember you, Señora," the woman said to Marta. "I am called Evelina. Isabel came down with a terrible sickness. I do not even like to say the word. She waited too long to tell me. I think she was trying to hide it, hoping it would go away. Silly girl! When she finally confessed I rushed her to the hospital. She did not want to go, but I made her. It's a very good hospital not far from here. They care for all my girls. Here is the address." She handed Lydia a card.

"She is there now?" Lydia said.

"Yes, and I warn you, Señora, you may not recognize her. I have visited her several times this month."

"Is she dying?" Paco asked.

"Take the address and go."

"What else can you tell me?" Lydia said.

"She was a fine girl, a hard worker, intelligent. She would have made a good businesswoman."

"Why do you say, 'was'?" Marta asked in an angry tone.

"Please, go to her."

Evelina ushered them out to the street and shook their hands. They could see she was genuinely concerned for Isabel. "If I can do anything, please let me know," she said, and embraced Lydia. "I'm sorry, dear."

Lydia again began to cry as she stepped into the carriage.

The driver drove directly there through an affluent neighborhood of gracious houses with neat landscaping. Paco again asked the driver to wait and they all went in. Paco got her room number at the information desk, and they walked up a flight of stairs to her ward. She was asleep in the third of four beds. The ward was clean with white walls and tile floors. Lydia liked the cleanliness, but Marta detested the sterile, forbidding atmosphere.

Isabel was pale and emaciated and her chest heaved as she breathed. Lydia stood beside her and put her hand on her forehead and stroked her hair back. Waking, Isabel looked up, momentarily confused. Then she smiled and said: "*Ay, Mamá. Que bueno.*"

"How are you feeling, *mi hija?* I have brought Paco and Marta. Actually they brought me."

She looked at both of them and smiled. Paco was surprised after the anger she had shown at their previous meetings. Marta and Paco bent down and kissed her. She held Paco's hand for a long time, not wanting to let go. They had to bend down close to hear her weak words.

A tall, thin, bald man entered wearing a white jacket and glasses. "Which of you is her mother?" he asked briskly, almost rudely.

"*Yo,*" Lydia said. "How is she, Doctor?"

"Come outside," he said, and turned and walked into the hall. Paco followed them out, and Marta stayed with Isabel.

The white, antiseptic narrow hall extended interminably with doors breaking the monotonous white walls. Nurses walked in and out of the rooms. Their nonchalance and the sickening, sweet odor of carbolic acid created a sense of doom and futility that nearly overcame Paco.

"She's very sick," the doctor said. "I don't know how much time she has left, but it isn't much."

"*Ay!*" Lydia said, numbly.

"We diagnosed advanced syphilis, but that is only part of the problem. She has developed serious complications. Her heart is erratic and she is bleeding internally. We have not found the cause, but her condition is grave and worsening."

"Is there nothing you can do?" Paco asked.

"Who are you?" he asked, looking down over his spectacles at Paco.

"Her father."

"Very little we can do, I'm afraid."

Still crying, Lydia pleaded, "Oh, Doctor, surely you can do something."

"You might have helped if you'd come earlier."

"I think you know what you can do with your judgments, Doctor," Paco said. "We need help now. If you wish to withdraw, say so."

"No need to get excited, Señor Iglesias. It's just that I see so many of these cases that ... How do you think it feels to be a doctor and not be able to help a young person like this?"

"I don't give a damn how you feel. Tell us what we can do."

"If you want to consult another doctor, there are many in Havana. I have already brought in four specialists to see her."

"They say the same?"

"I'm afraid so. I'm sorry."

Turning to Lydia, Paco said, "What do you want to do?"

"I do not know."

"Frankly, her despondence hasn't helped," the doctor said. "Having you here might help."

"I will stay with her," Lydia said. "If you have to go back I will telegraph every day."

"We will stay a few days, Lydia."

Without looking at the doctor Lydia returned to Isabel's room. Marta was sitting by the bed talking with Isabel. Lydia took another chair and sat beside Marta.

"Sit here so you can be close to Isabel," Marta said, getting up. "I will come back later."

"No, please, Marta. Stay," Isabel said.

Paco was standing by the door ready to leave, but he moved a chair and sat beside Marta, who had one hand to her forehead. "Are you all right, Marta?"

"Just a little weak."

Paco took her hand. It felt cold.

"Tell me about Matanzas," Isabel whispered.

Marta looked at Lydia, and Lydia began, "Genio has left for Oriente to join Macéo's army. Ignacio practically runs the farm by himself. He has turned out to be a brilliant manager. You would be proud of him, Isabel."

Paco thought he was hearing a phantom voice, not the same Lydia who had spewed hatred and anger for so many years.

"Magdalena is well, still sewing a lot, especially since you left. I think not having you to talk to and boss around has left her life empty. She misses you terribly. My aunt is getting old, but she still works, still as tough as ever. The driver often talks of you. He is a nice man. I have always liked him, though I barely know him. Ignacio has Manuel and Enrique jumping. They complain, but they respect him. I suppose you know Genio got married. They say his new wife, Celia, is lovely. They are expecting a baby. Both are revolutionaries."

Paco and Marta exchanged glances of astonishment.

"Lydia, I would like to go to the hotel for a while and rest," Marta said. "Stay with Isabel."

"Yes, yes. We have much to catch up on."

"Let us walk around the neighborhood, Marta," Paco said. "It will be good to see the city together."

"If you don't mind, Paco, I'd like to rest first."

"You are upset about Isabel."

"I do not know, but I am very tired."

The next morning Marta felt normal. Their daily schedule became two or three hours with Isabel followed by strolls in the areas around the hospital and the hotel. By week's end Isabel was talking with more animation. She seemed happier. Lydia stayed by her bed and returned to the hotel only to sleep a few hours.

On their last morning in Havana, Paco and Marta drove to the hospital to see Isabel and Lydia. Paco told Isabel he had to return, but would be back as soon as he could. She smiled and thanked him.

"And thank you for bringing Mamá," she whispered.

As Paco and Marta were leaving, Lydia stopped them at the door. "May I stay, Paco? I have money saved and can move to a cheaper hotel. I do not need such luxury."

"Keep your room as long as you like. I will tell the concierge to bill me for your expenses. Also I will arrange for a driver to take you anywhere you want to go. Just tell the concierge. It will be added to the bill. And I will leave an envelope with cash in your mailbox. I ask only that you keep me informed."

"Thank you, Paco. I promise. One thing: could you ask Magdalena to come? I think Isabel would like to see her."

"Of course. I will reserve a room for her."

"No. My sister can stay in my room." Then she reached and kissed him on the cheek. "Forgive me for everything, Paco, and you, too, Marta."

Paco hugged her. "Now we must go. Out train leaves in an hour."

Lydia kissed Marta, they embraced and Marta and Paco departed.

*

For five weeks Lydia described Isabel's decline in daily telegrams to Paco. She had lost weight, her breathing had become worse, and her bleeding had continued. Paco had to fight off the temptation to visualize his daughter, but the specter of an emaciated face with skin stretched over bones and lips receding to expose large teeth haunted him. With each telegram less emotional and more factual, Paco grew angrier.

"Look at this," he said to Marta. "She is reverting to the old, hard Lydia. Feels nothing."

"Perhaps she is finally accepting reality, Paco. You will have to accept it too."

Paco wanted to be with his daughter, and Marta encouraged him to go, but he felt it was somehow not right. And he did not want to confess to feeling uncomfortable spending so much time with Lydia.

"Magdalena is there to share the pain. I am sure Lydia would prefer to be alone with Isabel. She has shown much compassion by including her sister."

Lydia's last telegram arrived during lunch. It was briefest of all:

> She is gone.
> Lydia

Paco handed it to Marta and began to cry. He had not cried through the entire episode, but he could hold it no longer.

Seeing him out of control, Marta's eyes flooded and she took his hand. In a strong voice she said, "*Vamos.*"

Paco nodded.

Ignacio had watched the scene with little visible reaction and then stood, walked to his father and put his hands on his shoulders. "Go, Papá. I will handle everything here."

"She is your sister," Marta said. "You come with us."

Ignacio tried to argue, but Marta held up her hand, and he said no more. To Marta this was not the time for business or ambition or rhetoric. It was the time to comfort his father and to bury Isabel.

Paco sent Ignacio to the telegraph office in Matanzas with two messages. The first was to Lydia and Magdalena at the Hotel Inglaterra:

> Will arrive this evening.
> Reserve us two rooms.
> Paco

The second was to Celia at her apartment:

> Isabel has died.
> Please tell Genio.
> We arrive this evening
> Hotel Inglaterra.
> Paco

Ignacio returned in less than an hour to find Marta packed and ready and Paco waiting in the living room. "Let's go."

Because of Isabel's deteriorated condition they buried her that evening. Pushing himself down the aisle of the church past rows of empty pews, through air thick with incense and the smell of burning candles, Paco repeated to himself that no parent should have to bury an offspring. It is contrary to the natural order. The air in the church was so full of regret that he could barely lift his feet out of the bitterness of each step, his heart crushed by the boulder within his breast. Later, he could not recall who attended or anything the priest said, nor did he stop to talk with him afterward. The cold, businesslike cleric was a stranger, one of the anonymous priests who served the hospital chapel.

During the burial Paco's mind began to clear, and he became aware of standing under a pitiful drizzle as the dank black earth swallowed his daughter. Everyone wore black, which added to the somberness of the dismal day. Years later, his clearest memory would be of the dozen black umbrellas shifting in unison with the wind like shiny black flowers in a breeze. The memory would be forever linked to another burial years before during an Asturian cloudburst in which cows all faced the same direction as if viewing some grand scene, and then, as the wind shifted, turned to keep the rain out of their eyes.

After the funeral Lydia, Magdalena, Ignacio, Marta, Paco and Celia went back to the hotel. Celia had telegraphed Genio, but he had not yet replied. They were eating their supper in the dining room when Genio walked in and removed his coat to shake off the water. Paco sprang up. As they met, Celia waited, knowing his father needed to see his son alone first. Genio's tears moistened his father's shoulder when they embraced. Paco kissed him on both cheeks and walked him to the table, not noticing the patrons' stares. As they sat, Marta told him everyone in the place had turned to watch them. Genio embraced Lydia and kissed her and said some words of comfort before going around the table hugging everyone. At Ignacio he stopped a moment to look at him, smiled, and embraced and kissed him. "I am glad to see you, my brother."

"I too, Genio. I hear they made you an officer."

"A lieutenant, but I couldn't wear my uniform here," he said, looking around. He turned to his father, "I couldn't make it sooner, Papá. I had to wait for the General to approve my pass, and then the train."

"General Macéo?" Paco said.

"Yes. He wanted to know how long I would be away."

"Sounds like an offensive soon."

"I cannot say, Papá."

"I know, son."

"You sure picked a good time to skip out," Ignacio said.

"Skip out?" Genio said.

"Out of danger. No need to court danger for nothing."

"Not for nothing, Ignacio. For *Cuba libre*."

"Don't be a fool," Ignacio said. "Nothing's worth your life. How can you *disfrutar* what you died for?"

"My children and family will. You, Ignacio, Mamá, Papá, Celia, my baby, all will benefit."

"Such fanaticism! To die is to lose everything. I can understand giving up something for others, but your life? Inconceivable!"

Paco looked at them agreeing with both. To risk one's life is the true measure of devotion and the most admirable human quality, but Ignacio was also right. Yet something about Ignacio's words goaded Paco. He agreed, but he could not respect reasoning rooted in such egoism. Genio had the more flattering view, but Paco would not encourage it for fear of losing another offspring. The argument burned him like a hot poker.

"Not fanaticism, Ignacio," Genio said, "commitment, devotion to duty."

"Who says it's your duty to risk your life?"

"I want to live as much as anybody, but each man must draw the line somewhere."

"Better you would have drawn it fighting for the hacienda. Now that's worth fighting for."

"Each has his calling," Genio said.

"You must be devoted to abandon your law degree," Ignacio said. "At least your education will keep you from hand to hand combat."

"The General put me on his staff, transmitting orders, filling out papers and attending endless meetings. I'd much rather ride out with the troops."

"Such devotion is sure to land you a soft job ... if your side wins, that is."

Paco hated Ignacio at that moment. His most oily and cunning side leaked through his grin.

"I'd never accept a job won with the blood of my comrades," Genio said. "I'd gladly ride into battle to prove myself the kind of man I have always admired." He looked at his father as he spoke.

"I remember Isabel pushing you around like one of her dolls. You never fought back then. You'll never change, Genio. Ride into battle with a rifle and waving a machete? It's beyond imagining."

"I can imagine it," Paco said, his chest heaving. "I am proud of Genio and the man he has become." He stood, feeling rage welling. Finally he said, "Stop your taunting, Ignacio, and your cruelty. Are you so anxious to lose a brother? I have just buried a daughter and I can't take anymore. Look at your aunt and Lydia and your mother and Celia. Can't you see how your brutality hurts them?"

The women had sat stone-faced throughout the discussion. Tears rolled down Magdalena's cheeks; Lydia's mind had strayed to another time and place; Marta was perspired and her face was pale, and she held her hand to her breast; Celia had tried to smile, but fooled no one.

"Forgive me, Lydia, and you too, Mamá, and Tía Magdalena, and Celia," Genio said, smiling sadly.

Looking down at his plate Ignacio said, "Me too."

Paco put his arm around Genio's shoulder and smiled at him. He wanted him to know how he felt. Ignacio looked back at him with eyes flooded with anger.

At the end of the meal they stood, and Paco walked Genio to the lobby. "How long can you stay?"

"I return tonight. My train leaves shortly after midnight."

"Good. We have time to talk."

"Forgive me, Papá, but Celia and I had planned to spend some time together."

"Of course."

*

On their first evening back at the farm, Marta, Magdalena, Celia and Paco were sitting on the front porch after supper to relax, as don Miguel's carriage appeared. Paco stepped down to meet him, walked him up the steps and presented him to Celia.

"Don Miguel was a close friend and neighbor for years. He owned the plantation to the south."

"I've come to express my sympathy to Lydia," he said. "And to all of you, of course."

"Thank you, don Miguel," Magdalena said. "You came from Havana?"

"I only learned of it in today's newspaper."

"A great tragedy," Magdalena said. "She was too young."

Having gone to fetch Lydia, Marta returned with her a few moments later. Lydia wiped her hands on her apron as she approached don Miguel.

"My sincerest sympathy for your great loss," don Miguel said, standing. "I cannot imagine anything worse than the loss of a child."

"Thank you, don Miguel. It was very kind of you to come."

Don Miguel held Lydia's hand for a long time until Paco asked him to sit down. Lydia turned and walked back to the door.

"Please stay, Lydia," Marta said. "You are the one Don Miguel came to see."

"But the kitchen ..."

"It will wait," Paco said, drawing a rocker from the other end of the porch. "Come, sit with us."

To everyone's surprise she sat and began to rock gently.

"How's Genio? I heard he joined the rebels."

"He missed the funeral, but joined us at supper afterwards," Paco said. "Did you know Celia is expecting?"

"Wonderful. Life has its compensations."

"Nothing can compensate for the death of a child," Lydia said.

"I only meant that life provides good things along with its tragedies. We must try not to forget the good."

"I will bring coffee," Lydia said.

"No," Marta said. "I will. You stay."

Lydia looked at her with a mixture of confusion and anger. In truth she did not want to talk with don Miguel, but Marta had spoken with an authority that froze her to the spot.

"And Ignacio?" don Miguel asked.

"In town," Paco said. "A young man must find people his own age."

"Ah, yes, but Matanzas is no Havana."

"He is too devoted to his work to go that far," Paco said.

"Will he join the rebellion too?"

"He hates it."

"Most young men I see are itching to fight for *Cuba libre.*"

Marta appeared with a coffee pot and demitasse cups. She set out five cups and saucers and poured black coffee into each. She handed one to Lydia, who reached for it tentatively, as if performing a sinful act. Paco plucked two cigars out of his shirt pocket, handed don Miguel one, took one himself and lit both.

As Lydia finished her coffee and set the cup on the table, she moved as if to stand, but don Miguel asked, "How do you feel about the revolution, Lydia?"

"I have no opinions, don Miguel. My work keeps me busy."

"How can that be?"

She sat back and thought for a minute. "My people will lose no matter who wins."

"Your people?" Paco asked, unbelieving.

"Negroes."

"You are one of us," Paco said.

"I am both, Señor Paco."

"I understand, Lydia," don Miguel said. "I, too, live in two worlds." Knowing his sexual inclination, they all sat shocked. "I'll say only that my family and some of my friends abhor my other friends, and I'm torn between them. Sometimes I would like to choose one group, but I don't want to alienate the other. Something like that touches everyone. You, Paco, are a staunch Spaniard, or have you finally become a Cuban?"

"I have always felt Spanish, but with the passing years I waver."

"My point exactly. In that regard, Lydia, we're the same, pulling for one group when it's threatened, and for the other when that one's threatened."

"It is not the same, don Miguel," Lydia said, with evident indignation. "Your people were not dragged here in chains."

"And we shall never be absolved of that sin," don Miguel said. "The white race will carry that infamy to its grave."

"My mother and my aunt told me they saw children and women thrown into the sea; others died of hunger and disease on the crossing, and none ever heard from their African families again. Neither of you carries that history in your soul."

Magdalena, who had remained silent throughout the discussion, said, "Why do you not put that behind you and live as one of us? It is what we have always wanted."

"Not our father," Lydia said. "I could not even call him Papá. Why should I expect more from others?"

"We have all tried to make you feel like family, Lydia. I think you know that," Magdalena said.

"Both my mother and my aunt repeatedly told me, 'Do not fool yourself. You will never be one of them. You will grow old and useless, and they will throw you out. The only way to endure is to know your place and ignore the hypocrisy.'"

"Oh, Lydia," Magdalena said, shaking her head.

"Strange how slaves embrace their bondage to avoid pain," don Miguel said.

"I am not a slave!" Lydia said.

"We're all slaves to our desires, our phantoms, our fears. There's something to enslave each of us, Lydia. Being born a Negro is no doubt the most oppressive slavery and the most difficult to overcome, but it's not the only kind."

"Lydia, after all we have been through together, you cannot believe we keep you to work for us. Of course Papá wronged you, but I am not Papá. Why can't you see that?" Magdalena rose and stood by Lydia and reached down and kissed her. "I want you to be fully my sister. It is your birthright."

Lydia began to weep as she looked into Magdalena's soft, brown eyes.

"Well, I must be going if I'm going to make the last train to Havana," don Miguel said, rising.

Paco stood and shook his hand. "And thank you for everything, Miguel," Paco said. "You are a true friend."

Marta thanked him also and began to gather the dishes. Lydia stood to help, but Magdalena held her arm and said, "Stay and talk with me, and do Marta the favor of letting her help."

Lydia smiled sheepishly and rocked.

*

During the two weeks that followed, people dropped in at all hours, especially after supper. And every evening Lydia joined them to watch the sunset and talk about Isabel and Genio.

The day after don Miguel's visit Magdalena set a place at the table for Lydia, who saw the table before breakfast and frowned at Magdalena. "Who is coming?"

"You, Lydia. From now on you eat with us."

"But ..."

"Do not argue, please. Now let me help bring in the breakfast."

By common consent Lydia continued to cook, and Marta and Magdalena helped her serve and clean up. By the time the stream of friends and relatives trickled off, a month had passed, and Lydia seemed comfortable in what she viewed as her new role as family member. She was surprised how much this simple change had loosened the dark, angry knot that had bound her life.

Five weeks after the funeral, Magdalena placed the last kettle she had washed on its wall hook, dried her hands on a towel and looked down at them. She had never seen her skin so wrinkled, rough and red. On her way to the porch to rest she stopped at her portrait. Observing the face in the portrait she passed her hands over her cheeks and neck. Then her eyes moved down to the youthful hands, white and soft, and down at her wrinkled, aging hands. With a smile she wiped her hands on her apron and walked out.

Paco devoured every newspaper for news of the war, which had inundated the island like a tidal wave. He scanned each article nervously, trying not to read carefully, hoping not to understand, as if each line might be hiding a bomb that would explode as his eyes brushed it. And this feeling would not leave him even though he had no reason to worry, for Genio was safely behind the lines. But out of this certainty would emerge Isabel's death to lure him into believing, no, knowing—for belief had burrowed itself into a malignant canker—that he would lose a son in retribution for evil deeds. And the belief or certainty or knowledge, whichever it was, pointed its finger of damnation.

The newspaper one day carried an article about a fierce battle in the mountains north of Santiago de Cuba. It had cost the lives of many men on both sides. He searched frantically for Genio's name, but found no mention of him. At the end of the column his hands were shaking with hollow relief. But perhaps he had been killed and they had withheld the news. The horrible feeling that hides beneath the sheer veil of rationality would not leave him—the image of him lying dead on a godforsaken mountainside.

He folded the paper, laid it down and went out back. He found Ignacio in the barn talking with Manuel and Enrique. From a distance he could see their arms waving as they talked with great energy. "What is it, Ignacio?"

"They do nothing but talk about the fighting. I just told them to do their talking on their own time."

Ignoring him Paco asked Manuel what he had heard.

"My sister's husband," Manuel said. "He has been wounded."

"How bad?"

"Lost a leg. She is sick with worry."

"Sorry. Genio is with Macéo."

"He's got a desk job behind the lines," Ignacio said, erect and with his chest out.

Paco's stare deflated him.

"All right, back to work," Ignacio said.

"One minute," Paco said, showing anger. "I happen to be interested, so let him talk."

"But they're only rumors, Papá."

"Go on, Manuel."

"She said quite a few men from Matanzas suffered wounds and a few died."

"My God! Do they know who?"

"She thinks maybe Genio, but she was not sure."

"Hurt or dead?"

"*No sabe.* Probably just injured. It is only a rumor."

Paco ran to his horse, saddled it and rode off toward Matanzas as the three men stood gaping.

As he galloped furiously toward town, Ignacio cried out, "Wait, I'm coming with you." Paco could not hear him with the wind rushing past his ears as he rode along the road that cut through a sea of cane.

He was half way to Matanzas before Ignacio caught up. Paco did not look at him, but continued at full speed.

"Where are you going, Papá?"

"To send a telegram."

Paco pulled the reins to a dusty stop in front of the small telegraph office, jumped down and ran inside. There was little furniture, only a counter that divided the room in halves. Behind the counter the operator sat at his desk, which held the telegraph key and other apparatus, including a glass jar of blue liquid with wires sticking into it. A large window by the desk illuminated the stark room.

"A telegram, quick."

The operator grabbed a pad of paper as Paco dictated:

> To Celia Iglesias,
> Heard rumors of fighting and casualties.
> Was Genio involved?
> Await your reply.
> Paco

The operator read it aloud for Paco's approval and then sat down and began to tap out the message. After less than a minute he said, "It is sent."

"Come, Papá. There's a café across the street."

Paco looked past him and said to the operator, "I will be back in a few minutes for the reply. Do not send it to my house."

The hour dragged like a heavy iron chain as Paco and Ignacio drank their coffee silently. Paco took out his large, gold pocket watch to check the time several times as Ignacio talked about the farm, but his words merely bounced off Paco's armor. Holding the bulbous watch in his hand, he recalled the day his father gave it to him. It has been so long ago, that day in Colosía. The last time I saw him, he thought. If I had known … The only word that shoved all others out of his brain was death. He prayed fervently, hoping God would feel moved, but helplessness gripped him by the throat. Ignacio talked and talked, and Paco prayed and prayed. Suddenly he stood and started to the door.

"It's too soon, Papá. She hasn't had time to get the telegram. They have to send it to her house. Let's have another."

Before Ignacio had finished Paco had crossed the street.

As Paco appeared in the door, the operator said, "Not yet, Señor. It will be a while."

"I will wait."

The man lifted a chair from behind the counter and handed it to Paco, who thanked him.

"Ignacio, why don't you go for a walk or something?"

"I'll stay with you, Papá. It's nothing but a rumor, you know. He's probably fine; having a glass of beer or a cup of coffee, smoking a cigar."

Paco said nothing.

Three hours later a message came over the machine and Paco stood to see if it was his. The operator nodded as he watched the message print out. He lifted the paper off the machine and handed it to Paco.

> Paco,
> Eugenio has been hurt.
> Don't know how serious.
> Please come.
> Celia

Paco handed it to Ignacio. "I leave for Havana on the next train. Tell your mother to come as soon as she can. Oh, and follow me to the station and take my horse back."

"Wait for Mamá."

"Did you not read the telegram? She wants me now."

The rail clerk said the train to Havana had just left. Paco's stern look startled the man. "But there is another in two hours."

"Wait for us, Papá. I'll bring her as soon as I can."

"If you get her here on time, we go together. Otherwise, she can follow."

"What about me?"

"Stay and take care of the plantation."

*

Paco was surprised to see the carriage drive up with Marta. He took her bag. "Hurry, it is about to leave."

"Ignacio told me what happened. What do you think?"

"Better not to think. Soon we will know."

The train ride was not the pleasant drive through rolling country that Paco had often enjoyed. The train rattled and rocked and shook and stung their jangled nerves. Saying little, Marta tried to crochet, but her hands shook too much. Paco stared out the window at the passing scene remembering Isabel. Traffic and city noises made the ride to Celia's apartment even tenser. At the door Celia embraced them both and began to cry.

"What is it?" Marta sid.

"I don't know. I got a telegram from his unit that said he had been wounded, but no details. Said I would hear more soon. I'm still waiting."

"Who can we ask?" Marta said.

"He's in the fourth regiment of General Macéo's outfit."

"How do you communicate?" Paco asked.

"By letter. I wrote his commander a month ago to learn where they had moved him." She walked to her desk and opened one drawer and then a second. "Here it is. Major Chávez." She handed Paco his address.

"I will telegraph him right away. Where is the nearest telegraph office?"

She gave him directions and he disappeared.

The operator took his message, read it back and sent it. It read:

> Major Chávez,
> Have heard my son,
> Eugenio Iglesias, is wounded.
> Please supply details.
> When may I see him?
> Francisco Iglesias

"I will wait for an answer."

"I have sent many of these telegrams, Señor. Soldiers never rush to respond. Better to wait at home. I'll send it to you as soon as I get it."

"Thank you."

A knock on the door woke them the next morning. It was loud, urgent, like the knock of police or an urgent message. Paco and Marta were in Celia's room and Celia was on the living room sofa. At the thought of an urgent message Paco jumped out of bed, grabbed his robe, and ran to the living room and almost knocked into Celia, who was already at the door. By the time he opened it, Marta had come out too and was standing by him trembling. A young black man, about twenty years old and wearing a tan suit and tie, stood with his Panama hat in his hand.

"Forgive me, but I knocked several times and heard no answer," he said. "I am Lieutenant Rafaél Martínez, a courier for Major Juan Chávez who has ordered me to deliver this letter to Señor Francisco Iglesias."

"I telegraphed him yesterday," Paco said, taking the letter. "I wondered why he did not answer." He opened the letter and sat on the newly recovered sofa, as Celia escorted Rafaél Martínez to a chair. Celia had moved into Genio's apartment and had redecorated it with curtains, a new sofa her parents had given them, and a vase of carnations for the kitchen table. She pulled open the curtains, and light exploded into the room. They squinted. Marta sat by Paco and put her hand on his shoulder. As he ripped open the envelope he felt her shaking. He read aloud:

> Dear Señor and Señora Iglesias,
>
> I write this in response to your telegram. I deeply regret to inform you that your son, Lieutenant Eugenio Iglesias, was killed in the service of his country. Eugenio was such a good and kind person and has become such a hero that …

Paco could not continue. With his eyes filling he began to sob and dropped the letter to the floor.

Rafaél Martínez picked it up and said: "*Con permiso,*" and continued to read:

> … has become such a hero that a letter cannot convey the magnitude of his deed or the respect and admiration of his comrades. As you may know, Eugenio was assigned to my staff. However, since his sister's funeral, he has pleaded with me to let him go out with the unit. Because he had had no experience or training in warfare I repeatedly declined his requests. Two days ago we marched out to meet a troop of Spaniards who were threatening a nearby unit. I left him in charge of Headquarters. Half an hour later he took a horse and rode out after us. He was so determined that my remaining staff could not stop him.
>
> He caught up with us, and I immediately ordered him back, saying that we needed him at Headquarters to receive and send messages and make decisions. He would not listen. He said if I did not let him fight I would have to arrest him because he would not return voluntarily. I threw up my hands and turned my attention to the enemy, which had begun an offensive nearby.
>
> He joined the first platoon that marched out. The rest I learned later from the men of that platoon. They arrived at the assigned point and began to dig in, where they could fire without being hit. They had barely begun, however, when a hidden unit of Spaniards stationed uphill from them began to fire down on them. They turned their machine gun on the very spot where the platoon had tried to hide. Three of the men were hit in the first volley. Immediately, Eugenio tore a hand bomb from the belt of one of the

men and ran through the trees around the enemy's position above his platoon. Because of the rocky terrain and the thick trees and underbrush they did not see him. He made his way up the hill from tree to tree and rock to rock to a spot about ten meters directly above the machine gun nest. My men could see him clearly, but fortunately the Spaniards could not. No one spoke or yelled a word as they watched him position himself.

At a spot directly above the enemy he lit the bomb and waited for the fuse to burn down. At the proper time he dropped it into the gunners' nest. The blast killed all of the men and destroyed the machine gun. My men cheered, "Genio, Genio!" Then they saw him fall and try to get up and fall again. Seeing he was hurt, one of the men ran to him as fast as he could, ignoring sniper fire, but Eugenio was already dead. A piece of rock or shrapnel had hit him in the neck and severed an artery. The man carried him back to us, and I had him taken back to Headquarters immediately.

Though your son had never before engaged in battle, he managed to accomplish what few men would have attempted. In so doing he saved the lives of two-dozen men. My troops compare Eugenio's heroism with that of our late leader, José Martí. We are proud of him and, to a man, send our heartfelt condolences.

Major Juan Chávez

"Why did he telegraph his wife that he had been wounded?" Paco asked.

"Seeing him trying to walk they thought his wound was not serious. Major Chávez immediately sent a man to Headquarters to report the situation and to bring help. It was an unfortunate error, and Major Chávez sends his apology."

"Were you there?"

"Yes, Sir. I helped get him back to headquarters. I will never forget Genio's face; it was one of complete repose. It was a great honor to know him, Señor Iglesias."

Paco wanted to yell or hit him, but he could do neither, for he could not lift his arms. He suddenly felt old.

"Where is he?"

"Major Chávez sent Genio's remains by train to Matanzas for burial. There was so little time, Señor. He dared not wait for your permission."

"Yes, thank you."

He looked at Marta and Celia, who were staring out the window, seeing nothing. Each felt she was hanging alone in the shade of a large, empty world.

"*Muchas gracias, Teniente Martínez.* You have been very kind. May we know the name of the man who went to help him?"

"He was an ex-slave who called himself Ali. Poor man limped, but what a fighter. Nothing could stop him. He had taken an interest in your son, helped him and made sure he was comfortable."

"Ali?" Paco asked numbly.

"Yes, his last words were to give you his condolences and to express his gratitude to you."

"My God!"

"He was killed in action this morning."

Turning to Marta, Paco said, "We must go home."

She stared at him not comprehending. As he took her in his arms to comfort her, she collapsed. He laid her on the sofa. As he did she opened her eyes and said, "It is too horrible. I cannot bear it. He was so young, so gentle, so innocent. Why? It is not fair, not fair."

"I know," Paco said, also crying. "But you are my rock, my strength. You must bear up. Come now; there is nothing we can do here. We must return to Matanzas to receive him." Holding her to him he could feel her heart racing. "Please, Marta, try to calm down."

Looking on, Lieutenant Martínez said, "If there is nothing further I can do …?"

"Thank you, lieutenant. Please thank Major Chávez for his kindness."

"I want to see Genio," Celia said. "Where is he?"

"They are taking him home," Paco said.

"Home?" She smiled, as if she had heard good news.

"Yes, Celia, and we must go to him."

"But he's dead, no?"

"Come with us, Celia."

"Poor Celia," Marta said, "Of course she wants to see him." She sat up and put her arm around Celia's shoulder.

"I can't think," Celia said. Then after a few moments, "Yes, I must go to him."

It took her a long time to pack, wondering whether she would return, whether to take Genio's things or wait till later. Much of the time she sat alone on the edge of her bed, thinking about Genio and what she would do and where she would go.

Seeing her on the bed looking out the window, Marta asked if she was all right.

"I don't know. What shall I do?"

Marta sat beside her on the bed. "It is too much to bear alone." Then they embraced each other and cried.

"Come, Celia. Later we will mourn; now we must go to Matanzas. I will help you pack."

"Thank you, Marta, but I'll do it. I'll leave Genio's things here until I return. By then I'll figure out what to do with them and with myself."

In late afternoon the three of them left the apartment and took a carriage to the train station. Memories of the carriage ride and the walk through the station to their train would later be lost in a fog of remorse, but they marched through their assigned tasks as if under orders from a high command. Paco bought Celia's ticket and they walked like leaden soldiers to their track. Once in the train Paco felt the world had vaporized before his eyes. He was walking through a dark, hollow tunnel toward the edge of eternity with no sight of the future and little concern for the past.

Less than an hour later the sun sank into a broad, green field of cane. Watching the familiar sight, Paco hoped the great torch would envelop the field in flames and him with it, so he could ride the flaming ball to the other life. The rhythmic rattle of the train almost put him to sleep with its deadening monotony—at first like bullets spitting out of a machine gun, then like rocks raining down to earth after a giant blast, then like the pulse of a great heart forcing his last drops of blood onto the Cuban ground for which he had fought so fiercely, each drop seeping into the earth. Paco wanted to jump from the train and run to that spot of earth and dig it up with his hands and put it back where it came from, and he recalled reading of God telling Cain that the voice of his brother's blood cried out to Him from the ground.

Without realizing what had happened, Paco was lifting Marta into her chair and the conductor was bringing her a glass of water. She tried to drink it, but, with the train's jostling, she spilled most of it. She said her throat felt dry. Paco held her head in his hands as his heart pounded like a machine gun and he felt he would explode into a thousand pieces.

Marta slept a while, or perhaps fainted again. Still holding her in his arms, Paco could not be sure, though her breathing gave him comfort. Through the window Ignacio stared back at him from the darkness beyond. Behind the image trees and fields shot past like apparitions. Ignacio's image was only Paco's reflection. Ignacio, my last child, the one who will carry on my name, my flesh, my fortune, my work, my life. The apparition stared at Paco wondering what he would do. As thoughts crowded the passing scene out of his vision, he could think only of Ignacio, his son and heir. Paco did not want to blame him, but he could not help himself. Hadn't he taunted Genio to fight, ridiculing him, daring him to do what he himself would never do? And Genio, the poor fool, had to prove his manhood by exposing it to enemies he had conjured for himself. Poor Genio! How many times had he said those words, poor Genio? So resolute that night at supper, so idealistic, so brave, so human, trying so hard to stifle doubt. Was he trying to hide his fear of cowardice? What meaning has he given to his last breath? He leaves a child who will never know him, like my father. And he leaves a widow who barely knew him. And Ignacio gets everything. I have Marta, only Marta, nothing else. Thank God for Marta. If not for her I would follow Genio to redeem the sons I created. She is my fortress, but this loss is too much. I must take care of her.

*

The first to arrive at the Iglesias home before the funeral were Manuel, Horacio and Hector, who had received a short leave to be with the parents of their comrade. None of the three failed to notice the striking portrait in the entrance, and they all found time to return there to admire it several times during their stay that afternoon.

After expressing sympathy, Hector called Paco aside. They were standing in the living room near the front window. "Señor Iglesias, may I say a few words of eulogy in the church?"

"Certainly, Hector. You probably knew him as none of us did."

Marta, standing a few feet away with one of the neighbors, heard Hector's request and took Paco into the kitchen a few minutes later.

"It is enough to endure the funeral of my son," she said. "I will not have it turned into a political rally."

"That did not occur to me."

He found Hector and asked him to follow him to his office, where Paco asked him what he had in mind for the eulogy."

"You all knew Genio as a kind, gentle boy. I knew him as an intellectual, a friend and a patriot. Why do you ask?"

"His mother and I do not want a political speech, Hector. This is a terrible time for us, and we do not want to turn his funeral into a circus."

"People should know what he did and what a sublime hero he was."

"That is only one side of Genio, Hector."

"But very important, especially now. If people don't act soon it'll be too late. They've got to know."

It was now clear Marta was right. "I cannot allow it, Hector. You were his good friend, and I would like to count you as mine also. But no speech."

"But, Señor Iglesias, to lay him to rest with platitudes will deprive these people of the truth at this most crucial hour of their lives."

"Do what you want in the street, but in the church, no."

"Many of your friends, plantation owners, still resist our revolution. This is a rare opportunity to talk directly to them."

"Let me put it this way: if you rise to talk at the funeral, I will personally throw you out. Is that clear?"

"Genio would be ashamed."

"I think he would be more ashamed of his friend."

Paco turned and went to talk with other mourners, anyone to take his mind off Hector. Seeing Marta he said, "You were right. He was planning a political speech, all right. I told him not to."

Tears welled. "Will he comply?"

"I told him I would throw him out if he tried."

"Good!"

The church could not hold all the people. Nearly everyone in Matanzas had heard of Genio's death and how he died and wanted to attend. Some did not see Genio's death as tragedy, but as his just reward for challenging the established government. To others, like Hector and his friends, Genio was a martyr. Paco saw Hector talking quietly to Manuel and Horacio for a long time before the funeral started, but none attempted to speak.

*

In the days that followed, multitudes filled their house with flowers and expressions of sympathy. The women of the family, especially Magdalena, would break into tears each time someone new came to visit. Marta kept calm throughout, which did not surprise Paco, but it made him wonder what was going on inside her. On one of those first evenings, the last person left, and Lydia brought Marta a cup of consommé. "*Toma, Marta. I just made it. It will make you feel better.*"

"Thank you, Lydia. I wondered where you had gone."

"I could not stand to talk to any more people. All I could think of was Isabel. Don Miguel was right: there is nothing worse than losing a child."

"Would you sit with me on the porch?"

"Some fresh air would be nice. How is Paco holding up?"

"I don't know. He doesn't say much, but I know he is about to explode."

"He is a good man, Marta. He has always treated me well, even when I did not deserve it."

"Thank you, Lydia."

"And how are you feeling now? Better?"

"I think so."

"I worried about you in the train."

"I wanted to die, but now …" She shrugged.

"I know well what you are going through. Tomorrow I go to Matanzas to buy some things. Come with me? It will be a distraction."

"Thank you, Lydia. I would like that. After breakfast?"

"*Bueno.*"

*

A month after the funeral Ignacio came galloping to the house shortly before lunchtime. He left his horse saddled behind the house and ran upstairs to his father's office. "Look at this," he said, out of breath.

"What is it?" Paco asked, trying to read while Ignacio talked.

"General Gómez has ordered all production on the island to stop, cane, tobacco, coffee, all manufacturing, everything!"

"Why?"

"A moratorium on all economic activity. That means no planting, no harvesting, no grinding, and no sugar. He's crazy. It'll ruin us and Cuba."

"Doesn't make sense," Paco said.

"We'll hire some guards."

"For what?"

"To stop them. They threaten to arrest all the owners and workers and to burn any plantation that doesn't comply."

"I cannot believe they would do that," Paco said.

"You want to gamble on your intuition?"

"Have they burned any yet?"

"Not that I know of, but …"

"Wait and see. In the meantime, act as if you know nothing."

"And if they come with torches?" Ignacio asked.

"Stop them and bring them to me."

"If you're wrong, we're dead."

"Not dead; just slowed. We have resources to carry us a long time even with no production. If they're serious, we might be better off going along than fighting them. In the meantime, I'll go to the Spanish Army Headquarters in Matanzas and ask for protection."

Ignacio did not agree, but he kept quiet and returned to the field.

The following day Manuel galloped toward the house, left the horse at the pump shed and knocked at the back door. He told Lydia that he had to see Paco immediately, and she asked him to wait while she ran upstairs to get him.

Guessing what had happened, Paco came down and met Manuel at the back porch.

"Soldiers, Señor Paco. They ordered Ignacio to stop the planting."

Without a word Paco ran to the barn, saddled a horse, and rode back with Manuel and found Ignacio standing before two soldiers dressed in white with white *guajiro* straw hats. Paco looked around and saw only these two.

"What's the problem?" he asked, calmly

"You will stop planting, Señor. General Gómez's order. If you do not, we will burn your hacienda."

"We?"

"Our company is bivouacked near here, Señor. The commanding major has sent scouts to warn all the planters in this area."

"This is our livelihood. How can he expect us to stop?"

"General Gómez gives the orders, Señor. I enforce them."

"We will stop until we can get some clarification from the general's men," Paco said.

"We won't," Ignacio said. "Nobody can make us."

"We'll stop!" Paco said, and turned to the men, who had crowded around them and the soldiers. "That is all for today. Go home until I call you. You will be paid for the day."

"But Papá, you can't do this. They can't bully us like that without a fight."

"Quiet, Ignacio!" As soon as the men started to leave, he climbed onto his horse and rode back to the house without looking back. Ignacio followed on his horse and stopped at the house just behind his father, while his father continued past, along the royal palm Matanzas road. Ignacio watched him ride out and smiled. Surmising his father was going to the Spanish Royal Army Headquarters, he followed and caught up to him about a mile down the road. "Going to the army?"

"Right. You may come if you wish." Paco did not slow down.

They dismounted a few minutes later at the headquarters near the center of town, and Paco walked in without knocking. Paco's furor surprised Ignacio. A sergeant looked up from his desk nervously and asked what he wanted.

"Who is in command here?"

"*Capitan López, Señor.*"

"I have to see him immediately. It is urgent."

"Who are you, Señor?"

"Francisco Iglesias, from the hacienda south of town."

"I will see if he is available." The sergeant walked to the door behind his desk, knocked and entered when a voice responded.

A minute later a tall, handsome officer in a neatly pressed uniform came out buttoning his jacket. "I am Capitan López, Señor Iglesias. Please come in and sit down." Paco introduced Ignacio as they walked into the captain's office, where they sat across from his desk. "Now, how can I be of service?"

"Rebel soldiers appeared at our plantation this morning and ordered us to stop planting."

"We have heard of General Gómez's order, but it is only talk. They will do nothing. Just continue planting."

"And if they burn my plantation as they threaten?"

"They won't. The rebels are panicking. They will not ruin their countrymen's livelihoods. Even they are not that stupid."

"You have not offered any assurance, Captain. If they burn my land, I will be ruined, and you will still sit in your office."

"What do you want?"

"Post soldiers at my hacienda and keep these trespassers from harming us and our fields."

"We can't post soldiers at every plantation."

"I am talking about the largest one in Matanzas Province and one of the few that the Americans have not bought. If they rout all local cane producers, there will be nothing for Spain to defend except American interests."

"Sorry, Señor."

"I am a Spaniard, and my country will not protect me from criminals who want to drive me out of business?"

"Perhaps I can have a platoon march through your place in a few days. That is the best I can do."

"That is not good enough, Captain."

The captain turned, looked out the window and said, "Didn't your son die recently fighting against Spain, Señor Iglesias?"

"That is right."

"Well, you might ask the rebels for help."

"How dare you talk to me, a Spaniard, like that? I am not responsible for the actions of my son."

The captain turned to face him and, with a smirk, said, "Perhaps you should control your family, Señor Iglesias."

"Genio was right. I am looking into the face of Spanish tyranny."

"Señor Iglesias, I …"

"Not another word unless you are ready to give me satisfaction outside, Captain."

Captain López smiled, turned and stood looking out the window behind his desk. Paco and Ignacio calmly walked out.

"What now, Papá?"

"Mount your horse and you shall see, Ignacio. You shall see."

In the hacienda Paco rode directly to the barn looking for Enrique or Manuel, but they were not there, so he galloped out to find them. Ignacio followed wondering what his father had in mind. Paco would say nothing. Ignacio asked several times, but the only answer was, "You shall see."

Paco found Manuel with the men who had been planting the new cane crop. Without dismounting he stopped and called Manuel aside.

"I need men who are not afraid to use guns."

"I have a gun, Señor Paco."

"Thank you, Manuel, but I need perhaps a dozen men."

"For what, Señor?"

"To guard the hacienda."

Manuel smiled approval. "Yes, Señor. I can find several who fought in the Ten Years War and who killed men with their own hands."

"Good. Dismiss the workers and pass the word to report back tomorrow morning. Then take Enrique and find these friends of yours as quickly as you can."

"Bring them here?"

"As soon as possible, Manuel. We have no time to lose."

As Paco turned his horse toward the house, Ignacio said, "What if the rebels come back?"

"They told us to stop. We stopped."

"I told you we should hire an army," Ignacio said with a touch of arrogance.

"It was wrong then. It is right now."

"You never take my side, do you?"

"Will you never grow up? I'm tired of the little boy who has to win at all costs. I act to save the plantation."

"Me too, Papá."

"Then be a man. You still have time to learn."

"I don't deserve that, Papá."

"You deserve what you earn. You want to run this place someday? Watch and learn."

"But I don't see why ..."

"I'm tired of your bellyaching. You cannot jump from foot soldier to general. Now shut up and watch; perhaps you may even grow up a little."

Paco kicked his horse's flanks and galloped off. Ignacio stayed back under the blazing sun for another half hour before he rode back.

That night after dark Manuel and Enrique showed up with eight men. Paco invited them into the back porch and asked them to wait while he fetched a kerosene lamp. Inside, he met Ignacio who had heard the noise and came to see.

"What is it, Papá?"

"Follow me."

Paco returned with the lamp, and Manuel and Enrique introduced each man, as Paco held up the lamp to study each face carefully. They were all tough, middle-aged men.

"Do you have guns?" Paco asked, after he had met them all.

They nodded. Two of them pulled out revolvers and held them up.

"Have you ever used them against men?"

"Yes, Señor," one said.

"In the war," another said.

"Have you ever shot a man?"

"Many. I even hit a few," the first man said, grinning maliciously.

"I need men who are willing to kill to defend this farm. If any of you does not feel he can do that, please drop out with no prejudice."

No one moved.

"Then report here at sunup with your weapons and bullets. I will reimburse you for any expenses, and I will pay you well if you perform well. Manuel and Enrique will verify that I am a man of my word. I hope you will not have to use arms; I would rather not spill blood. Also understand that you are not fighting for *Cuba libre* or for Spain. My political leanings do not matter, and neither should yours. If you fight, it will be to protect this hacienda and for no other purpose. Is that clear?" They all nodded and he said, "Go then, *hasta mañana.*"

Ignacio stayed after his father had gone inside. The men seemed as enthusiastic and eager for excitement as he was. As they dispersed Ignacio asked Manuel what he thought.

"Your father inspires loyalty."

"But do you think we'll fight?"

"The rebels? I don't think your father wants to. Knowing him, I am sure he has it calculated."

That evening Paco announced at supper that he had hired some men to help in the fields. He spoke in matter-of-fact tones as if he were hiring a new carriage driver. "In case you see strange men tomorrow, don't be surprised or alarmed. They are only temporary."

After his father's verbal thrashing of the previous day, Ignacio did not venture to ask what his father expected to happen the next day. Instead he stayed home that evening hoping Paco would reveal something. He did not, and Ignacio went to bed early knowing he would sleep poorly with his heart racing. The women had no idea of Paco's plan and said no more about his announcement. As usual, they all retired to the front porch to discuss the day's activities over coffee.

The next morning, as the sun was dislodging itself from the horizon, Paco and Ignacio found the eight men in the barn with Manuel and Enrique. Each man had either a pistol or a rifle, and each carried a machete at his side. It was still cool and they had left their horses saddled.

Paco gathered them together and said, "Wait here in the shade of the barn. When rebel soldiers appear, Manuel, you or Enrique will ask them to wait while the other comes to fetch me. Then I will lead you out to the field for a confrontation. Meanwhile, stay quiet and out of sight. If they do not appear by sundown, I will dismiss you until tomorrow."

For most of the morning the men stayed in the barn smoking cigars and talking. By midmorning the sun had made its presence felt, and Lydia brought out lemonade. Though they knew they would be paid whether they acted or not, they were all anxious to do something. Some fidgeted as they talked and joked; others sat quiet on the ground, waiting. Each man had a large-brimmed straw hat for protection from the sun. Some cleaned their guns or rifles; others simply waited. As the sun reached its zenith where it exhaled its flames down on them, Manuel rode up. "They are here! I will call *Señor* Paco. Saddle up."

Within minutes Paco and Ignacio were riding toward the field with the men behind them. The field was partly planted in the black, rich earth. Paco thought of the crop they might lose and what it would cost them, as well as of the possibility of losing the plantation. Reaching the soldiers, Paco stopped, dismounted. His men did the same and stood behind him. Paco approached the group of rebels in their motley white outfits and wide-brimmed straw hats. "Who is your leader?" he asked in a loud voice.

A large man, about thirty with long light hair, a brown moustache and face brown from the sun, walked to Paco. "I am sergeant Pedrada."

"Leave now with your men and nobody will get hurt," Paco said.

"We warned you yesterday, and you disobeyed the General's order, Señor Iglesias. You are all traitors and will face firing squads."

All eight of Paco's men lifted their rifles and pistols out of their holsters and stood holding them, and the rebels did the same. The two groups stood facing each other a few meters apart.

"So I am a traitor for protecting my property," Paco said. "You come here and threaten me and my property, and you are heroes."

A voice came from the rebel group: "Did you say Iglesias, Sergeant?"

"I don't give a damn who he is. He disobeyed the order," Sergeant Pedrada said.

The man emerged from the group and stood beside the sergeant.

"I haven't asked for your opinion," Sergeant Pedrada said. "Get back in formation."

"But, Sergeant ..."

"Shut up," the sergeant yelled. "I'll deal with you later."

"But Sergeant, I think this is the father of Lieutenant Eugenio Iglesias."

The sergeant looked at the private and then at Paco. His expression changed from anger to bewilderment. "Are you, Señor?"

"Yes."

"Sergeant, do you realize ..." the man said.

"Shut up!" Sergeant Pedrada said. "Of course I realize who he is. Leave me alone." Then turning to Paco, "I'm very sorry, Señor Iglesias. It is an honor to meet you. Your son was a great hero." He extended his hand to Paco and shook it vigorously. Then he turned to his men: "*Vamos!* This man is the father of the hero of Oriente. His farm is not to be touched."

"But the order, Sergeant," another man said, barely audibly.

"I shit on the order!" Sergeant Pedrada yelled. "Move out."

Paco and the men stood throughout the exchange with determined faces and their guns at the ready. As the rebels rode off Ignacio took off his hat and scratched his head. The men holstered their firearms, some disappointed, some relieved.

Paco had considered this possibility and had pondered how to bring it up in the showdown, but he had not expected such an easy resolution. He turned to the men and said, "You've done your duty. Come to the house for your pay. Manuel and Enrique, resume planting."

He rode off with Ignacio a horse's length behind and the others behind him. Paco still had not spoken to Ignacio. At the house Paco asked the men to wait on the back porch and strode upstairs two steps at a time. After a few minutes he returned with a pouch, gave each man twenty-five pesos and a hearty handshake. "Thank you, men. You have earned your money, and I have kept my property."

"This is more than we earn in a month," one of them said. "And we did nothing for it, Señor Paco."

"Must you die to earn your pay? You faced them like men, and you did your job well. You have my thanks. If I need you again, Manuel and Enrique know where to find you."

They all walked to the barn, retrieved their horses and rode off. As they passed the house, each waved at Paco, who was still on the back porch smiling.

"That was great, Papá!"

"Have you learned anything, Ignacio?"

"Yes, Papá. You're smarter than I thought."

"Come in and we will open a bottle of cognac."

"Good idea."

CHAPTER 8 - NINE YEARS LATER, 1905

*

American Intervention Brings Close to Cuban War of Independence

*

Deccember 10, 1898: Treaty of Paris Signed. Spain Withdraws from Cuba

*

January 1899: General John R. Brooks Named First U.S. Governor of Cuba

*

Constitutional Delegates Fight Over U.S. Demand for Platt Amendment

*

1901: Delegates Approve U.S. - Style Constitution

*

May 20, 1902: Tomás Estrada Palma
Named First Cuban President

*

Even after all his years in the tropics, Paco still marveled at the sky. With the sun about to set, a golden glow spread over the land. The cool breeze blowing through his office window made him feel alive.

Through Ignacio's persistence they had broken into sugar distribution, selling directly to the United States and several other countries. But Ignacio's obsession for total control still worried Paco. The young man seemed willing to do anything to keep his life's goal from slipping through his fingers. Marta encouraged Paco to let Ignacio have it, but Paco would not. "He will wait till I die as a son should. Truthfully, Marta, If only he were not so anxious, so ruthless, I would have turned it over to him years ago."

"I know, Paco, but ..."

"A business cannot have two heads, especially when one of them is Ignacio. He will wait."

Paco sat down to supper that evening feeling good in spite of the battering of his fifty-seven years. Having suffered from indigestion for years he ate with caution, which was nearly impossible with his voracious appetite and the women's passion for conjuring fancy meals. But all in all, it had been a good day and, since good days were less frequent now, he enjoyed those that came his way.

Over the years their seating arrangement at table had changed. Lydia and Magdalena shared one side across from Ignacio, who had his side to himself; Marta and Paco sat at opposite ends. Lydia was still in charge of the kitchen, but now she allowed Marta and Magdalena to help serve. Paco encouraged them to hire a servant, but they would not hear of it.

Lydia had made Paco's favorite: red snapper baked with onions and green peppers. As he helped himself from the large platter, Ignacio turned, as he usually did, to politics. Paco always shuddered when Ignacio started because his diatribes seemed endless. The man who so hated the revolution now hated the new Cuban Republic even more.

"Think about it: the war ended in 1898; then the Americans ran the country for four years. It's been three years since they left, and they still control us. We should have let them annex us. We have all the disadvantages of American control and none of the benefits."

"It takes time to establish a government," Magdalena said through an understanding smile.

"They've had plenty time," Ignacio said, banging his hand on the table so hard it rattled the wine glasses.

Paco tried to enjoy the fish, but Ignacio had begun to gather strength. "The Americans helped," Paco said.

"They certainly did," Magdalena said.

"Sure. They jumped into the war when it was all but over. You think because they love us? They said they stayed after the war ended so they could teach us how to run our country efficiently. Bah! They jsut wanted to dig in. They didn't bother to annex us because they got everything they wanted without having to bother with an unruly colony. We are their lackeys, slaves almost."

Lydia raised her eyes and said, "That is exactly right."

"But only because we allow it," Ignacio said. "It's time to do something."

"What do you have in mind?" Paco asked.

"Nothing! To hell with politicians. I work for us."

"Then why such anger?"

"Because it affects us. The Americans spent the years before the war buying up all the land they could get. They own most of the island. Where does that leave us?"

"What's the difference? We still have ours. You must admit they know business. Sugar production has never been better."

"True, but as long as they run the show they'll milk us dry."

"Havana is as corrupt as ever," Lydia said. "It makes no difference who runs the country."

"It wasn't this bad with Spain in control," Ignacio said. "This government is only marginally Cuban. They're all puppets and thieves, and the Americans pull the strings."

"I got a letter from Celia today," Marta said. "She is well, and so is little Eugenio. It doesn't seem possible that he is already in third grade."

"So cute," Magdalena said. "Slender like his mother, and has his father's eyes."

"Let's go to Havana," Paco said. "It's been weeks."

"Not right now. I have something for Celia I want to finish."

"The crocheting?"

"It is turning out beautifully."

"I know this is not the time to bring it up, Papá, but my hands are tied."

"You are right, Ignacio. This is not the time."

"But you never want to talk."

"Not now."

Ignacio slammed down his fork and stood. "I've got a lot to do before morning." He walked out.

"You have not finished," Magdalena said.

He was already out the door.

He saddled his gray stallion and galloped off toward Matanzas. The wind echoed in his ears as he spurred the horse and whipped it with the reins, as if he were in a race with death. He stopped at a small house in the center of town, left the horse, ran up the steps, and opened the door without knocking.

A beautiful young Negro woman with thick, brown hair that stood out as if she were electrified was sitting in the living room reading a book. The way he burst in made her jump. Then she smiled and stood to meet him. The room was simple but elegant with lace curtains and doilies on the table and chairs and a small Persian-looking carpet in the middle of the floor. Ignacio kissed her full lips and pressed her to him. He lifted her, she wrapped her legs around him, and he took her to the bedroom and threw her on the bed and furiously undressed. She responded by shedding her nightgown and slipping under the light cover. He pulled back the cover and looked at her for a moment, then he got on her with no words exchanged between them and in a moment they were entangled in each other, puffing and grunting.

With no prelude their copulation lasted only a few moments. Regaining his breath he turned on his back, took a cigar from the humidor on the night table and lit it, musing on the simple furniture that Haydée kept so clean and so neatly arranged. He had bought it all and began mentally to tally the prices of the items in the room. Soon his thoughts turned to the plantation and his father's refusal to give him his rightful inheritance, and how much more money he will manage when he takes over.

"What's the matter, Ignacio?"

He blew out a large cloud of smoke. "Why do you ask?"

"You were so anxious and finished so quickly. I barely had time to catch my breath."

"If you didn't like it, too bad."

"I didn't say that, Ignacio. But you seem troubled."

"The same old thing. I don't want to talk about it."

After a nervous moment she said, "I have some news."

"If it's not good I don't want to hear it."

"Please don't be angry, Ignacio … I'm going to have a baby."

He sprang out of bed and looked down at her. "How could you?"

Haydée curled up and started to cry.

"Don't start that shit. I don't want a baby, understand?"

"It won't be any trouble."

"You didn't hear me, Haydée. I won't have it."

"What do you want me to do?"

"I think you know."

"How can you be so mean?"

He took a long pull on the cigar as she turned away and remained silent for a long while.

Finally she said, "I won't kill my baby, Ignacio."

As he dressed, Ignacio could see the anger building in her eyes, but he said nothing.

"Where are you going?" she asked.

"Home."

She got up and put her arms around his neck and tried to kiss him, but he pushed her away. "Not our baby," she said.

He looked in her eyes and said, "Go back to Camagüey or wherever you want. I don't care where; just get the hell out of Matanzas. Understand?"

She started to cry again and cried all the while Ignacio was dressing.

"How do I know it's mine?"

She became hysterical, jumped from the bed and came at him and began to hit him with her fists. He grabbed her arms and she kicked him, so he pushed her toward the bed and sat her down. "Listen, Haydée, it's your baby and your problem. I never want to see it or you, and I don't want to know anything about either of you. If you need money, write and I'll do what I can, but never tell anyone I'm the father. Understand? A one-way ticket to Camagüey will be waiting under the name Haydée Gómez at the train station. Treat me right and I'll treat you right."

"My parents are good people. I won't need anything from you."

"As you wish." He dressed and looked at her, smiled, took fifty dollars from his wallet, and laid it on the night table. "Write if you need more."

*

Next morning Ignacio did not show up for breakfast. Paco found him in the barn talking politics with Enrique.

"Gentlemen," Paco said. "How goes the cutting?"

251

"Good," Ignacio said. "Papá, I have to get out there."

By his tone Paco knew he was still angry, and he stopped him. "Wait, Ignacio. Let us talk first."

"About what?"

"I know what you want, son, but it is not yet time. I am still strong and able."

"And I am stronger and more able."

"That is a matter of opinion." Paco realized he had opened a door he had wanted to keep closed. "But even if you are right, youth is not always best in a business as large as ours."

Enrique silently walked away.

"Oh, no? Who brought in all the new business, and the overseas distribution network? Who started selling directly abroad?"

"You have done well, Ignacio, but you have many years ahead of you. I have fewer, and I want to *disfrutar*."

"Is that what this place is to you? A plaything?"

"I have not done badly, Ignacio. Each man makes his contribution. No man builds a business like ours by himself. Each of us builds on what he is handed."

"Nothing has been handed to me, Papá."

"You're running the farm. What more do you want?"

"You know the answer to that."

"Well, to be honest, you are not ready."

"What the hell does that mean? I'm nearly twice as old as you were when you took over."

"But I was settled with a wife. You are still a boy, pursuing boy's things."

"You mean Haydée, I suppose."

"For one thing, yes. Aren't you ever planning to settle down?"

"You had a mulatta on the side, Papá, and everybody knew it."

"That was quite different, Ignacio, and you know it."

"All I know is you've held me back all my life, and I'm tired of it."

"You do not understand what happened back then. It was nothing like what you are doing, keeping a woman in Matanzas and flaunting her as if she were a grand prize for your grand penis. Any man can have that, and many do. It takes only money to have a mistress; no brains are required. But most important, it shows little responsibility to keep a woman to whom you make no commitments."

"So it was all right to sleep with a slave under your own roof?"

"Have you no respect?"

"The sister of your benefactress?"

Paco moved toward him and looked up into his face. "*Cabrón! Sinvergüenza!*" he yelled. "I wish you had acquired a trace of your brother's humanity!"

"You want me to be like that nincompoop?"

The blindness overtook Paco and he lunged at him. He saw nothing but Ignacio's chest, for his eyes landed there with only one thought: to flatten him, to pulverize him, to smash him to dust. Paco suddenly found himself on the ground, his jaw aching, with his son, tall and lean, standing over him.

"I knew it would come to this, Papá. You should have learned by now that I'm not Genio. I won't be pushed around."

Still on the ground, his stomach and jaw aching, Paco watched him walk away. Ignacio walked to his stallion, saddled him, and rode off without looking back. Paco stood with some difficulty and brushed the dust and sand off his clothes. It took him several minutes to reconstruct what had happened, then he did not want to think about it.

He passed Magdalena and Lydia talking over coffee in the kitchen. They stopped as he passed through, slightly bent over.

"Are you all right?" Magdalena asked.

He said nothing and continued up to his office and closed the door behind him. Slumped in his chair he must have spent an hour looking out the window at his land, the men in the distance planting new cane, Enrique standing to one side watching them, then Ignacio riding up to him on his gray stallion and dismounting. It was all happening before his eyes on his land under his control, and for the first time he realized he no longer controlled anything outside his skin. He lit a cigar and smoked it down to a stub over the next hour before he rose to look at the papers on his desk.

Paco said nothing of the incident to Marta. In truth he did not want even to think about that awful encounter, and he did not want to excite her needlessly. He thought of it as an encounter rather than a fight, but it was no less than a fight, and he had lost, and he would have to deal with that before he could face himself.

Three days later, after supper, Paco asked Ignacio to come to his office to talk. They had not spoken since that morning at the barn, and Ignacio had remained aloof, not hurt, merely angry. He turned his steely gaze to his father and, patronizingly, said, "Fine."

Paco excused himself and walked up the stairs with Ignacio behind him. Paco closed the door and asked him to sit. The air was more formal than either enjoyed with little chatting or friendly banter. Ignacio looked at his father with that same strange smile, for he knew what Paco would say.

"I have thought it over, Ignacio, and I have decided to retire and turn over ownership of the farm to you. Of course Magdalena will have to agree."

"I understand."

"I will keep an interest in the profits with which to support your mother and me."

"That's just."

"Good. I will talk with Magdalena to see if she is willing. You understand that she, too, must have a share since she is half owner."

A cool breeze blew in through the window.

"Of course. What share do you want?"

"Twenty percent for me and twenty for Magdalena. That will leave you controlling interest with sixty percent. Also I have left your mother and you as my beneficiaries. I will ask Magdalena to name you as a beneficiary also, so eventually you will be sole owner."

A smile of relief crept across Ignacio's face. "I appreciate that, Papá. I'm sorry for the other day. I said and did things I shouldn't have."

"So did I and we are both sorry."

They stood and shook hands, and Ignacio embraced his father. Paco shuddered at his son's cold body.

As Ignacio left, Paco asked him to leave the door open and to ask Magdalena to come up. He walked to the window and stood with his face in the breeze. The slight chill took him back to his early years in Asturias. He had perspired while talking with Ignacio; the soft breeze caressed his face like loving hands, and he felt the most profound relief he could remember. Such a simple act, he thought, and we can both begin to enjoy life.

Marta and Lydia looked surprised when Ignacio abruptly told Magdalena to go up and then walked back to the barn. Magdalena jumped to her feet and went to Paco's office.

"*Que pasó?*"

"I have business to discuss if you feel like it. Otherwise, we can talk tomorrow."

She nodded, and he explained the proposal he had made Ignacio. "He has wanted this for a long time, Magdalena. I think he can handle it as well as I have, perhaps better."

"As long as Lydia and I can continue to live comfortably in this house, where I have always lived, whatever you decide is fine with me."

"Thank you, Magdalena. I will have the lawyer draw up the papers tomorrow. I would like you to come too, so that you will understand everything."

"Thank you, Paco, but that is not necessary. I have every confidence in you."

"Please, Magdalena. I want you to."

"Of course."

Paco again went out to the porch and asked Marta if she wanted to take a stroll. She stood and led him down the steps smiling. "And Magdalena?"

"I have turned the plantation over to Ignacio. I wanted Magdalena's approval."

Marta stopped and embraced him. "I am very glad, Paco. It is what he always wanted. He is intelligent and a wonderful manager; the responsibility will let him feel like a man. Oh, Paco, I'm very happy."

Paco smiled and marveled at how she could love such a spoiled boy. "Let us plan a vacation."

"Wonderful. Where?"

"How would you like to visit Asturias. It's been a long time."

She hugged him and he felt her tears on his neck. "Let me rest a moment," she said. "Too much excitement." After a few moments she resumed walking.

"Is something wrong?"

"Oh, no. I'm so happy, Paco. It will be good for all of us. He has a good heart. Let us go back now? I would like to sit on the porch and watch what is left of the sunset."

"Of course."

*

During the next three weeks Paco explained the minute details of his bookkeeping system to Ignacio, most of which Ignacio had already figured out, including the agreement with Paco's Uncle Eugenio about promising to keep Magdalena and Lydia. Ignacio had performed every job on the place and had studied family dynamics at close range. He did not need to listen, but he gladly humored his father. It was the bookkeeping that he dug into with glee. He had scanned the entries many times and carried much of the data in his head, but that morning Paco took him systematically through every step, explaining how and why he kept each account, marveling at how easily Ignacio grasped everything. Paco then opened a bottle of Spanish brandy he had kept for special occasions and poured two glasses.

"It is early yet, but I want to toast you, my son. May you make your place in this world." He raised his glass.

Ignacio drank and returned the toast, "And to my father, who has taught me everything I know."

Paco drank, silently wishing he had been able to teach his son the important part of a good life. He lifted two cigars from his humidor and handed one to Ignacio. He knew Ignacio liked his cigars and never missed an opportunity to smoke one.

"Your old humidor. I remember it as a boy."

"It is two years older than you. I wrote my father to send me some cedar and some oak from Peñamellera. He thought I was crazy. Before the logs arrived I received a letter from him asking how it could be that Cuba has no cedar or oak. I wrote back saying we had plenty, but I wanted Asturian logs. I hired a master wood crafter in Havana to make that table behind my desk. With the leftovers he made the humidor."

"I've always admired them, Papá."

"One day they will be yours, Ignacio, but not yet. Some things will remain mine for a while longer—without argument, I hope."

"Of course not, Papá."

Suddenly they heard the sound of something heavy falling to the floor in Paco's bedroom next door. They ran in, opened the door, and found Marta on the floor with a crochet needle and some thread clutched in her hands. Her face was pinched in pain.

"What happened, Marta? Marta?" Paco tried to make her talk, but she was unconscious. "Quick, Ignacio, get the doctor. Hurry!" But Ignacio was already racing down the stairs two at a time. Paco lifted her onto the bed and heard horse's hooves pounding. Glancing out the side window he saw Ignacio raising a cloud of dust along the road.

In a few moments Lydia and Magdalena ran in. Magdalena put her hand over her mouth and fainted into a chair. Lydia went immediately to Marta and felt her pulse. "She is alive."

"What is it?"

She shook her head. "Heart?"

"Oh, God! Ignacio, please hurry."

"He has already gone," Lydia said.

By then Magdalena regained consciousness, realized what had happened, and began to cry.

In less than an hour the doctor arrived and Ignacio took him to the bedroom. Paco, Magdalena, and Lydia all jumped to their feet.

"She collapsed on the floor, Doctor. We heard her from the next room and ran in."

"Yes. Ignacio told me." The doctor felt her pulse. "Uh-huh." Then he put his stethoscope to her chest and listened and moved it and listened and moved it again and listened.

"What is it, Doctor?" Paco could barely control himself.

"Her heart. A coronary thrombosis, I'm afraid. We'll have to monitor her for a while to see what develops."

"Can't you do something?"

"I'll give her something to calm her and try to stabilize her heart, but … we'll see."

For three hours they sat in the room waiting with the doctor for a sign that Marta would respond. Seeing her so motionless, the doctor walked to the bed and placed his stethoscope on her chest again and then shook his head. Slowly he rose and walked to Paco. "She's gone, Paco. I'm very sorry."

The words might have been in a foreign language for the impression they made. Paco looked dazed into the doctor's face. It was impossible to know what was boiling in his brain, but it was clear he had not understood or perhaps refused to understand. The doctor gave him a sedative, which he took passively and lay down beside Marta. In minutes he was asleep. An hour later he woke screaming. Lydia ran in and found him shaking Marta's shoulders, trying to revive her.

"Stop it, Paco." But he would not.

She slapped his face, and he stopped and looked up at her. "She is dead, Paco. Now come."

*

"Papá wants to make the funeral arrangements, but he is not able," Ignacio said that evening.

"Let your father do something; the distraction will help him," Lydia said.

"Haven't you seen him? He looks like a mummy, staring at us as if we were all strangers."

"Yes," Magdalena said. "Lydia is right. Let him do what he wants."

Paco stayed in his bedroom all that day like a prisoner looking out his cell window, feeling removed forever from the world. Out his window lay another world in which workers came and went and overseers yelled orders. But in his room Paco felt like a man condemned to loneliness with prison guards to lead him from meal to meal. Watching soft, puffy clouds move languorously, he tried to imagine Marta looking down on him. He opened his liquor cabinet, took out a bottle of brandy, filled a glass and drank it down hoping to wash away the loneliness of a world suddenly devoid of substance.

The next morning Ignacio came for him and helped him dress for the funeral. Ignacio led his father downstairs and out to the carriage where Magdalena and Lydia waited.

At the funeral Lydia sat on his left with Magdalena beyond her and Ignacio on his right. Paco could not comprehend Ignacio's kindness and the way he had handled everything with such efficiency and sensitivity. Sobbing every time she heard Marta's name, Magdalena was little help. The way she attracted attention revolted Paco. He wanted to think of Marta and his future and try to understand his anger at the woman he loved. She did not want to die, he told himself. But nothing helped allay the feeling that she had abandoned him.

As he tried to find the thread ends in his unraveled world, and the priest droned through the mass, and Magdalena mumbled the rosary over and over fingering her beads, Lydia reached for Paco's hand and held it on her lap. He knew Lydia had grown to love Marta, but her sudden tenderness surprised him. As always, she held her head high and her jaw clamped firmly, ready for action. Isabel's funeral must be rumbling in her mind, he thought. She rubbed Paco's hand warmly and tenderly. A strange coldness ran through Paco as the fleeting memory of those days long ago flashed before him, those evenings she had come to him with such love and devotion, and then stopped suddenly because she no longer needed his services. He withdrew his hand and passed it over his head to dissimulate. He did not look at her, but tried to listen to the Latin, which over the years he felt he understood. The congregation would rise and repeat a chant or response; then they would sit. After communion, Paco kneeled with his hands clasped on the back of the pew before him and again felt Lydia's hand reach over and cover his. He sat back before the others and remained sitting until the ceremony ended. Throughout the ritual he saw the priest's face only once or twice. Only his back presented itself to the congregation, and Paco hoped that neither he nor anyone else had seen this ridiculous woman trying to hold his hand. They would see it as no more than a kind gesture, but he knew better.

On their way out, Magdalena commented on the priest's beautiful oration. Paco had heard little of it, but he nodded agreement. What he had heard sounded trite: words he could have said about anybody.

Outside Lydia would not leave his side. Magdalena stopped to talk with some of the other ladies and left Paco and Lydia to greet the mourners together. Paco did not like her posing as his companion any more than he liked her gestures in the church, but he said nothing. People stopped to offer condolences for over half an hour. Finally the crowd dwindled and Lydia said, "Come, Paco. I will prepare your favorite meal."

"I do not have hunger, Lydia, but thank you."

"Do not be a child. You must eat." Turning to Magdalena she said, "Come, Magdalena, time to go home."

Without changing her clothes Lydia went straight to the kitchen, put on her apron, and went to work. As Paco walked up the stairs, Magdalena said, "Rest now. I will call you when lunch is ready."

An hour later she went to his room and knocked. He did not answer. She turned the doorknob. It was locked. "Paco, lunch."

Hearing no answer, she knocked again, waited a few seconds and said, "Come now, Paco. You must eat."

After several minutes with no response she walked down to the kitchen and said, "He has locked himself in his room and will not answer."

"Such a child. I will bring him."

Lydia's knock was stronger than Magdalena's, but it brought the same response. Knocking harder she said firmly, "Do not be a child, Paco. Lunch is ready."

Paco opened the door slightly. "Leave me alone."

"But your lunch."

"You eat it."

"But, Paco." Before she could say another word he closed the door, and she heard the key turn in the lock.

Lydia returned to the kitchen and told Magdalena.

"He wants to be alone, Lydia. He will soon get hungry and come out."

"Ignacio will not eat either," Lydia said. With her lip curled she walked into the kitchen and fixed a plate for herself, brought it to the table and sat down to eat. Like a puppet Magdalena did the same.

By nightfall Magdalena again tried to talk to Paco and again got no response. As she turned to walk away, she heard his voice through the door, "Bring two bottles of brandy."

"But Paco, you must eat something."

Lydia said, "Do not take it. That will bring him out."

"No, Lydia. I must respect his wish."

"Nonsense! Starve him out."

Magdalena opened the pantry and took out two bottles of Paco's good brandy and took them to his door. "They are by the door, Paco."

He opened the door, reached down for the brandy and closed the door behind him. She heard the key turn in the lock.

That evening, long after sunset, Lydia fixed him an omelet and took it to his door and knocked. "Paco, I have made you something to eat. I leave it by the door. Please take it."

Half way down the stairs she heard his door open and close.

That night, Magdalena told Ignacio about his father's strange behavior. He said he would talk to him. A few minutes later he returned to the living room. "I see what you mean. He must feel terrible. Leave him alone."

*

For six days Paco lived in his room consuming only brandy and an occasional meal. Most of the meals Lydia left outside his door remained there until she took them away to leave another. Four times in those six days he opened the door and took in the tray of food. Each day he requested another bottle or two of brandy. After the second day they brought him what he requested without comment.

Late in the afternoon of the sixth day, Paco emerged shaved and wearing a suit. Magdalena stopped him as he walked down to the back porch. "*Ay*, Paco. I am so happy to see you. Are you feeling better?"

"I'm going out."

"But Lydia has supper."

"I'm going out."

"Lydia and I want to help you through your ordeal, Paco. She is preparing baked snapper."

As if she had not spoken he started toward the barn to get the carriage. Magdalena stopped him. "Do not offend her, Paco. She means well. Eat something and tell her how good it is."

"Why should eating out offend her?"

"Paco, you have no idea how much she loves you and wants to please you. It is not good to live alone." She looked down at her hands. "Believe me, I know."

Paco stood in shock at hearing those words. "*Por Diós, Magdalena,* it's been less than a week."

"I just want to see you happy. You have suffered an indescribable loss, but you must move on."

"You pushed Lydia on me forty years ago. I realize you want to help your sister, but has it occurred to you that my happiness is too high a price to pay for her well-being?"

"I love you both, Paco. I only want to see you both happy."

"How stupid do you think I am?"

"I do not understand. It is so easy to be happy, to do what is right. All those years Lydia chose to be a slave she could have been my sister. Why did she hurt herself? It was wrong. I do not understand. You both suffer, and I want to help, not make you sad or angry. You could be happy here with Lydia and me and your son. What is wrong with that? I do not understand. I am not intelligent, Paco. I seem to hurt people even when I try to help them, but life could be so good and simple if only people did what was right."

Paco did not feel like arguing. In fact, through her goodness she had hurt nearly everyone around her. "You are the kindest person I have ever known, Magdalena, but you cannot push people where they do not want to go."

"I should not have interfered ... I meant no harm ... It just seemed so simple ... But every time I try ... Please forgive me."

"There is nothing to forgive."

"Please try to see the good in Lydia."

Paco's warm, soft smile solidified into a stony glare. He looked at her for a moment fighting anger and said, "I go to Matanzas for supper. Tell Lydia whatever you like."

"But ..."

Paco did not stay to hear her response, but walked to the barn, where he asked one of the workers to hitch up the carriage. He waited and then drove off alone.

He returned after midnight through the back door and found Magdalena and Lydia in the living room.

"How late you are, Paco," Magdalena said. "Did you have a good time?"

"*Buenas noches,*" he said, and went to the dining room and, for a minute, leaned against the chair at his place at the table and then turned and walked up the stairs clutching the banister with every step.

On the way to his room he noticed Ignacio's room light still on. He thought it unusual for Ignacio to be up so late; then he went to his own room to get ready for bed. He took off his jacket and tie and heard a soft knock at the door, a knock so soft it raised its fist out of ancient memory. "I'm almost ready for bed."

"It's Ignacio, Papá."

"Oh, come in."

"I hear you went out this evening."

"Not spying on me too, I hope."

"Oh, no, just worried."

"Well I am fine. I had supper with don Miguel and two other friends in Matanzas. We had a good time talking and finishing off a bottle of brandy. Anything else you want to know?"

"Actually I'd like to talk if you feel up to it."

"I feel fine."

"You look a little ... well ..."

"If you mean drunk, you are right. Now what is the problem?"

"Some advice?"

Looking at his son with one eye to get a single image, Paco had never seen such intensity of feeling. He took his son's arm and led him to one of the chairs near the window and sat at the other. "A brandy?"

"Yes, thank you."

Paco poured two glasses. "Sounds serious."

"It's not easy, Papá."

"Well, are you going to tell me?"

"The girl I have in Matanzas."

"Haydée?"

"May I have a cigar, Papá?"

Paco nearly knocked over the humidor reaching back over the table, but recovered it and extracted two cigars. "You have noticed, I brought it in from my ... your office along with the brandy."

"I don't know if it's me or what, but it's so ... there's no passion, no closeness. I go to her, we undress, and ... well, you know ... afterwards she wants to talk, and all I want to do is leave. She's very beautiful, but I don't love her, whatever that means. I just ... you know ... she gives me what I want."

Only the brandy could have eased Paco's embarrassment, especially as it was the first time Ignacio had dared such intimacy. "How does she feel about it?"

"She says she loves me. She likes to talk and sit together beforehand, but I'm already excited when I get there. Talking distracts me. She calls it 'warming up,' but it cools me off. I don't want to talk to her about me, about intimate things."

Paco had always thought this boy's coldness had sprung from ambition and a single-mindedness that would not allow anything else to intrude. But even through an alcoholic haze he realized the lack of feeling had been there before the ambition, before boyhood, possibly before birth. "Much of the fun of lovemaking, son, is playing around, at least for me."

"Not for me. Is something wrong with me, Papá?"

"I have never seen Haydée. What does she look like?"

"Beautiful, voluptuous, almost as tall as I, a full-blooded African, but unbelievably attractive. We walk down the street together, and every man we pass turns to stare. Some even say things. I suppose it should make me angry, but it doesn't. She likes it."

"Love means wanting to be with her. Do you?"

"I want her desperately sometimes … but no, not just to be with her. She's a woman like the others. They all have the same equipment."

"When I was a young man, well meaning friends and family advised me to try many girls before settling on one, but I never wanted anyone else. I loved your mother since childhood. Some men, perhaps most, follow that advice, though." His eyes filled.

"I've had dozens, Papá. I enjoy them all, but they're all pretty much the same."

"You seem to see a woman as someone to satisfy your appetite, like a steak. You couldn't fall in love with a steak." Paco liked the analogy and laughed aloud. "A woman is different. The right woman becomes part of you." Struggling to hold back tears, he poured another glass of brandy, held up the bottle and looked at Ignacio questioningly.

Ignacio shook his head.

"Children provide wonderful satisfaction. They fill a deep desire to leave some of your self that will live beyond you. A piece of immortality, I suppose. That's why losing a child is so terrible." He emptied the brandy glass and poured another. "Besides producing offspring, a wife is your companion and friend, as much a part of you as your arm or your head. You become one person."

"I've never felt anything like that."

Moving to stand, Paco said, "I hope you will one day; however, you will have to do that without my help."

"There's more, Papá."

Although the brandy had taken its toll and his monolog had drained him, he felt he had to hear him out, so he sat and sipped. "Go on."

"The last time I saw her was three weeks ago, before Mamá died. She told me she was pregnant. I wanted her to abort it, but she wouldn't."

"And?"

"I sent her home. Told her I'd send money, but only if she doesn't name me as the father."

"What did she say?"

"She cried. Why do they always cry, Papá?"

Paco shook his head and turned to reach for the bottle, but could not focus on it. Even with one eye closed he could not direct his hand to it.

Ignacio picked it up and filled his glass for him and said, "I told her I'd leave a one-way ticket to Camagüey at the train station."

"Did she leave?"

"Yes."

"Now what?"

"What do you mean?"

"Another mistress to spread your seed west toward Pinar Del Río?"

"You're making fun of me."

"There is no fun in this, Ignacio. I merely ask if you intend to continue."

"What else?"

"I've had too much brandy for profound thoughts."

"Damn it, Papá, I have a problem."

"Sounds like you have the solution."

"But you don't like it?"

"Have you ever cared about what I like?"

"You never refused advice before."

"You are thirty-three years old, Ignacio, a little old for seeking advice, but here it is: become a human being."

"Meaning?"

"You made a baby, paid off the mother, and threw them both out. God knows what will become of your son or daughter. Does it not bother you that you will never know your child, your very flesh?"

"Her parents were slaves, Papá. I can't marry her. I don't owe her that."

"I'm not thinking of her."

"The baby won't starve."

"It will hunger for a father."

"With her looks she'll find someone."

"You asked for advice; that's it: become a human being." He stood, walked to his bed, turned down the cover, and fell in. "I'm tired and drunk, Ignacio. Perhaps tomorrow." With Ignacio looking on he fell asleep.

Hours later he opened his eyes. The room was spinning. He remembered the brandy. He could feel blood coursing through his temples. Not sure he could stand, he tried and got as far as the window. With the room still in motion, his head throbbing, and the odor of burnt cane and fermented juice blowing through the window, his stomach rebelled. He ran to the dresser, removed the pitcher from the pan, and let loose into the pan. After standing bent over the pan for several moments with his hands on the dresser top, he stood as straight as he could and walked back to the window for air and saw the moon embedded like a hatchet in the horizon. With the red sphere as backdrop the trees and cane came eerily alive.

The odors of the pressing plant seemed less potent now. He had grown accustomed to those odors and even managed to convince himself he liked them. But now, at that moment, he knew he had lied to himself. The smell was indeed revolting, a sickening sweetness overlaying sour corruption. But no man would build his life around an odor, no matter how vile. Yet, it would be good to wake up one morning and not smell it, or better yet, never smell it again. Perhaps one day he might remember it fondly, he said to himself; and then he muttered, "But I doubt it." At that moment he realized he had spent those days enclosed in his room nearly smothering in the silence of Marta, with only that dark, sickening odor to let him know he was still alive. She had smelled it too, he told himself. Surely it had revolted her, but she said she did not mind. She had breathed it and lived in it because it had become hers. Paco tried to formulate an image of her face but could not. He began to weep.

He must have spent half an hour watching the moon pull itself out of the horizon and slip ever so slowly into the sky like a drunken bat trying to take flight after its daylight repose. As Paco watched he wondered, as he had a thousand times, how he would live without Marta. He had walked through the living room that evening and looked into the dining room for Marta's chair, forever to remain empty. She had filled the room with her absence. He had walked up to their bedroom hoping to find her sewing and had stood at the window trying vainly to imagine her face against the moonlit sky. During his fitful sleep he had felt for her several times. Now, awake at the window he listened to the sounds of the night and recalled a day in his childhood in Colosía when he was five or six years old. A cat had given birth to kittens in a nest by the back wall of his house. Wanting to help them he moved the kittens into a box in his room to keep them dry and warm. With no visible emotion the mother cat followed him in and, with her teeth, picked one up by the scruff of the neck and walked it back to her nest as little Paco watched. Then she returned and picked up another and moved it, and then another, and another. When she had laid the last kitten in her nest she returned to look again, saw none, and returned to her family, gently lay around them and nursed them. Watching the process with fascination he concluded that cats cannot count. But I am not a cat, he thought. I know she is gone; why do I keep expecting to find her.

Looking up at the white moon, he felt a weight lift from his breast: I have shaken off one ghost, the terrible struggle with Ignacio. Perhaps I can shake off the more deadly one, my responsibility for him. Ghosts have only the life I give them. Since he was born Ignacio had dominated Isabel and his older brother ruthlessly, thinking only of himself. In a way he has dominated me for years, but no more. At the age of Christ on the cross, this man-child still thinks only of himself. I can detest the man he has become without detesting myself. Last evening he exposed the core of his soul, and it was cold, corrupt, whiskered. I think it emerged fully formed at birth. No father could have diverted him from his destiny.

Late night sleeplessness had long plagued Paco with irrational fears, and he had learned that fears diminish with the rising sun. But this was no ordinary night. Looking through the window at the great beacon of the night he finally accepted that he had done all he could for his wife and sons and must now live the remainder of his life. Isabel was his greatest regret, and he would never pardon himself for abandoning her. He wanted to believe he could not have changed her, but that was too great a stretch.

The moon had quenched its red glow in the cool, dark sky. Paco returned to bed and fell asleep.

*

He should have felt terrible the next morning, but he rose refreshed and reached to the small table next to his bed and picked up the old watch his father gave him. Because of its bulk he had used it rarely, mainly on formal occasions. It was hardly worth the trouble to carry to work, but his father had held it in his hands and his grandfather a century before. Pushing the stem of the bulbous timepiece, the face cover flipped open to show a few minutes before seven-thirty. They would all be waiting for him, but he did not hurry; they would not start without him. He emptied the pan out the window, rinsed it from the pitcher, wiped it clean, and washed his face and shaved. As he lathered his face and then stropped the razor, anticipation overtook him. What will I face? Ignacio waiting for my reaction to his nocturnal confession; Lydia's seductive routine; Magdalena playing along with her; trying to visualize Marta in her vacant chair; not worrying about planting and cutting and pressing and all the other duties of *hacendado;* and the acrid smell of the cane mills.

Ignacio will handle it well, he thought, but if not, it will not be my problem. This house is filled with loneliness and death. Marta couldn't even say goodbye. No; I must remember that she did not wish to die.

He rinsed the lather off his face, put on a white shirt and necktie, lifted his white linen suit off its hanger, and pulled on the trousers and then the jacket. He took two suitcases from under the bed and laid them open on the bed and then looked in the mirror, straightened his tie and walked downstairs smiling at the morning into which he was about to walk.

As he expected, Magdalena, Ignacio and Lydia were waiting, and they all smiled as he sat down.

"Why is Marta's chair gone?"

"Sorry, Paco," Magdalena said. "I thought it would remind you."

"I have not forgotten her, Magdalena."

She rose and moved the chair to its place at the opposite end of the table.

He nodded approval. "Now, how are you? The sun shines and the breeze blows across the cane fields."

"You feel better," Magdalena said. "I am very happy. You have been through much."

"I feel quite well. Lydia, would you please pass the eggs?"

"Of course, Paco. I made them the way you like: solid whites and soft yolks."

"You are too good to me."

"Nothing is too good for you, Paco."

Ignacio's eyes moved back and forth between Lydia and his father. He wondered if something had revived between them.

"You look well, Lydia. Is that a new dress?"

"Yes. I bought it last week. Do you like it?"

"It becomes you. Stand and let me see … turn … yes, very nice."

Lydia's smile spread across her face. She looked almost girlish. "Thank you, Paco. I hoped you would like it."

"Everything under control, Ignacio?"

"Sure, Papá. I'll relax when the planting's finished. Maybe go to Varadero Beach for a few days."

"Good. Human beings need rest."

Anger flashed across Ignacio's eyes; then he smiled at Magdalena and Lydia and continued eating.

"You know, Magdalena, the first time I walked into this house your portrait almost knocked me over."

She smiled. "Really?"

"I fell in love with it that very moment. It was the most beautiful woman I had ever seen." She blushed and Paco continued, "Then you walked into the living room and made the picture look like a pale imitation."

"You are embarrassing me."

"You have aged beautifully and gracefully. You still put the portrait to shame."

Lydia looked puzzled and annoyed; her sister glanced at her apologetically.

"I almost forgot Marta that day. The way Tío Eugenio scowled, he must have noticed."

"Oh no, Paco. He was never jealous."

"Any man with a wife like you would be either jealous or an idiot."

"*Ay*, Paco, this flattery makes me feel bad; truly."

"Forgive me, Magdalena. I did not intend that."

"What will you do now?"

"Continue to live as God requires ..."

She smiled and winked at Lydia.

"... in Asturias. It's time I returned to my homeland."

"How?" Magdalena asked.

"On the next sailing."

"It takes time to adjust and find peace. Mourning takes time. Too much has happened, and you must cope with it."

"All quite true, Magdalena, but I have an irresistible desire to see those cold, green mountains."

Lydia squinted, her eyes hidden behind dark anger. "Have you any family there, Paco?" she asked. "Your parents died years ago."

"My brother and his wife and his four children I have never met and lots of cousins, most of them strangers."

"I hope it is not because of me, Papá."

"Nothing so complicated, Ignacio. I just want to."

After breakfast Paco excused himself and went upstairs.

"I have much work," Ignacio said and walked toward the back porch. In a few minutes Paco heard a light knock on his door. "Come in," he said, expecting Lydia. He stood bent, laying clothes neatly into the open suitcases. He had enjoyed the sisters' reaction to his announcement and was curious to learn how far they would go. He turned and saw Ignacio wearing his most serious face and said, "Oh."

"Why, Papá?"

Paco continued laying shirts and socks in one of the bags. "As I told you."

"I don't understand."

"There is no mystery."

"I guess the trip will do you good. I'm surprised you haven't gone back sooner."

"Did you want to talk about something?"

"About last night: you're right. I'm too rigid. We'll work together after you return. Between us we'll make this farm the gem of the island."

"Thank you, Ignacio, but I do not plan to return."

"But this is your home. Everything you have is here."

"It is yours now. You will not need me."

"But I do, Papá."

"Without your mother, I am no longer the same man. I have another life to live, and I am anxious to learn who I will become."

"What will you do?"

Paco shrugged. "Perhaps help my brother's family, improve their lives, find happiness. Who knows? I only know that I cannot stay here and remain alive."

"I need you here, Papá."

"I have passed thirty-eight good years here. Now I leave you in charge with full confidence."

"Genio was your favorite, wasn't he?"

"No, you were until I finally understood him; then it was too late. Look, Ignacio, My self remains here in you. I have sown my seeds in hopes that they would take root. You are the only one left. All my hopes and descendants reside in you. What I said last night: it is your only hope and mine. I am not leaving to get away from you or anyone else. I simply want to return to the land that bore me, where I met the only woman in my life. The trajectory of your life ascends as mine descends. Asturias is the home of my ancestors; my heart longs for her. Perhaps I will find only ghosts, but I must look."

His eyes filled. He shook his head and resumed packing. For the first time in years Ignacio looked like a little boy, hands in his pockets, eyes on the floor. Until that moment he had felt sorry for his father. Now he realized that his father pitied him, and that hurt even more than his father's disdain.

"Ignacio, I have done what I could for you. I have taught you what I could. You must make your own life. Mine has turned out well, not perfect, but well enough. I hope yours does too; but remember: you get no second chance."

Ignacio embraced his father as he had never before and held him until Paco felt his son's tears on his neck. "I'll try, Papá. I will. I promise."

After lunch four days later, Paco sat at the table in his room, took out a piece of paper and wrote a note:

> "Dear Ignacio, I wish you success in your life and the farm, especially the former, for it is by far the more important. I depart with love, and I assure you that your mother loved you very much also.
>
> "I leave you my watch. My father gave it to me when I left Colosía. It is old and primitive and has little value, but it was my father's, and I want it to be yours.
>
> "Goodbye.
>
> "September 17, 1905."

269

Paco rubbed his thumb over the face of the watch and remembered his gruff father's sad face the day he handed it to him on the road outside their house in Colosía. Paco's grandfather had taken it off a French soldier he had shot on the outskirts of Madrid. The child Paco had tried to imagine what it would feel like to kill a man and then take his watch for a souvenir. Perhaps his father had wondered the same thing, but he never spoke of it. Paco felt both pride and horror in his grandfather's courage. He smiled with satisfaction at the watch and at the years he had carried it. Perhaps it was his only link to a past he could never know; he stroked the same face his grandfather had stroked and felt he was touching that grandfather who had died a boy. Such useless objects as these speak of history in a wordless language. What had it meant to that poor young Frenchman? Had his father given it to him? Those parts of its history lie buried in the ashes of time.

Paco laid the watch on the table as he reread his note and realized he had said nothing about his grandfather and the Frenchman. He started to rewrite the note, but decided not to bother knowing that Ignacio had no interest in mundane details. Genio was different; he would have wanted to know.

He folded the note, slipped it into an envelope, wrote Ignacio's name on the outside and left it on the dresser with the watch and chain over it. Ignacio will find it, he thought. He might even enjoy it.

*

Except for the narrow opening into the Florida Straits, Havana spreads her arms around her huge, sprawling harbor. That massive body of water lies nestled, as in a womb, safe from the world outside. In that harbor with its smells and sounds, ships have taken sustenance to and from the city for four centuries.

Paco boarded the ship an hour before departure after empty goodbyes and dry kisses. Ignacio and Magdalena seemed sad; Lydia had stayed home to tend to her duties. After waving goodbye to Magdalena and Ignacio from the deck one final time, Paco strolled around the ship to survey the city. In his nearly forty years in Cuba, this was the second time he had seen Havana from the bay. The wind changed suddenly, and he caught the acrid-sweet odor of the cane fields and walked to the other side.

He was on the port side when stevedores slipped the cords off their mooring. At first the movement was so gradual that he did not realize they were moving. Almost imperceptibly the detached ship slipped languidly a short distance into the harbor and then rotated nearly one hundred eighty degrees to face the channel. It seemed like a mirage to Paco because he did not see the tugboats straining to move the great vessel. Standing at the railing he watched the city move around him as if on a spinning platform. He recalled the night his room had spun in a sea of brandy, but this motion was real. The ship completed its turn and began its slow slide through the tight opening between the two great Spanish fortresses. As it slid along the narrow channel between El Castillo de La Punta and El Morro Castle and into the racing Florida Strait, Paco felt he was being reborn.

Over the next half-hour the loud, bustling metropolis dwindled to a quiet sprinkling of honeycombed structures aflame in the setting sun. An hour later the great city dissolved into a gray smudge on the horizon between cobalt sky and turquoise sea. Pushing past the choppy tropical gulf as it emptied into the tumultuous blue Atlantic, Paco recalled the day in Gijón where waves crashing against the rocks nearly shook the explorer out of him. Only Facundo's taunting had prevented him from aborting his quest and succumbing to the Spanish army. Many times over the years he had wondered where life might have led him as a soldier. Fighting young rebels like Genio, perhaps? He had imagined he could conquer the world—a conquistador, Facundo had said. Now he would leave that dream to Ignacio. At fifty-six, trying to foresee his future, he recalled how, as a boy, he wondered what kind of man he would become. Now he understood that destiny yanks you this way and that, with no warning of what is waiting around the next bend in the road. Living, he thought, is like moving across this great ocean in the dark of night.

Two hours later, still standing at the rail outside his first class stateroom, he went inside and changed into a dark gray suit. Taking his old beret out of his suitcase he put it on and returned to the deck. The old black felt cap smelled of moth balls, but it still fit after thirty-eight years. Marta had saved it for him, knowing he would one day return. Now, dressed for Spanish weather, his eyes moved with the huge swells that could easily swallow the ship. Such power! This ocean is truly power without restraint. As he looked into the water imagining sea monsters and other brute life, Lydia and Magdalena sprang into his thoughts. He smiled to himself.

The sun had set into the ship's wake leaving night free to invade defenseless sky. Paco realized he had spent the afternoon at the rail. Now, with no moon yet, he could see only the water's bared teeth as the ship knifed eastward. Feeling finally relaxed, his mind wandered:

Where is Marta? Certainly not up there in that darkness. The northeastern horizon has dissolved in blackness, but I know the ancient mountains of Asturias are there. Perhaps I will find her in those mountains. He thought of the ruins of an old Visigothic castle high above Covadonga.

It was surely bold and majestic and strong in its day; all *conquistadores* eventually weaken, crumble, and die. Perhaps I can find contentment among shards of memories and the optimism of youth. Youth doesn't realize its ignorance, and old age wraps itself in sour memories it calls wisdom. The water rises and falls in profound, gentle undulations. How deep it must be? What lives down there? *No importa!* By morning it will be blue again and rough and beautiful.

Hearing a series of bell tones and a voice, "Call to supper," he recalled the Spanish proverb: *El muerto al Hoyo, el vivo al pollo.* (To their grave with the dead; the living to their bread.)

END

Printed in the United States
61427LVS00004B/103-291

9 781425 953386